Positively Pricked

A Novel

SABRINA STARK

Copyright © 2018 Sabrina Stark

All rights reserved.

ISBN-13:

978-1719112000

ISBN-10:

1719112002

CHAPTER 1

The senator was screaming like a girl. Funny, I felt like screaming too, but for entirely different reasons.

On both sides of the long, carpeted corridor, doors swung open as hotel guests leaned their heads out to gawk at the commotion. I couldn't exactly blame them. After all, it wasn't *every* day you spotted a bare-chested billionaire dragging a senator by his ankle.

The senator was still screaming. "Help! Somebody!"

With my notebook in-hand, I scrambled to keep up. Desperately, I called out, "What are you doing?"

The senator stopped screaming only long enough to holler back, "I'm being assaulted! What the fuck does it look like?"

Dumb-ass. I wasn't talking to him. I was talking to my employer.

Yes. That would be the billionaire.

If I weren't so horrified, I might've noticed that his dark tailored slacks clung oh-so perfectly to his tight butt and trim waist. And while I was at it, I might've *also* noticed that his muscular back and shoulders looked annoyingly fine as he dragged Mister Grabby-Ass – a.k.a. the senator – down the long, ornate hall.

As they passed a random door on their left, a couple of teenage girls swiveled their heads to stare at the traveling spectacle.

They were still staring when I scrambled past their doorway. As I hurried forward, one of them called out after me, "Hey, was that–?"

"No comment!" I yelled, hoping to keep the publicity to a minimum.

Probably too late for that.

Already, the other girl was finishing the question. "Zane Bennington? Oh, my God. I think it was."

Damn it.

Unfortunately, the dragger *was* Zane Bennington, and he wasn't just my employer. He was the guy who'd been making my life miserable for weeks. He was a prick. An asshole. A stone-cold ruthless bastard with no redeeming qualities whatsoever – well, except for his face. And his body. And yeah, maybe his massive fortune.

But other than that, the guy had zero going for him.

Hustling away from the girls, I called out to Zane's receding back. "Where are you taking him?"

Zane – yes, we *were* on a first name basis, but that was another story – didn't answer. He didn't even pause. He just kept plowing forward, ignoring me *and* the guy twisting and screaming behind him.

By now, the friction had wreaked havoc on the senator's fancy suit jacket. Already, it was tangled up around his torso, like some sort of melted bobsled. He gave a particularly girlish scream. "Call security!"

Oh sure, like that would help.

Security here was top-notch, but Zane owned this hotel, so if security came running, it wouldn't be to rescue the senator, as much as he might need it.

I yelled, "Damn it, Zane! Will you *please* stop?"

Thanks to a whole series of implausible events, I was Zane's public relations manager, and it was proving to be more than a full-time job. The guy didn't care who he offended, or what anyone thought of him.

But even for Zane, this was a bit much. Until now, he'd confined most of his anti-social behavior to general assholery as opposed to outright assault.

How on Earth would I explain *this*?

They were moving so fast that I could barely keep up. But then again, I *was* wearing high heels and a long fitted skirt. Unless I wanted to grab the bottom of that skirt, and hike it up thigh-high, sprinting was out of the question.

So instead, I rushed along behind them – too slow to catch up, but too fast to pretend that I wasn't part of this impromptu parade.

Maybe I should've felt bad for the senator.

But I didn't.

I couldn't.

I barely knew the guy. And yet, just yesterday evening, he'd gotten all grabby after a few cocktails too many. For all *I* knew, he didn't even remember.

But *I* did.

If I weren't so busy scurrying down the hall, I might've shuddered with revulsion. But instead, I kept on going, trying like hell to forget the feel of his hand squeezing my ass, and then worse, going in for the crack.

It was this particular recollection that led to a new discovery. Turns out, you *could* shudder and scurry at the same time. *Go figure.*

As I watched, Zane rounded the corner, still dragging the senator behind him. The way it looked, they were heading for the elevators – my steps faltered – or, *oh crap*, the stairwell.

I said a silent prayer. *Please be the elevators. Please be the elevators…*

I called out, "Don't you dare take the stairs!"

Whether Zane heard me or not, I had no idea. With a muttered curse, I kept on going, praying that the next sound from the corridor *wouldn't* be the bumpity bump of the senator getting tossed down the stairway.

A split second later, the screaming stopped, and I almost feared the worst. I rounded the corner just in time to see Zane yank the senator up by his jacket and shove him hard against the wall between the two nearest elevators.

Zane was tall and powerfully built. As for the senator, he'd been a pro football player back in the day. But those days were long gone, and the only thing he tackled now were women half his age.

Oh sure, he still *looked* imposing, but looks, I decided, could be deceiving. And besides, the guy holding him against the wall was pretty imposing himself. If I were a betting gal – which I wasn't – I'd have put all my money on Zane.

Now that I'd actually caught up to them, I wasn't quite sure what to do. After all, Zane wasn't dragging the guy anymore, so that was good, right? Silently, I edged forward, hoping to catch Zane's elbow and maybe gently ease him away from the senator.

I was halfway there when Zane finally spoke. In a voice filled with menace, he leaned closer to the senator and said, "If you *ever* touch her again, I'll break off those fucking fingers." His grip visibly tightened. "And then, I'll shove them down your fucking throat."

I froze. *What?*

Again, Zane shoved the senator against the wall. "Are we clear?"

I stood in stunned confusion. Who on Earth was he talking about?

He couldn't mean *me*.

Could he?

No. He couldn't. Definitely not.

If I weren't so stressed, I might have laughed at the mere thought. After all, Zane hated *me* just as much as I hated *him*.

And seriously, wasn't *I* full of myself? Like Zane would go to any trouble on my behalf.

Probably, I decided, the senator had gotten grabby with someone else, like maybe an important guest or, heaven forbid, Zane's latest squeeze, whoever she was *this* time.

I tried to think. I'd ditched the senator just after midnight, which left plenty of time for another round of slurring and ass-grabbing with whatever random female happened to cross his path next.

Still, we had security for that sort of thing. So why would Zane Bennington – who owned not only this hotel but countless others worldwide – take such a personal interest?

Trying to make sense of it all, I studied Zane's face in profile. For as long as I'd known him – which, granted, wasn't forever – he'd been the epitome of control.

And yet, he didn't look in control now.

He looked ready to break the senator in two. When the senator offered no coherent response, Zane gave him another shove and repeated his question, more slowly this time. "Are. We. Clear?"

The senator swallowed. "I, uh, what?"

More confused than ever, I stepped toward them.

Instantly, the senator's gaze snapped in my direction. He called out,

"Jane! Go on! Tell him!"

My steps faltered, and I heard myself ask, "Tell him what?"

The senator gave me a pleading look. "Tell him that you liked it. You know, that it was voluntary."

My jaw dropped. *Wait, what?*

I gave a confused shake of my head. I *didn't* like it. The senator was a creep, and besides, until just last night, he'd been engaged to someone else – someone I might've called a friend. But that wasn't the thing that had me reeling.

It was the implication of what he'd just said.

My gaze shifted from the senator to the guy holding him against the wall. As if feeling my gaze, Zane slowly turned to look. And when he did, I saw something new in his eyes – a possessive spark that caught me totally off guard.

My breath caught. *Oh, my God.* This *was* about me.

But why?

Was it because I worked for him?

No. That couldn't be it. Thousands of people worked for him, and I'd never seen him behave anything like *this*.

Still, it didn't make any sense.

I mean, he didn't even *like* me. Cripes, Zane Bennington didn't like anyone – as I'd learned so quickly on the night we'd met – when I'd been a lowly catering assistant and he'd been – well, Zane Bennington, the mystery man who had everyone talking.

CHAPTER 2
THREE MONTHS EARLIER

My gaze drifted across the room. For a total prick, the guy sure had a lot of friends.

Naomi gripped my arm. "Don't."

Startled, I turned to face her. "Don't what?"

She lowered her voice. "Don't look at him."

And just like that, my gaze snapped back in his direction, not that it did a lick of good. He was absolutely swarmed, leaving me nothing to see but the very top of his head, covered in thick, bronze hair that would've made a movie star weep with envy.

Surrounding him were men in designer suits, bejeweled women in sultry dresses, and, on the outskirts, a couple of random reporters trying to edge their way into the inner circle.

The way it looked, they weren't having much luck.

I almost sighed. I could *so* relate. My own luck? It was so deep in the toilet that I'd need a plunger just to say hello.

Naomi's grip on my arm tightened. "Hey, Jane."

I was still focused on the crowd. "Yeah?"

"You heard me, right?"

Absently, I felt myself nod. In truth, it was hard to hear much of anything over the sounds of live jazz and the hum of excited voices – *rich* voices with upper-crust accents and laughter that sounded almost rehearsed.

These were important people, and they darn well knew it.

As for me, I was just a catering assistant – in other words, a total nobody. But packed in the mansion's enormous living room were plenty of somebodies, including the biggest somebody of them all – Zane Bennington, who, if the rumors were true, was an absolute asshole.

I turned to Naomi. "Why shouldn't I look? I mean, it's not like he saw me or anything."

"It's not *him* I'm worried about." Naomi looked past me, and her mouth tightened. "It's *her*."

Reluctantly, I turned to look. Sure enough, Ms. Hedgwick – the sharp-faced woman who'd let us into the mansion a few hours earlier – was giving me the stink-eye again.

I felt warmth rise to my cheeks. *Damn it.* She *had* warned us, hadn't she?

Her instructions – delivered with such cold precision – still rang in my ears. *"Don't talk to him. Don't smile at him. Don't look at him. And whatever you do, don't do anything to draw his attention. Is that clear?"*

Of course, I'd nodded. I mean, what else could I do? It's not like I'd gain any brownie points by explaining that if Zane Bennington wandered over for a caviar canape – or whatever – that I couldn't exactly fling it onto his plate with a grunt and a frown.

Besides, I smiled at practically everyone. Looking to prove it now, I summoned up a tentative smile for Ms. Hedgwick.

Her posture stiffened, and she didn't smile back.

Instead, she turned away, glowering as she headed toward the front entrance, probably to give the parking attendants another dose of holy hell for that incident with the catering van.

Next to me, Naomi murmured, "I told you so."

Again, I turned to face her. "Well, I wouldn't have *been* looking if you hadn't just mentioned him."

Naomi flashed me a sudden grin. "Liar."

She was right, of course. Yes, I would've looked, but hey, I wasn't the only one. Even now, all eyes in the room kept drifting in his direction. I could practically hear their thoughts. They were wondering the same thing that I was wondering.

Were the stories true?

Obviously, some of them were. Yes, he was obnoxiously good-looking with a killer body. And yes, he'd arrived from nowhere to claim the vast family fortune that had fallen so violently into his lap. And yes, he'd been caught in some alcove with Senator Wilson's new fiancée, who'd tried to explain away their half-naked encounter by claiming it was some sort of wardrobe malfunction.

Wardrobe malfunction, my ass.

I knew the fiancée. We'd gone to the same university. But where *she'd* graduated straight into the arms of Senator Wilson, *I'd* graduated to the sad realization that the job market sucked, rent was expensive, and the clock was ticking.

Unless I wanted to move back to the family farm, I needed money like *now*. I loved the farm. And I loved my family. But skulking back like a runaway child was too humiliating to consider.

Besides, things weren't all bad. The catering gig paid a lot better than the job I'd just given up. Plus, I'd been officially converted to full time. That was something, right?

Naomi's voice interrupted my thoughts. "You know, he's only twenty-eight?"

I gave another nod. I *did* know, but it was still hard to fathom. Twenty-eight-years old. That was only five years older than I was.

I bit my lip. Where would *I* be in five years?

And then, there was the scarier question. Where would I be in five days? I gave an involuntary shiver. Headed for trouble, that's where, unless I could scrounge up enough money for this month's rent.

Sometimes it was hard to smile when the rent was due – no, *overdue*. Feeling suddenly overwhelmed, I looked toward the nearest window. Outside, it was dark, leaving me nothing to see but my own reflection.

Yup, there I was – Jane Compton.

A plain Jane? I wasn't quite sure.

I was no runway model, but I wasn't bad-looking in that girl-next-door sort of way. Of course, I'd look a lot better without the frilly white apron, and better still if my hair wasn't knotted up so tight that my scalp literally ached.

As for my feet, well, they ached, too, but that had nothing to do with my appearance. It was because I'd been on those feet since the crack of dawn, finishing up my other job.

Yeah, that was me, living the good life, all right.

In the background, I heard Naomi say, "Oh shoot, there goes another candle."

I turned to look. Sure enough, the chafing candle underneath the nearest stainless steel warmer had gone out, leaving the crab cakes in serious danger of growing cold.

Already, Naomi was rummaging around below the cloth-covered serving station, saying, "Good thing we brought extras."

Had we? I didn't remember, but then again, I wasn't the one who packed the supplies.

After five minutes of rummaging, Naomi looked up and frowned. "I must've left them in the van. You wanna run out and look?"

Did I ever.

I'd been surrounded by people for hours, and I was dying for a little peace and quiet.

Unfortunately, that's *not* what I found in the back parking area. I found *him* – Zane Bennington, who proved beyond a shadow of a doubt that at least one rumor was true.

He *was* an asshole.

Totally.

☐

CHAPTER 3

I was still crawling around in the van's cargo area when something thudded against the back bumper.

I froze, wondering what had just happened. I glanced toward the rear cargo doors, and was just about to fling them open, when something made me hesitate.

It was the sound of male voices. At least one of them was slurring. Drunk? It sure sounded like it. Determined to avoid them, I clamped my mouth shut and waited for them to pass.

But they didn't.

Instead, they stopped somewhere near the back of the van and kept on talking.

"Oh yeah?" the drunk guy slurred. "What? You think you're one of us? Well, lemme tell you something. You're not." He gave a derisive snort. "And you're never gonna be."

The other guy gave something like a laugh. It was a low, dangerous sound that made me shiver in the cold, dark van. "Got that right."

I felt my eyebrows furrow. Whoever the second guy was, he sounded stone-cold sober.

The drunk one demanded, "What's that supposed to mean?"

"You're smart enough. You'll figure it out."

"I don't *wanna* figure it out. I want you gone. We all do." His voice rose. "So why don't you get the fuck outta here?"

"I'll tell you why." An edge crept into the sober guy's voice. "Because it's *my* house."

My breath caught. *Oh, crap*. Now, I knew who the sober guy was. It was Zane Bennington. It *had* to be. Along with the massive fortune and business empire, he'd inherited several estates, including this one.

"*Your* house?" the drunk guy said with a nasty laugh. "Yeah, well, not for long."

Zane's voice remained cool. "We'll see about that."

"No! *You'll* see."

Holding myself very still, I glanced around the cluttered van. I *so* didn't want to eavesdrop, but it's not like I could jump out *now*. Not only would it be incredibly awkward, I'd probably get tossed out on my ass – if not by Zane Bennington, then definitely by Ms. Hedgwick.

And damn it. I needed this job, now more than ever, considering that I'd already quit my other one.

I said a silent prayer. *Just go away.*

But they didn't. Outside the van, they were still going back and forth, first about the estate, and then about the chain of luxury hotels that bore the Bennington name. The way it sounded, the drunk guy's dad was planning some sort of hostile takeover.

Funny, I was a feeling a little hostile myself. Of all the places for them to argue, why here? The estate probably had fifty rooms. Couldn't they just pick one and talk there instead?

Idiots.

Afraid to move, I was still on all fours, and my knees were starting to ache. I felt like a dog ready to bolt.

If only I could.

Already, I'd been out here for way too long, and the delay wasn't even my fault. Normally, the back of the van was neatly organized, with every box and bin in a predictable place. But thanks to that earlier incident, the whole cargo area was a giant mess, with boxes and bins strewn everywhere.

And I just *knew* there were meatballs rolling around somewhere.

I could only imagine how messy the van would look under decent lighting, but all *I* had was a small keychain penlight, and the thing was practically useless. Even now, its narrow beam illuminated next to nothing.

I hesitated. Maybe that was a good thing. I couldn't see the mess, and *they* couldn't see *me*. If I were smart, I'd keep it that way. On instinct, I cut the light and tried not to breathe.

Outside, the guys were still arguing. Or – more accurately – the drunk was arguing with Zane, who said only enough to keep the other guy ranting. Why, I had no idea. Already, the guy was repeating himself.

For the third time, he slurred, "Everyone hates you. You know that, right?"

"Uh-huh. Now tell me something I *don't* know."

"All right." The guy gave a drunken laugh. "You're an asshole."

"Sorry, try again."

The drunk paused. "What?"

"*That*, I already know." Zane's voice hardened. "Now tell me something I don't."

Another pause. "I've gotta pee."

I rolled my eyes. *Fine. Whatever. There's a dozen bathrooms. Go find one.*

The night was cold. Naomi was waiting. And I *still* needed to find the candles.

Stupidly, all I could think was, "I hope they like cold crab cakes."

Outside, I heard a quick zipping noise, followed by the distinct sound of – *What the hell?* – liquid splashing against the side of the van.

Oh, my God. Was the guy seriously *peeing* on the catering van? I gave a disgusted shudder. *Talk about unsanitary.*

Searching for a silver lining, I reminded myself that it could always be worse. At least, he hadn't said he had to poop. I made a face. *Not yet, anyway.*

When the splashing stopped, I said yet another silent prayer. *Just go. And I don't mean number-two.*

Sounding more sloppy than ever, the drunk mumbled, "Man, it goes right through ya, you know?"

Whether Zane knew or not, I had no idea, because a new voice sounded in the distance. It was a male voice, filled with hearty good cheer. "Hey, *there* you two are!"

From near the bumper, I heard a muttered curse. But from who? Zane? Or the drunk? I couldn't be sure either way.

A moment later, the new voice, sounding much closer now, said, "So, what are you two young bucks up to?"

I gave another eye-roll. *Young bucks. Seriously?*

I wanted to scream in frustration. Outside, the crowd was growing, not shrinking, which meant that I was more trapped than ever.

Fearful of rocking the proverbial boat, I was *still* on all fours. My hands were freezing, and my thin pants were doing nothing to pad my knees from the cold metal of the van's floor.

When neither of the "young bucks" responded, the new guy said, "I hear you caused quite a ruckus."

The drunk mumbled, "So?"

"So, I called James. He's waiting with the car out front."

The drunk whined, "But I'm not ready to go."

The stranger gave a friendly chuckle. "Still full of piss and vinegar, huh?"

I gave another shudder. *Nope. Not piss, anyway.* I tried to think. Was the car-wash still open? *Doubtful.* It was, after all, nearly midnight – or later, for all I knew.

The new guy said, "Hey, uh, Teddy?"

"Huh?"

"Your, uh, fly's open."

The drunk guy muttered, "Son-of-bitch." I heard another zip as the guy said, "Fuck, Zane. Why didn't you tell me?"

Zane replied, "Because I wasn't staring at your cock."

"Oh yeah?" the drunk said. "Well, I wasn't staring at yours either." He snorted. "Asshole."

The new guy spoke up. "Aw c'mon guys. No harm, no foul, right?"

I frowned. *Yeah, tell that to the van, buddy.*

Finally, after some additional back-and-forth, Teddy the Drunk shuffled off with a belligerent promise to deal with Zane later – whatever that meant.

I gave a quiet sigh. And then, there were two.

The new guy said, "Hey, thanks for looking out for him."

"I wasn't looking out for *him*," Zane said. "I was looking out for *me*."

The new guy chuckled. "Yeah, who needs a scene, right? I'm just glad you got him outta there when you did."

When Zane said nothing in response, the guy added, "Listen, I know that you and your granddad weren't close, but he was a fine man." His tone grew sympathetic. "And it was a damn shame what happened to him."

I tried to recall. What *had* happened to him?

The stranger was still talking. "But I guess when your time's up—"

"Fuck you," Zane said.

Long pause. "Pardon?"

"You heard me."

The new guy cleared his throat. "Hey, if you wanna talk…"

"I don't."

After a long, awkward pause, the guy tried again. "I'm just saying, I know it's gotta be overwhelming – with the hotels, the houses, hell, the financials – but if you ever need a shoulder to lean on…"

"I don't."

"Yeah, well…" The other guy hesitated. "I'm just saying, I know there's a lot on your plate."

"Right," Zane said. "*My* plate. Not yours. Speaking of which, you're moving."

"What?" the guy said. "What do you mean?"

"I mean," Zane said, "the house on Longwood. It's mine now. So get the fuck out." In a voice that held the barest hint of a smile, he added, "By Monday."

The stranger gave a strangled laugh. "Oh come on. You're not serious?"

"Yeah? Why not?"

"Because we've been living there for years. It's our family home. The deed – it was just a technicality. I mean, everyone knows it's our house."

"Not anymore."

"You're joking."

"Do I *look* like I'm joking?"

The stranger gave a low curse and was silent for a long, terrible moment before saying, "Even if I agreed – and I'm not saying I do – we couldn't possibly move by Monday. I mean, come on. That's only two days away."

"Right. So you'd better get packing."

"But that's not even legal."

"So sue me."

"Maybe I will," the stranger said. "You *do* know that I'm a lawyer, right?"

"I don't care if you're the fucking president. You're in *my* house, and I want you gone."

"Is that so?" The stranger gave a derisive snort. "Why? Aren't the other houses enough?"

"No. They're not."

"But—"

"Move. Or I'll have it done for you."

"What the hell?" the guy sputtered. "You can't do that."

"Yeah? Watch me."

"But what about Teddy? He's your cousin, for God's sake."

"So?"

"So that's *his* house, too."

I tried to think. Teddy? As in Teddy the Drunk?

Zane replied, "Not my problem."

The stranger was silent for another long, awful moment, and I held my breath, wondering what on Earth he'd say next. Cripes, what *could* he say?

In the background, I could still hear the muted sounds of music and laughter coming from inside the house. But out here, no one was laughing – not me, not the stranger, and definitely not Zane.

Asshole.

Finally, the stranger gave a long, sad sigh. "You know, it really pains me to say this, but if your grandfather were alive, he'd be utterly ashamed of you."

"I know," Zane said. "But he's not. So fuck off."

It was one of the strangest things I'd ever heard. He didn't even sound angry, just matter-of-fact. It was truly chilling.

The other guy made a scoffing sound. "Is that all you can say? Fuck this and fuck that?"

When Zane made no reply, the guy practically spat, "Look here, you ingrate. I don't know how they do things in the dirt *you* crawled out of, but around here, we treat people with dignity and respect."

"Yeah?" Zane said. "Well in the dirt, you've gotta earn it."

"And I haven't?" the guy said. "You *do* know I spent three decades working for your family."

"So?" Zane said. "You didn't work for *me*."

"But I worked for your grandfather. I was his right-hand man."

"Yeah. And he's dead. So like I said, *Bob*, get the fuck out."

I tried to think. *Bob? Bob who?*

Outside the van, Bob spoke again. "You *do* recall it was *me* who threw you this party, right?"

Oh, crap.

That Bob?

The stranger *had* to be Robert Something-or-Other, the silver-haired gentleman who'd been so friendly when we'd been setting up.

At the time, I didn't even realize that he was the one throwing the party, but in hindsight, I should've. After all, he'd taken a pretty keen interest in all of the details.

I closed my eyes and said a silent prayer that he'd already paid the catering bill, because if he hadn't, I had a horrible suspicion that we were about to get stiffed.

Outside, Bob was sounding more frustrated with every passing moment. "And let me tell you," he was saying, "it wasn't cheap."

In a deadpan voice, Zane said, "I noticed."

"Jesus," Bob muttered. "If you were gonna toss us out, why didn't you say so earlier?"

"Because I'm saying it now."

"But the band, the catering – hell, the parking attendants – they weren't free, you know."

"Again, not my problem."

Bob made another scoffing sound. "Listen here, you reprobate. If you think I'm leaving that house, you're dead wrong."

"Is that so?"

"Damn straight. In fact..." Bob paused a long moment before blurting out, "You'll get the house over my dead body."

"You think that can't be arranged?"

"What?"

"Lemme ask you something, *Bob*." Zane said the guy's name like it was some sort of insult. "You got a good security system?"

"What? Well, uh, yeah. Of course."

"Uh-huh," Zane said. "You do know those things fail all the time."

"Yeah, well not mine."

"Except it's not yours. Is it, Bob?"

"What?"

"It's *mine*. Funny how that works."

"What is this?" Bob said. "A threat? Because lemme tell you something. I'm not afraid to fight you."

"Is that right?"

The guy cleared his throat. "I mean in court, like civilized people, not that *you'd* know anything about that."

"You're right," Zane said. "I wouldn't." That now-familiar edge crept back into his voice. "So if I were you, I'd get packing."

After a few more minutes of back-and-forth, the conversation ended with a string of profanity and fading footsteps as Bob stomped off, leaving a trail of curse words in his wake.

I gave a quiet sigh. *And then, there was one.*

My legs were cramped, and my hands felt like ice cubes. Desperately, I waited for the sounds of additional footsteps – *Zane's* footsteps, heading away from the van.

But I heard nothing.

And the longer I waited, the more I started to doubt myself. Maybe he'd already wandered off. After all, Bob's departure hadn't been terribly quiet. For all I knew, Zane had left at the exact same time. Maybe, he was already back inside the house, or wherever jerks went when they weren't spreading their misery.

And yet, I still waited.

Finally, when I couldn't stand it another moment, I crawled silently toward the back cargo doors and listened.

Nothing.

Slowly, I reached up and lifted the nearest door-handle. Praying for the best, I gave the door a gentle push. It swung outward maybe half a foot before it stopped, bumping into something on the other side.

I gave a little gasp.

No. Not some *thing*. Some *one*.

Oh, no.

CHAPTER 4

In a panic, I yanked the door shut and scooted backward inside the van. On the way, I bumped a stack of boxes and sent them tumbling. A sudden clatter – the sound of metal cascading onto metal – made me cringe in absolute horror.

Yup, there went the extra silverware.

But it wasn't the silverware I cared about. It was the noise.

So much for silently hiding out.

I gave a mental eye-roll. *Yeah, right.* Like I hadn't already been busted.

What now?

Should I hunker down and hope he goes away? Or crawl out and face the music?

In the end, I didn't have to do anything, because a moment later, that same cargo door swung open, and there he was – Zane Bennington himself.

His gaze was sharp, and his mouth was tight, which was a shame really, because he had a nice mouth. Or rather, it *would've* been a nice mouth if his lips weren't compressed into a hard, ominous line.

Our gazes locked across the short distance, and I felt myself swallow.

I was still on all fours, and I had to crane my neck to stare up at him. He was tall and broad-shouldered, with that obnoxiously thick hair, and cheekbones that made me just a little bit jealous. His suit was dark and tailored – obviously expensive – with a white button-down shirt, open slightly at the collar.

In every possible way, he looked like a million bucks, which was almost funny, because if the stories were true, he was worth way more than a million – probably more than a billion counting all the assets.

And yet, he wasn't much older than I was.

Talk about lucky.

Him, not me.

Still, I tried to smile. "Uh, hi."

He didn't smile back, not that I'd expected him to. In a dangerously quiet voice, he said, "Get out."

I blinked. "What?"

"You heard me."

Suddenly, I didn't *want* to get out. True, the van was a cluttered freezing mess, but the guy in front of me was something else entirely. I mumbled, "That's okay. I'm good."

His gaze hardened. "You think."

Was that a question? It didn't *sound* like a question. I cleared my throat. "You're probably wondering who I am, huh?"

From the look in his eyes, he knew exactly who I was – an insignificant bug to be flicked off his pricey jacket.

Into his silence, I said, "I'm just the caterer."

No. That wasn't quite true.

I tried again. "Well, not the caterer-caterer. I mean, I'm just the assistant, one of several, actually – because, you know, it's a pretty big party, huh?"

Right. As if he didn't know. This was his place, after all.

His cool gaze swept over me, and he looked decidedly unimpressed.

Then again, I *was* hunkered out, doggie-style, in a van.

I sat up in the confined space and tried to ignore the random fork or whatever that was poking against my right ass-cheek. I ran a nervous hand down my frilly white apron and said, "The thing is, I was looking for a candle."

His jaw was so tight, it was a wonder he could even speak. "A candle."

I hesitated. Was *that* a question? Again, I wasn't quite sure. "Right. You know. The kind you put under a serving thingie to keep it warm?"

Damn it. The thingie had a name. Normally, I knew the name, but the guy was looking at me with such loathing that I was finding it hard to think.

He moved a fraction closer. "The doors," he said, "why were they shut?"

"You mean the van doors?" I gave them a quick glance. "I shut them because it's freezing out."

If the answer satisfied him, he sure as heck didn't show it. "It's April."

Yes, but it was *early* April, and this was Indianapolis, not Tampa. And besides, springtime or not, the night was unseasonably cool. Somehow, I managed to stammer, "Right. But it's dark, and there's a breeze."

Right on cue, that same breeze ruffled the ends of his thick hair, making him look like a some kind of movie star in one of those annoyingly sexy slow-motion shots. It was especially annoying now, because *this* guy wasn't moving at all. Instead, he was eyeing me with open hostility.

Like an idiot, I started blathering. "So, you see, I shut the doors to keep it out – the breeze, I mean. I would've fired up the van – you know, for the heat – but I didn't think it would take so long to find the candles." I gave a nervous laugh. "I don't suppose you have any on you?"

He didn't even crack a smile. "Who do you work for?"

So much for softening him up with humor.

"Vista Catering." I pointed vaguely to my right. "It's, uh, written on the side of the van, actually."

His gaze didn't waver, and he made no reply.

I cleared my throat. "If you don't believe me, just look." I plastered on another smile. "Go on. I'll wait."

Or, I'll run screaming into the house for my purse and car keys.

Stupid? Probably. But the guy was making me nervous, and not only because he'd caught me eavesdropping. For all his money, there was something about him – something barely civilized – lurking underneath his rich, glossy surface.

One thing I knew for certain, this was a guy who wasn't afraid to break a few eggs. And right now, I was feeling like a giant chicken.

In front of me, he still wasn't moving. He repeated his question, more slowly this time. "*Who* do you work for?"

I was freezing and tired – and yeah, maybe a little scared. I hated being scared. In fact, I decided, I wasn't going to be, not tonight.

When I spoke, my voice came out snippier than I intended. "Vista Catering. You *did* hear me, right?"

"I heard you."

"But what? You don't believe me?"

"No. I don't."

Damn it. The way it looked, there was no way on Earth that I'd be leaving with my catering job still intact. Oh sure, anything was technically possible, just like it was technically possible that I might win the lotto someday, well, if I ever splurged on a ticket, that is.

I sighed. *Oh, screw it.*

If I was going to get tossed out anyway, there was no point in groveling. "You know what?" I said. "You're right. I was just hanging out here for fun. I mean, why would I be out watching a movie or something when I could be crawling around in a van, looking for a stupid candle in a pile of forks."

He gave the van's floor a perfunctory glance. "If that's your story, it needs work."

"It wasn't a story," I told him. "It was sarcasm. You *did* catch the tone, right?"

His gaze narrowed. "I caught *something*."

Again, I felt myself swallow. "What?"

"And I don't know *what* she is," he continued, "but I'm gonna find out." He flicked his head toward the main house, where the party was still going strong. "Now, get your ass back to work."

I blinked. "Excuse me?"

"You heard me." He glanced toward the house. "Wherever your station is, find it. And don't leave until I say so."

I stared up at him. "Until *you* say so?" Okay, I knew that he was the customer and all, but I wasn't his servant. "You can't talk to me like that."

"Why not?"

"Gee, I don't know. Because it's rude?"

"You think I care?"

No. He didn't. That much was obvious.

Asshole.

Probably, I should've been relieved. After all, if he was ordering me back to my station, there was at least *some* chance I'd get to keep my job. If I were smart, I'd probably scurry back inside and count my blessings.

I bit my lip. *Damn it.* I *was* smart. I had a bachelor's degree in public relations. With honors, too. My stomach sank. And what was I doing? Working as a catering assistant.

True, it was honest work, and I didn't mind it most of the time. But under the guy's scornful gaze, I was starting to feel like a giant loser – not because of my job, but because my degree had cost so much, and netted me so little.

And now, I just had to ask, "Let's say I *do* go back inside. What then?"

His eyebrows lifted. "*If* you go back inside?"

"I mean…" I hesitated. "Are you gonna tell on me?"

"The person I'd tell is *me*."

"Well, yeah, sort of. But I mean are you gonna tell my boss?"

"I *am* the boss."

Talk about arrogant. And besides, that wasn't even true. Not really. I mean, it's not like he *owned* the catering company.

I made a sound of frustration. "Oh, come on. You know what I mean."

He studied my face. "Do I?"

Okay, that was definitely a question, even if it was obviously rhetorical. "Listen," I said, "I don't want to go back in there, only to find out that I'm fired later." I lifted my chin. "If I'm getting bad news, I'd rather hear it now and be done with it."

A shadow crossed his features, and the van suddenly felt ten degrees colder. "Trust me," he said in a voice that inspired zero trust. "Losing your job is the least of your worries."

Was that a threat? It sounded like one. Still, I met his gaze head-on. I wasn't afraid of him, or at least that's what I kept telling myself, even as alarm bells kept ringing in my head.

No – not alarm bells – a phone – *his*, apparently, because it sure as heck wasn't mine. I knew this, because I had no cell phone. Well, not since last Tuesday, anyway.

This was yet another long story.

As I watched, he reached into his front pants pocket and pulled out a cell phone. After glancing briefly at the display, he pulled it to his ear and said, "What?"

He listened for a few moments before disconnecting the call without so much as a goodbye. He tucked the phone back into his pocket and eyed me with renewed scorn. "You're still here."

Yes. I was.

"Well, yeah," I stammered. "I haven't found the candles."

"Fuck the candles."

I tried not to flinch. "What?"

"Your station," he said. "Find it. *Now.*" And with that, he turned and walked away, but not toward the house. Instead, he walked in the opposite direction, heading toward the rear of his property.

Through the open cargo door, I watched him as he strode across the narrow parking area and into his massive back yard. He kept on going, making his way around the swimming pool, past the pool house, and into the woods beyond.

I felt my eyebrows furrow. *Well, that wasn't weird or anything.*

I couldn't see him anymore, but I *could* feel the remnants of our encounter, haunting me like a bad dream.

Jerk.

And where was he going, anyway?

Inside his estate, there had to be at least a hundred guests. Was he ditching them?

It sure looked that way.

I blew out a long, unsteady breath. He was right about one thing – forget the candles. If I hadn't found them by now, they obviously weren't out here. And besides, I'd been gone far too long for a simple errand.

I scrambled out of the van and slammed the door shut behind me. With my heart still racing, I dashed back through the rear entrance and returned to my catering station – well, what was left of it, anyway.

And it wasn't good.

CHAPTER 5

Dumbstruck, I stared down at destruction. *What on Earth had happened?*

Where the serving station used to be, all that remained now was a giant mess. Oh sure, the table was still there, but it was now lying on its side, surrounded by broken dishes, scattered food, and toppled serving trays.

Even the chafing dishes were upended, along with all of the edibles that we'd been so determined to keep warm. As far as the lit candles, they were nowhere in sight, but I *did* spot a few burn marks on the formerly pristine tablecloth, which happened to be covered in stains and wadded up into a loose blob.

In the middle of everything was Naomi, who was crouched on the floor, plucking crab cakes off the ornate rug.

I stared down at her. "What happened?"

Only barely glancing up, she tossed a crab cake into a nearby wastebasket and said, "Don't ask."

I looked around. Except for the catering mess, the party hadn't really changed. In the far corner, the jazz band was still playing. Around us, the guests were still laughing and drinking. On the room's opposite side, Ms. Hedgwick was back at her old spot, giving me another dose of the stink-eye.

Well, that was nice.

Returning my attention to the mess, I crouched down beside Naomi and followed her lead, plucking food off the rug and tossing it into the trash. Trying to lighten the mood, I said, "I guess we should look on the bright side, huh?"

She stopped in mid-motion to ask, "What bright side?"

"Well, we don't need those extra candles anymore." I gave her an encouraging smile. "So, that's good, right?"

Naomi only frowned. Under her breath, she muttered something that sounded suspiciously like, "Fuck the candles."

Like so many other things tonight, it was déjà vu all over again. It seemed like the perfect time to repeat my question. "So what happened?"

Naomi sighed. "There was this guy, drunk off his ass, and—"

"And he flipped the table?"

She gave me an annoyed look. "No. He went careening *into* the table when our 'gracious host' body slammed him."

My jaw dropped. "You don't mean Zane Bennington?"

"Who else would I mean? It's his place, right?"

I glanced around. Yeah, it *was* his place, and it was absolutely fabulous.

He *so* didn't deserve it, especially considering how callously he was willing to toss others out of *their* home. I felt my jaw clench. That guy? What *he* deserved was a giant kick in the ass.

Hoping for the best, I asked, "So did the guy body-slam him back?"

Naomi tossed another crab cake into the trash. "No."

My shoulders sagged in disappointment. "Well, did he at least hit him or something?"

"You mean did the drunk guy hit Zane Bennington?" Naomi paused. "He *threatened* to hit him. Does that count?"

Damn it. I muttered, "Not really."

I considered the timetable. Odds were pretty good that the drunk was Teddy, the guy who'd been arguing with Zane outside the van. What he actually looked like, I had no idea, but I'd definitely recognize his voice – well, if he slurred, that is.

How he sounded sober, I could only guess.

Mulling all of this over, I continued plucking food off the rug while Naomi went in search of cleaning supplies.

As I worked, I eyed the rug with growing concern. It was creamy white with black and tan swirly patterns. And yet, as ornate as the patterns were, they did nothing to hide all of the food stains.

Probably, I should've been happy. Like everything else, the rug looked beyond expensive. If the stains didn't come out, Zane would surely need to replace it, and it wouldn't be cheap.

Good.

My joy lasted like five whole seconds before I gave a silent scoff. A new rug? The expense would be pocket change for a guy like Zane Bennington.

Probably, he'd simply send out a servant to buy a new one. Or more likely, a servant would send a servant, because let's face it, Mister Fancy-Pants probably had a million better things to do – like kick puppies or burn down orphanages.

Jerk.

I was still plucking food off the carpet when the sound of throat-clearing made me look up. Standing over me was the senator's fiancée, dressed to kill in a sleek black dress and big diamond earrings that looked like the real deal.

She looked down to ask, "Do you have any more crab cakes?"

I hesitated. Was that a serious question? I mean, she *did* see the mess, right? I said, "Excuse me?"

She sighed. "I *said*, do you have any more crab cakes?"

I glanced around. Yeah, I had dozens, assuming she didn't mind scraping them off the rug. But telling her that would be a mistake, so I gave her an apologetic smile. "I'm sorry, but they're not really edible."

And did she smile back?

No.

She didn't.

Instead, she made a little huffing noise and said, "But they're the senator's favorite."

Oh, please. If the rumors were true, the senator's *real* favorite was something called a cheerleader sandwich.

Still, I forced another smile. "Gosh Tiffany, I'm really sorry, but—"

She stiffened. "*What* did you call me?"

"Uh, Tiffany?"

She was frowning now. "That's a little personal, don't you think?"

I stared up at her. Surely, she remembered me. In college, we'd had at least ten classes together, maybe more. After all, we'd majored in the same thing. Hoping to jog her memory, I said, "Well, I remembered your name from –"

"From the papers, I know." She gave a toss of her ice-blonde hair. "But that hardly makes us friends."

Now, *I* was the one frowning. "What?"

"I'm only saying, just because you've seen my name in the society pages, that doesn't put us on a first-name basis."

I felt my eyebrows furrow. Society pages? Was that even a thing anymore?

I tried to think. The last time I'd handled an actual newspaper was when I'd been unpacking some rummage sale coffee cups. And even *that* newspaper had been old and yellow, with more coupons than actual news.

I was still kneeling at Tiffany's feet. Suddenly, I didn't like it. I stood and brushed the crumbs off my apron. She was taller than I was, and I still had to look up to meet her gaze. But then again, she *was* wearing heels higher than the Empire State Building.

I crossed my arms. "What *should* I call you?"

She shrugged. "I dunno. Maybe 'Miss'?"

I almost laughed. "Seriously?"

"Or, if you want to make it more personal, you could always go with Miss Bedford." She lifted a hand and wiggled her fingers, making her massive diamond engagement ring sparkle in the light of the chandeliers. "Until I'm married, that is." She gave me a thin smile. "And *then,* you can call me Mrs. Senator."

Okay, that *had* to be a joke. Ever the optimist, I forced a laugh. "Good one."

She blinked. "A good what?"

I studied her face. So that *wasn't* a joke?

Could she seriously not remember me? I tried to think. I'd run into her just last month at a nearby book store. She'd recognized me just fine *then.*

And then it hit me.

At the book store, I'd been just another customer – an old college classmate. Now, I was the poor slob plucking seafood off the floor. Apparently, that put me so far below the future Mrs. Senator that we weren't even on speaking terms, even as acquaintances.

How lovely for her.

Probably, I should've let it go, but for some reason, I just couldn't. "Oh come on," I persisted. "I sat next to you in graphic design."

Her mouth tightened. "So about those crab cakes? That's a 'no', then?"

Oh, so that's how it was.

I pointed to the floor. "There's a couple. Want me to toss them onto a plate for you?"

She didn't even look. "They're not for *me*. They're for the senator."

Oh, for crying out loud. First of all, he was a *state* senator. And second of all, assuming Tiffany even made it to the altar, she'd be wife number four. "Fine," I said. "Want me to toss them onto a plate for *him*?"

She glanced at the floor, and her brow wrinkled. "Are they still warm?"

Oh. My. God. She wasn't seriously considering it? I said, "Well, they *do* have a nice coat of lint."

She frowned. "Can't you scrape it off or something?"

I gave her a disgusted look. "Are you serious?"

She lowered her voice. "I mean, like so he wouldn't know?"

"Oh, he'd know," I said. "And if he didn't, I'd tell him."

Her gaze narrowed. "You wouldn't."

"I would."

"Well, this is just great." She made a sound of frustration. "I can't go back without them. He gets all super-intense when he's hungry." She gave another huff. "And he's in the worst mood already."

No doubt, he was. After all, his fiancée had just been caught dry-humping the host. That would be enough to put anyone in a bad mood.

Still, why was she confiding in me of all people? After all, it's not like we were on a first-name basis or anything – as I'd been so recently informed.

Summoning up my last ounce of professionalism, I pointed to my left. "You *do* know they've got shrimp cocktail in the solarium."

She perked up. "Really? Why didn't you say so?"

"I just did."

"Oh, fine," she muttered. "Whatever." And with that, she turned and flounced away, heading toward the solarium. As for me, I returned to the floor and tried to count my blessings.

Oh sure, I might be plucking food off the carpet, and sure, I might've just been shunned by a former classmate, *and* yeah, I'd been caught eavesdropping by our not-so gracious host.

But it could always be worse, right?

Probably, that was the wrong question, because – almost as if I'd willed it personally – things did get worse, thanks to who?

Zane Bennington – the biggest prick in the universe.

CHAPTER 6

A voice, cool and masculine, sounded from the darkness. "Going someplace?"

I stifled a gasp. It was nearly three in the morning, and I'd finally hoofed it out to the rusty heap that passed for my car.

I whirled toward the sound and spotted him a few feet away, watching me from the shadows.

It was Zane Bennington, wearing the same clothes as before. But where *I* felt wrinkled and worn out, *he* looked just as glorious as he had three hours earlier – the last time he'd caught me by surprise.

Like everything else tonight, it simply wasn't fair. I gave him an annoyed look. "Yes, in fact. I'm going home."

"Don't tell me you forgot."

"Forgot what?"

"You *know* what."

I did know, but I refused to give him the satisfaction. Instead, I gave him a loose shrug and utter silence.

Take that, you jerk.

The sidewalk was wide and lined with trees. Probably, it was designed so that rich, happy couples could walk hand-in-hand and admire all of the estates that lined the super-exclusive gated neighborhood.

Unfortunately, I was in no mood to appreciate any of it. I wasn't rich. I wasn't happy. And I certainly wasn't part of a couple. Even my last date had been months ago, because seriously, who had the time?

Not me.

Not lately, anyway.

Into my silence, Zane said, "We had a deal."

"What deal?"

"You. Not leaving 'til I say so."

I lifted my chin. "It's only a deal if both people agree. And besides, you weren't around."

It was true. For once, timing had been on my side – or so I'd thought. When my shift had finally ended, Zane had been nowhere in sight. At the time, it seemed like a lucky break. I should've known better.

The street was very quiet, with no traffic and only the faint sound of wind rustling the trees. As I watched, Zane moved closer until we were sharing the same stretch of sidewalk.

He said, "I'm around now."

I felt myself swallow. *Yes. He was.* And he was even more imposing then I remembered. I took an involuntary step backward and almost tripped on the curb. I caught myself just in time, but only by grabbing the nearest thing within reach, which happened to be my side-view mirror. Of course, it came loose and crashed onto the pavement, where it shattered into like five pieces.

I stared down at the destruction. *Damn it.* How much would *that* cost? I looked back to Zane. "That was *your* fault."

If the accusation bothered him, he didn't show it. "Was it?"

"You know it was."

I waited him for him to argue. But he didn't. Instead, he gave my rust-bucket a perfunctory glance and said, "Your car sucks."

Yeah, it did. But did he really need to rub it in? Under my breath, I muttered, "Not as much as *you*."

His eyebrows lifted. "You don't care about your job much, do you?"

Well, this was just great. I made a sound of disbelief. "What is that? Another threat?" I threw up my hands. "You know what? Fine. Tell my employer. I don't care."

He studied my face for a long moment. "You're lying."

He was right. I was.

I *did* care. But there was no way I'd ever admit it now, not when it was too late to take it back. So instead, I doubled down. "It doesn't even matter," I told him. "I'm off the clock, so I can say whatever I want."

Technically, this was only half true. Yes, I was off the clock, but insulting the customer was – How shall I put it? – strongly discouraged.

He made a forwarding motion with his hand. "All right. Go ahead."

I gave him a perplexed look. "Go ahead and what?"

"Say it."

"Say what?"

"Whatever you want."

It was an obvious trap, and I refused to throw myself into it. "Oh sure," I said. "Like I'd fall for that trick."

"It's no trick," he said. "I wanna know what you think."

I almost laughed in his face. "No, you don't."

"Try me."

I was dead on my feet and beyond ready to leave. In a moment of utter insanity, I heard myself say, "All right. I think you're an asshole."

Startled by my own stupidity, I clamped my lips shut and waited for the fireworks. But none came.

Instead, he gave a slow nod. "And?"

"And what?"

"What else?"

I hesitated for only a split second before saying, "And a jerk."

"And?"

During the last three hours, the night had grown even colder. I wore no coat, and the icy breeze should've had me shivering. Funny, I *had* been shivering until he'd shown up.

But now, under the weight of his gaze, I felt myself growing warm, and not only in my extremities. If I were being totally honest, an embarrassing amount of heat was settling somewhere just south of my stomach.

How humiliating.

But in my own defense, there was something about him that was drawing me in. It wasn't his money, and it wasn't his looks. And – this was a biggie – Lord knows, it couldn't be his personality, because let's face it, he was the biggest prick I'd ever had the misfortune of meeting.

And yet, there *was* something.

Suddenly, I was almost afraid – and not because it was the middle of the night or because it was just the two of us, standing alone in the near darkness.

It was because, for the first time, I detected the faint hint of laugh lines around his eyes and dwelled on the sweet fullness of his lips. My heart gave a traitorous flutter. *Oh yeah*. There was definitely something about his mouth. It didn't *look* like it was made for frowning. It looked like it was made for kissing – I swallowed – kissing *me?*

I blinked. *What the hell?*

I felt my gaze narrow. If this was some sort of game, I didn't want to play it. For one thing, I didn't have the time. And for another, he *had* to know exactly what he was doing to me – what he'd do to almost *any* girl with a pulse.

He might be a prick, but he wasn't stupid.

So, what was this, anyway?

The silence stretched out between us, crackling as our gazes locked and held.

I couldn't read his expression, and maybe that was a good thing. For some reason, I thought of him with Tiffany – a.k.a. the future Mrs. State Senator.

They'd been caught in the coat room with her dress hiked high, and his hands heading for ground zero. I hadn't seen their encounter, but I'd heard plenty from my fellow catering assistants as well as from all those party guests who didn't mind gossiping in front of the help.

The help.

That was me.

And Zane was… well, trouble, that's what.

I mumbled, "I've gotta go." And yet, I made no move.

He said, "I've got a question."

"What?"

"Why didn't you tell anyone?"

"Tell anyone what?"

He flicked his head toward his estate. "What you heard."

Obviously, he meant the ugliness I'd overheard from inside the van. No doubt, it would've made for a good story, and yet, I hadn't told a soul.

But that was no big mystery. I said, "I don't gossip."

"Why not?"

I stared at him. What kind of question was that? It was like asking why I didn't eat soup with a fork. I wasn't an idiot. No, I used a spoon for the same reason I resisted the urge to blab about things I'd overheard by mistake.

Who needs a mess, right?

When I made no response, he frowned. "And why'd you walk out alone?"

I glanced around. "You mean out here? To my car?"

He gave my car a dismissive glance. "If that's what you're calling that thing."

Well, that was charming.

I gave him an annoyed look. "Oh, so now you're insulting me?"

It shouldn't have been a surprise. He insulted everyone – or so I'd heard.

"I wasn't insulting *you*," he said. "I was insulting your car." He spared it another glance before saying, "Don't tell me you *like* that thing."

I felt my jaw clench. "Hey, that 'thing' got me here just fine, so maybe you should show it some respect."

Why on Earth was I sticking up for my car? I absolutely hated it, probably even more than he did, because *I* was the one stuck driving it. The car wasn't just ugly. It was practically useless. The heat was iffy, the upholstery was ripped, and its gas mileage seriously sucked.

Still, the car wasn't *his* to insult.

And why was I still here?

His frown deepened. "You make a habit of this?"

I wasn't quite sure what he meant. "A habit of what?"

"Being careless."

My jaw dropped. "You're one to talk."

After all, *I* wasn't the one who knocked over the serving station.

His gaze shifted, as if taking in our surroundings. "And where's your partner?"

"What partner? You mean Naomi? She's driving the van back."

"And the others?"

"You mean the other catering assistants?" I gave a bitter laugh. "They left an hour ago."

"And you didn't?"

"No, because I got stuck trying to clean that stupid rug, not that it did any good."

To add insult to injury, it wasn't even *my* idea. Naomi and I had been all packed up and ready to leave when Ms. Hedgwick marched up to tell us that we couldn't go anywhere until we'd cleaned up *all* of our mess, *including* the rug.

It was so unfair. I mean, it's not like *we* toppled the table.

Again, I felt my gaze narrow. In fact, the table had been toppled by Zane, who apparently, wasn't done making my night miserable.

His cool voice interrupted my thoughts. "Fuck the rug."

And there it was – another dose of déjà vu. It was just like his comment about the crab cakes, but only worse, because it was three hours later, and I felt so damned grubby.

I gave him my snottiest smile. "I can't, because I'm too tired from 'fucking' the crab cakes."

My words hung in the air, and I felt color rush to my cheeks. I didn't seriously just say that. *Fuck the crab cakes?* That sounded weird and stupid, and yes, obscene in a truly disgusting way.

Plus, now that I thought about it, he hadn't said "Fuck the crab cakes." He'd said, "Fuck the candles."

Totally different.

Worst of all, I swear, I saw amusement flicker in his eyes until it was replaced by something else.

Sadness?

No. Contempt. Or something just as bad.

Either way, I'd had enough. I said, "What do you want, anyway?"

As an answer, he held out his hand, palm up. "Your phone."

"What?" I gave him a perplexed look. "Why?"

"I'm gonna key in my number."

Okay, now I was really confused. "And why would you do that?"

"So you can call me when you're fired."

My stomach clenched. "What?"

"When you're fired," he said, "call me."

I was glaring at him now. "I'm not gonna be fired." I swallowed. *Was I?*

"Or, if you want," he added, "you can key it in yourself."

Key what in? His phone number? This had to be a joke. I gave him a stiff smile. "Gee, thanks."

"You're welcome."

I made a scoffing sound. "I didn't mean it."

"Good."

I studied his face. What kind of response was *that*? Looking at him, I had no clue, and I was in no mood to try to figure it out.

With a sigh of irritation, I turned away and yanked my keys out of my purse. With nervous fingers, I fumbled for the one that would unlock my car door.

The car was so old, it didn't even have keyless entry, and my hands shook when I tried to insert the key into the lock.

It wasn't even because of the cold. It was because of him – the prick standing just a few feet away. With my back turned, I couldn't see him, but I could feel his eyes on my back, watching and mocking as I yanked open my car door and hesitated as I remembered the side-view mirror.

Reluctantly, I looked down. And there it was – or what was left of it. I tried to think. Would it be cheaper to have it repaired, or to just get a new one?

The thought of scooping it up was beyond humiliating. And yet, I'd feel like a slug if I just left it lying in the gutter like a discarded condom.

Heat flooded my face. *A condom?* Where on Earth had *that* thought come from?

Trying not to dwell on it, I crouched down and plucked the mirror pieces off the pavement, and then tossed them onto the passenger's side floor. Afterward, I slid into the driver's seat and yanked the car door shut behind me.

My car started on the first try – thank God. Still, I wasn't taking any chances. As fast as I could, I shifted into gear and slammed my foot on the gas. My car lurched forward with an embarrassing amount of clunking and rattling.

But at least I was on my way.

Against my better judgment, I snuck a quick glance in the rear-view mirror. Zane Bennington was still standing there, looking like every girl's impossible dream.

But so what? Dreamy or not, he was living proof of everything that was so unfair in this world. The guy had it all, and what was he doing with it?

Tormenting *me* of all people.

And thanks to him, I now had something else to worry about. *Was I going to lose my job?*

No. I wasn't. I returned my attention to the road and kept it there. As far as the job thing, he was just toying with me.

He *had* to be.

Right?

CHAPTER 7

From my open front doorway, I stared down at the small decorated cake that my sister held out in front of her. On the cake, in small scripted letters, was a single word, written in festive pink icing.

I read the word out loud. "Congratulations?" I looked up. "To who?"

Charlotte gave an exaggerated eye-roll. "To you. Who else?" She was standing on my front doorstep looking ten times more awake than I was. "Now, c'mon," she said. "Let me in, so we can celebrate."

I rubbed at my aching eyes. It wasn't yet noon, and I'd gotten only a few hours of sleep. I loved my sister. And I loved cake. I should've been delighted.

Damn it. I *was* delighted. Charlotte still lived with my parents and was attending nursing school an hour south. I hadn't seen her in weeks.

Still, I would've been even *more* delighted if only she'd surprised me a few hours later. After my odd encounter with Zane Bennington, I'd slept like crap and was feeling the effects.

Still, I tried to smile as I stepped aside and held the door open wider to let her in. "What are we celebrating?"

She didn't move, and her gaze dipped to my clothes, as if noticing them for the first time. "I didn't wake you, did I?"

I was wearing a long T-shirt and my comfiest sweatpants. The outfit was, sadly, my jammies. Reluctantly, I admitted, "Actually, you did."

"Oh." She lowered the cake. "Sorry. But I just figured…" She paused. "I mean, it *is* noon."

It wasn't *quite* noon, but I wasn't going to quibble. I motioned for her to come inside. "Yeah, I know. So it's a good thing you showed up, huh?"

She hesitated. "Are you sure?"

My eyes felt like sandpaper, but I tried not to show it. I really *was* glad to see her. "Definitely. I mean, I can't sleep *all* day, right?"

Finally, she laughed. "Well, not alone, anyway."

I tried to join in the laughter, but the comment still made me think. Zach and I had broken up how long ago? Five months? Or was it six? Either way, I'd been sleeping alone for so long that I'd started wearing sweatpants to bed. They weren't sexy, but they *did* keep me warm when the nights grew cold.

And last night had been particularly chilly.

Finally, Charlotte stepped into the house. "So what happened?" she asked. "Did you oversleep?"

"I guess. Maybe."

She gave me a perplexed look. "You *did* get my message, right?"

"There was a message?"

Charlotte sighed. And then, as if shaking off a minor irritation, she smiled. "Never mind." She began heading toward the kitchen, and I trudged behind her, trying my best to shrug off my grogginess.

When we reached the kitchen, Charlotte placed the cake in the middle of the table and said, "You wanna grab some plates?"

Obviously, there was something she wasn't telling me, and it didn't take a genius to figure out what. "Let me guess," I said. "You called the landline, and got Paisley. Am I right?"

Paisley was my roommate, or at least, she was supposed to be. But lately, she'd been making herself scarce, and I knew why. The rent was due five days ago. Coincidentally, it had been exactly five days since I'd seen her last.

Nodding in answer to my question, Charlotte pulled out a chair and sat. As I put on a pot of coffee, she went on to tell me that she'd called my place yesterday. I hadn't been home, but she'd caught Paisley, who'd grudgingly promised to pass along Charlotte's message that she'd be stopping by.

Charlotte concluded by saying, "You know, you *really* need to get a cell phone."

"I *have* a cell phone."

She perked up. "So you found it?"

"No." I forced a smile. "But I will."

In the meantime, I was using the landline, which oddly enough was one of the few things included with the rent – excluding long distance, of course. So thanks to an old cordless telephone, I could still make and receive calls.

In theory, anyway.

I glanced at the charging station, where the cordless telephone was supposed to be. The station was empty.

Well, this was just perfect.

No phone. No message. No rent.

And I just knew that if I opened the pantry, I'd also find practically no groceries, even though I'd been buying far more than my share.

Charlotte's voice interrupted my thoughts. "Just accept it. Your cell's gone."

I gave the charging station another glance. The way it looked, my cell wasn't the *only* phone that was missing. I looked back to Charlotte and said, "It's not *really* gone. It's somewhere in the house."

Hopefully.

Charlotte looked unconvinced. "If you say so."

Finally, I was feeling more awake. "But wait, you said you called *yesterday*?"

"Yeah. Around five."

My gaze narrowed. "So she *was* home."

"You mean Paisley? Yeah. Why?"

I made a sound of annoyance. "Because she hasn't been around."

Charlotte laughed. "You say it like it's a *bad* thing."

I knew what Charlotte meant. Paisley was a little on the dramatic side. And I *hated* drama, just like I hated it when Paisley cranked up the thermostat, even when she was on her way out the door.

Still, I *had* to catch up with her. It was, after all, my best shot at snagging the rent money. I looked to Charlotte and explained, "I've been calling her for days, but she hasn't been answering. And of course, I know why."

Charlotte's eyebrows lifted. "Because she's too busy boning her professor?"

"No." I hesitated. "Well, yeah, probably. But that's not what I meant. I *mean* she's avoiding me because the rent's due."

Charlotte was frowning now. "So she stiffed you? Again?"

I tried not to look as worried as I felt. "Well, technically, she always pays, so I'm sure I'll get it eventually."

After a lot of begging, pleading, and yes, occasionally stalking.

Charlotte gave a derisive snort. "Yeah. Like two months late."

This was only a slight exaggeration. "So anyway," I said, "yesterday, I get *so* desperate that I call her cell phone from this catering gig – meaning a number she wouldn't recognize – and she *finally* answers."

"So you tricked her, huh?" Charlotte gave a slow nod. "Nice."

"Oh yeah, she just 'loved' that," I said. "But anyway, she tells me that she's out of town."

"Really? Where?"

I gave a dismissive wave of my hand. "She didn't say. But the point is, she tells me that she'd just *love* to give me the rent money now, but she can't, because she's gone 'til Wednesday."

Charlotte made a scoffing sound. "And you actually bought that story?"

"Not really," I said. "But it's not like I've seen her around, so I can't really call her on it." I felt my jaw clench. "But then *you* tell me that she was home just yesterday, maybe right here, in this kitchen."

"And you seriously didn't know?"

"How would I?" I asked. "I was at work."

"But if she's not home, where does she sleep?"

"Well, not at the good professor's house, that's for sure."

The professor was married. According to Paisley, he and his wife had some sort of understanding. I wasn't buying it. Not only was the guy a total cheater, he was a pompous, smarmy ass.

"Yeah," Charlotte said. "I'm sure his wife would just 'love' a big ol' sleepover."

My gaze drifted to the fridge. Taped on the front of it were both of my work schedules, written on two separate index cards.

I stalked to the fridge and yanked both of them off. I crumpled up the first one and tossed it in the trash. After all, I'd finished that job just yesterday. The other card, I folded up and set aside, with plans to put it someplace less visible.

Obviously, I'd been making it way too easy for Paisley to know when I was coming and going. And, during the last few weeks, my schedule had been particularly hectic.

Until just yesterday, I'd been holding down two jobs – a part-time job at a donut shop and the catering gig, which had only recently been converted to full-time. Now, finally, I had one full-time job instead of two part-time ones.

Thank goodness.

My gaze drifted to the cake, and I felt a wave of guilt wash over me. I'd been so lost in my griping that I'd completely lost sight of the fact that this was apparently supposed to be some sort of celebration.

I gave Charlotte an apologetic smile. "Sorry."

"For what?" she asked.

"For ruining the celebration."

"You're not ruining it," she said. "You're making it more interesting." She leaned forward. "Tell me. Is Paisley still claiming to be a psychic?"

I had to laugh. "Probably."

I turned and pulled out two of my best dessert plates, along with a couple of forks and a big knife. I set everything on the table and then went back for two mugs of coffee.

Finally, I claimed the seat across from my sister and asked, "So what are we celebrating?"

"Oh, stop it," she said. "You *know* what. Your promotion."

"Oh, that? It's not really a promotion." I couldn't help but sigh. "And it's *still* just a dead end job. I mean, it's not like I'm using my degree."

"So? You're still meeting interesting people, right?"

Instantly, a vision of Zane Bennington popped into my head. *Oh yeah*. He was definitely interesting, in a giant rich prick sort of way.

I gave an epic eye-roll. "Sure. And I'm serving them crab cakes. I mean, it's not like we're rubbing elbows or anything."

"Eh, who cares?" she said. "At least you're not making donuts anymore."

Well, there *was* that. In truth, I loved donuts, but getting up at the crack of dawn to make them wasn't my idea of a good time, especially after working a late-night catering gig.

But forget the donuts. I had cake. And a wonderful sister who'd made a special trip to make a celebration out of nearly nothing. If that wasn't a reason to smile, what was?

I was just about to cut into the cake when I heard a noise that made me pause. It was a thud. And it had come from somewhere inside the house.

Paisley?

Or someone else?

CHAPTER 8

I leaned across the kitchen table and whispered, "Did you hear that?"

Charlotte's coffee cup was halfway to her lips. She froze in mid-motion. "Hear what?"

I listened more carefully. Somewhere inside the house, a door creaked. I glanced toward the sound. "Shh! I think it's her."

Silently, Charlotte returned her cup to the table and whispered, "Paisley?"

I nodded. It had *better* be Paisley. If not, I had bigger problems than a deadbeat roommate.

Charlotte whispered, "And why are we whispering?"

"Because I'm trying to think of a plan."

"Screw planning," Charlotte said. "Just march out there, grab her by the hair, and say, 'Pay up, bitch. Or else.'"

I stared at my sister. In my whole life, I'd never heard her call anyone a bitch. Ignoring *that* pesky detail, I asked, "Or else what?"

Charlotte hesitated. "I don't know." She glanced away. "You could always slap her around or something."

I was still staring. My sister wasn't the violent type either – or at least, not that I knew of. I asked, "Is that a serious suggestion?"

She gave a small shrug and mumbled, "Well, it's how they do it in the movies."

I rolled my eyes. "Good to know."

And yet, Charlotte was correct about one thing. I didn't really need a plan. I just needed the money. And I wouldn't get it by sitting around the kitchen table while Paisley snuck out to who-knows-where.

As quietly as I could, I pushed back my chair and stood. I looked to my sister and whispered, "Wait here."

"No way." Already, Charlotte was pushing back her own chair. "I want to see this, especially if it gets slappy."

"It's *not* going to get slappy," I told her. "The last thing I need is more drama."

"But what about backup?" she asked. "You need that, right?"

I looked at my sister. She was twenty-one years old and barely over five feet tall. And yet, I was pretty sure she could kick Paisley's ass all by herself if it came down to it – not because my sister was a brute, but because I knew Paisley. She'd crumble like a cookie at the first sign of any real threat.

I whispered, "I'll be fine. Let me handle this. Please?"

With obvious reluctance, Charlotte sat back down. "Oh, all right," she muttered. "But I'll be listening, just in case."

Silently, I turned and tiptoed away. A minute later, I found Paisley with her hand on the front doorknob and an oversized tote bag slung over her shoulder. The way it looked, she was on the verge of leaving.

I felt my gaze narrow. *Not so fast, buttercup.*

I called out, "Going someplace?"

The question had barely left my mouth when it occurred to me that this was the exact same thing that Zane Bennington had said to *me* last night, when I'd been trying to make my own escape on the street outside his house.

But this was totally different. Paisley owed me money. I owed Zane Bennington nothing.

Paisley was still facing the front door. Her long blond hair was in a loose ponytail and was dyed pink on the edges. She was wearing black skinny-jeans and a red flannel shirt several sizes too big.

Probably, the shirt belonged to the professor. The guy dressed like a lumberjack and screwed like a donkey – or at least, that's what he sounded like when he climaxed.

Yes, the walls *were* that thin.

And why was I thinking about this?

In front of me, Paisley still hadn't moved. Either she was planning to bolt, or she was busy thinking up her next excuse.

I crossed my arms and waited.

With a loud sigh, Paisley finally turned around. "Actually, yes," she said. "I *am* going someplace. And I'm in a hurry, so—"

"Great," I chirped. "If you wanna toss me the money, I'll grab it fast so you can be on your way."

She put on her confused face. "What money?"

As if she didn't know. "The rent money."

She frowned. "But I already told you, I'll get it to you on Wednesday."

"Uh-huh." I gave her a look. "Because you were *supposedly* out of town."

Her mouth tightened. "Are you calling me a liar?"

"I don't know," I said. "*Are* you out of town?"

"Oh, so now you're making fun of me?"

Was I? Probably, a little. But seriously, she had it coming. "Listen," I said, "I don't want to be a nag, but the rent was due five days ago. And I can't keep paying your share on top of my own."

"What are you saying? That I'm a deadbeat?" Her voice rose. "I've *always* paid. You know that."

"Maybe," I admitted. "But you've never paid on time."

At this, she had the nerve to look insulted. "I have, too."

Now, it was my turn to sigh. "Fine. Other than the very first month, you've never paid on time."

"Oh, so you're keeping track? Is that it?"

"Of course I'm keeping track. I have to. The lease is in my name."

"So?"

"So if it's not paid, *I'm* the one in trouble."

"Oh, please," she said. "You are not. You act like someone's gonna drag you off to jail or something." She rolled her eyes. "God, you are so dramatic."

My mouth fell open. "Me? *I'm* the dramatic one?"

"Well, you don't see *me* giving *you* a hard time, do you?"

What the hell? "You don't think it's hard when you don't pay your share of the rent?"

"Oh, for fuck's sake." Paisley hurled her tote-bag onto the floor. "I *have* paid. Every single month. Do we seriously need to go through this? *Again*?"

I eyed her bag. It was open at the top, and I spotted a familiar-looking wine bottle nestled among her clothes.

I felt my gaze narrow. "Is that my wine?"

She looked down. "What do you mean?"

I pointed. "That bottle of cabernet. Is that the one I just bought?"

"How would *I* know?" she said. "It's not like we go shopping together."

I considered the empty pantry and equally empty fridge. "It's not like *you* go shopping at all."

"I do, too," She pointed down at her legs. "I just bought these jeans." She gave me a thin smile. "Goes to show what *you* know."

Well, that was rich. I gave the jeans a good, long look. I wasn't a huge shopper, mostly because I was always broke. But I *did* know that whatever she spent on those jeans could've contributed at least *something* toward this month's rent.

Through gritted teeth, I said, "And *when* did you buy them?"

"Yesterday." She gave my sweatpants a scornful glance. "I mean, I'm not gonna go around like *that*."

Paisley was like a machine with two settings – bitch or crybaby, with very little in between. It was pretty obvious where the dial was set today.

I told her, "These are my *sleeping* clothes."

She gave a derisive snort. "Yeah, and no wonder you're alone."

Stupid or not, her words stung. It shouldn't have mattered. After all, this *was* Paisley, the perpetual grad student who was sleeping with her professor. Correction, her *married* professor.

Still, I didn't know what to say. I was still searching for the perfect comeback when I heard a familiar voice behind me call out, "And no wonder *you're* about to get slapped."

I whirled around to see my sister glaring at my roommate. I gave Charlotte a pleading look. "I'm *not* going to slap her."

"Oh yeah?" Charlotte said. "Well maybe *I* am." She looked back to Paisley and said, "Now, pay up." She hesitated for a long moment before mumbling, "Or else."

I tried to look on the bright side. At least she hadn't called Paisley a bitch. Well, not yet, anyway. I looked back to Paisley. Trying to tone everything down, I said, "Look, just give me what you can, okay?"

Paisley looked from me to my sister. I looked from Paisley to Charlotte. Charlotte looked from me to Paisley. The tension in the room crackled like a firework about to explode.

It was Charlotte who finally broke the silence. She looked to my roommate and demanded, "And where's the message, Paisley?"

Paisley said, "What message?"

"When I called yesterday, you *promised* to give Jane the message. You even *claimed* you were writing it down."

Paisley was glaring again. "I *did* write it down."

"Oh yeah?" Charlotte crossed her arms. "Then where is it?"

As an answer, Paisley turned and stalked toward the kitchen. I followed after her, with Charlotte on my heels. At the kitchen counter, Paisley lifted the phone's charging station and sure enough, underneath it were a couple of scribbled notes.

Paisley grabbed them and thrust them out in my direction. "There." She turned to Charlotte and said, "You can apologize any time now."

Charlotte gave a bark of laughter. "In your dreams."

I spoke up. "But Paisley, I don't get it. Why'd you put them *there*?"

Paisley replied, "That's where we always put them."

"No, we don't." In truth, we didn't put them anywhere. No one ever called for Paisley – well, at least not on the landline. And, as far as I knew, these were first actual messages that Paisley had bothered to write down.

Paisley said, "I'm not talking about you and me. I'm talking about my parent's house, when I was growing up."

"And you didn't think to tell me?"

"I shouldn't have to tell you," Paisley said. "It's common sense. And you know what else?"

"What?"

"I'm getting a little tired of being your secretary."

Next to me, Charlotte muttered, "Good thing, since you suck at it."

I turned to my sister. "Charlotte, please. You're not helping."

Across from us, Paisley threw up her arms. "You know what? Screw this shit." She elbowed her way between me and Charlotte and then kept on going, heading toward the front door.

I didn't try to stop her. Why bother? It was pretty obvious that she wasn't going to pay up, at least not right now.

I looked to Charlotte. I adored my little sister, and I was fully aware of how lucky I was that she cared enough to stick up for me. But still, I had to say it. "You promised to stay in the kitchen."

She gave me a shaky smile. "I *am* in the kitchen." She pointed toward the kitchen counter. "See?"

I sighed. "You know what I mean."

"Oh, all right," she muttered. "But she was a total bitch to you." Charlotte's tone softened as she added, "And in a way, this is all my fault."

I shook my head. "It's not your fault. It's Paisley's."

Still, I knew what Charlotte meant. Paisley was the sister of Charlotte's ex-boyfriend. This connection was how Paisley and I had become roommates in the first place. It all happened just seven months ago, when I'd found the perfect rental house, *this* house in fact, a cute little two-bedroom in a decent neighborhood with lots of old, stately trees.

The house even allowed pets.

In my dreams, I had time to grill hamburgers in the shaded back yard and walk a cute little fuzzball of a dog to the nearby park. In those dreams, I could *also* afford plenty of dog food and the occasional vet bill.

But reality had turned out to be so very different.

Now, I could barely afford food for myself, much less medical care of the human variety. Good thing I was healthy, or I'd be really screwed.

And here, my roommate – someone recommended by my own sister – had turned out to be a deadbeat drama queen.

As if reading my mind, Charlotte said, "She was a lot nicer before. Honest."

I gave Charlotte a look. "And how many times did you meet her?"

"I dunno." Charlotte glanced away. "A couple."

I didn't push the issue. In reality, it was mostly *my* fault, not Charlotte's.

To think, I'd actually believed Paisley's assessment of her prior roommate. Supposedly, the former roommate had been, in Paisley's words, a total downer.

Since I was on the cheerful side, it sounded like Paisley and I would be a perfect fit. Now, *I'd* become the downer – the one who nagged about the rent and griped about the groceries.

Still, I tried to look on the bright side. I'd finally gotten my phone messages. That was something, right?

The crumpled notes were still in my hand. I looked down and scanned the top one. It had only three words. *Charlotte. Noon. Tomorrow.*

Charlotte snatched the note and gave it a quick read. "Talk about vague," she said. "It doesn't even say where. I mean, what if I were meeting you for coffee or something? I'd still be there waiting."

I tried to laugh. "And I'd still home be in my jammies."

In unison, Charlotte and I looked down to my sweatpants. I couldn't help but recall Paisley's snide comment. Oh sure, it was easy for *her* to talk when she spent *her* rent money on herself, while I spent mine on, go figure, actual rent.

Pushing that thought aside, I glanced down at the second note. It took me only a split second to read it. And yet, I felt compelled to read it again, and then a third time afterward.

I was shaking my head. This note was even more concise than the first. In fact, it had only two words. But they packed a wallop.

You're fired.

CHAPTER 9

Seven hours later, I was standing on Zane Bennington's front doorstep. For the third time, I reached out and slapped at the doorbell. With growing impatience, I listened as the deep, melodious chimes echoed from inside the mansion.

The doorbell was obnoxiously loud, and yet, I could barely hear it over the happy yips of the two hounds pawing at the nearest front window. They'd nudged aside the curtains and were slobbering all over the glass.

Good.

If I was lucky, they'd leave some nice scratches, too.

When they saw me looking, I swear, they smiled. They weren't huge, but they were definitely hounds – or whatever someone called short-haired, floppy-eared dogs that were completely out of control.

When I leaned in for a closer look, the darker one gave a particularly happy yip.

Any other time, I might've smiled. But not today. And not here. Still, a very tiny part of me couldn't help but feel at least a little guilty, because I'd gotten their hopes up for nothing.

I called out, "I don't *have* any freaking meatballs!"

The dogs stopped yipping for only a split second before starting up again. I told them a second time, but they *still* looked happy.

Goobers.

I tried to look on the bright side. Maybe if they got *really* excited, they'd pee on the curtains. And if I got especially lucky, Zane wouldn't even notice until next week, when the stink really set in.

That would show him.

I pulled my attention from the dogs and smacked the doorbell again. Hell, I could do this all night. I mean, it's not like I had a job to go to or anything.

Jerk.

In the back of my mind, I realized that the odds of him actually answering his own door were slim to none. But surely *someone* would answer eventually.

And whoever that someone was, they'd need to fetch the ass-hat who'd torpedoed my catering job. Or, they'd need to call the police – because I wasn't going anywhere until I saw Mister Fancy Pants in person.

And then what? Honestly, I wasn't quite sure. But I *did* know that if nothing else, he deserved a piece of my mind. He wasn't a customer anymore – not to me, anyway – so I could be as rude as I wanted.

As I continued slapping away at the doorbell, his words from last night echoed in my brain. *"Call me when you're fired."*

Oh, I was going to call him all right.

Already, I had a good selection of names. On impulse, I decided to work my way through the alphabet, starting with *asshole*.

I slapped the doorbell again and started making a mental list.

Bastard.

Cockwaffle.

Dick.

I hesitated. What begins with the letter "e?"

I tried to think, but nothing came to mind. *Damn it.* This was no good. If I was already stumbling on "e," what would I do when I reached "x"?

While pondering this, I kept slapping away at the doorbell.

Eater of shit?

No. That was cheating.

Enema...? I paused. *Bag?*

No. That was just stupid.

Praying that inspiration would strike later, I skipped over "e" and moved on to "f."

Happily, this was an easy one. *Fuck-face.* In the spirit of things, I awarded myself bonus points for using the right letter twice.

By now, I had a pretty good rhythm going. *Slap, wait. Slap again.* My palm was stinging, and my breath was coming in short, angry bursts. By now, I was so angry that I barely heard the dogs even as they yipped away in the background.

On some level, I realized that I was about to make a spectacle of myself, but I couldn't bring myself to care.

I was still working my way through the alphabet.

Prick.

Quack-head.

Rat-face.

Admittedly, my standards were falling with every letter, but still, I kept on going.

Shit-bag.

I was so lost in my own anger that it took me a moment to realize that a large shadow had crept up behind me, darkening the front door beyond my own silhouette.

I stopped slapping and whirled around. And there he was – Mister Fancy Pants himself. Except he didn't *look* fancy. And he wasn't wearing pants, not technically, anyway.

Instead, he was wearing black running shorts and some sort of dark hoodie that wasn't even zipped. Without thinking, I zoomed in on his torso. Where a shirt *should've* been, I saw a wet muscular chest and, below that, glistening washboard abs.

Heat flooded my face, and I yanked my gaze upward. His hair was dripping wet, and a small white towel was draped over the back of his neck.

I stared in utter confusion. Darkness aside, it was only April and unseasonably cold. It wouldn't be swimming weather for at least two months. But that wasn't the only thing that made me pause.

It was his appearance. Last night, he'd looked every inch the billionaire. Now, he was a damp, disheveled mess. Unfortunately, he was also a *hot* mess, as much as I hated to admit it.

Well, this was just great.

I was so flustered that the next word on my list shot out of my mouth. "Turd!"

CHAPTER 10

I froze, even as the word echoed out between us.

Damn it. I'd been planning to start with the letter "a", and now, the whole thing was ruined, just like my catering job.

From inside the house, the dogs sounded happier than ever. Oh sure, they could afford to be happy. They didn't need jobs.

But I did.

Ignoring the yipping behind me, I ditched my list of names and went straight to the point. I glared at Zane and demanded, "How could you?"

He looked entirely unruffled, well, except for his hair, which looked annoyingly sexy in spite of its damp disarray.

He eyed me with apparent disinterest. "How could I what?"

"Oh come on. You *know* what." Even after a dozen phone calls to the catering company – using Charlotte's cell phone no less, since both of my phones were *still* missing – I'd learned very little about my abrupt termination.

All they'd been willing to tell me was that there'd been a serious customer-complaint. They wouldn't even say from who, but it was laughably easy to guess. After all, there'd been only one person who'd known I was about to get fired.

It was the jerk standing right here in front of me, barefoot no less. I felt my eyebrows furrow. "And where are your shoes?"

"Does it matter?"

"No."

"Then why'd you ask?"

"Oh, forget it. You can guess why I'm here." My voice rose. "I was fired today. There, are you happy?"

He studied me for a long, silent moment. Funny, he didn't *look* happy. But then again, I'd never seen him smile. For all *I* knew, this was his version of jumping for joy.

But damn it, I *wanted* an answer. "Well?" I crossed my arms. "Are you?"

His gaze shifted to my car, parked a few paces away in the turnaround. "No."

My arms dropped to my sides. So he *wasn't* happy? Really? Could a prick like him actually feel regret? Cautiously, I said, "And why not?"

He was still looking at my car. "Because I've gotta fire the guard."

Huh? "What guard?"

"The guy at the gate."

Oh, no. He couldn't mean the guy who'd let me into the neighborhood. I swallowed. Could he?

Zane looked back to me, and his expression darkened. "There's a gate out there for a reason."

His words felt like a slap. "Oh, yeah?" I said. "And why's that? To keep the riff-raff out? Is that what you're saying?"

Ignoring my tirade, he looked back to my car and muttered, "Shit."

I forced a bitter laugh. "Look, I'm *ever* so sorry that my car offends you, but if you hadn't gotten me fired, I wouldn't even *be* here, and neither would my car." I glowered in his general direction. "And just so you know, it has a nice, long history of not starting, so if you're really lucky, it'll be here all week."

To my infinite frustration, he was *still* looking at my car. *The jerk.*

Under his lack of attention, my rant was losing momentum fast. Lamely, I finished by mumbling, "And it would serve you right."

Finally, he returned his attention to me. "And where will *you* be?"

I didn't get it. "What do you mean?"

A note of sarcasm crept into his voice. "Are *you* staying too?"

I gave him my snottiest smile. "That depends. Are *you* leaving?"

"No."

I lifted my chin. "Then I'm not staying." Of course, it was a stupid thing to say. I mean, it's not like I'd been invited or anything. But that wasn't the point. He needed to know that I hated *him*, just as much as he hated *me*.

In fact, I hated him more, because *he* hated everyone, while all of *my* hatred was reserved just for him.

Wasn't *he* special?

He looked past me, toward the dogs, who, if anything, sounded happier than ever. "Good to know," Zane said. "Are we done?"

Were we? This hadn't gone anything like I'd expected. On the drive over, I'd spent a lot of time fantasizing about this particular moment. By now, I was supposed to be basking in the warm afterglow of telling him off.

I searched my heart and mind. *No afterglow.*

Talk about disappointing.

But I wasn't ready to give up. Not yet.

I kept my feet rooted to his doorstep and tried to think.

What now?

In my fantasies, this encounter had always ended in one of two ways – either with him begging for my forgiveness *or* getting so angry that he made an ass of himself.

But there he was, not on his knees and somehow managing to look sinfully delicious when anyone else in his shoes – or rather *lack* of shoes – would look like a drowned rat.

More annoyed than ever, I demanded, "And why are you wet?"

"Does it matter?"

Oh, great. This again? I made a sound of frustration. "Fine. Don't tell me."

"All right."

Perversely, now I *really* wanted to know. "It just seems to me," I persisted, "that after you made me so miserable, the least you could do is answer a simple question."

He gave me a quick once-over. "You don't look miserable to me."

"Well, I am."

"And why's that?"

Oh, for crying out loud. "Weren't you listening? You got me fired."

"And you *liked* that job?"

Not particularly. But I *was* fond of eating and paying the rent. "That's not the point."

"That's no answer."

I made a scoffing sound. "So? You won't give *me* any answers." As I spoke, I tried not to notice that the water droplets were easing down his abs in a way that was stupidly distracting.

And why wasn't he freezing? He *should* be freezing. Unless…?

My gaze narrowed. "You were in the hot tub, weren't you?"

I should've known. It was the only thing that made sense. Probably, the tub's temperature was set so high that this whole standing-around-in-the-cold thing was some sort of cool-down. Probably to him, the air felt brisk and refreshing.

That *had* to be it. And stubbornly, I wanted him to admit it. "I'm right, aren't I?"

"No."

Damn it. "Are you sure?"

He gave me a look. "I was swimming."

"Oh." I paused. "So the pool's heated?"

"No."

I couldn't help but stare. "Seriously? Aren't you cold?"

"What do *you* think?"

"I think you're crazy."

"Trust me." His voice grew deadpan. "You have no idea."

He was right. I didn't. And I never would, because if I had my way, I'd never be seeing him again. With that in mind, I said, "Good. Because I don't want to."

Huh?

Even *I* wasn't sure what that meant. Regardless, it was definitely an exit line. So with my head held high, I marched past him, heading toward my car, only to feel my steps falter halfway as a terrible realization hit home.

I whirled around and said, "Wait!"

To my surprise, he'd barely moved. But it was easy to guess why. He wanted to make sure I was long gone before ducking into the warmth of his mansion.

I gave him a hard look. *Not yet, buddy.*

I stalked forward until we were standing within arm's reach. I said, "You're not *really* going to fire that guy, are you?"

"The guard? Hell yeah."

My stomach sank. "But you can't."

"I can," he said. "And I will."

Damn it. This was all because of me and my stupid car. I couldn't let that happen. "But..." Desperately, I looked around. "It can't be just *your* decision. I mean, the neighbors get a say-so too, right?"

"Wrong."

"But—"

"The guy's gone. Forget it."

Crap. I tried again. "But he was really nice."

Zane's jaw tightened. "Was he?"

"Definitely. So you should keep him." I shoved aside my loathing, and summoned up a hopeful smile. "I mean, nice is good, right?"

"For a guard?" Zane eyed me with cool contempt. "No."

"But he's not really a guard-guard," I said. "He's more of a welcome wagon, or like a greeter in a grocery store."

Zane gave me a look. "He's supposed to be a guard, not a welcome wagon."

"Well, yeah, but he wasn't *that* welcoming. I mean, I had to *really* talk him into letting me through."

This wasn't a lie. On the dashboard of my car, I still had a parking pass from last night. Unfortunately, the pass was for one night only, and tonight wasn't the night.

Still, when I'd explained to the guy that I had some important unfinished business, he'd been surprisingly cooperative. *Damn it.* The guy had done me a favor. And now, he was going to lose his job. With growing desperation, I said, "You can't fire him. It's not right."

Zane's expression hardened. "Uh-huh. Tell me something."

"What?"

"The guard, did he ask for anything?"

Oh, crap. "Uh..." I *so* didn't want to say. Stalling, I asked, "Like what?"

Zane gave me another hard look but said nothing.

"All right, fine," I muttered. "He *might've* asked for my phone number."

"And did you give it to him?"

I stiffened. "That's not really any of your business. And besides, why would you care?"

"Think. You'll figure it out."

His gaze met mine, and that annoying warmth came creeping back. I was obscenely aware that his lips were full, and his eyes would've been so amazing, if only he smiled once in a while. I mean, those faint laugh lines had to come from something, right?

I heard myself say, "I honestly don't know."

His gaze shifted to my car, and he frowned. *Again.*

Well, so much for that whole smiling fantasy.

He looked back to me and said, "Now, tell me something else."

"What?"

"Did you give it to him?"

"My phone number? Well, like I said, that's not really any of your business."

"So you *did* give it to him."

He hadn't phrased it as a question, which was fine by me. It was time to give him a taste of his own medicine. "Does it matter?"

"Yeah. It does."

"But why?"

"Because," Zane said, "I want to know how cheap he was bought off."

My mouth fell open. *God, what a jerk.* I wasn't sure what exactly he was implying, but it sounded vaguely obscene, like I'd blown the guy for a parking pass.

Already, I was glowering again. "Hey, it's not like I had sex with him, if that's what you're getting at."

In truth, the guard wasn't even my type. And even if he were, I wasn't a "do-it-in-the-guard-shack" kind of girl. I was more of a "take-it-slow" kind of girl. And even then, I had to be in love.

Zane said, "Good to know."

I didn't know what that meant, but I was beyond insulted. I felt a sudden urge to slap him. In truth, I'd never slapped anyone in my whole life. But if I *were* to get slappy, I decided, I knew exactly who I'd be slapping first.

For once, that person wasn't Paisley.

Unfortunately, it was the same person whose cooperation I now desperately needed, so I swallowed my rage and gave him a pleading look. "Seriously, don't fire him." Somehow, I managed to choke out a single world that stuck like a chicken bone, lodged in my throat. "Please?"

His gaze hardened. "No."

I made a sound of frustration. "Oh come on. There's gotta be something I can say to change your mind."

"No," he said. "There's not."

"Oh, come on." I eyed him with growing desperation. "What? You want me to beg or something?"

He made a forwarding motion with his hand. "If you want to, go ahead."

I blinked. "Go ahead and what?"

"Beg."

I stared in utter disbelief. Was he serious? He couldn't be. And yet, he didn't look like he was joking. A nervous laugh escaped my lips. "Beg who? You?"

"I don't see anyone else around."

I drew back. "Forget it."

He gave a tight shrug. "Done."

Forget slapping. I wanted to kill him. "So, what are you saying? That if I beg, you'll let him keep his job?"

"No," Zane replied. "I'm saying that if you decide to beg, I'm not gonna stop you."

I felt my gaze narrow. "God, you are *such* as jerk."

He didn't even flinch. "If that's your version of begging, it needs work."

"Oh, for God's sake," I said, "I'm not gonna *beg* you."

"Well, there you go." And with that, he turned away, heading up his front steps. When he took the final step, the back of his hoodie hiked up just a fraction, and I stifled a gasp. Tucked in the back of his shorts, I swear I saw what looked like the handle of a gun.

No. It couldn't be. I mean, if nothing else, wouldn't he be in danger of getting the gun all wet? Or worse, shooting his own ass off?

I almost scoffed out loud. *Like I'd get so lucky.* Summoning up my last remaining shred of dignity, I extended both hands and flipped him the double bird – not that he saw it or anything, since I was technically flipping off his backside.

Still, it *did* make me feel a fraction better as I turned and marched, once again, to my car, where I got inside and slammed the door shut behind me.

Cursing the whole time, I fired up the engine and hit the gas. In a perfect world, I would've squealed out of the driveway, leaving a nice patch of rubber in my wake.

Unfortunately, my car wasn't the squealing type, unless you counted the brakes. So I settled for rattling out of his driveway in my rusty heap, praying like hell for a nice oil leak – anything to make him pay.

As I drove off, I considered the folly of everything I'd done. The only person paying for this little excursion was the security guard – some total stranger who'd given me a break. And now, I needed to warn him, because if I didn't, I'd have yet *another* thing to feel crappy about.

And, like everything else, this was all Zane Bennington's fault.

CHAPTER 11

With growing dread, I rattled back to the neighborhood entrance and turned into the small parking area that was located just a short walk away from the guard shack.

If I was planning to give the guy bad news, I figured the least I could do was deliver it in person rather than shout it out my car window as I made my own escape.

Night was falling fast, and I was eager to get this over with. With my stomach in knots, I got out of my car and approached the guard-shack on-foot.

In spite of its small size, the so-called shack looked a lot nicer than most of the homes in my current neighborhood. Its exterior was a rich, red brick with fieldstone accents. It had a single door and several cheerful-looking white-trimmed windows, complete with window panes and fancy green shutters.

The building was cute, like a gingerbread house for rich people. Unfortunately, I was in no mood to admire it. My feet felt heavy, and my shoulders slumped. The guard hadn't yet appeared in any of the windows, and I was grateful for the reprieve.

My thoughts grew darker with every step. How on Earth was I going to tell him? It's not like I could simply blurt out, "Sorry, dude. You're about to be fired, but thanks ever so much for the help."

Just shoot me, now.

I was still a few steps away when the shack's narrow door flew open, and the security guard rushed outside. He was big and muscular, with a thick neck and close-cropped hair. He slammed the door behind him and gave me a big friendly smile. "Hey, you're back."

I tried to smile in return, but my face refused to cooperate. "Uh, yeah. See, the thing is…" I pushed a nervous hand through my hair. "I've got something to tell you, and it's kind of important."

"Oh yeah?" He moved closer. "In public or private?"

Well, I didn't want to shout it from the rooftops, that was for sure. "Uh, private, I guess?"

He grinned. "I like the sounds of *that*."

Oh, crap.

The way it looked, he was expecting *good* news. I couldn't imagine what. Heck, on the way in, I hadn't even given him my phone number. Instead, I'd explained – truthfully, I might add – that my cell phone was missing-in-action, which meant that any cell number of mine would be pretty useless until the phone itself reappeared.

None of this had been a lie. And yet, I'd phrased it carefully to spare his feelings. The sad truth was, the guy simply wasn't my type.

And now, I could hardly meet his eyes. "It's not exactly *good* news."

Talk about a massive understatement.

The guy was still smiling. "Hey, I'll take what I can get." He gave a rueful laugh. "You ever have one of those days?"

I blew out a nervous breath. "Oh, yeah."

He gave the guard shack a quick glance. "But I'm a little tied up at the moment. You wanna come back in a half-hour?"

No. Definitely not.

Already, my stomach was knotted so tight, it literally ached. In a half-hour, I might lose my nerve entirely. Plus, this neighborhood was literally the last place on Earth I wanted to be. After all, I'd lost my own job today, thanks to a certain prick who lived within these oh-so-exclusive gated grounds.

I shook my head. "Actually—"

He held up a hand. "Hold that thought." He turned and looked toward the long, winding road that led up to the neighborhood. On that road, a pair of headlights was heading our way.

The guard tossed a quick apology over his shoulder, and rushed back into the guard shack, slamming the door shut behind him.

Damn it.

From the shadows, I watched the headlights get closer until they stopped just outside the gated barrier.

A moment later, the barrier slid aside, and the headlights, which belonged to a sleek dark sedan, eased through the opening and kept on going.

When the gate slid back in place, I waited, expecting the guard to return. But he didn't. Instead, he opened the window facing me and called out, "So, see you in a half-hour?"

Crap.

"Actually," I said, moving toward him, "we can talk at the window if that's all right."

He held up a hand, as if to ward me off. "Sorry. Not now."

I stopped moving. *What? Why?* I glanced around, wondering what I was missing. I assured him, "I can make it quick."

"Quick's no good," he said. "Besides, I've gotta finish up here first."

Double crap.

I glanced toward my car. Even if I wanted to stay – which I totally didn't – what was I supposed to do for thirty whole minutes?

I lived on the opposite side of town and was beyond eager to leave. I gave the guy a perplexed look. "So you want me to wait in my car?"

He looked toward my car and frowned. "Nah, that's no good." Suddenly, he perked up. "Hey, I know. You could go on a walk or something."

I stared at the guy. *A walk? Now?* I looked longingly at my car, ugly as it was. It would be so easy to just hop into that thing and drive off, leaving this whole mess behind. After all, nothing was technically stopping me – except my own sense of decency, which was feeling severely strained at the moment.

I looked to the gated barrier that blocked the exit. Last night, the exit gate had opened automatically – or at least, that's what I'd assumed.

But what if the guy in the shack had to open it? What if last night, I'd only *thought* it was an automatic process? How awful would *that* be, to force the issue with a guy I'd just gotten fired, even if he didn't yet realize it.

Again, my shoulders slumped. Who was I kidding? I wasn't going anywhere until I'd given the guy a heads-up.

After all, it was the least I could do.

And who knows? Maybe he *wouldn't* be fired. Maybe, if I gave him an advance warning, he'd be able to prepare some sort of argument that would save his job.

Or maybe – and this was a big maybe – Zane wasn't seriously planning to fire the guy at all. Either way, I needed to tread very carefully or risk doing more harm than good.

I looked down to my feet. It could be worse. At least I was wearing tennis shoes.

As if sensing his victory, the guard called out, "All right, see ya then!" A split second later, the window slammed shut, cutting off any further conversation.

Well, that was nice.

Without much enthusiasm, I decided to take the guy up on his suggestion. If nothing else, the time would go a lot faster if I was doing something. Plus, it was a cool night, and the heat in my car was iffy at best. At least if I walked, I reasoned, I'd be generating my own body heat.

So with a sigh, I turned back and started walking down the wide tree-lined sidewalk. As I moved deeper into the neighborhood, I tried to tell myself that a stroll through this rich fantasyland would be the perfect thing to distract me from my troubles.

After all, I loved to walk, and I loved to look at houses. Maybe this wouldn't be *so* bad.

Boy, was *I* wrong – because, as it turned out, Zane Bennington had even more misery to fling my way.

CHAPTER 12

As my feet moved forward, my head was constantly in motion, taking in all the massive homes, with their interesting architecture and manicured lawns, all clearly visible thanks to crazy amounts of accent lighting.

The way it looked, nobody in *this* neighborhood ever worried about the electric bill – or any other bill for that matter.

I saw very few cars, but that wasn't terribly surprising, considering that each and every home had a three-car garage at the bare minimum. But the cars I *did* see? Well, they probably cost more than the little house I was currently renting.

Heck, they probably cost more than the farmhouse I'd grown up in. As a kid, I'd been surrounded by acres of open fields. At the time, I'd barely realized that gated neighborhoods like this even existed.

Now, walking along the quiet street, I was overly aware, and I couldn't help but wonder, were these people happy?

I thought of Zane Bennington. *He* wasn't happy. That much was obvious. But why not, when he had the world at his feet?

The guy wasn't just a prick. He was an idiot, too. He *had* to be.

As I strolled along, there was one house I was determined to avoid – *his* house, if it could be called that. *No.* To call Zane's place a house was like calling the Titanic a boat. I felt my lips curve into a slow, evil smile. If only I had a giant, portable iceberg.

Take that, Zane Bennington.

I'd been walking maybe fifteen minutes when I spotted a street sign that made me pause. The name of the street sounded vaguely familiar, but I couldn't seem to place it. Hoping to jog my memory, I said the name out loud. "Longwood."

And then it hit me. While I'd been hunkered down inside the catering van, I'd overheard Zane Bennington tell that Bob guy that he had to move out of his family home, which happened to be on *what* street?

Longwood. I was sure of it.

But was it the *same* Longwood? If so, it made no sense. Last night, Bob had summoned a driver to take Teddy home. But why would he do that if they lived within stumbling distance?

Suddenly curious, I turned and headed down Longwood, noting that the homes on this street were still amazing, even if they weren't nearly in the same league as Zane's.

But then again, none of them were.

I snuck a quick glance at my watch. Probably, it was time to turn around.

And yet, I didn't.

Instead, I came to a complete stop as I spotted something that made me frown. It was a giant moving truck, parked up against the curb, just a few houses ahead.

Racked by indecision, I turned to glance in the general direction of the guard shack. And, then I returned my gaze to the truck.

As I watched, a couple of big guys in brown uniforms emerged from somewhere beyond my sight, carrying an antique table across the front lawn. Together, they loaded the table onto the truck and then returned to the house. A minute later, they emerged again, carrying an antique armoire, and then, a Victorian fainting couch.

My heart sank. Someone was definitely moving, all right.

I tried to tell myself that it was probably someone else – someone entirely unconnected to Zane-the-Prick Bennington. And whoever that someone was, they were probably moving because they wanted to – not because some heartless bastard had kicked them to the curb.

That *had* to be it.

After all, Zane had given Bob until Monday to move, and it was, –

oh, crap – Sunday night. I heard myself sigh. Who was I kidding? The way it looked, I was getting yet another first-hand glimpse of needless misery, thanks to you-know-who.

It was beyond depressing. And yet, like a fly to a big steaming pile of crap, I found myself moving closer, hoping against hope that I was wrong.

I wasn't.

Of course.

I knew this, because when I passed – working like crazy to keep my gaze straight ahead – I saw from the corner of my eye a man who looked sadly familiar. It was Robert or Bob What's-His-Name, the silver-haired gentleman who'd been so actively involved in the catering setup.

He was standing on the front lawn, wearing khaki pants and a dark sweater. He watched the movers in stoic silence as they loaded an ornate side table onto the truck.

Surrounding him were a stunning array of Victorian antiques. I knew, because my mom had a fondness for them, even if the very best pieces were well beyond her price range.

The way it looked, these antiques were headed to a new home.

Just like Bob.

It was depressing as hell, and yet, I tried to tell myself it could always be worse. At least nobody was sobbing out on the front lawn.

Turns out, I spoke too soon.

The house was on a cul-de-sac, which meant that I'd need to turn around and pass the same house yet again only a few minutes later, from the opposite side of the street. When I approached it the second time, Bob wasn't alone. Instead, he was standing with a waifish young woman, who looked to be around my own age, or possibly younger.

She wore a stylish red dress and had thick, dark hair, done up in some sort of fancy twist. She was leaning against Bob and crying her eyes out, not bothering to hide it. She pulled away only long enough to choke out, "But this is *our* house."

Who was she? His daughter? A trophy wife? Or something else?

Bob pulled her close and mumbled something that I couldn't make out.

Whatever it was, it didn't make her happy. She stepped away to glare at him. "I don't *want* a better place," she yelled. "I want *this* place! You promised!"

Through the outburst, I kept my eyes straight ahead, pretending not to see or hear as I strode along the sidewalk. In truth, I was wishing that I hadn't witnessed any of this. Already, I'd had more than enough misery for one day.

But I had to face facts. More misery was definitely coming. After all, I still had to give the security guard *his* bad news.

I trudged onward, feeling guiltier with every step. Behind me, the woman's voice carried across the distance. "He's such an asshole!"

I heard myself gasp. I don't know why. It's not like I believed that rich people never cursed. It was just that, well, I didn't think they cursed on their front lawns like Jimmy the Shank – the crazy welder who lived three doors down from my current residence.

I kept my head down and kept on walking. The young woman's voice rang out again. "I hate him!"

Yeah, you and me both, sister.

On instinct, I picked up the pace. After all, there was nothing I could do, and I had my own bad news to deliver. As I moved, I snuck another quick glance at my watch. *Damn it.* The half-hour had been up five minutes ago.

I broke into a jog, and then into a run, practically sprinting, until I was within sight of the guard shack. And then, fearful of arriving sweaty and breathless, I deliberately slowed my pace.

Better late than disgusting, right?

I was still a good distance away, walking in the shadows of the trees, when the guard emerged from the shack, looking a little sweaty and breathless himself.

He tugged at his collar and looked around, as if searching for someone in particular.

Me?

That was *my* guess.

I was just about to call out to him when he abruptly turned and hurried back into the shack. He emerged a moment later with a buxom brunette in a skin-tight black dress.

Leading her by the hand, he hustled her toward the small parking area, where a cute little sports car was parked near my old beater. I tried to think. Had the car been there earlier?

Yes.

It had.

Definitely.

Not that I'd paid it much attention at the time.

Unsure what to do, I came to a complete stop. I watched as the guard gave the woman a lingering hug, complete with a whole lot of ass-grabbing – by him, not her.

In a totally perverse way, I was actually glad for the guy. If nothing else, his night wasn't *all* bad, which was more than I could say for myself.

And heck, given what I was about to tell him, he'd need all the cheering up he could get.

From the shadows, I watched the brunette climb into her car and shut the car door behind her. Soon, the car backed out of its parking space and turned – not toward the exit as I'd anticipated – but rather *into* the neighborhood.

A moment later, the car sped past me and kept on going. As for the guard, he returned to the shack, whistling a happy tune.

Weird.

Little did I know, things were about to get a whole lot weirder.

CHAPTER 13

To give the guard some semblance of privacy, I waited ten extra minutes before approaching the guard shack. But when I arrived, it didn't take long for me to wonder why I'd bothered.

After greeting me with a smile this side of creepy, he flicked his head toward the shack and asked, "So, you wanna go inside, check it out?"

I gave a mental shudder. *No. Definitely not.*

After all, I wasn't quite sure what he and the brunette had just done in there, but I *did* know that I wasn't eager to bask in the stale afterglow.

Still, I tried to smile. "No. But thanks." I glanced around. "We can talk out here, if that's all right."

"Aw come on," the guy said. "I got a space heater and everything." He lowered his voice. "Don't tell on me, but I also got half a bottle of merlot. You interested?"

Half a bottle? I could only guess who drank the first half. But it didn't even matter. I hated merlot. And even more so, I hated where this was going. "Actually," I said, "I'm just here to give you a heads-up."

He grinned. "So, you wanna give me head, huh?"

I drew back. "What?"

He gave a bark of laughter. "Sorry. Bad joke."

I bit my lip. "Uh, yeah."

"Although," he continued with a sly wink, "I'm not saying I'd turn you down."

I stared at the guy, wondering what on Earth I should say to *that*. The way he acted, this was my lucky day, like it was *so* hard to find a guy willing to accept an impromptu blow job.

It was definitely time to set him straight. Speaking very slowly and clearly, I said, "What I'm here to give you is a heads-*up*." I stressed the word, "up" and repeated it twice for good measure. "Up. *Up*. You heard me, right?"

"Oh, don't be like that," he said. "I was just kiddin' around." He glanced down at his crotch. "Not that I'd complain."

My jaw clenched. "Good to know."

He leaned forward. "Is it?"

I leaned back. "No."

For the briefest instant, I wondered if Zane Bennington might've been right all along in wanting to fire this guy.

But damn it, he *couldn't* be. Because Zane Bennington wasn't right about anything.

Still, in spite of my hatred for Zane, even *I* could see that I might've misjudged the guard at least a little.

Okay, a lot.

How depressing.

I tried to think. Maybe it wasn't so much that Zane was right. Maybe, it was just that, well, *I* might've been a teeny bit wrong.

See? That was totally different.

I looked to my car. "You know what? On second thought, I'd better get going."

The guy frowned. "Why?"

Because you're creeping me out, that's why.

But I didn't say it, because at this point, all I wanted was to be on my way.

Abruptly, the guy said, "You know, your hair looks a lot better tonight."

Obviously, he meant compared to last night, when he'd issued me the original parking pass to work at Zane's party. Feeling suddenly self-conscious, I reached up to smooth my hair away from my face. I mumbled, "What?"

He was still looking at my hair. "Yeah, it's all long and pretty." He laughed. "Last night? Eh, it wasn't a good look. I'm not a fan of the bun, you know?"

I wasn't a fan of the bun either, but I *had* been dealing with food, which left two options – wearing a giant lunch-lady hairnet or wrapping my hair up in a tight bun. If the guy thought the bun was bad, I could only imagine what he'd think of the lunch-lady look.

But I didn't bother explaining. Instead, I muttered, "I've gotta go," and then, I turned away.

"Wait," the guy said. "Where ya goin'?"

I was already walking to my car. "Home."

Unable to take a hint, he turned and followed along beside me. "Hey," he said, sounding almost peeved now, "I let you in when I wasn't supposed to."

I kept on walking. "So?"

"So, you know how this works, right? I do *you* a favor. You do *me* a favor…"

Abruptly, I stopped and gave him a sharp look. "I don't get it," I said. "Earlier, you asked for my number, and you were actually pretty nice. And now you're all…" I let my words trail off, because I wasn't quite sure how to put this.

"Yeah," he said, "because your story was bullshit."

"What?"

He made a scoffing sound. "That whole 'I lost my phone' thing? What? You thought I *bought* that story?"

"It wasn't a story," I said. "It was true."

He snorted. "Yeah, right."

"It was," I insisted, and then immediately thought better of it. This guy didn't deserve an explanation, not anymore. I looked toward the guard shack. "And what were you doing in there, anyway?"

"What do you mean?"

"With that chick, the one who just left."

"Hey, that 'chick' knows how it works." Under his breath, he added, "Unlike *you*, who wants favors for free."

Unbelievable.

I said, "I *thought* you were just being nice."

"I was," he said. "So why don't *you* be nice to *me*?"

Ick. With a sound of disgust, I turned away, heading once again for my car.

And once again, the guy followed along beside me. "Hey," he said, "I'm sorry, all right? I was just kidding, like I said before."

Sure, he was. I kept on walking, barely listening as he blathered on about my apparent inability to take a joke.

When I reached my car, I pulled my keys from my pocket and jammed the car-key into the lock.

The guy said, "I could've been fired, you know."

I had to laugh, even as I yanked open my ugly, rusted car door. "Oh, I know."

"What's so funny?" he demanded.

There were so many ways I could've answered that question. I might've told him that it was absolutely hilarious that I'd spent any energy at all in trying to save *his* job when I'd lost my own job today.

I might've told him to enjoy the guard-station while he could, because it wasn't going to be his love-shack for much longer. I might've also told him that he was a giant douchebag and that he reeked of stale coffee and old cigarettes.

But I didn't say any of those things – not because I didn't have the nerve, but because a new voice sounded from the shadows.

It was Zane's voice, low and ominous, saying only two words. "Get out."

CHAPTER 14

In unison, the guard and I turned to look.

I spotted Zane, standing a few paces away. He was wearing dark pants, a dark jacket, and an expression so dark that I instinctively backed up.

But I had no room. My butt hit the side of my car, and my keys slipped from my fingers and clattered to the pavement.

I didn't even look down, and neither did the guard. Both of us were still staring at Zane, who eyed the guard with cold contempt.

The guard practically gulped, "Mister Bennington."

Zane said nothing, but his look said it all. He was *not* pleased.

The guard looked to me and said, "Mister Bennington's right. You should probably get going."

Zane spoke again. "No. Not her. *You.*"

The guard's eyebrows furrowed. He looked to Zane and said, "But I've got two hours left on my shift."

Zane's expression didn't change. "Not my problem."

It seemed a funny thing to say. After all, it *would* be Zane's problem if there was no one around to let people in or out of his neighborhood.

Wouldn't it?

The guard tried again. "But—"

"But nothing," Zane said. "Get the fuck out. *Now.*"

The guard turned accusing eyes on me. "This is *your* fault."

I almost laughed in his face. "*My* fault?"

Okay, maybe the guy did have a point. After all, Zane had decided to fire him nearly an hour ago, thanks to my careless confession on his front lawn. But there was no way the guard could know that.

So, why was he blaming *me?*

And seriously, what did he expect? He'd just been caught red-handed, away from his station, putting the moves on someone who obviously wasn't interested.

It's not like I put a gun to his head.

The guard turned back to Zane and said, "But I was just escorting her to her car. It's in my job-description. She asked me to." He turned back to me and urged, "Go on. Tell him."

What a total crock.

I made a scoffing sound. "No way."

He gave me a pleading look. "Why not?"

"Because it's a lie."

The guard leaned closer and said in a low whisper, "C'mon. Help a guy out, will ya?"

Like the sap I was, I almost wanted to say yes. I liked helping people. And I hated Zane Bennington. But even *I* knew that lying for the guy would be a huge mistake, especially if I cared one bit for whatever random female crossed his path next.

Besides, from what I knew of Zane, lying for the guy wouldn't do a lick of good, anyway.

I crossed my arms. "No."

His nostrils flared, and he reached out, as if preparing to shake some sense into me. His hands never made it, because suddenly, he was yanked back by a shadowed force.

That force was Zane Bennington, who had crossed the short distance and pulled the guard away – all in the blink of an eye.

Already, he'd spun the guy around, giving him a hard shove in the opposite direction. The guy stumbled backward before catching his balance. His mouth opened, as if preparing to lodge some sort of protest. But then, he apparently thought better of it. He clamped his mouth shut and looked from Zane to me. His gaze narrowed, and he looked almost ready to spring.

Zane said, "Whatever you're thinking, don't."

After a long, tense moment, the guard lifted his hands in mock surrender and took a single step backward. "I wasn't thinking anything."

Zane flicked his head toward the guard shack. "Now, get your shit and go. You're fired."

"But..." The guard shook his head. "You can't fire me."

Zane gave him a look. "I can. And I did."

"But, uh, I don't work for you."

"Right, you're done," Zane said. "So get the fuck out."

The guy cleared his throat. "I mean, I was hired by the Board of Governors."

I wasn't familiar with the term, but I could only assume that he meant something along the lines of a home owners' association. After all, this did seem like the kind of place that would have one.

"So really," the guard said, "I work for them."

"Not anymore," Zane said.

"But—"

"Get out," Zane said, "or I'll toss you out."

From the look on Zane's face, he was willing to make good on the threat. Still, it was one of the strangest things I'd ever seen, because for all of Zane's harsh words, he looked in absolute control.

And for some reason, that was ten times more terrifying than if he'd completely lost it.

I looked from one guy to the other. In spite of the guard's beefy size, he was decidedly outgunned in the face of Zane's quiet menace.

Already, the guard was stepping backward. "But my ride's not here."

Zane flicked his head toward the road. "So walk."

The guard looked down and muttered, "Son-of-a-bitch."

Zane took a single step closer. "What's that?"

"Nothing," the guard said. And then, with a final muttered curse, he turned and trudged to the guard shack. He opened the door, went inside, and emerged a moment later, carrying an uncorked bottle of wine and a big, brown backpack, bursting with who-knows-what.

He slung the backpack over one shoulder and gave me one final, disgruntled look as he turned away and began trudging toward the road that led into the neighborhood.

Watching him go, I couldn't help but feel at least a little sad. It was true that Zane probably did the right thing – as much as I hated to admit it – but it was still such a sorry sight that I almost felt like crying.

And I wasn't a cryer.

Who knows? Maybe it *wasn't* because of the guard. Maybe it was because, well, today had been one giant crap sandwich, and I'd had just about enough. All I wanted now was to be home, away from all of this, away from *him* – the guy who'd brought me nothing but trouble.

I glanced at the exit gate and wondered if I'd need someone to open it. If so, I was screwed, unless – *damn it* – my gaze shifted to Zane. Would *he* open it for me?

He was the only person around, and I yet hated the idea of asking him for anything.

Summoning my last bit of optimism, I decided that the gate would open automatically, if only I pulled up my car. With that in mind, I turned away, intending to get the hell out of Dodge.

But before I could climb into my car, Zane's voice cut through the shadows. "What the hell were you thinking?"

CHAPTER 15

His question caught me off guard, and I froze in mid-motion. What the hell was *I* thinking? What kind of question was that?

I whirled to face him. "What?"

Standing in the shadows, Zane's eyes were hard, and his mouth was tight. "I told you that guy was trouble."

My jaw dropped. "You did not."

He stepped closer. "You want some advice?"

"From you?" I tried to laugh. "No."

"Yeah? Well, you're getting it, anyway." He looked toward the road, where the guy was already out of earshot. "When you know someone's trouble, you don't stand alone with them in the dark."

I made a sound of disbelief. "Well, that's rich."

"Meaning?"

"Meaning, you've caused me ten times more trouble than the guard. And here I am, alone with *you*." I gave him a thin smile. "So, if you wanted to warn me, maybe you should've warned me about yourself."

His jaw tightened. "Then consider yourself warned."

He was standing almost within arm's reach, and something about his statement – or maybe something about him – sent a shiver down my spine. And yet, to my extreme annoyance, the shiver felt warm, more like a caress than a warning.

And that only irritated me more.

My tone grew sarcastic. "Gosh. Thanks ever so much. Now, if only someone had warned me yesterday."

Before I'd lost my job.

Before I'd witnessed people getting tossed out of their home.

Before making this stupid trip out here at all.

In front of me, Zane said, "If you see him again, you avoid him." He gave me a hard look. "Got it?"

"Who? The guard?" I gave Zane a hard look right back. "You know that was at least partly your fault."

He looked anything but contrite. "Yeah? Why's that?"

"Because here, you act like he's a big raging pervert, but you never thought to do anything about it?" My voice rose. "Until *now*?"

He gave me another long look, but said nothing.

"I mean, come on," I persisted. "How long have you known?"

Zane moved closer until he towered over me in the near darkness. Already, I had nowhere to go, and it suddenly struck me that the guy standing before me now was a million times more dangerous than that stupid guard on his worst day.

I don't know *how* I knew. I just did.

Still, I refused to back down. "Well?" I said. "How long?"

"Before you showed up?" Zane's gaze met mine. "An hour. Maybe two."

I blinked. "What?"

"I had a visit."

Curiosity got the best of me. "From who?"

His gaze shifted to the guard shack. "From someone who wasn't supposed to be here."

Obviously, he couldn't mean the guard. So who was he talking about? For some reason, I couldn't seem to let it go. "Yeah, but who?"

I'd barely finished the question when a car – coming from *inside* the neighborhood – sped up to the guard shack and squealed to a stop, not in the parking area, but on the side of the street.

I recognized the car immediately. It was the same little sports car I'd seen passing me a few minutes earlier. Sure enough, the now-familiar brunette emerged from the car and slammed the car door shut behind her.

She stalked to the guard shack and went straight for the door. She twisted the doorknob and gave a hard tug.

Nothing happened.

"Hey!" she hollered through the door. "I know you're in there! Open up!" When nothing happened, she raised her arms and started pounding with both fists. "Hey, jackass!" she yelled. "You owe me! You fucking liar!"

I looked to Zane, wondering what he'd do. But the way it looked, he wasn't going to do anything, except eye the woman with barely concealed revulsion.

I whispered, "Shouldn't we tell her? You know, that her boyfriend's gone."

Slowly, his gaze shifted to me, and his eyebrows lifted just a fraction. "Boyfriend?"

Heat flooded my face. Okay, I didn't *really* think they were boyfriend-and-girlfriend, but I wasn't sure how else to put it.

I gave a loose shrug and mumbled, "Or whatever."

At this, Zane looked like he just might smile. But he didn't. Instead, he turned back to the guard shack and watched as the woman stalked to nearest window and pressed her face to the glass. She cupped her hands around her eyes, as if to better see inside. What she saw, I could only imagine.

I whispered, "Do you think he locked the door?"

Zane gave a tight shrug. "Probably."

I couldn't help but wonder why. As a responsible safety measure? Or as a final "screw you" to Zane for giving him the old heave-ho?

That reminded me of something. I asked, "And how could you fire him if he didn't even work for you?"

"Easy," Zane said. "Two words. 'You're fired.'"

"But won't someone get mad? I mean, what'll happen? You know, with the people he *does* work for?"

"Nothing," Zane said. "They'll piss and moan, and I'll tell them to fuck off. End of story."

It suddenly struck me that this was pretty much what he'd done with my job. After all, I hadn't worked for Zane directly either, and he'd still gotten *me* fired, even if he hadn't bothered to do it personally.

The jerk.

At the guard shack, the woman was yelling again. "I know you're in there! And just so you know, that merlot sucked ass!"

In spite of everything, I wanted to snicker. In my book, *all* merlot sucked ass.

At the guard shack, the woman stopped yelling and looked around. I knew the exact moment she spotted us, because her eyes widened to epic proportions, and she smiled so big, it was almost scary.

Next to me, Zane muttered, "Fuck."

I looked from Zane to the woman and back again. I felt a slow, evil smile spread across my face. I lifted my hand and hollered out, "Yoohoo! Over here!"

Under his breath, Zane said, "What the hell are you doing?"

"Why, introducing you, of course."

"You wouldn't."

I was still smiling. "I would."

And I did. After the woman scurried over, I gave her a warm welcome and said, "Have you met Zane Bennington?" I flicked my head in his direction. "He's a gazillionaire, you know."

The woman sidled closer to Zane and gave a little shimmy of excitement. "Oh, I know," she gushed, batting her eyelashes up at him.

"And he's single," I helpfully added.

The woman gave a little squeal of excitement. "I know!" She turned to Zane. "I just *love* your hotels. They're soooooo luxurious." She leaned toward him. "I'd just *love* a private tour." Her eyes brightened. "And you know what? I've never been to Paris, but I'd just *love* to go sometime."

I gave a happy sigh. "Oh, well, I'd better get going." And then, true to my word, I swooped up my keys, got into my car, fired up the engine, and pulled away, leaving Zane staring after me.

As for the woman, she paid me no attention at all. Instead, she kept her gaze firmly on the so-called gazillionaire, even as he ignored whatever she was saying.

I pulled my car up to the exit gate and said a silent prayer that the gate would slide open automatically, which, thank heaven, it did.

And, then, I was on my way.

As for the guard, I spotted him maybe a mile up the road, lugging that same brown backpack and yelling into his cell phone. Oh, sure, I couldn't hear him over the sounds of my rattletrap of a car, but his contorted face told me all I needed to know.

Whoever he was talking to was a getting an earful.

I was just glad it wasn't me.

Funny to think, I'd just had one of the crappiest days of my life, and yet, I couldn't help but smile. Revenge – who cared about serving it cold, when you could dish it up, nice and hot, thanks to a rabid fangirl and her merlot-swilling sidekick.

I gave it some thought. Maybe the guard wasn't so much a sidekick as an accomplice. I considered what Zane had said, about getting an unwanted visitor at his house. He couldn't have meant the brunette, because from what I'd seen, their first actual meeting had been the one I'd initiated.

Had there been another girl? Before that one? And what was the guard doing, anyway? Trading access for blow-jobs?

I decided not to think about it.

I was just glad to see Zane inconvenienced, even if only a little. The bastard had it coming, and a whole lot more besides.

The only upside was that I'd never have to see him again – or so I thought.

Turns out, I saw him just an hour later. But at least *this* time, it wasn't in person.

CHAPTER 16

When I walked in through my own front door, the television was blaring, and the whole house reeked of burnt popcorn. I found Paisley and Professor Lumberjack on the living room sofa, watching Paisley's favorite celebrity gossip channel.

The professor was big and burly, with thinning hair and a red beard that almost perfectly matched his red flannel shirt.

In the nearby armchair sat Charlotte, with her arms crossed and an expression I was all too familiar with. It was her "I'm-not-going-anywhere-and-you-can't-make-me" expression.

Funny, she'd been wearing the exact same look earlier when I'd left the house to confront Zane. Over my objections, she'd insisted on waiting for me to return. The only real surprise was that she wasn't waiting alone.

I looked to Paisley, cuddled up next to the professor. She was making an obvious point to ignore me, which I thought took a lot of nerve, all things considered.

I gave her an annoyed look. "I thought you were going out of town."

Paisley's eyes remained glued to the screen. "You'd like that, wouldn't you?"

"That depends," I said. "Does this mean you have the rent money?"

Next to her, the professor muttered, "Rent."

My gaze narrowed. "Excuse me?"

"Rent," he repeated to one in particular, "it's only a tool for exploitation."

I felt my jaw clench. *Speaking of tools.*

"No," I said, as if speaking to my least-favorite half-wit. "Rent is the thing that keeps us in this house."

"Exactly," he said.

Oh, for God's sake.

I looked to Charlotte, who was glowering in their direction. I gave her an apologetic smile. "I'm sorry I'm late. That took longer than I thought."

"That's all right," she said. "It's not *your* fault."

Actually, it was my fault, but the way it looked, Charlotte was focusing all of her hostility on the dynamic couch-duo.

With more than a little trepidation, I asked, "So, what's been going on here?"

It was Paisley who answered. "Your sister's being a major pill, that's what."

Charlotte turned to me and said, "And your roommate ate all the cake."

I asked, "What cake?" And then, it hit me. "Oh, my God. Not the cake *you* brought?"

From the sofa, Paisley gave a dramatic sigh. "Look, if you wanted to save it, you should've put your name on it or something."

Through gritted teeth, I said, "My name *was* on it."

"It was not," Paisley said.

Now, I was glowering, too. "Well, it said 'congratulations.' My name was implied."

The professor muttered, "Implications don't pay the rent."

What the hell did that even mean?

I snapped, "And neither does your side-squeeze."

With a little gasp, Paisley whirled around on the sofa. Glaring daggers at me, she demanded, "What did you just call me?"

It was too late to back down now. So instead, I repeated it. "His side-squeeze."

Paisley jumped up from the couch and looked to the professor. "Did you hear that? Aren't you gonna say something?"

We all looked. For once, I was actually sort of interested in what the guy might say.

Finally, he said, "I refuse to dignify that with a response."

Paisley's mouth fell open. "So you're not gonna stick up for me?"

The guy settled deeper into the couch. "You're a strong, independent woman. You shouldn't need *me* to defend your honor."

From the armchair, Charlotte said, "That's because she doesn't have any."

Paisley turned to Charlotte and yelled, "You take that back!"

Charlotte stood. "Make me."

I yelled, "Shut up! All of you!"

Surprisingly, they did.

I pointed to the TV screen, where the flash of a familiar face had just claimed all of my attention. I said, "I wanna see this."

Paisley frowned toward the screen. "But you hate this show."

She was right. I did. And I hated the guy whose face had just appeared *on* the show. But I was also dying of curiosity.

They were introducing a new segment. It was about who else, but Zane "the Prick" Bennington. Of course, the gossip reporter didn't call him that. No, *she* preferred to use nicer words, like "sudden sensation" and "reclusive mystery man."

I muttered, "How about arrogant ass?"

Paisley, who'd already plopped back down onto the couch, said, "Shut up. I'm trying to watch."

I gave her an annoyed look. That was supposed to be *my* line.

Still, I watched in silence as the segment began by explaining that just last month, Zane Bennington had arrived seemingly out of nowhere to claim the massive Bennington fortune and assume control of the family's vast hotel empire.

This all happened, she explained, on the heels of Zane's grandfather, Lloyd Bennington, dying of a sudden stroke.

The story itself might've been pretty standard, except for the fact that Zane had been completely out of the family picture – unlike the other Benningtons, who'd been household names forever.

I watched in grim fascination as the show detailed how Zane's two uncles – both notorious, aging playboys – had died earlier this year in two separate incidents within hours of each other.

One had died in a freak boating accident on the French Riviera, while the other had died when his private helicopter crashed in the Mojave Desert.

The reporter went on to say, "Sources close to the family tell us that Lloyd Bennington was heartbroken at the loss of his two favorite sons. According to these sources, this double tragedy, along with ongoing upheavals in his business empire, almost surely contributed to his death."

The reporter briefly mentioned a third son, the youngest, who happened to be Zane's father. Without elaborating, she quickly moved on to Zane himself.

This only piqued my curiosity. Was Zane's father still alive? And if so, why didn't *he* inherit?

I leaned forward, dying to hear what she'd say next. But already, the program was going to a commercial. *Damn it.* This was part of the reason I hated this show. It always left me hanging just as things were getting interesting.

As the commercial droned on, Charlotte said, "Maybe Zane did it."

"Did what?" I asked.

"You know. Offed his uncles."

From the sofa, Paisley said, "Offed?"

"Yeah," Charlotte said. "Like, he killed them so he could inherit." She looked to me and asked, "What do *you* think?"

Paisley said, "How would *she* know?" She gave Charlotte a smug smile. "You should've asked me. I know way more about celebrities than she does."

Charlotte said, "Oh yeah? Have *you* met him?"

"No," Paisley grudgingly admitted. "But she hasn't either."

"Hah!" Charlotte said. "That's what *you* think."

"Oh, get real." Paisley turned to me and said, "You have not met him." When I made no response, she frowned. "Have you?"

The way I saw it, it wasn't anything to brag about. Still, I said, "Actually, I worked at one of his houses last night." Under my breath, I added, "…back when I *had* a catering job."

Paisley brightened. "Oh, is that all? Gee, *I* could've done that."

I gave her a dubious look. Catering jobs were hard work. Paisley was on some sort of work-study program as part of a financial-aid package. From what I'd seen over the last few months, it involved very little work *or* study.

I couldn't resist telling her, "I think they're hiring. Maybe, you should apply."

She drew back. "What? You mean work in…" She made a face. "…food service?"

I gave an enthusiastic nod. "Yeah, and think of the glamor." My tone grew sarcastic. "You could meet rich, famous guys."

Next to her, the professor announced, "I just had a paper published."

We all turned to look. When no one said anything, he mumbled, "I'm just saying, I'm kinda well-known myself."

It suddenly struck me that I had no idea what subject the guy even taught. Cripes, I didn't even know his name – mostly because Paisley always referred to him simply as the professor.

I briefly considered asking for more details, but quickly thought better of it. When it came to Paisley and the professor, I knew far too much already.

Charlotte pointed to the TV. "Shhh! It's back on."

I looked to the screen, and there he was, Zane Bennington. It was a live-action shot of him entering the Bennington's flagship hotel, located in downtown Indianapolis, where the company was also headquartered.

In the news footage, Zane looked obnoxiously rich and successful, just like any other hotshot business mogul, well, except for the fact he was a few decades younger and a whole lot sexier.

The bastard.

And yet, as the segment continued, I couldn't help but lean forward, more curious than ever.

Who was this guy, anyway?

CHAPTER 17

Silently, we all watched as the reporter gave us a virtual tour of some of the most famous Bennington properties.

This included a stunning parade of hotels, along with restaurants, mansions, a horse farm in Kentucky, plus a ranch out West, along with a villa in Tuscany, and a penthouse suite in New York.

The whirlwind tour ended with some exterior shots of the estate right here in Indianapolis, where Zane's grandfather had apparently been living until he died.

It was strange to think I'd just been there, chewing out the property's new owner, for all the good *that* did.

When the show ended, I hated Zane even more – not because I was jealous, but because the guy was such an ass. In fact, the show's final scene was a long slow-motion shot of Zane, flipping the camera the double-bird.

He'd been standing on the same front porch where I'd visited him today. But unlike earlier, he'd been perfectly groomed and dressed in a pricey suit and tie. He would've looked every inch the billionaire, if only he weren't making such an immature, obscene gesture.

The thought had barely crossed my mind when I recalled something that made me a teeny bit uncomfortable. I'd been making that *same* gesture at him, less than two hours ago.

But that was totally different, I reasoned, because in my case, Zane totally had it coming.

To no one in particular, I said, "You know, he's gonna run that company straight into the ground."

Charlotte said, "I dunno. They went through a really rough patch a couple years ago, but the company's doing great now."

I turned and gave her a perplexed look. "How do you know?"

She glanced toward her cell phone, sitting on a side table. "I had to do *something* while you were gone."

I couldn't resist asking, "So, did you learn anything else? Like about his dad?"

"Oh yeah," Charlotte said. "Get this. The guy's like some mountain man or something."

I felt my eyebrows furrow. "Mountain man?"

Charlotte nodded. "Totally. He lives in a cabin in the U.P."

I asked, "What's the U.P.?"

"The upper peninsula of Michigan. Didn't you know?"

I wasn't familiar with the abbreviation, but I did know that northern Michigan was sparsely populated and known for producing people a lot tougher than I was.

I said, "So the U.P. has mountains?"

Charlotte gave it some thought. "I dunno. Maybe. But you don't need a mountain to be a mountain man."

On this, I decided she had a point. I asked, "What about his Mom?"

"Oh, she died forever ago."

For the first time, I felt a twinge of sympathy for the horrible Zane Bennington. "Really? How?"

"A car accident," she said. "The way it sounds, Zane was just a baby."

And there it was – another annoying twinge of sympathy. The guy hadn't even known his mom? Was *that* why he was such a jackass? It didn't excuse his behavior, but it might explain some of it, if only a little.

Damn it. I didn't want to feel sympathy for him. After all, plenty of people had horrible things happen to them, and *they* didn't all turn into raging jackasses. And besides, Zane was loaded. On top of *that*, he had a job, with the best job title of all – C.E.O. It didn't get any better than that.

In contrast, I had no job, no title, and no idea how I'd be paying the rent.

With that in mind, I followed after Paisley when she stood and began heading alone toward the kitchen.

I was hoping that if it was just the two of us, maybe we could discuss the rent situation like two reasonable adults.

Those hopes were squashed like a bug on a windshield.

In less than two minutes, our so-called discussion devolved into a whole lot of name-calling – from Paisley, mostly – which caused Charlotte to barge in and return the favor by calling Paisley, among other things, a deadbeat cake-hog.

From there, it went decidedly downhill.

The confrontation finally ended with Paisley marching back to the living room and yanking the professor off the sofa. As Charlotte and I watched, she dragged him out the front door, hollering over her shoulder that she was tired of living with a total nag.

By then, I was so spent that I had nothing left to say.

As for Charlotte, she had plenty. "Oh yeah?" she hollered back. "Well, maybe *she's* tired of living with a pink-haired lumberjack fucker!"

Oh yeah. It was totally one of those days.

After Paisley squealed out of the driveway, I shut the front door and shuffled silently to the sofa. With a sigh, I sank down where the professor had been lounging just a few moments earlier. If nothing else, he'd kept the spot warm. That was something to be thankful for, right?

I reached up to rub my temples. Who was I kidding?

It was sad day when you had to be thankful for the second-hand warmth of your roommate's married boyfriend.

I leaned back and closed my eyes, wondering what on Earth I was going to do now. I still had five months left on my lease, and that wasn't even the worst of it. I had plenty of other expenses, too – student loans, an outstanding car repair bill, and cripes, even a cell phone contract, which really sucked, considering that I had no phone.

For what felt like the millionth time, I heard myself murmur, "It'll *eventually* turn up, right?"

From somewhere in the living room, Charlotte said, "If you're talking about your phone, the answer is no."

I sighed. "No?"

"Sorry," Charlotte said. "It's time to accept it and move on."

Stupidly, I repeated, "Move on?"

"Yeah. Buy a new one."

Like that was so easy. I opened my eyes to look at her. She'd reclaimed her spot in the armchair, and was scrolling through her own cell phone.

It must be nice.

I just had to ask, "And how am I supposed to buy anything without a job?"

"Don't worry," Charlotte assured me, "you'll find one."

I gave her a dubious look. "Just like I found my phone?"

"That's totally different," she said. "Your phone's been missing for what? A week?"

"More or less." I was still convinced that it wasn't truly lost. After all, I was pretty sure I'd misplaced it right here, in this house, on a day I hadn't gone anywhere.

Damn it. The phone might still turn up. It *had* to.

Back when money hadn't been quite so tight, I'd splurged on the latest model, and there was no way on Earth that I could afford to replace it *now*.

Charlotte said, "And besides, you'll have a new job before you know it."

I tried to smile. "You really think so?"

"Definitely."

But Charlotte was wrong. Nearly a month later, I was still very much unemployed and getting more desperate with every passing day.

In fact, one Tuesday afternoon, I got *so* desperate that I sold my integrity for pasta primavera and a basket of bread sticks.

CHAPTER 18

Tiffany was all smiles as she scurried toward me in the department store. "Oh, my God!" she squealed. "It's been ages. How *are* you?"

I glanced around. "Me?"

But already, Tiffany had barreled into me and wrapped me up in a hug so tight that I could barely breathe. She laughed like I'd just said something funny. "You are *such* a kidder."

I wasn't a kidder. I was confused as hell. The last time I'd seen Tiffany had been at that disastrous catering gig, when she'd acted like we were practically strangers. That had been nearly a month ago, and I hadn't forgotten, even if *she* had.

I pulled away and eyed her with suspicion. "What are you doing?"

She lifted both arms, showing off a colorful array of festive shopping bags. "Shopping, what else?"

I recognized the bags, and not only because they'd just been poking me in the sides. Every single bag sported the name or logo of some upscale shop that was well beyond my price range.

Of course, everything was beyond my *current* range, considering that I had no money and none coming in any time soon.

Unlike Tiffany, I wasn't here to shop. I was looking for a job.

Already, I'd hit dozens of stores, in hopes that someone was hiring. No such luck.

Tiffany gave me a sunny smile. "So, you wanna grab some lunch and catch up?"

At the mere mention of lunch, my stomach gave a traitorous grumble. Looking to conserve my money, I'd been living on rice and

Ramen noodles for the past couple of weeks. By now, I was so hungry for something different that even food court nachos sounded sinfully delicious.

Still, I shook my head. "I can't."

Tiffany frowned. "Why not?"

Because I can't afford it.

But I'd die before admitting such a thing.

And besides, that wasn't the only reason for declining Tiffany's invitation. My empty wallet aside, it was because Tiffany and I weren't on speaking terms, as she'd so nicely informed me at Zane's place, back when I'd been plucking crab cakes off the carpet.

I told her, "Because we're not friends, remember?"

Tiffany blinked. "What? Why not?"

"Oh, for God's sake," I said. "Don't act like you forgot."

"Forgot what?"

As if she didn't know. I crossed my arms and waited.

"Oh, all right," she finally said. "But what did you expect? There *are* protocols, you know."

I felt my gaze narrow. "What kind of protocols?"

"Well…" She glanced away. "Like chatting with the help. It's like a *huge* faux-pas."

I stiffened. *The help?* "Hey," I said, "I was a catering assistant, not a leper."

Tiffany sighed. "I know. Honest. But the senator, he's *so* image-conscious. Do you know, he got all mad at me yesterday when I started chatting with some parking valet?" Tiffany gave a sad shake of her head. "Which totally sucked, because he was super-cute, too."

Obviously, she wasn't talking about her fiancé. Still, I couldn't resist tweaking her at least a little. "Sorry, who's cute?" I put on my clueless face. "The Senator?"

"Oh, him?" She sagged a little. "Not really. I mean, he's a little too hairy to be cute-cute." She brightened. "But he *was* a big football star. So that's good."

I had no idea what to say. The senator was clean shaven and nearly bald. This posed a rather disturbing question. *Hairy where?* But I didn't ask, because I was pretty darn sure that I didn't want to know.

Tiffany leaned a fraction closer and whispered, "But can I be honest?"

"Uh, well…" In truth, I wasn't sure how much more honesty I could take. And yet, I gave a short, jerky nod.

What was I? A masochist or something?

Tiffany glanced around before saying in a hushed voice, "Just between us, I'm thinking of trading up."

Curiosity got the best of me. "Really? To who?"

Tiffany's gaze grew dreamy. "Zane Bennington."

I froze. Just the mere mention of that dreaded name was enough to make me want to break something, like an arm – *his* preferably.

My mouth tightened. "So are you two a thing now?"

"I wouldn't go *that* far," she said. "But we *could* be, right?"

What could I say to *that*? "Sure, why not?"

Once again, Tiffany was all smiles. "And I was thinking that maybe you and I could chat about it over lunch."

She was thinking wrong. The last thing I wanted now was to hear anyone gush about Zane "the Prick" Bennington. Already, I'd been hearing that name far too often. It seemed like every time I turned on the news, there he was, pissing someone off – or, on the flipside, doing a new business deal or schmoozing with some actress or runway model.

And, if that weren't bad enough, he was doing most of these things right here in Indianapolis, as opposed to the usual places, like New York or L.A.

By now, I had a theory. All those jet-setters were coming to him, because he wouldn't go to them.

I just knew it.

In front of me, Tiffany asked, "So, do you like sushi?"

Seafood? Immediately, I thought of those stupid crab-cakes and how awful she'd treated me the last time I'd seen her.

I shook my head. "No. Sorry." I made a move to step past her. "I've gotta go."

"Wait!" Tiffany sidestepped to block my path. "It doesn't *have* to be sushi. We can go anywhere you want." She gave me a pleading look. "The truth is, I could *really* use someone to talk to."

I almost didn't know what to say. Even in college, Tiffany and I hadn't been more than casual friends. Why would she confide in me of all people?

As if reading something in my expression, she said, "Do you remember that time you caught me with Buster Hogan in the stall?"

Did I ever. Even now, three years later, the image was burned into my brain. I'd opened the last stall in the library's second-floor women's restroom, only to catch a good eyeful of Tiffany and Buster doing the nasty.

I still didn't know why they picked *there* of all places. And in truth, I didn't *want* to know. With more than a little trepidation, I said, "Uh, yeah?"

"Well, you never told anyone."

This wasn't quite true. I'd told Charlotte. But that was like putting it in the vault, because we had a strict no-blabbing policy on shared secrets.

"Yeah?" I said. "So?"

"So I know that I can trust you, you know, with girl-talk stuff."

It was actually a pretty nice thing to say. "Uh, thanks."

"And besides," she added, "we travel in totally different circles now, so it's not like you could tell anyone important."

I gave her a look. "Oh, that's nice."

"I know, right?" She gave me another sunny smile. "So, how about Italian? Everyone likes *that*."

My stomach gave another traitorous grumble. *Damn it.* I *did* like Italian, but it hardly mattered. I still couldn't afford it.

Almost as an afterthought, Tiffany added, "Oh, and I'm totally treating. I *did* mention that, right?"

CHAPTER 19

Yes. I *was* a food-slut.

But in my own defense, Tiffany had refused to take no for an answer. And honestly, I was running shamefully low on dignity.

"So anyway," Tiffany was saying, "I'm thinking that if he likes blondes, I'm a total shoe-in."

I wasn't so sure. From what I'd seen on the news, not to mention an embarrassing amount of gossip blog posts, Tiffany would have some serious competition. I asked, "But what about that model?"

Tiffany frowned. "Which one?"

I tried to think. There was that leggy brunette, and maybe a couple of blondes. I couldn't recall any of their names, but that was no surprise. I wasn't big into high fashion, especially with everything so far beyond my budget.

I said, "Actually, I'm not sure. Maybe someone who goes by just one name?" Yes, I *was* playing the odds. I mean, they *all* went by one name these days, right?

"If you're talking about Maven," Tiffany said, "I'm not even worried. She's a total diva. And besides, you *know* she's just using him."

I had no idea which model was called Maven. But did it matter?

Probably not. After all, it's not like I'd ever meet her.

Still, I said, "Using him? You mean for his money?"

Tiffany laughed. "No. Not *that*."

"Oh," I said. "For his looks?"

Tiffany leaned forward. "Guess again."

"Um…" I tried to think. "His last name?"

After all Bennington was pretty high up there in the name-recognition department. That sort of thing would matter to a diva, right?

Tiffany gave another laugh. "No. That's not it."

"Well, it couldn't be his charm," I muttered.

Tiffany lowered her voice. "It is, if you're talking about the charm in his pants." She gave something like a giggle. "I felt it, you know."

I froze. "It?"

Tiffany nodded. "Oh yeah. It was just through our clothes, but…" Her eyes became dreamy. "Oh. My. God."

Instinctively, I drew back. I *so* didn't want the details.

We'd already eaten, and my stomach couldn't handle another thing – especially dirty details on Zane Bennington's anatomy.

I glanced down at the table, now littered with soiled napkins and dirty plates. I'd just devoured a full plate of pasta primavera plus that whole basket of bread sticks – well, minus the one that Tiffany had nibbled on. Plus, there'd been that cannoli for desert and a nice little mint to finish everything off.

Damn it. I wanted to keep it all down, not send it right back up again.

I didn't know why, but I was surprisingly disturbed at the image of Tiffany making a grab for the prick's, well, prick, actually. Just the thought made my stomach lurch in a way that was decidedly unnatural.

It was really strange, too, because I'd just spent a full hour listening to Tiffany go on and on about how she was considering ditching the senator for Zane. None of *that* had made me feel sick.

Then again, *that* part of the conversation had been pretty clinical. The way it sounded, Tiffany had this whole mental spreadsheet mapped out, stating the pros and cons of each guy.

When it came to wealth, fame, influence, and looks, Zane was the clear winner. But the senator did have one huge thing going for him – he'd already popped the question. He was the proverbial bird-in-the-hand, while Zane was still firmly in the bush.

Across from me, Tiffany picked up her nearly empty wine glass and drained the rest of her zinfandel. She returned the glass to the table and said, "Did I mention I'm seeing him tonight?"

My stomach gave another lurch.

Damn it.

Still, I tried to shrug it off. "Oh, really? You mean like on a date?"

"I wouldn't call it a date-date." She grinned. "But I *am* meeting him at the hotel later on."

"Oh." In my stomach, that sick feeling grew and twisted. Why? I had no idea. Breadstick overload? That had to be it. Hoping to steer the conversation away from Zane's privates, I made myself ask, "Which hotel?"

She gave me a look. "His. Of course."

"Oh." Yeah, that was probably a stupid question. After all, the guy owned the most luxurious hotel and conference center in the whole city. Why on Earth would he slum it anywhere else?

Across from me, Tiffany pulled out her cell phone and frowned. "Oh, shoot. I've got a manicure at two." She reached into her purse and pulled out a few bills. She tossed them onto the table and said, "Sorry to run, but can you settle up here?"

Before I could even think to answer, she was already on her feet, blowing me an air kiss and scampering off to wherever. I looked down at the bills and did a quick calculation. If nothing else, she'd made good on her deal.

The cash was enough to cover both of our lunches, plus a nice tip for the waitress. Still, looking at the bills, scattered among the dirty dishes, I couldn't help but feel at least a little weird about it. After all, I'd just let someone I didn't particularly like treat me to lunch, just because I was hungry.

There was only one cure for that, I decided – to find a job of my own, like now. With that in mind, I spent the next couple of hours, going from business to business in hopes that somebody was hiring.

Finally, thanks to a chance meeting with a former neighbor, I had my first solid lead. There was only one problem.

I hated the thought of pursuing it – and all because of you-know-who.

CHAPTER 20

I stared at my former neighbor. "Wait, did you say the *Bennington* Hotel?"

Standing with me in the library, Lydia nodded. "Yeah, my uncle's a manager in the main kitchen."

My shoulders slumped. "Oh."

Lydia and I used to live in the same apartment building. We'd lost touch after I'd moved, but meeting her by chance seemed like the best luck ever, until like thirty seconds ago.

"Why?" she asked. "Is that a problem?" She hesitated. "You *did* say you'd take anything, right?"

It was true. I had said that.

We'd been chatting for maybe ten or fifteen minutes when I'd asked her if she happened to know of anyone who was hiring. In what felt like amazing luck, she told me that she knew of a big hotel that was ramping up its catering staff.

Best of all, they were looking to fill those positions right away. The timing was perfect, and the way it sounded, the pay wasn't half-bad, at least by food-service standards.

There was only one problem. The job happened to be at the one hotel I was determined to avoid.

Lydia gave me a sympathetic smile. "If it makes you feel any better, I'm working as a barista."

That made me pause. "But wait. What about your art degree?"

"What about it?" she said. "I paint on the side, but…" With a shrug, she let her words trail off. "Well, you know how it is."

I *did* know. Still, I was curious. "But the job you just mentioned… Don't take this the wrong way, but if it's so great, why aren't *you* interested?"

"Oh, that's an easy one," she said. "You know how I'm working at that coffee shop? Well, the owner's really great. She lets me hang my paintings on the walls, *with* a price tag."

"Oh, so you sell them?"

Lydia frowned. "In theory." She glanced away. "I mean, I haven't sold any yet, but you never know, right?"

I nodded. "Right. Definitely."

"But how about you?" Lydia said. "Why don't *you* want this job?"

"It's not that I don't want it," I explained. "It's just kind of complicated."

I glanced toward the nearby copy machine, the one I'd been using to print off more copies of my resume. I wasn't even sure why I bothered. After all, you didn't need a resume for low-level service jobs.

But in my own defense, I'd been applying for plenty of professional jobs, too. The only difference was, for those jobs, I usually applied online, because that's what most hiring agencies insisted on.

In front of me, Lydia asked, "Complicated how?"

I sighed. "Well, the truth is, I've met the hotel's owner, and let's just say we kind of hate each other."

Her eyes widened in obvious surprise. "You don't mean Zane Bennington?"

And there it was, that dreaded name again. "Uh, yeah. Actually, I do."

"Wow." Lydia was grinning now. "You lucky dog."

"Hardly." I tried to laugh. "You *did* hear the part where we hate each other?"

"But you actually met him?" She leaned forward. "What was *that* like?"

"Awful."

"Awful how?"

"Oh come on," I said. "Everybody knows he's a giant prick."

Lydia's lips curved into a mischievous smile. "Well, what *I* heard was that he *has* a —"

I held up a hand. "Don't say it."

Lydia laughed. "Oh come on. That's just gossip, anyway. And besides, it doesn't matter. You'd probably never see him."

"With *my* luck? I'm not so sure."

"Oh, come on," she said. "What, you think he spends his time in the kitchen? Like, take my uncle. He's only seen Zane Bennington once, and that was only because he happened to be outside when Zane's limo pulled up."

"You mean outside the hotel?"

Lydia nodded. "He has an office on the top floor. I hear it's pretty amazing."

My shoulders sagged. "That's too bad."

"Why?"

"Because I'd rather see him working in the basement." I smiled. "A nice, damp one. With rats. No. Not just rats. Giant man-eating rats."

"Boy, you really *do* hate him, don't you?" She hesitated. "And you said the feeling's mutual?"

Now, it was my turn to laugh. "Actually, I'm pretty sure he *has* no feelings."

"Then you should apply for the job. Honestly, I doubt you'd ever see him."

There was a certain comfort in that, and I *did* need the money. So when Lydia plucked a resume off my stack, and promised to pass it along to her uncle, I did what I should've done in the first place. I thanked her for the help and said a silent prayer that I'd actually get the job.

In what felt like terrific luck, I received a call the very next day from a nice lady in the Bennington's Human Resources Department. And just like that, I had an interview scheduled for the very next afternoon.

I didn't ask with whom, because I just assumed that it would be with Lydia's uncle, or maybe with a generic H.R. person.

Big mistake.

I arrived at the Bennington Hotel fifteen minutes early, and was ushered straight into the nearest elevator, where my escort, a thin, dark-haired woman, hit the button for the very top floor.

Watching this, my stomach sank. *He* was on the top floor, well, assuming that he was in the office today.

Damn it. I *so* didn't want to run into him, especially here, where he'd surely torpedo my job interview – or worse, kick me straight to the curb.

And I *so* needed this job.

In a desperate bid for reassurance, I turned to my escort and said, "I know this is a funny question, but by any chance, do you know if Zane Bennington is here today?"

She gave me a perplexed look. "Excuse me?"

Quickly, I added, "It's just that I met him a few weeks ago, and I was wondering if I might run into him again."

I held my breath and waited for the answer. *Please say no. Please say no…*

She eyed me up and down, frowning at my plain brown dress and no-nonsense shoes. Looking more perplexed than ever, she asked, "Was that a joke?"

I shook my head. "No, why?"

"Because he hates jokes. So if I were you, I'd stick to the basics."

And with that, she turned straight ahead, sending me the clear signal that our conversation was over. That was fine by me. Suddenly, I wasn't feeling so chatty.

I was getting a terrible feeling about this – a feeling which proved totally justified less than two minutes later, when I was ushered into the most luxurious office I'd ever seen. And who did I spot, sitting behind a massive desk in front of the giant floor-to-ceiling windows?

Zane "the Prick" Bennington.

Of course.

CHAPTER 21

My steps faltered, and I almost fell flat on my face. I looked down and spotted something on the floor. It was a red high-heeled shoe, lying on its side.

What the heck?

Zane's cool voice broke through my confusion. "If you want it, you can have it."

I looked up. "I can have what?"

"The shoe."

"What, why?"

"Because she's not coming back."

Well, that wasn't disturbing or anything.

I gave Zane a look. The bastard looked utterly at ease. And why *shouldn't* he be? He owned this hotel. Hell, he owned the whole block. And that was only here, in this city.

Worldwide, he probably owned hundreds of places just like this.

Plus one red shoe.

I just *had* to ask, "Whose is it?"

"Does it matter?"

Again, I looked to the shoe. It wasn't quite a stiletto, but it was pretty darn close. If it could talk, I knew exactly what it would say, and it *wasn't* "Hey, let's have a nice conversation at the library."

No. That was a "fuck-me" shoe if I ever saw one.

I tried to look on the upside. At least it wasn't a bra and panties.

My gaze narrowed. "What happened to the rest of her?"

Zane gave something like a shrug. "Don't know. Don't care."

Well, that was nice.

He motioned me to the single chair facing his desk. "Sit."

I didn't want to sit. I wanted to storm out. And yet, for some reason, my feet weren't cooperating.

He added, "Please."

The small courtesy surprised me, and just when I was ready to consider the slight – *very* slight – possibility that he wasn't a total prick *all* of the time, he continued, "Or leave. Your choice."

I stiffened. "Do you *have* to be so rude?"

If the question fazed him, he didn't show it. "Yes."

Funny, I hadn't expected an answer. I heard myself ask, "Why?"

"Because I'm an asshole."

I blinked. "What?"

For the briefest instant, he looked almost ready to smile. But of course, he didn't. Instead, he leaned back in his chair and said, "It's what I hear."

I wasn't going to argue. Still, I felt compelled to point out the obvious. "But you don't *have* to be."

"Wrong." He glanced at the visitor's chair. "So are you staying or going?"

I gave the chair a good, long look. It was a nice one, made of rich brown leather, with armrests and everything. But sitting anywhere near Zane Bennington seemed like a very dangerous idea – and not only because he was such a jerk.

Already, something was glaringly obvious. I might've been surprised to see *him*, but *he* wasn't surprised to see *me*.

No matter how I sliced it, that couldn't be good.

I turned and looked at the door behind me. At the sight of it, my brow wrinkled in confusion. The door was shut. Funny, I didn't remember shutting it. Maybe my escort had discreetly closed it after showing me in?

Or maybe Zane had one of those super-secret buttons under his desktop.

Reluctantly, I turned back to Zane. He was wearing a suit and tie.

He should've looked civilized. And yet, he didn't.

Oh sure, his suit was obviously expensive, and it fit him perfectly. His hair was unruffled, and his face was clean-shaven.

And yet, there was something in his eyes, or maybe in the set of his jaw, that told me he wasn't your average C.E.O.

But then again, I'd known that already, hadn't I?

I had no clue what was going on, but I did know that someone like Zane Bennington wouldn't be conducting interviews for a lowly kitchen job. So why was I here?

His last question hung in the air. *Was I staying or going?*

I still didn't have an answer. It was true that I desperately needed a job, but it was *also* true that I hated this guy, and not only because he was a total prick. It was because, in some weird, twisted way, he intrigued me in ways that were decidedly unnatural.

Talk about messed up.

And I *still* didn't have an answer. I tossed his own favorite phrase right back at him. "Does it matter?"

"To me?" He glanced away. "No."

At this, I felt an embarrassing surge of disappointment, but for the life of me, I couldn't figure out why. I really did loathe him. Still, I summoned up a thin smile and said, "Good." And with that, I turned and began marching toward the door.

Behind me, he added, "But it *will* matter to you."

My steps faltered, and I turned to ask, "Why?"

"Because," he said, "I'm about to offer you a job."

☐

CHAPTER 22

I was so shocked, I could hardly speak. Okay, maybe I shouldn't have been terribly surprised. This was, after all, supposedly a job interview.

But we hated each other. And I couldn't help but notice that no actual interview had taken place.

I felt my gaze narrow. "What kind of job?"

As an answer, he made a point of looking at the empty chair. His message was loud and clear. If I wanted to learn more, I knew exactly where my butt belonged.

Damn it. I *did* want to learn more. But who wouldn't?

With as much dignity as I could muster, I marched to the chair and sat.

He looked at me for a long, penetrating moment before saying, "You don't like me."

This, of course, was a massive understatement, so I didn't bother denying it. "You're right. I don't."

I waited for him to ask why. But he didn't. Instead, he gave a slow nod and said, "Good."

I felt my brow wrinkle. "Good? Why is that good?"

Ignoring my question, he said, "I need to know something."

Yeah, welcome to the club, buddy.

But I didn't say it, mostly because I was dying to hear what he'd say next.

He leaned forward and asked, "How good are you at pretending?"

I blinked. "What?"

"Pretending," he repeated. "Are you any good at it?"

Nope. Definitely not.

And yet, I was almost tempted to lie. But I couldn't, because in all honestly, I wasn't terribly good at *that* either. Stalling for time, I said, "Pretending what?"

"You ever hear the expression, 'good cop, bad cop.'?"

"Of course," I said. "I mean, I know the basic premise."

After all, I'd seen my share of police shows. In them, one officer would pretend to be nice and reasonable, while his partner would be a total hard-ass. Together, they'd wear the suspect down until he confessed, whether because he feared the bad cop, or because he trusted the good cop.

Zane said, "You wanna guess which cop I am?"

I almost snorted. "I don't need to guess."

"Right."

I gave him a perplexed look. "Wait a minute. You're hiring someone to be what? Your own personal 'good cop'?"

"In a sense."

"But why?"

"It's complicated."

I resisted the urge to roll my eyes. "I bet."

The longer we talked, the more this felt like a joke. Over the last month, Zane Bennington had brought me nothing but misery. And the way it looked, he still wasn't quite done.

Once again, he leaned back in his chair. "Over the next few months, I'm gonna be ruffling a few feathers."

I wanted to laugh. A guy like Zane Bennington? He wouldn't be content with merely ruffling a few feathers. No. Not *him*. He'd ruffle the whole bird. Hell, a flock of birds. And then, he'd eat the birds for dinner. Raw. With a side of gravel.

Because he was just that awful.

I said, "So, let me get this straight. You're hiring some sort of good-cop, feather smoother? Is *that* what you're saying?" I gave a nervous laugh. "Because that's one heck of a job title."

But Zane wasn't laughing. "That's not the title," he said, "although, if you wanna throw it on a card, be my guest."

"What card?"

"A business card."

"Oh." *Damn it*. I should've known that. "So, what *is* the title?"

As an answer, he reached into his top desk drawer and pulled out a single sheet of paper. He slid it across the desk in my direction.

I reached out and picked it up. On the sheet was a single typewritten paragraph under an official-looking job title. I read the title out loud. "Personal public relations manager." I looked up. "Seriously?"

My degree was in public relations. It was true that I hadn't done a whole lot with it, but it seemed an odd coincidence – unless it wasn't a coincidence at all.

I said, "Is this for real?"

As usual, he ignored my question. He pointed to the sheet and said, "Read the first word again. Out loud."

I glanced at the sheet. "Personal?"

"Right. Which means you're employed by me, not the company."

Technically, I wasn't employed by anyone, not yet. And I couldn't help but notice that he seemed awful certain that I'd accept any offer.

For some stupid reason, maybe old-fashioned pride, I didn't like it. And yet, I could see why he'd be so sure of my acceptance. I was, after all, an unemployed catering assistant with an old car and no other prospects.

I bit my lip. In truth, this would've been my dream job if only it involved working for someone else.

Even in college, I'd worked my share of menial jobs – fast food, retail, whatever, anything for tuition. One thing I'd learned the hard way – no matter how great a job might seem, it totally sucked if your boss was an asshole.

I studied the guy across from me. He returned my gaze with no discernable emotion. In truth, it was a little unsettling.

I looked down and quickly scanned the rest of the job description. It was pretty standard for this type of work. It involved setting up interviews, answering media inquiries, and dealing with the public as needed.

I saw nothing about pay and benefits.

As I stared down at the sheet of paper, I couldn't help but recall that Zane was the guy who'd gotten me fired from my last job. And now, he was offering me a new one?

It didn't make any sense.

If he'd been anyone else, I might've chalked it up to pity or regret. But this was Zane Bennington. He had no pity, and he wouldn't know regret if it bit him on the ass. No. He was the kind of guy who'd evict an entire family – of relatives, no less – from their family home just because he could.

That wasn't the only thing that bothered me. Other than a brief summer internship, I had nearly no experience. But this *wasn't* an entry-level job. It was the kind of job that someone worked their way up to.

I was inexperienced, but not naïve. Zane could hire anyone. So why me?

I recalled that old saying. If something sounds too good to be true, it probably is. I pulled my gaze from the description and looked to Zane.

I just had to ask, "What's the catch?"

He sat, watching me, from his side of the desk. Behind him, the sky was blue with fluffy white clouds. But when it came to Zane, there was nothing fluffy about *him*. He looked hard and impervious, even as he studied my face with his usual cool detachment.

He never did answer my question. Instead, he casually informed me, "You start on Monday."

I made a scoffing sound. "Aren't you forgetting something?"

"What?"

"I haven't accepted."

"No. But you will."

"Oh yeah? Why?"

"You want the blunt answer? Or the polite answer?"

I couldn't help but smirk. "The polite answer."

"All right. You'll accept because it's a good opportunity, and you damn well know it."

"And that's the *polite* answer?"

"Now, you want the blunt one?"

I wasn't so sure. And yet, I felt myself nod.

He said, "Your car's a heap. Your rent's chronically late. Your student loans are kicking your ass, and that extension you applied for last week? Let's just say, it's not gonna pan out."

My jaw dropped. Last Tuesday, in a fit of desperation, I'd applied for a hardship extension on my biggest student loan. As far as I knew, the application was still pending.

And now, he was telling me that it was going to be declined?

I felt my gaze narrow. "How do you know?"

"Guess."

I wanted to strangle him. "You didn't seriously sabotage me?"

"You think I wouldn't?"

"Actually, I think you would, but I can't imagine why you'd go to that much trouble." I looked away and muttered, "Unless you're *trying* to ruin my life." I was still looking away when the rest of his statement caught up with me.

I looked back to him and said, "Wait a minute, how did you know all that?"

"You think I'm gonna hire someone without checking them out?"

I was glaring at him now. "You had no right."

"Wrong," he said. "You gave me the right."

"I did not."

Again, he reached into his desk drawer. He pulled out another sheet and held it out in my direction.

I snatched it from his hand and looked down. It was a printout of an on-line application – one of many that I'd submitted over the last few weeks. But the application wasn't with Bennington Hotels. It was with one of the most exclusive hiring agencies in the whole city.

He said, "You see that box by your digital signature?"

I did see it. I'd agreed to a background check as part of the application process. Still, it felt like a dirty trick.

I gave Zane a hard look. "A background check doesn't give you permission to pry, at least not like that."

"Wrong again," he said. "Now, you want some advice?"

"From you?" I crossed my arms. "No."

"Yeah? Well, you're getting it anyway." His tone grew harder. "Read the fine print. *Always*."

The longer this little interview – or whatever this was – went on, the worse I was feeling. It wasn't just his attitude. It was the way he'd spelled out my financial shortcomings like I was some sort of loser.

I felt my jaw tighten. *Damn it.* I wasn't a loser, and I refused to feel like one.

Suddenly, I didn't care whether this was a good opportunity or not. And I didn't care that I had no other offers. With one swift motion, I tore the application in two and tossed it onto his desk.

Take that, you prick.

He didn't even look down. "That's a copy, you know."

"What?"

"It's a copy," he repeated. "Lesson two. Always keep the original."

Once more, I felt like strangling him. Of course, I knew the application wasn't the original, because I'd submitted the whole thing by computer.

Technically, there was no original, as he obviously realized. So what was this, anyway? Just another way to make me feel stupid?"

I told him, "I don't need any lessons."

"If you say so."

"I *do* say so." My mouth tightened. "And you know what? I'm leaving."

"All right." His gaze shifted to the door. "No one's stopping you."

"Good." And with that, I stood and turned away. I marched toward the door with my head held high and a silent promise to not look back.

I'd made it only halfway when my foot snagged something in my path. Before I even realized what was happening, I'd done a full face-plant onto his fancy carpet, yelping, "Son-of-a-bitch!"

I scrambled to my feet and turned to glare – first at him, and then at that stupid "fuck-me" shoe, lying near my feet. On impulse, I picked it up and hurled it straight at him – or at least, it was *supposed* to go straight at him. But my aim sucked, and the shoe went careening into his desktop lamp.

The lamp toppled and crashed to the floor. To my infinite frustration, it didn't even break.

How unsatisfying.

And through all of this, Zane hadn't even moved, not even a

twitch. Instead, he sat, watching me with his usual cool detachment.

Asshole.

My face was flaming, and my breath was coming in short, angry bursts. In a fit of pique, I yelled, "That was *your* fault!"

His eyebrows lifted. "The shoe or the lamp?"

"Both!"

"Lesson three —"

"I don't need another freaking lesson!"

Once again, he leaned back in his chair. "You're awful mouthy for a new hire."

His calmness grated on me, and I had a nearly uncontrollable urge to yank off my own shoes and hurl them straight at his head, one by one.

But I didn't – mostly because I couldn't afford to replace them.

So, with what little dignity I could muster, I took a deep, calming breath. And then, I coolly informed him, "I'm not your employee. And I'm *not* going to be."

Prick.

He said, "You think."

"No," I told him. "I *know*. There's a difference."

"Right."

"And," I said, "in case you're too stubborn to realize it, I'm declining your offer."

He looked utterly unfazed. "You can't 'til you see it."

"I *have* seen it," I said. "You just showed it to me."

"You saw the description. You didn't see the offer."

I gave a snort of derision. "So what? I don't care what you're offering. The answer's still no."

But as it turned out, that was a total lie.

CHAPTER 23

Charlotte was still staring at the sheet of paper. "Is this for real?"

I took another swig of my wine. "Apparently."

"What do you mean, apparently? On the phone, you said you accepted."

I'd called her an hour ago, after I'd first gotten home. Based on the timing, Charlotte had obviously left my parent's house the moment I'd told her the news.

I knew why. She thought I was losing my mind.

She was right, of course.

I blew out a long, shaky breath. "Yup."

"Shouldn't you be, like, *happy* or something?" Again, she looked to the paper. "I mean, holy crap."

I blew out another breath. "Yup."

"That's a lot of money."

I took another drink. "Yup."

She eyed my half-empty glass, and then, the half-empty bottle. "I thought you hated merlot."

"Yup."

"So why'd you buy it?"

"I didn't. It's Paisley's."

Charlotte gave a snort of laughter. "You're kidding."

"Nope."

I wasn't a big drinker, but I liked to keep a bottle of wine on-hand, just in case. Sometimes, it was just in case company showed up. Other times, it was just in case you accepted a job offer from the biggest prick on the planet and wanted to drown your anxiety in a bottle of cabernet.

Unfortunately, Paisley had swiped my emergency bottle weeks ago, and I'd been too broke to buy a replacement. So here I was, drowning my worries in cheap merlot.

Or heck, it might be expensive merlot. It's not like I could taste the difference.

Charlotte picked up the bottle and took a closer look. "But where'd you find it? I mean, the way you talk, she never stocks the pantry."

"Got that right," I muttered.

"So where was it?"

I glanced toward the back hallway. "In her bedroom."

Charlotte was grinning now. "No way! You went through her bedroom?" She leaned forward. "So, did you ransack it or what?"

I hadn't been looking for the wine. In truth, I didn't even realize she *had* wine. No. What *I'd* been looking for was the cordless telephone.

Eventually, I'd found the phone under her pillow, but only *after* I'd found the bottle of merlot, hidden under her bed, where I'd *also* found three cans of soup, a box of saltines, and an unopened bag of corn chips.

I looked to the bag, which was now sitting, half-empty, on the kitchen table. I pushed the bag in Charlotte's direction. "Corn chip?"

She burst out laughing. "Don't tell me. Are those Paisley's too?"

I reached out and grabbed a handful of chips. I popped them into my mouth and mumbled, "They're mine now."

Charlotte studied my face. "Should I be worried? Because you look like you might be losing it."

"Oh, please." I gave a weak laugh. "I'm not losing it. It's gone."

In fact, I was pretty sure that I'd lost my sanity the moment I'd signed that job offer. But the salary – not to mention the perks – had been impossible to resist. Obviously, none of this was an accident. The way it looked, the paperwork had been drawn up long before I arrived in Zane's office.

I couldn't help but wonder, why me?

Obviously, there was something Zane wasn't telling me. But what?

Charlotte leaned closer and squinted at my face. "I hate to ask, but did something happen to your nose?"

Again, I reached for my glass. "Oh yeah." I took a good, long drink and returned the now-empty glass to the table.

"Well?" Charlotte said. "What happened?"

I sighed. "Rug burn."

"Seriously?"

I reached up to touch the tip of my nose. Oh sure, the carpet in Zane's office had *looked* all soft and plush, but it was a different story when you smashed your face into it.

I muttered, "Stupid carpet."

The only upside was that the rug-burn had been barely visible at first. In fact, my nose hadn't gotten truly red until that hot bath and, yes, too much merlot.

By Monday, my nose would be as good as new.

Or at least, I sure hoped so. It would, after all, be my first day on the job – a job I'd only taken because the offer had been impossible to resist.

And here, I thought I had integrity.

Turns out, not so much.

But then again, integrity wouldn't pay the bills. And it wasn't like I'd taken a job beating orphans. The truth was, this would've been my dream job, if only someone else had offered it to me.

Still, it reminded me of that Italian lunch with Tiffany. Apparently, I could be bought with pasta and bread sticks – or in the case of Zane, a six-figure salary and a whole bunch of perks.

I leaned back and closed my eyes. "I'm a job slut."

"What?" Charlotte said. "So, he expects you to—"

My eyes snapped back open, "God no. I didn't mean it *that* way."

And yet, an image popped into my brain. The image was of me and Zane, sprawled across that giant desk of his. *Damn it.* It was an image I didn't need, and not only because, inexplicably, I was wearing those stupid red heels and not much else.

Charlotte said, "Then what *did* you mean?"

As for Zane, in my unwanted fantasy, he'd been wearing that same expensive suit, minus the shirt. Funny though, the tie was still there. And it looked way too good against his bare, muscular chest.

I mumbled, "Huh?"

Charlotte made a sound of frustration. "When you called yourself a job slut, what were you talking about?"

"Oh." I snapped back to reality. "That? I just mean that I hate the guy, and yet, when I saw that offer…" I let my words trail off into something like a sigh.

"Tell me something," Charlotte said. "Do you regret it?"

"Yes." My shoulders slumped. "And no."

"So it can't be *all* bad," she said. "And by the way, whose car is that?"

"The one in the driveway? It's mine. Sort of."

"Seriously?"

I reached up to rub the back of my neck. "Well, it's not like my name's on the title or anything. It's more like a company car."

"Wow, it looks brand new."

"Uh, yeah. I think it is." It wasn't just brand new. It was sleek and luxurious, with leather seats and an engine that purred like a kitten.

"I knew it!" Charlotte said. "I swear, when I walked by, I could *smell* how new it was."

I knew what she meant. It *did* have that new-car smell. As for my old heap, it was somewhere in the depths of the Bennington parking garage, where I'd been allowed to store the thing indefinitely.

It was all such a whirlwind, I still didn't know what to think.

After I'd accepted the offer, I'd been sent down to Human Resources, where I'd been given a choice of cars and a key to the executive suite. And then, in the strangest development of all, I'd been assigned a personal shopper, who'd hustled me from store to store, buying suits, dresses, shoes, and all of the accessories I'd need for the new position.

Even now, my closet was packed with more clothes than I'd ever owned in my whole life.

I honestly didn't get it. Why would Zane go to so much trouble, when he could simply hire someone who already had the wardrobe, not to mention the experience needed for such a high-profile position?

Charlotte said, "Hey, can I ask you something?"

"What?"

"Aren't you worried you're gonna get fired?"

"No." I tried to laugh. "I'm worried I *won't* get fired."

"Oh come on," she said. "I'm serious. I mean, look what happened with the catering thing. You were just there doing your job, and the next thing you know, you're out on your ass."

"I know." I gave a long, sad sigh. "But at least the dogs were happy."

"Dogs? What dogs?"

I eyed my sadly empty wine glass. Would it be *so* bad if I refilled it? Already, I wasn't feeling so great, but I *was* awful thirsty.

As if reading something in my expression, Charlotte snatched the bottle out of my reach and set it on the other side of the table. She gave me a no-nonsense look and repeated the question. "What dogs?"

"*His* dogs," I said. "Flint and Lansing." I gave a little wave of my hands. "There was this incident. Don't ask."

But she did. And of course, I *had* to tell her.

☐

CHAPTER 24

"Well," I began, "when we showed up, it was absolutely crazy with people everywhere."

"You mean like party guests?" Charlotte said.

"No. With workers, like me." I made little air quotes. "The help."

"And…?"

"And they even hired a valet parking service. I have no idea where they parked the cars, but the whole setup was really official, with guys in fancy red uniforms and everything."

"But what does that have to do with you?" Charlotte asked.

"I'm getting to that," I said. "So anyway, Naomi and I are unloading our stuff. And I *might've* left the van open, which wouldn't have been a problem, except, well, there were these two crazy hounds."

Charlotte said, "Flint and Lansing?"

"Right. *His* dogs, apparently. And get this. Somehow, they end up *inside* the van."

"Somehow?" Charlotte laughed. "You mean through the door you left open?"

"Oh, fine. Yes. Probably. But anyway, they're rampaging through the whole cargo area, causing this huge ruckus, and some 'helpful' valet guy decides the only thing he can do is – get this – shut the van door."

"You're kidding." Charlotte looked horrified. "He trapped them *inside* the van?"

"Right. And I just wanna clarify, I wasn't even out there when this happened."

"Where were you?" she asked.

"Inside the house, getting everything set up. But then, I hear all this yelling."

"From who?"

"Everyone," I said. "But mostly, from this event planner – Ms. Hedgwick. Apparently, she'd hired some 'dog-wrangler' to keep the dogs entertained, and she was hollering for the guy to get out there and do his job."

Charlotte's eyebrows furrowed. "Dog wrangler?"

"Actually, I don't know what his official title was, but he was supposed to keep the dogs somewhere else, where they wouldn't cause any trouble."

"Like where?"

"I dunno. But trust me, they had plenty of space." I waved away the distraction. "So anyway, like I said, I hear all this yelling, so I run out there, and everyone's standing around the van, doing nothing but listening."

"To what?" Charlotte asked.

"Mostly clattering and barking."

"So what'd you do?"

"So I go to the back of the van, fling open both doors, and there they are." I tried not to smile. "The hell hounds."

"So they were vicious?"

I thought of the dogs, with their excited eyes and floppy tongues. I felt a warm, happy glow as I recalled them slobbering all over Zane's front windows. "No. But they *were* insane. And snacky."

"Snacky?" Charlotte cringed. "You don't mean –?"

"Yup," I said. "For party food."

"But wait, I thought you already hauled it into the house."

"Not all of it," I said. "In fact, that's why I left the stupid van door open in the first place. We had more stuff to take in."

"Like what?" she asked.

"Like, we had these little meatballs, some bacon and artichoke wraps, these cute little finger sandwiches, all kinds of stuff."

Charlotte said, "And the dogs got into it?"

"Not all of it. But enough to make a huge mess." In spite of everything, I couldn't help but smile at the memory of how happy they'd looked, frolicking among the catering goods.

"So," Charlotte prompted, "what'd you do?"

"Well, at first, I don't do anything, because I'm sure they're gonna bolt out of there any minute."

"But they don't?"

"No," I said. "They don't. And they won't, even *after* I call to them. I mean, there they are, surrounded by meatballs."

Charlotte winced. "You don't mean they—"

"Got into them? Yeah, they totally did. The other stuff was sealed up pretty good, but the meatballs broke from their container and rolled all over the place."

"So *then*, what'd you do?"

"Well, I've got to get the dogs outta there, right? So I hop into the van and grab a wad of meatballs off the floor."

"A wad?"

"You know, a handful. And I start tossing them out the back of the van. And I'm yelling, 'Fetch, doggie, fetch!'"

Charlotte laughed. "Doggie?"

"That was before I knew their names."

"Well, that explains everything," she said. "So did they? Fetch, I mean?"

"Not at first, because they've got all this meat *inside* the van. I mean, they'd be stupid to leave, right?"

Charlotte rolled her eyes. "Totally."

"So anyway, before I know it, I've thrown like fifty meatballs. And they're scattered all over the parking area." I sighed. "And I might've hit a valet or two."

Charlotte was laughing again. "You didn't."

"Hey, you know I've got the worst aim in the world." I glanced away. "And if you think I can't throw a meatball, you should see me throw a shoe."

"Wait," Charlotte said. "Why would you throw a shoe?"

I waved away the question. "Don't ask."

Charlotte was shaking her head. "I can't believe I'm just hearing this. Why didn't you tell me sooner?"

"Honestly, it was a little embarrassing."

"Just a little?" She looked beyond amused. "So why are you telling me now?

My gaze shifted to the wine. "I dunno."

Charlotte leaned forward. "Is there anything else you wanna confess?"

"Like what?"

"Admit it." Her tone grew teasing. "You think Zane Bennington's hot, don't you?"

Once again, an image of Zane flashed in my mind. As usual, he was beyond sexy, with that thick hair, gorgeous cheekbones, and a body to die for. With an effort I shoved aside the image and reminded myself that he was *not* a nice person.

I gave an irritated sigh. "Of course, I think he's hot. But he's a total jerk, so it doesn't count."

Charlotte gave me a knowing smile. "That's what *you* think."

Already, I'd had enough of Zane Bennington. I didn't want to talk about him, and I sure as heck didn't want to think about him.

Already, he was haunting my thoughts far too often. Oh sure, most of those thoughts were homicidal, but every once in a while, a different kind of thought burrowed its way into my brain.

Like just now.

And it was pretty darn annoying.

Deliberately, I changed the subject. "Back to the catering thing, it was such a total nightmare."

"It wasn't *all* bad," she said. "Like you said, the dogs were happy, right?"

"Oh yeah. *They* had a lovely time. Me, not so much."

"So I've gotta ask," Charlotte said. "How do you know you weren't fired for *that*?"

It was a good question. And lucky for me, I had a good answer. "Because," I explained, "everything was mostly smoothed over until Zane got involved. And with the dogs, these things happen, right?"

Charlotte gave me a look. "Not to normal people, they don't."

"Hey, I'm normal."

But Charlotte was shaking her head. "You're not normal." She gave me a cheery smile. "You're better than normal. You're unique."

"You mean like a snowflake?" I frowned. "I'm not sure that's a compliment."

"Well, look on the bright side," she said. "With the money you're making now, you can afford your own dog." She grinned. "And maybe a wrangler, too."

"I don't need a wrangler," I said. "I need a psychic."

"Why?"

"Because I still don't know why Zane hired *me* of all people."

"Did you ask?"

"Sure."

"And what did he say?"

"Nothing. As usual."

"Who knows? Maybe he likes you."

"Him?" I said. "Not a chance."

"Why not?"

"Because he hates everyone. And he might even hate *me* more than he hates most people."

"That can't be true," she said. "If he hated you, he wouldn't have hired you."

I bit my lip. "Unless it's some sort of punishment."

"Oh come on," she said. "Do you know how many people would kill to be in your shoes?"

I *did* know, which only made me feel worse, because on some level, I knew I should be thrilled. And yet, I wasn't. I couldn't be.

It wasn't only because I didn't like him. It was because, in spite of what my sister might think, I knew there had to be some nefarious reason he'd hire *me* of all people.

Maybe he wanted to see me squirm.

If so, he definitely knew exactly what he was doing, because my first day proved even more uncomfortable than I'd anticipated.

CHAPTER 25

"You're late," he said.

He was right. I was. But it wasn't entirely my fault. Paisley, who I'd barely seen over the past few weeks, had parked behind me in the driveway sometime in the middle of the night, and then, she'd caused a giant stink this morning when I woke her up to ask her to move her car.

And of course, she'd taken her own sweet time.

As a result, here I was, fifteen minutes late for my very first day on the job. *Damn it.* I had to say it. "I'm sorry." The words stuck in my throat like a giant chicken bone, even as I promised, "It won't happen again."

His eyebrows lifted. "You sure about that?"

"Yes. Definitely." It wasn't even a lie. From now on, I decided, I'd park on the street, if that's what it took.

I hated feeling rushed, and here I was, nearly breathless after practically sprinting from the elevator to the executive suite. I'd arrived only thirty seconds ago, and still had no idea where my own desk was, assuming that I had a desk at all. Unfortunately, I'd had no time to ask before I'd been hustled straight into Zane's office, where he'd been waiting behind that huge desk of his.

Unlike me, *he* didn't look rushed or harried. No. He looked like a million – wait, make that a *billion* – bucks. His suit was cut perfectly to his broad shoulders, and his tie was dark gray with subtle flecks of red – probably to match his devil horns.

Oh, I couldn't see them. But I *knew* they were there.

He stood. "There's a breakfast meeting in five."

I was still catching my breath. "Five minutes?"

He gave me a look. "What do you think?"

I gave him a look right back. Of course, it *had* to be minutes. After all, in five *hours*, it would be mid-afternoon. My question had been mostly rhetorical. But seriously, did he have to be such a jerk, even about such a little thing?

Then again, this was Zane Bennington.

I gave him my sweetest smile. "Oh. So it's in five *days*."

He didn't smile back.

Stubbornly, I kept my smile plastered in place. "Or maybe, it's weeks."

He still wasn't smiling, but I was getting pretty used to it. I added, "You strike me as a planner."

This wasn't quite true. In reality, this buttoned-down billionaire seemed like a different guy than the one I'd met during our earlier encounters.

I wasn't even sure why I was tweaking him. It was beyond stupid, and yet, whether it was due to nerves, or because he had it coming, I couldn't seem to stop myself.

He said, "It's five minutes. And you're coming with me."

Suddenly, I wasn't smiling anymore. Already, I'd gotten attached to the idea that he'd be rushing off to a breakfast meeting, and *I'd* have the chance to pull myself together.

No such luck.

On top of that, breakfast wasn't sounding so great. I'd had coffee in the car, and even *that* wasn't sitting right. The idea of any food whatsoever made me feel just a little bit queasy – partly because of nerves and partly because last night, I'd found another bottle of merlot, this one hidden in the back of the linen closet.

One sip led to another, and here I was, dreading the idea of breakfast. Still, I wasn't completely stupid. Even *I* realized that breakfast meetings usually had very little to do with the actual food.

I tried for another smile. "Great. Where's the meeting?"

"Here."

I glanced around. "In your office?"

"No. In the restaurant downstairs."

If he meant Claudette's, it was one of the very best restaurants in the whole city. But I'd always known it as a dinner place – not that I'd ever eaten there personally. For one thing, I couldn't afford it. And for another, the place was notoriously hard to get into.

"Claudette's?" I said. "I didn't even realize they served breakfast."

"They don't," Zane said. "But they are this morning."

"Oh." I couldn't imagine why, unless Zane had personally arranged it. "So they're opening just for you?"

"They will if they know what's good for them."

Was that a joke? Doubtful.

Before I could even think to ask, Zane flicked his head toward a side table and told me to drop everything but my computer – a sleek little tablet that I'd been assigned, along with a new cell phone, right after signing the employment paperwork.

More confused than ever, I set down my purse, along with the brown-bag lunch that I'd brought for later on, assuming that I'd be able to eat at all.

And then, we were off.

In the elevator on the way down, Zane – without bothering to look at me – gave me a quick rundown on who we were meeting with. Apparently, it was with the owner of a shipping company who handled most of the international transports for the Bennington Hotels.

Zane said they had several issues they needed to resolve and mentioned that the guy had been a problem.

I gave Zane a sideways glance. Speaking of guys who'd been a problem.

But that wasn't the thing that was bothering me now. At the moment, I was terrified of screwing up, especially because I didn't really know what was expected of me. After all, Zane had mentioned nothing about media involvement, press releases, or anything related to my actual job description.

Reluctantly, I turned to look at him. "I've got a question."

He kept his gaze straight ahead. "What?"

"Is there anything specific you'd like me to do at this meeting?"

"Yeah." A ghost of a smile crossed his features. "Keep him from hitting me."

The smile – if that's what it truly was – caught me off-guard. "Seriously?"

And just like that, the smile was gone. "No."

"Oh, so that was a joke?" A nervous laugh escaped my lips. "So he's *not* going to hit you?"

But Zane wasn't laughing. "He can try."

"Wait, so you *weren't* kidding?" I felt myself swallow. "Am I *really* supposed to keep him from—"

"No."

"No?"

"If it's heading that way," Zane said, "you stay out of it."

Well, that was a relief.

Sort of.

But it told me nothing about why I was attending the meeting in the first place.

Searching for clues, I asked, "Will anyone from the media be there?"

"Not if they know what's good for them."

What did *that* mean? I had no idea, so I tried again. "Okay…So, will I be writing a press release or something?"

"No," he said. "But we might need to counter his narrative if the meeting goes south."

I gave a slow nod. Finally, I understood. "So we're talking damage-control? You mean like crisis-management, right?"

"Something like that."

As last, I had a sense of what my role would be, and I breathed a sigh of relief. I hated feeling clueless, and I'd been swimming in unfamiliar waters ever since I'd been hired.

Unfortunately, my relief was short-lived, because less than five minutes into the meeting, I was seriously worried that Zane *would* get hit.

And why? Because he totally had it coming.

CHAPTER 26

We'd just settled into our seats when the owner of the shipping company looked to Zane and said, "I was real sorry to hear about your grandfather."

Zane leaned back in his chair and gave the guy a dismissive look. "Yeah, I bet."

I looked from Zane to the poor sap who'd just made the mistake of acting like a decent human being. His name was Marco Sarkozy, and apparently, his family owned Ace Transports – the company that had been handling Bennington freight-shipping needs for three decades. As for Marco himself, he was a heavy-set, middle-aged man with a ruddy completion that was looking ruddier with every passing moment.

His eyebrows furrowed. "What?"

Zane shrugged. "I'm just saying. Sucks he's dead, huh?"

"Well, uh, yeah," Marco said. "As I said on the phone, you have my deepest condolences."

Zane made a low, scoffing sound. "I *mean* it sucks for you."

Marco gave a confused shake of his head. "Sorry, I'm not following."

Watching this appalling exchange, I wanted to say something – anything – to break the growing tension, but honestly, what could I say? *I'm sorry my boss is a jerk?*

I *was* sorry, but it's not like I could do a darn thing about it.

Zane tossed the guy a menu. "If you want breakfast, you'd better hurry."

Marco blinked. "What, why? Are they closing soon?"

"They'll close when I want them to." Zane glanced at his watch. "I'm thinking ten minutes."

"Ten minutes for what?" Marco asked. "To order?"

"No," Zane said. "To order, eat, *and* fuck off."

And there he was – the uncivilized tool I'd become all too familiar with. *So much for that whole buttoned-down billionaire thing.*

By now, Marco's cheeks were beet-red. "Sorry?" He reached up to tug at his collar. "I, uh, think you lost me there."

"If you want," Zane said, "you can skip the first two."

Marco shook his head. "The first two what?"

"Steps," Zane replied. "Go straight to 'fuck off', save the chef some trouble."

If I weren't so horrified, I might've scoffed out loud. *Like Zane cared about the chef.*

As Marco stammered out some incoherent response, I gave our surroundings a nervous glance. The place was beyond posh, with pristine white tablecloths and fresh flowers on every table. And yet, ours was the only table that was occupied.

The whole situation was entirely surreal, and yes, incredibly awkward.

Desperately, I was wishing that someone else had joined us for this godawful whatever-it-was. But no, there were just us three – me, the prick, and the poor slob who was still stammering.

I recalled what Zane had told me during my job interview. He'd warned me that he'd be ruffling a few feathers, and said that he wanted me to play the good cop to his bad cop.

Was I supposed to be doing that *now*? I gave Zane a sideways glance. I didn't know what he was thinking, but I *did* know that he wasn't above pulling out a night stick and beating the guy senseless.

I mean, if you'd kick someone out of their house, you were capable of anything, right?

I spoke up. "You know what we need?"

Zane's cool gaze remained on Marco. "What?"

Oh, crap. I didn't know. "Hang on," I said, reaching for my menu. I gave it a quick once-over. Turns out, it was the menu they used for their Sunday brunch. My gaze bounced from item to item. Finally, it landed on the beverage section, where the top item caught my eye. Before I could even think, I'd already blurted out, "Mimosas."

I wasn't even sure what a mimosa was, but it sounded tropical and maybe even boozy. Either one sounded like a very good thing.

Zane's gaze shifted to me. "Mimosas."

Was that a question? I hated how he did that, said things that *could* be a question, but were missing the question mark. Desperately, I looked to Marco. "*You'd* like a mimosa, right?"

Marco was literally sweating now. "Uh—"

Zane's voice cut across the table. "No. He wouldn't."

Marco cleared his throat. "Actually—"

"Fuck off," Zane said.

And just like that, Marco was back to stammering again.

With growing desperation, I called out to our water. "Excuse me?" When he rushed over, I said, "Could we get a round of Mimosas?"

The waiter's gaze shifted to Zane. "Mister Bennington?"

Zane spared the guy half a glance. "No."

My face burst into flames. *Talk about humiliating.*

The waiter lowered his voice. "I'm sorry sir, but…" He hesitated. "Is that a 'no' for everyone? Or just for you?"

Zane's gaze flicked briefly to me. "Bring *one*." His voice hardened. "To go."

The waiter frowned. "I'm terribly sorry, but—"

"But what?" Zane said.

"Well, you see…" Now, the waiter's face was red, too. "We're not allowed to do that."

Zane's jaw tightened. "Why not?"

"Because uh, it's against the law." Quickly, he added, "Because of the alcohol."

Oh, no. Now, I'd gotten the waiter in trouble, too.

I spoke up. "That's all right. Forget I asked." I gave the waiter what I hoped was a reassuring smile. "Maybe we'll just have a round of orange juice then?"

Again, the waiter's gaze shifted to Zane. "Sir?"

"*One* orange juice." Zane looked to Marco. "And like I said, to go."

Across the table, Marco managed to say, "That's all right. I, uh—"

Zane said, "It's not for *you*, dickhead."

At this, Marco's face flushed so red, he looked like a human tomato. "What the hell?" He pushed back his chair and stood. "What *is* this, anyway?"

It was a train-wreck, that's what.

Once again, Zane leaned back in his chair. He gave Marco a long, cold look. "I dunno. You tell me."

Marco glared down at him. "Hey, *dickhead. You* were the one who called this meeting."

"That's right," Zane said.

"For what?" Marco demanded. "To be an asshole? Is that it?"

Zane replied, "Pretty much."

Marco's jaw dropped. "What, why?"

Zane looked almost bored now. "Why not?"

Marco stared in apparent disbelief. "You've got to be joking. I flew in from the coast." His voice rose. "On *four* hours' notice."

"Yeah?" Zane said. "Sucks to be you." He flicked his head toward the entrance. "Now get the fuck out."

The guy looked ready to lunge across the table. "Or what?"

In a surprisingly calm voice, Zane said, "Or I'll toss you out."

I didn't know what to say. Did he mean personally? Or that he'd call security? Zane was tall and well built. No doubt, he *could* toss the guy out, if that's what he really wanted to do.

But why would he?

None of this was making any sense.

I felt myself swallow. If I was supposed to be playing the good cop, I was failing miserably, because I had absolutely no idea what to do.

Across from us, Marco demanded, "But what about our contract?"

"What about it?" Zane said.

"You said you wanted to discuss it."

"Oh, yeah. That's right," Zane said, as if remembering something long-forgotten. "I tore it up."

Marco gave a confused shake of his head. "What are you saying? You can't just tear it up. It's not like it's a piece of paper you can—"

"It is. And I did," Zane said. "So fuck off."

It was at this moment that I heard a quiet male voice just over my right shoulder. "Miss?"

I turned to look and saw the waiter, holding two plastic to-go cups, each with a lid and a straw. He whispered, "I've got your drinks."

Drinks? As in more than one? I felt my brow wrinkle in confusion. "I'm sorry, what?"

"The drinks," he repeated. "The ones you ordered."

"Oh." In truth, I hadn't meant to order anything for me. I'd been ordering them as a social thing, something to break the tension. By now, the thought of drinking anything whatsoever made me almost want to throw up.

Still, what could I do? With a whispered thanks, I reached out and took the drinks from his outstretched hands.

As he handed the cups over, he leaned close and said in a whisper so low, I could barely hear it, "Officially, they're both orange juice, but…" He hesitated. "Just don't get me in trouble, okay?"

With who? Zane? Or the law? Either way, the guy looked scared to death. My heart went out to him. Obviously, neither one of us wanted to be here, in the middle of whatever this was.

Before I could formulate any sort of response, the waiter turned and rushed away, as if beyond eager to get the hell out of Dodge.

I could *so* relate.

The meeting ended less than a minute later when Marco stormed off, promising Zane that he'd see him in court.

And then, there was just the two of us – me and my new boss, the biggest prick in the universe.

Heaven help me.

CHAPTER 27

I glanced toward the entrance, where Marco had disappeared only moments earlier.

Next to me, Zane was still sitting, which, like so many other things, caught me off guard. For some reason, I figured that Zane would've already been on his feet, hustling both of us toward the elevator.

But he wasn't.

Instead, he was watching the entrance with cool detachment, even as the sound of a thud, quickly followed by a crash, echoed from somewhere beyond our sight, probably in the hotel lobby.

I just had to ask, "What do you think *that* was?"

Zane's gaze remained on the entrance. "Don't know, don't care."

"I bet it was a plant," I said. "Or maybe one of those tall tables with a vase of flowers on top."

Zane's gaze shifted in my direction, but he made no reply. I didn't even know why I was babbling to him of all people, and yet, I couldn't seem to make myself stop.

For some stupid reason, I just had to explain, "See, the thud would be from the table, and the crash would be from the vase." I hesitated. "Unless the vase was plastic."

Zane was still looking at me. "Plastic," he repeated.

I'd seen the vases on the way in. "Well, they didn't look like plastic," I said, "but you never know, right?"

Once again, Zane said nothing. He didn't have to, because his look said it all. *Shut the hell up. I'm thinking.*

I was still holding the two drinks. Desperate for something to do, if only to keep myself from blathering, I lifted the drink in my right hand

and took a good, long pull.

Hello, Mimosa.

And yup, it was definitely alcoholic. Champagne and orange juice? So *that's* what a mimosa was. And why on Earth was I drinking on my first day on the job? Before noon, no less.

It wasn't good for business *or* my stomach. And yet, I couldn't resist taking another pull, even as I prayed that I'd be able to keep it down.

Zane said, "If you get drunk, I'm not holding your hair."

As if I'd let him.

I took a final, defiant slurp before setting the drink on the table. "You won't need to," I informed him.

He gave me a dubious look. "And why's that?"

"Because…" I smiled. "I've got a scrunchie in my purse." Oh, sure, the purse was upstairs, but that was beside the point.

His gaze shifted to my hair, which I'd worn loose today, letting it fall in waves over my shoulders. He didn't look *entirely* disgusted, but that was probably just the mimosa talking – to *me*, not him.

He was still looking at my hair. "What the hell is a scrunchie?"

"It's like a glorified rubber band."

Now, he looked disgusted. "A rubber band."

"Well yeah," I said, "but it's covered in cloth." I paused. "Or maybe it's *made* of cloth. Anyway, it's all thick and fluffy, so it doesn't pull your hair out in gobs." I cleared my throat. "Well, not *your* hair. I mean, *my* hair…"

Yup, I was definitely blathering now. It was long past time to stop. Lamely, I finished by mumbling, "…because your hair's too short for a scrunchie." And with that, I clamped my lips shut and tried to pretend that the mimosa wasn't wreaking havoc on my nervous stomach.

He said, "You want breakfast?"

I gave a small shudder. "Not really."

"Good," he said, "because we've got another meeting in five."

My stomach sank to the floor. I wasn't sure I could take another meeting, especially if it was anything like the first one.

Unfortunately, it was.

Oh sure, it wasn't *quite* as bad, but it wasn't a walk in the park either. The only difference was *this* meeting, along with several more afterward, took place in Zane's office, where he told a whole new set of people to fuck off.

Why he wanted *me* there, I had no idea – unless it was to torture me in front of strangers, which, knowing Zane, wasn't exactly out of the question.

By noon, I was utterly exhausted and more confused than ever. I still had no idea what I was supposed to be doing or where I'd be doing it. After all, I hadn't been shown to anything resembling a desk.

No doubt, a dark and dreary cubicle awaited me somewhere in the building, assuming that I actually managed to keep this job for more than a single day. I was, after all, just a little bit tipsy.

After the umpteenth person stormed out of Zane's office, I just had to ask, "Am I supposed to be doing something?"

"Yeah," Zane said, "planning for the fallout."

Oh, there'd definitely be a fallout. Already, Zane had been threatened with a whole bunch of lawsuits and a shocking degree of physical violence. I bit my lip. "About that last guy…" I hesitated. "You don't *really* think he'll send people to your house? Do you?"

Zane looked oddly unconcerned. "He can try."

If I cared about Zane at all – which I totally didn't – I'd have been just a little bit concerned. That last guy had looked ready to pop. And just before storming out, he'd told Zane flat-out that he'd better watch his back – here *and* where he lived.

Before I could stop myself, I asked, "Is that why you carry a gun?"

Zane's mouth tightened. "What?"

"Well, I'm just saying, when I stopped by your house a few weeks ago, I couldn't help but notice that you had a weapon in your swimsuit." I froze. *Damn it.* For some reason, that statement sounded wrong, and yes, slightly X-rated. Quickly, I added, "I mean, in the *back* of your swimsuit."

Oh, crap. Was that worse or better?

My face was burning, even as I tried to pretend that I was just making normal conversation.

"You met the guard," Zane said. "What do *you* think?"

Me? I thought the guard wouldn't look nearly as good in a swimsuit.

Where had *that* idea come from? I gave a small shake of my head. "Uh, sorry? What do I think of what?"

"About the guy manning the gate. You think someone like him is gonna keep an eye out?"

"Well, not anymore," I said, "since you fired him and all."

Zane's expression darkened. "Yeah. And he had it coming, as you damn well know."

This was true, even if I hated to admit it. Unsure what to say, I did the smart thing for once and kept my mouth firmly shut.

Zane looked toward the window and said, almost as if speaking to himself, "I've got enemies."

A nervous scoff escaped my lips. "Yeah, I bet."

Slowly, he turned his gaze back to me. "Meaning?"

"Well, I'm just saying, I think you'd catch more flies with honey."

He looked at me for a long moment before saying, "I'm not catching flies. I'm catching monsters."

I studied his face. The way it looked, he was actually serious. I just had to ask, "What kind of monsters?"

"Trust me. You don't wanna know."

He was wrong on both counts. I *didn't* trust him. And I *did* want to know. Of course, *some* of it wasn't a huge mystery. Already, I'd seen how he treated people.

Was it any wonder he had enemies?

I considered every person he'd offended, abused, or threatened during our short acquaintance. First, there'd been Bob, the guy he'd kicked out of his family home. And then, there were all of the people we'd seen today. Every single one of them had been friendly coming in, and raging as they left.

I could totally relate.

And yet, it was almost sad. The way all those people talked, they thought Zane's grandfather had been a hell of a guy. So how was it, I wondered, that his grandson had turned out to be such a jerk?

I tried to look on the bright side. Maybe today was some sort of trial by fire. Maybe, assuming that I kept this job at all, things would be a lot more peaceful going forward.

But surprise, surprise… They weren't.

CHAPTER 28

By some miracle, I survived the first couple of months with my sanity mostly intact. Zane hadn't been kidding about damage-control. During those first few weeks in particular, it felt like I was jumping from one crisis to another as Zane ripped up contracts, renegotiated previous deals, and took a wrecking-ball to countless longstanding relationships.

Afterward, there was almost always a fallout, with Zane being the primary target of whatever media storm ensued.

This was where I came in.

I smoothed ruffled feathers and spun things the best I could – which, honestly wasn't all that great.

It's not that I was plagued by incompetence, or even my own inexperience. Mostly, it was that Zane didn't seem to care one bit what anyone thought of him.

It was like the guy had a reputation death-wish or something.

As for me? I felt like a firefighter, armed with only a squirt-gun, as my billionaire boss lit too many fires for me to put out. Already, my name had appeared in countless media outlets throughout the country, not to mention several overseas.

And why was *my* name appearing?

The reason was simple. Zane absolutely refused to be interviewed, even by friendly outlets with a history of favorable news coverage. So that left only me, his spokesperson, to deflect whatever controversy blew up on any given day.

Probably, this strategy was for the best, considering that Zane had that annoying habit of telling people to fuck off.

Still, it was a strange arrangement. Bennington Hotels had its own public relations staff, and it was absolutely huge, with a team of writers, spokespeople, media buyers, graphic designers, and who-knows-what - else.

But, as Zane had warned me during my so-called job interview, I worked for him and *only* him.

I didn't get it. From what I gathered, he owned most of the corporation all by himself, so why wouldn't he just use the regular staff? Oh sure, technically, they were focused on the larger hotel operation, but surely, they would've done a much more comprehensive job than just one person, meaning me – a recent college graduate with little experience, not to mention issues of my own.

My primary issue? I couldn't stop thinking about him – my boss, my tormenter, and yes, my least-favorite sparring partner, meaning the verbal kind. As far as anything physical, I was determined to keep my distance.

That part was easy, considering that Zane appeared to be screwing his way through the phonebook, assuming that the phonebook was filled with the names of supermodels, actresses, and other stunners who made me feel like some sort of generic lump in comparison.

One Tuesday around noon, I was mulling all of this over while nibbling on crackers at my desk, which, as it turned out, was located in a spectacular office right next to Zane's.

Even now, I could hardly believe the office was mine.

I had a huge window, my own coffee maker, and a front-row seat to all of the comings and goings of the billionaire next-door.

As much as I loved the office – which I totally did – I knew exactly why I'd been assigned this one, and not the dark and dingy cube I'd been expecting. It was because here, Zane could summon me with a series of knocks – no, *not* on my office door, but on the wall that divided our two offices.

Just like Zane, it was unconventional – and rude as hell.

I was still dwelling on this when a knock, this time on my partially closed office door, made me look up. Carla, the receptionist, poked her head through the opening and asked, "Can I come in?"

"Sure," I said, waving her inside. Even though I'd been working here for weeks, I'd found it surprisingly difficult to make any friends, even with Carla, who was friendlier than most.

It's not that anyone was rude, exactly. It was just that for some unknown reason, everyone seemed to be walking on eggshells whenever I tried to talk to them. Granted, this wasn't often, considering how busy Zane had been keeping me. And yet, it was a little strange.

I'd never had problems making friends *before*.

Carla stepped into my office and shut the door behind her. With a worried frown, she hurried to my desk and said in a hushed voice, "There's a visitor."

Her worried expression told me all I needed to know. "Let me guess," I said. "The vlogger's back?"

Just yesterday, Carla had been the one to inform me that a celebrity vlogger was camped out in the executive lobby and was refusing to leave without interviewing you-know-who.

As usual, Zane had been entirely uncooperative, even though the vlogger was a rabid fan-girl who was promising tons of favorable coverage in return for just five minutes of his time.

In the end, even after hours of waiting, she received exactly zero minutes, and she hadn't been happy. If she was back for more, that would definitely explain Carla's nervous demeanor.

But already, Carla was shaking her head. "No. It's not her." She bit her lip. "It's someone else." Looking more worried than ever, she whispered, "It's a guy. For you."

I felt my eyebrows furrow. "For me?"

She nodded. "In the executive lobby."

She looked almost afraid.

Hoping to calm her nerves, I tried to make a joke of it. "It's not an ax-murderer, is it?"

"I, uh, don't think so."

Well, that was reassuring.

I gave her a perplexed look. "But you don't know who it is?"

She shook her head. "He wouldn't say. He said it's a surprise."

Now, I was almost afraid, too. "A work surprise?"

Again, Carla shook her head. "The other kind."

"What kind is that?" I asked.

She leaned close and whispered so low, it was a wonder that I heard her at all. "The personal kind."

Okay, now I was *really* confused. I'd been far too busy to date, and other than a few visits with Charlotte and a mother's day weekend at my parents, I'd been doing nearly nothing outside of work.

Obviously, there was something I was missing. I looked to Carla and asked, "And why are you whispering?"

Her gaze shifted toward Zane's office, just beyond our shared wall. She mouthed, "You know."

I shook my head. "I'm sorry, but I don't..." And then it hit me. "Ohhhhh…You mean because I'm at work?" I waved away her concern. It was true that Zane was a hard-ass, but he was surprisingly decent when it came to visitors showing up during lunchtime.

Just last Friday, I'd had Charlotte up for lunch in my office. And Zane – in a rare moment of civility – even had the decency to say hello and refrain from cursing for five whole minutes.

But now, in front of me, Carla was looking more uncomfortable with every passing moment.

Looking to ease her concerns, I gave her a reassuring smile. "It's okay. It's lunchtime, right?"

Again, her gaze shifted to the wall. She chewed on her lower lip for ten whole seconds before whispering, "Well, then you'd better hurry while he's on that telecon."

I didn't know which telecom she meant, but it was easy to guess who she was talking about. "You mean Zane?"

She froze. "Uh, right. Mister Bennington."

Around here, everyone called him Mister Bennington – well, everyone except for me. But there was a good reason for that.

It stemmed from an argument during my second day on the job. After yet another tense meeting, where I'd tried – and failed – to help keep things civilized, I'd flat-out demanded to know if there was something else I was supposed to be doing.

Zane's response had caught me totally off guard. "Yeah. You can pretend I'm not an asshole. And while you're at it, call me Zane."

The first part of his request was hard, because in truth, Zane *was* an asshole. As for the second part, *that* was easy, because I'd always thought of him as Zane – not Mister Anything – probably because I'd first met him outside the office.

In front of me, Carla was still looking tense and uneasy.

"Don't worry," I assured her as I got to my feet, "it's not a big deal, honest."

Unfortunately, that turned out to be a big, fat lie.

CHAPTER 29

My visitor was big, bearded, and burly. He was gripping a vase of flowers with his right hand and the handle of a brown briefcase with his left.

It was Professor Lumberjack, except today, he'd ditched the flannel in favor of tan slacks and a brown sports coat with dark elbow patches. For once, he looked more like a professor than a guy who cut down trees for a living.

When he spotted me emerging from the door behind the reception desk, his face broke into a wide smile. "There you are."

I stared at the guy. *Yes. Here I was.*

But where was Paisley?

Not here, apparently.

I hadn't seen her in days, probably because the rent was due the day after tomorrow. For once, my checking account contained more than enough to cover it, but that didn't mean I was willing to pay Paisley's share on top of my own.

Aside from catching up on my own bills, there were too many other people who could use a little something extra. There were my parents, who hadn't gone on a vacation in forever. And then, there was Charlotte, who was working her way through nursing school. As soon as I got caught up on my finances, I vowed, I'd treat all of them to something special.

But when it came to Paisley, I couldn't afford to be stupid. Sure, I had a great income *now*, but how long would it last? For all I knew, Zane would be telling *me* to fuck off tomorrow. Or next week. Or whenever the mood struck him.

After all, he did have that history.

In the executive lobby, Professor Lumberjack – I *still* didn't know his name – thrust the flowers out in my direction. "For you."

I blinked. *Huh?*

We were still several paces away from each other, with the tall reception desk acting as a barrier between us. I glanced at Carla, who'd returned to her usual spot behind the desk.

She was making an obvious effort to look at anything but me or my flower-toting visitor. I could see why. After all, I was pretty darned uncomfortable myself.

Reluctantly, I looked back to the professor and said, "For me? Why?"

He lifted the flowers a fraction higher. "An office-warming present."

I'd had this job for two months now. My office was plenty warm already. Still, I reluctantly circled the reception desk and summoned up an awkward smile as he handed me the vase.

Trying to be polite, I gave the flowers a perfunctory sniff and murmured the appropriate noises about them being lovely or whatever.

In truth, I hardly knew what I was saying. Against all hope, I told myself that maybe the flowers *had* to be from Paisley, too.

After all, stranger things had happened, right?

The professor leaned closer and said, "So, you got time for lunch?"

I felt my brow wrinkle. "With who?"

I wasn't even playing dumb. This little visit was so out-of-character that I felt certain I was missing something. Like maybe Paisley would be joining us?

In front of me, the professor gave a hearty smile. "With me. So do you like Chinese?"

"With *only* you?"

"Yeah. There's a place down the street. I hear they have great egg-rolls."

Screw the egg-rolls. I felt my gaze narrow. "Where's Paisley?"

He shrugged. "I dunno."

Shit.

Happily, there were no other visitors in the lobby. This made it only slightly less awkward when he added, "I saw you on TV last night. You looked *really* good." He gave me a sly wink. "And smooth, too, like melted butter."

I *so* didn't want to encourage this. "I looked like butter?"

"No, I mean you handled it smooth, like a real pro, when the reporter was asking you about the fight."

I knew which fight he meant. Thankfully, it hadn't been the physical kind. But it *had* involved a whole lot of yelling – all on the part of Zane's latest victim, a hotshot land developer whose condo-construction plans were squashed when Zane refused to sign on the proverbial dotted line.

I'd handled *that* part of the interview just fine. But when the reporter started asking about Zane's latest dinner companion, some spokesmodel named Serena, I didn't have a lot to say.

So I'd pulled out the only response that didn't get me in trouble.

No comment.

I swear, it was becoming my catch-phrase.

In front of me, the professor said, "And you look *really* good today." His gaze dipped to my legs. "That skirt looks nice on you."

I glanced down. I was wearing a tailored skirt, along with a creamy silk blouse. I *did* love the outfit, but I could hardly take credit, since I hadn't picked it out *or* paid for it personally.

No. The clothes had been selected by the shopper and paid for by Zane – or his company. I still didn't know which, and in truth, I tried not to think about it.

Absently, I mumbled, "Thanks."

"I always thought you were gorgeous..." The professor chuckled. "...even if you did dress like a troll."

Now, *that* got my attention. "What?"

He held up a hand, palm out. "Hey, I meant it as a compliment."

Okay, first of all, he'd seen me dressed like a "troll" because he and Paisley had this annoying habit of coming in so late that I was already in my pajamas – which lately, yes, *had* consisted of comfy sweatpants and a T-shirt. But that didn't mean I *always* dressed that way, not even for bed.

In truth, I would've loved to lounge around in sexy lingerie, but lingerie was expensive, and I'd always been too busy or too broke for those kinds of luxuries.

And besides, who was he to talk? He was like Paul Bunyan without the ax – or without the big blue ox, for that matter.

I felt my gaze narrow. "And what about your wife?"

He gave it some thought. "She dresses, okay, I guess."

Oh, for crying out loud. "That's not what I meant." I felt my jaw tighten. "I meant, where is *she* today? Would *she* be joining us for lunch?"

He looked away and mumbled something that I couldn't make out.

I gave an impatient sigh. "What?"

He looked back to me and said, "She, uh left me, actually."

"Oh." I felt sympathy for only a split second before reality kicked in. The guy was a cheating, pompous toad. If he wanted sympathy from *me*, he was barking up the wrong tree.

I said, "What about Paisley?"

He gave loose shrug. "We've got an understanding."

What a crock.

When I made no reply, he said, "So about lunch…?"

I was still holding the flowers. *He* was still holding his briefcase. I looked to Carla. *She* was holding a pen, but doing absolutely nothing with it.

I knew why. She was listening to every word, even if she was still making a point not to look.

It was long past time to end this. I looked back to the professor and said, "No."

His eyebrows furrowed. "No what?"

"No to lunch and whatever else you're thinking."

"What do you mean?" He had the nerve to look offended. "I'm just here as a friend."

Call me skeptical. After all, no one needed "an understanding" to have lunch with a friend.

I looked to the flowers. He'd claimed they were an office-warming present. But they didn't *look* like an office-warming present.

They were a lush, romantic shade of red, including the vase. It's not that I didn't like the color. I loved it, in fact. But I wasn't stupid. This wasn't the kind of arrangement you bought for a friend – *or* the roommate of the girl you'd been banging on the side.

No. Those were fuck-me flowers.

For some reason, I thought of that stupid red shoe, the one I'd tripped over in Zane's office. I hated that shoe. I hated the flowers. And I especially hated the fact that a byproduct of Paisley's poor judgement had infested my workplace.

I gave the professor a no-nonsense look. "I think you should go."

His mouth tightened. "But what about lunch?"

"I already ate."

He was frowning now. "Then why didn't you say so?"

"I did. Just now."

He looked to the flowers. "But what about those?"

They felt like poison in my hands, and I wanted to fling the whole arrangement right in his face. But I didn't, because the last thing I needed now was a scene at work.

So instead, I asked, "Do you want them back?"

He was still frowning. "What would *I* do with them?"

You could shove them up your ass, that's what.

But I couldn't say it, not here. So instead, I gave him a thin smile and suggested, "You could give them to Paisley. Or to your wife."

He stiffened. "*Ex*-wife."

"Oh, please," I said. "You're separated, and just barely. And what about Paisley?"

"What about her?" he asked.

"Is *she* your ex, too?"

He sighed. "Can I be frank?"

"No," I said. "Definitely not."

Ignoring me, he confessed, "She's a bit of a drama-queen, if you know what I mean."

"Really?" My tone grew sarcastic. "I had *no* idea."

He nodded. "Oh, but she is."

God, how clueless *was* this guy? I made a point of looking at the reception area door. "You really need to go."

He didn't budge. "What if I don't?"

I stared at him. What kind of question was that? We had security. They were top-notch. Technically, I could call them right now and have Professor Lumberjack tossed out on his ass.

I was *so* tempted.

But that was hardly the way to avoid a scene. So instead, I said, "Please. Just go, okay?"

When he *still* didn't move, I marched past him toward the big glass door that led out of the reception area. I yanked the door open wide and said, "Thanks for stopping by. But I *really* need to get back to work."

He still didn't budge. "But I just got here," he whined.

Damn it.

With growing desperation, I said, "I'll talk to you later, okay?"

His gaze narrowed. "When?"

Double damn it. "Tonight. Whenever." Just leave already.

But he didn't. Instead, he muttered, "Oh, shit."

I was momentarily confused until I heard something that made *me* curse, too. It was Paisley's voice shrieking out from somewhere behind me. "I knew it!"

CHAPTER 30

I whirled around and came face-to-face with Paisley, who was wearing an annoyingly familiar black dress – mine, in fact. Her eyes were wild, and she was trembling with apparent rage.

She practically spat in my face. "You bitch!"

I drew back. "What?"

"I *knew* you liked him!"

Obviously, she meant the professor. But she was crazy. I didn't like him. I barely knew him, and I wanted to keep it that way.

In the calmest voice I could muster, I said, "Sorry, but you've got it all wrong."

Her gaze zoomed in on the flowers, and she gave a snort of disbelief. "Do I?"

I looked down at the flower arrangement still clutched in my hand. My fingers were tight around the neck of the vase, and for the briefest instant, I wanted to hurl the whole thing, vase and all, straight at the professor. Or cripes, even onto the floor.

Instead, I thrust the flowers out in Paisley's direction and said, "If you want them, you can have them."

She eyed the flowers with obvious disgust. "I don't want them. They're used."

Behind me, the professor mumbled, "They are not. I got them an hour ago."

God, what a dumb-ass. I turned toward him and said, "You know what? Why don't you and Paisley go out to lunch and settle this like adults?"

Behind me, Paisley demanded, "What are you saying? That I'm immature?"

Oh, for crying out loud. Once again, I turned to face her. "I'm not saying anything. I just think the two of you need to settle this somewhere else."

"Oh suuuure," Paisley sneered, "you'd like that, wouldn't you?"

"Yes, actually." I glanced toward the professor. "And besides, your boyfriend was just leaving."

Paisley gave a little sniff. "That's right. *My* boyfriend, not yours."

I muttered, "Thank God."

Her gaze narrowed. "What's that supposed to mean?"

"Nothing." Or least, nothing I wanted to discuss here.

At work.

In front of an audience.

I was still holding the door, and I couldn't help but wonder what would happen if I just let it go. Would it smack Paisley in the face? And if so, would it knock any sense into her?

Her beloved professor was a cheater and a creep. Whatever Paisley was feeling, he wasn't worth it – not that *she* was any prize herself.

I snuck a quick glance at Carla. She'd given up on pretending not to notice and was now watching the theatrics with obvious concern. I could totally relate. I was getting pretty concerned myself.

So far, I'd been incredibly lucky that Carla was the only person witnessing this spectacle. But my luck couldn't last forever.

I gave the professor a pleading look. "You said you wanted Chinese, right? Well, Paisley loves Chinese."

"I do not!" Paisley said.

Liar. Just last week, I'd splurged on Chinese takeout on my way home from work. After walking in through the front door, I'd set the takeout on the kitchen table, and dashed into my bedroom to change. Five minutes later, I'd returned to find the food mostly gone – into Paisley's mouth.

I gave Paisley an irritated look. "Oh, stop it. You own your own chopsticks."

"So?" she said. "That doesn't prove anything." Her voice became shrill. "You think you're an expert on me? Well, you're not. So stop pretending that you are!"

She leaned around me to glare at the professor. "I *knew* there was someone else."

Under my breath, I said, "Yeah, his wife."

In unison, Paisley and the professor said, "*Ex*-wife."

Well, at least they agreed on *something*. Probably, these two deserved each other. Regardless, I wanted no part of it.

Once again, I glanced at the door that I was still holding. Probably, I should let it smack *me* in the face, if only to put me out of my misery.

I looked back to Paisley and said, "Honestly, I don't even like him."

"You do, too," she insisted. "I see the way you look at him."

"Oh, please," I said. "I don't even know his name."

Behind me, the professor said, "You do, too."

I turned to tell him, "I do not."

"Oh come on," he said, looking decidedly disgruntled. "It's Fergus."

Huh. Weird. I definitely would've remembered *that*.

The professor pointed to the flowers. "It's on the card."

I looked down. Attached to the arrangement was a little red envelope with no name on the front. In my haste to get rid of the guy, I hadn't even opened it.

In a flash, Paisley reached out and snatched the envelope away. She ripped it open and pulled out a small pink card. She let the envelope flutter to the floor as she pulled the card closer to read it.

When she finished, she gave a little gasp. She looked up and yelled, "You pig!"

At me.

Not at him.

What the hell?

My heart was racing, and my stomach was in knots. This couldn't be happening. Not here. Not now. Fearing the worst, I looked to Carla.

Sure enough, she was already reaching for the phone. When she saw me looking, she said, "I'm calling security."

"No!" I blurted out.

She froze in mid-motion. "No?"

"Everything's fine," I told her. "I'll handle it."

Behind me, Paisley yelled, "Oh yeah? Just like you handle his cock?"

I almost shuddered. The guy was *so* not my type. I turned to tell her, "I haven't even touched him. And I don't want to. So just give it up."

"Give *him* up, you mean?" Her voice broke. "Well, I'm not gonna. So *you* give him up."

"Fine," I said. "Whatever. But you *really* need to go."

"Why?" She gave a choked sob. "So you can screw him on your desk?"

By now, I almost felt like sobbing too, but for entirely different reasons. Already, I could see my job slipping away, consumed by drama that wasn't even my fault.

I turned to glare at the professor. "You," I said. "Get out. *Now.*"

"Why me?" he demanded. "*I'm* not causing a scene."

Behind me, Paisley was crying openly now. "You've got everything," she sobbed, "and I've got nothing." She finished by wailing, "Not even Fergus!"

I turned and stifled a curse. Rounding the corner just behind her was someone new. It was a guy in his early thirties, with blond hair and a slight build. He was wearing a suit and tie, and had his cell phone pressed to his ear.

He stopped in mid-stride and stared at the scene in front of him – Paisley sobbing, me holding the door, and behind us, the professor doing who-knows-what.

The guy's brow wrinkled, and he said into his phone. "I'll call you back later, okay?" He put the phone in his pocket and turned his full attention to us. He asked, "Is there a problem?"

There were so many problems, I hardly knew where to begin. Still, I stammered out, "No, this is just—"

Paisley sobbed, "She stole my boyfriend!"

Damn it. "I did not," I said through gritted teeth, "as I've already explained."

But Paisley wasn't done yet. She wailed, "And she's a liar, too!"

The stranger's gaze zoomed in on me, and he frowned like he actually believed her.

I told him, "I'm not a liar."

And why was I even explaining myself to this guy? After all, he was a total stranger – or so I thought, until he said, "I know you from somewhere."

Did he? I didn't think so. Maybe he'd seen me on TV?

Paisley turned to the guy and said, "Oh, great. Have *you* fucked her, too?"

I wanted to strangle her. "Listen," I snapped, "I don't need this. Not here. So why you don't take your drama somewhere else?"

The guy's frown deepened. He looked to me and said, "Can't you see she's upset?"

Oh yeah. I could see. And I could hear. Probably, so could everyone within a five-mile radius. I snuck another quick glance at Carla. She was still holding the phone's receiver, as if unsure what to do.

That made two of us.

And of course, it wasn't lost on me that the guy who'd caused all of the trouble, Fergus the Lumberjacking Professor, was letting *me* bear the brunt of this attack.

I turned to him and said, "Didn't you hear me? I told you to get out!"

Once again, he didn't budge. "But we're not done," he insisted.

I wanted to scream in frustration. "With what?"

"Plans," he said. "You said we'd meet up later tonight."

At this, Paisley gave another sob. "I knew it." And then, obviously speaking to the stranger, she said, "And she's my roommate, too."

I didn't even turn to look, but in the background, I could hear the new guy making soothing sounds to my sobbing roommate. "Oh, come on," he was saying, "You're worth ten of her."

Well, this was nice.

Paisley gave another choked sob. "You really think so?"

"Sure," he soothed. "And you don't need this. You know that, right?"

After a pause and a stifle, Paisley mumbled, "I guess so."

As for me, I was still glaring at the professor. "Get out," I told him, "or I'll have you thrown out."

He lifted his bearded chin. "No."

I made a sound of frustration, "What do you mean, 'no'?"

In the background, the new guy was still talking to Paisley. "Now come on," he soothed, "give me a smile." There was another sniffle, followed by another pause. A moment later, the guy said, "See? It's not so bad."

Turns out, he was wrong. It was bad. Very bad. Because the door behind Carla had just swung open, and there he was – my boss.

And he didn't look happy.

CHAPTER 31

An ominous silence descended hard and fast, broken only by the sound of a single sniffle coming from Paisley.

We were all looking at Zane, who stood silently in the doorway. His jaw was tight and his eyes were hard as he assessed the scene in front of him.

I sucked in a breath. There was something about him, something quiet and ruthless, that made me want to take a couple of steps backward. But I didn't, unlike Professor Fergus, who was backing slowly away, whether he realized it or not.

I wanted to say something, but nothing came to mind. Already, I was mentally packing my bags – or boxes, as the case might be. Fortunately, almost nothing in my office was mine, not even the coffee maker. The only things I'd need to grab were my purse and favorite coffee mug, and maybe the half-eaten crackers that were supposed to be my lunch.

How depressing.

It was Carla, still holding the phone's receiver, who finally broke the silence. "Mister Bennington…"

Whatever she'd been planning to say next died on her lips as Zane snapped his gaze in her direction. She blanched and returned the phone to its cradle without another word. She looked absolutely terrified, probably for the same reason I was.

Hello, unemployment line.

A wave of guilt washed over me. Probably, *I* was doomed no matter what, but Carla didn't have to be. This wasn't her fault. She was just an innocent bystander. And worse, she'd actually been trying to do her job, until she'd been stopped.

By me.

I spoke up. "Carla had nothing to do with this."

Zane turned his gaze on me, and my mouth suddenly went dry. Desperate for a distraction, I snuck a quick glance at Fergus, who eyed my boss with something that looked an awful lot like fear.

Reluctantly, I looked back to Zane. He still hadn't responded to my statement, and I felt the sudden need to elaborate. "She wanted to call security, but I, uh, wouldn't let her, actually." I cleared my throat. "So this is my fault, not hers."

Behind me, Paisley said, "That's for sure."

I wanted to turn around and slap her. Who knows, maybe I *would* be slapping her before the day was done.

One thing about Paisley, she had no idea when to quit.

And, as if that weren't bad enough, the new guy jumped on the bandwagon by calling out to Zane, "Your *employee* slept with *her* boyfriend." He said "employee" like the word *really* meant disease-ridden ho-bag.

Zane's gaze shifted to Fergus. "You the boyfriend?"

Fergus gave a tight nod.

I spoke up. "And just for the record, I *didn't* sleep with him, not that it's anyone's business."

"Liar," Paisley said.

The urge to get slappy grew just a little bit stronger. To no one in particular, I announced, "I don't even like him."

"Oh yeah?" Paisley said. "Then why'd you accept the flowers?"

Without bothering to look at her, I said, "What was I supposed to do? Throw them in his face?"

Paisley muttered, "Well, you didn't have to take them."

Through this entire exchange, Zane's gaze remained firmly on the professor, who'd taken a few more steps backward. He glanced toward the door and mumbled, "Well, uh, I guess I should get going."

I gave him an annoyed look. "So *now*, you're willing to leave? I've only been asking you for fifteen minutes."

The professor stiffened. "It wasn't *that* long."

Behind me, the new guy called out, "So *this* is how you run things?" Under his breath, he added, "I don't know why I'm surprised."

Obviously, this was directed at Zane, who paid the guy no attention. He was still focused on Fergus, who seemed to wilt under the weight of Zane's stare. Silently, the professor began sidestepping his way toward freedom.

He looked utterly ridiculous, but then again, I probably did, too. I was still holding those stupid flowers *and* the door. Without thinking, I released the handle, letting the door swing inward.

Unfortunately for the professor, this is when he decided to make a break for it. The door smacked him in the face, and he stumbled backward, saying "Hey! What'd you do *that* for?"

"I, uh..." Had I done that on purpose? Honestly, I couldn't be sure either way. But I *did* know that I wasn't feeling terribly guilty about it.

Behind me, Paisley said, "Oh, my God. Are you okay?"

I wanted to roll my eyes, but I didn't, even as the professor bolted forward and yanked the door open as wide as possible before dashing through the opening like a robber of the smash-and-grab variety.

I turned just in time to see him scurry down the hall, with Paisley darting after him, calling out, "Do you need a ride?"

Together, they disappeared around the corner, leaving me to deal with the fallout on my own. No doubt, this was for the best, and yet, I couldn't help but think they were weasels for doing so.

And once again, I was holding the stupid door – but only because it had been either that, or let it smack *me* in the face. As for the new guy, he was staring, slack-jawed, after the two escapees.

"See?" I told him. "They totally deserve each other."

With that, I reluctantly turned back to Zane. He was eyeing me with an expression that I couldn't make out. But he definitely wasn't thrilled.

Yeah, welcome to the club.

But I didn't say it. In fact, I didn't say anything. I wanted to, but no words came to mind.

Zane said, "My office. *Now.*"

For once, I couldn't exactly blame him for being so rude. I let go of the door and trudged forward, letting the guy behind me grab the door-handle – or not. At this point, I hardly cared who got smacked by the stupid thing.

The whole situation was incredibly depressing. I'd kept this job for just a couple of months. And as much as I hated to admit it, I'd actually come to like it a lot more than I'd been expecting.

Oh sure, Zane was impossible, but even that made the days a lot more interesting. And then, there was the pay. I'd definitely be missing that, especially when it came time to buy groceries and what-not.

Zane turned away and began stalking back toward his office, leaving me to follow after him. From somewhere behind me, I heard the new guy call out, "Hey, we had a meeting!"

"Later," Zane told him without even bothering to look.

Whether the guy heard him or not, I had no idea. But I *did* hear Carla offer the guy coffee or water and assure him that Mister Bennington would be with him in a moment.

But first apparently, "Mister Bennington" would be dealing with me.

CHAPTER 32

When his office door shut behind us, I felt myself swallow. I waited, expecting for him to stride to his chair and take a seat, leaving me to stand before him, like some sort of criminal awaiting judgment.

But he didn't. Instead, he turned to me and said, "Tell me."

Confused, I stared up at him. "Tell you what? That I'm sorry? Because I am. Really."

And I meant it, too. After all, this was supposed to be a place of business, not a place of roommate-boyfriend drama.

He frowned. "What the hell?"

I gave a confused shake of my head. "Is that another way of saying, 'Apology not accepted'?"

"Fuck the apology."

"Excuse me?"

"What I *want* is the guy's name."

Now *that* surprised me. "What? Why?"

"Fergus," he said. "That's the first. What's the last?"

At that moment, I wasn't sure that telling him would be such a great idea, even if I knew, which happily, I didn't. "Actually," I said, "I don't know."

He gave me a look and waited.

"Honestly," I said, "it's not like we're close."

His gaze dipped to my hands, and his mouth tightened. I looked down and wanted to cringe. *Oh, crap.* I was still holding the flowers. I was so frazzled, I'd practically forgotten.

Stupidly, I tried to explain. "They were, uh, some sort of office warming present."

"Is that so?"

I bit my lip. "Yes?"

He gave me a dubious look. "Uh-huh."

"Well, that's what he said, anyway."

From the look on Zane's face, he wasn't thrilled with *this* answer either. He said, "We have security for a reason."

"I know." I sighed. "And Carla wanted to call them, but…" I hesitated. "I didn't want to cause a scene."

Zane gave me a good, long look before saying, "A scene."

My nerves were frayed, and my stomach was in knots. I heard myself say, "You know, it's really confusing when you do that."

"Do what?"

"Ask a question without a question mark."

He looked toward the window and muttered, "Fuck the question mark."

When he kept looking out the window, I turned my head to see what I was missing. But I saw nothing new, just the usual stunning view of the city below and the clouds above.

I looked back to Zane and studied his face in profile. His eyes were hard, and posture was tight. He was still looking away when he said, "Next time, call *me*."

Okay, now I was really confused. "Why would I call *you*?"

He looked back to me and said, "Because I don't give a flying fuck about causing a scene."

In spite of everything, I almost laughed, because it was so terribly true, as I'd seen way too often.

Zane said, "You think I'm kidding?"

"No," I said. "I think it's pretty obvious."

"Meaning?"

"Meaning you create more scenes than anyone I know."

"Do I?"

"Definitely. Almost everywhere you go, there's a scene."

"Maybe," he admitted. "But not by me."

I gave it some thought. In a weird, twisted way, I knew what he meant. He might curse. He might break deals and tear up contracts. He might even insult whoever he was talking to. But it was never Zane who lost his cool.

It was always the other guy.

Even today.

And yet, for a moment there, I hadn't been so sure.

It made me wonder what else was going on. Normally, I spent a lot of time with him, but this morning, he'd been holed up in his office, doing who-knows-what.

I just had to ask, "Is something wrong?"

"Yeah," he said. "Some bearded fucker was harassing my—" Abruptly, his words cut off, as if he wasn't quite sure what to call me.

Beyond curious, I waited, wondering what he'd say.

Finally, he said, "Employee."

I wasn't sure why, but the word felt oddly unsatisfying.

As a nervous reflex, I tried to make a joke of it. "What? You forgot my job title?"

His gaze met mine, and he was quiet for a long moment before saying, "Something like that."

Slowly, it was dawning on me that I hadn't been fired, and the way it looked, I wasn't going to be. One thing about Zane, he didn't beat around the bush.

No. If he planned on firing me, he'd have told me right away, and maybe added a nice "fuck off" to seal the deal.

That was, after all, his style.

And yet, as long as I'd known him, I'd never seen him curse out an employee, not even me.

That reminded me of something. "Carla's not in trouble, is she? Because I wasn't kidding. She had nothing to do with it."

"You think I don't know that?"

"No." I hesitated. "Or yes. I don't know. I'm just saying, I don't want to cause her any problems."

His jaw tightened. "If you wanna worry, worry about yourself."

At something in his look, I felt myself tense. Maybe I'd been reading his reaction all wrong. Maybe I *was* about to get fired. Bracing myself for the worst, I asked, "Why's that?"

"Because, when things settle down, I'm gonna ask you for a favor."

If I weren't so confused, I might've laughed. I couldn't imagine Zane "asking" me for anything. Normally, he just barked out commands, like some kind of dictator.

I felt my gaze narrow. "What kind of favor?"

"I'm not asking you *now*."

What did *that* mean? He wasn't going to tell me? What was this? Some new form of torture? "But—"

"You owe me," he said.

"For what?" I asked. "Not firing me?"

"No," he said, "For not beating that fucker's ass."

I drew back. *Woah*. I hadn't seen *that* coming. I felt my brow wrinkle in new confusion. At the moment, I hardly knew which Zane I was dealing with – the billionaire businessman or the so-called reprobate, as Bob had called him on that very first night.

I just had to ask, "But wait, why would it be *me* owing you a favor?"

He gave a tight shrug. "Why not?"

"Well, if anything, wouldn't it be Fergus?" When Zane said nothing, I added, "You know. The, uh, 'fucker'?"

Zane moved a fraction closer, and his gaze locked on mine. In a quiet voice, he said, "No."

"No?" My lips felt suddenly dry, and I felt my tongue dart out, as if to wet them. I was feeling things, stupid things.

At the moment, Zane Bennington didn't feel like my boss – or even like the jerk who'd been making my life miserable for months. But what he *did* feel like, I wasn't quite sure.

Around us, the office felt big and quiet, like it was only the two of us in the whole building, or cripes, even the whole world.

I gazed up at him, wondering what on Earth was going on – and not just with me. With him, too. Because he wasn't acting like his normal prickish self.

After a long, drawn-out moment, it was Zane who broke the silence. "Remember, you owe me."

At that moment, stupid or not, I swear I would've given him

anything he asked for – starting with my panties and ending with who-knows-what.

I gave a nervous laugh. "Oh, please. Maybe I *wanted* you to beat his ass."

"Yeah?" he said, looking suddenly intrigued. "Good to know."

Weird. He looked like he actually meant it.

I said, "You *do* know I was kidding, right?"

It wasn't even a lie. Although a part of me would've loved to see the good professor pummeled for all the trouble he'd caused, I wasn't the violent type, and I wasn't the kind of person to encourage violence either.

Zane said, "We'll see."

"We'll see what?" I asked.

"What the fucker does next." And then, almost as an afterthought, he added, "And by the way, we're going to New York."

I felt my eyes widen in surprise. "We are? For what?"

"Interviews." he said, not looking too happy about it.

I almost didn't know what to say. "Seriously?"

For weeks, I'd been fielding countless requests for in-studio interviews, mostly from nationally syndicated shows, based out of New York. Apparently, Zane was in hot demand – from morning shows, business channels, and even a slew of entertainment programs.

After all, he was the hot, new thing – an unknown entity, a human wrecking ball, and yes, a billionaire bachelor with a thing for supermodels.

Who *wouldn't* want to interview him?

He was fascinating. And maddening. And surprisingly successful, in spite of his annoying tendency to piss people off.

By now, I knew a lot more about the Bennington corporate structure. Technically, it was a publically traded corporation, but Zane was the primary shareholder, which meant that he controlled practically everything.

When he'd taken control of the company after the death of his grandfather, stock prices had plummeted, leaving many to wonder how low the value would go.

But lately, things had been on a definite upswing as the company exceeded projected earnings and upped its guidance for the next quarter.

Was *that* the reason for Zane's sudden announcement?

Trying to make sense of it, I said, "So you've changed your mind? Is that what you're saying?"

"More or less."

Based on his earlier refusals, I almost couldn't imagine. "So you *want* to do those interviews?"

"Want?" He shook his head. "No."

I waited for him to elaborate.

He didn't.

I tried again. "But you're going to do them, anyway?"

"Apparently."

"But why?" I asked.

"I've got my reasons."

"Is it because things are going so well? With the company, I mean?"

"No," he said. "It's because I've got other business in New York, and it's too late to cancel."

I still wasn't following. "Cancel what?"

"Other business," he repeated, "just like I said."

Well, that was informative.

Still, I knew better than to push my luck. "Okay," I said. "So when are we going?"

Again, he looked to the window. "Tonight."

My jaw almost hit the floor. "Tonight? Why so sudden?"

He was still looking away. "Because things happen."

Talk about a non-answer. "But I'm not even packed."

"If you need help, I'll send someone."

I didn't need help. I needed information. "And how long will we be gone?"

He turned once again to face me. "As long as it takes. A week, maybe two."

What the hell?

This was just like him.

Two whole weeks?

On just a few hours' notice?

What if I had kids? Or dogs?

Come to think of it, *he* had dogs. What was he planning to do with them? I asked, "What about Lansing and Flint?"

A shadow crossed his features. "They're staying with my dad."

His dad lived in a cabin hours away. "So they're not living with you anymore?"

"No," he said. "Not now."

"Why not?"

"It's not safe."

"You mean at your place? Why not?

"Because I'm not there."

I recalled all those threats. The way it sounded, he was actually taking some of them seriously, at least when it came to his dogs. This posed an unsettling possibility. Zane Bennington might, in fact, be human after all.

Crazy, I know.

The thought had barely crossed my mind when his expression hardened. "About the trip," he said, "if you're thinking of saying no, forget it."

I stiffened, and all those warm feelings vanished in the face of his rudeness. He didn't *need* to warn me. After all, I wasn't stupid. Even *I* realized that I was incredibly lucky to still have a job.

I looked toward the door. "Well, I guess I should get packing, huh?"

"Later."

I gave him a perplexed look. "Sorry, what?"

"You're needed here."

I could hardly believe my ears. "Until when?"

"'Til *I* say so."

And, like the jerk he was, he didn't "say so" until after five o'clock, which left me almost no time to get ready, even if I *did* use the time as best as I could, returning a flurry of phone calls from media outlets who'd been seeking interviews.

Still, it was almost like Zane was making me scramble on purpose – which, knowing him, he probably was.

And why?

Just because he could.

As usual.

CHAPTER 33

Paisley was still glaring out the front window. For the third time, she grumbled, "It must be nice."

I was still dashing around the house, trying to get my things in order. In our driveway, a company limo was waiting. It was the same limo that had shuttled me from the office an hour earlier.

As for my company car, it was in the Bennington parking garage, where I'd be picking it up upon my return.

Whenever that would be.

Paisley said, "Why do *you* get a limo? I mean, it's not like *you're* anyone important."

She was right. I wasn't. But Zane had been adamant, and *not* in a nice way. Of course, I knew why. He didn't trust me to make it to the airport on time, and I was dangerously close to proving him right.

In his usual charming way, he'd told me, "Seven o'clock. Be ready."

Or else.

He hadn't said it, but it was definitely implied.

I glanced at my watch and cringed. Already, it was five minutes to seven, and I still wasn't quite ready to go. I felt stressed and anxious for a whole host of reasons.

For one thing, the limo had been idling in the driveway forever, and no matter how many times the driver had assured me that waiting was part of his job, I felt guilty and awkward just the same.

And then, there was Paisley. I'd arrived home just after six o'clock to find her in the living room, looking not exactly civil, but not nearly as hostile as I'd been anticipating.

Turns out, Professor Lumberjack, or Fergus, or whatever I wanted to call him, had somehow managed to convince Paisley that the flowers had been for her all along. Supposedly, he was only bringing them to *me*, so I could give them to *her* when I arrived back home.

What a load of crap.

And yet, Paisley had gobbled it up like a hound in a van full of meatballs. She was still wearing the black dress – the one she'd borrowed from me without even asking.

From the window, she said, "You *do* know, you could've saved me a lot of heartache if you'd just told me right away."

I was hardly listening as I scanned the living room, looking for the last item on my list. I asked, "Have you seen my phone charger?"

Paisley made a sound of annoyance. "Didn't you hear what I just said?"

Of course, I'd heard, but I didn't have time for this discussion – or for the other discussion that we'd need to have when I returned.

The lease on the house was up in just a couple of months, and I wasn't planning to renew. The way I saw it, I'd rather move to an entirely new place than suffer through another year with a deadbeat drama queen.

I said, "Sorry, but I'm in a hurry."

"Whatever," she muttered and returned her attention to the window. "I guess nobody cares that I spent the whole afternoon crying my eyes out."

I cared, but only because she'd used up all of my tissues, plus the last of the toilet paper. *Again.*

With growing desperation, I lifted the nearest sofa cushion and did a quick scan for the charger. All I saw were a few pennies and remnants of burnt popcorn.

Well, that was nice.

I lifted the other cushion, only to be disappointed again, unless I considered two nickels a marvelous find. I tossed the cushion back in place and frantically looked around, wondering where on Earth my charger could be.

Funny, I could've sworn I'd set it near the sofa. In fact, I was almost sure of it. My gaze drifted to Paisley, and I felt my jaw tighten.

She wouldn't.

Would she?

I tried again. "My charger, you seriously haven't seen it?"

Slowly, she turned around and smiled in a way that made me almost nervous. "I don't know," she said. "Have *you* seen my bottle of merlot?"

This again?

"Oh come on," I said. "That was weeks ago. And I replaced it."

"It wasn't just one bottle. It was two."

"Right," I said through gritted teeth. "And I replaced both of them."

"You couldn't *really* replace them," she said. "They had sentimental value."

"Oh for God's sake," I said. "It was a generic wine, not a love letter."

Paisley's smile twisted into a smirk. Mimicking my tone, she said, "It was a phone charger, not a space ship." She turned back to the window and said, "See how that works?"

Yes. In a roundabout way, I did. And it was one of the reasons it had taken me so long to pack. In a fit of paranoia, I'd gone through the whole house, especially my bedroom, gathering up everything of special importance to me – family photos, old letters, and the few pieces of decent jewelry that I owned.

I'd stuffed all of these things into an extra suitcase with the intention of taking everything with me, rather than leaving it here in the house, where Paisley could do who-knows-what with it.

If the missing phone charger was any indicator, my paranoia had been totally justified. Trying to look on the bright side, I reminded myself that the charger – unlike those other things – was entirely replaceable.

"Fine," I told her. "Keep the charger. I don't care."

"I don't care either," she said, even as a knock sounded at the front door. "And just so you know," she added, "the door's not for me, so *I'm* not getting it."

"Good," I told her, "because I'm leaving anyway."

I grabbed my stuff and hustled to the door. When I flung it open, the limo driver gave me an apologetic smile. "I'm sorry, but Mister Bennington's instructions were very explicit." He pointed to his watch. "And it *is* seven o'clock."

Technically, it was six fifty-eight, but it wasn't worth quibbling over. So instead, I assured him that I was ready and that there was no need to apologize. After all, *I* didn't want to be late either.

Soon, we were off, heading toward the airport as I tried not to imagine what kind of trouble surely awaited me – first in New York, and then back home, whenever I returned. After all, I'd be out of town at least a week, which left Paisley plenty of time to wreak havoc on the home front.

I had no doubt, she'd do just that.

I might've spent the rest of the night dwelling on this, if I weren't soon distracted by something even more disturbing. It was the sight of my boss getting practically slobbered on – and *not* from his dogs.

CHAPTER 34

We were only fifteen minutes into the flight, and already, I was wishing for a parachute.

Or a barf bag.

Across from me, the leggy brunette leaned closer to Zane and practically cooed, "I just *love* your plane."

He gave her a dismissive glance. "It's not mine. It's the company's."

"Oh, stop," she laughed, reaching for his arm. "You *are* the company."

This much was true, but I was in no mood to give her credit. Already, she'd taken seventeen selfies – yes, I *was* counting – and had made so many sexual innuendos, that I was starting to wonder if her dialogue was pulled straight out of a porno.

Right on cue, she pressed her lips to Zane's ear and said in a husky whisper, "Do you think we're a mile high?"

I tensed. The reference was obvious – and pretty darn disturbing, considering that I was sitting directly across from them, facing them no less, in the luxurious seating area.

This was only my fourth flight in my entire life, and it was proving to be the most uncomfortable, in spite of it being my very first on a private jet. Oh sure, the seats were leather, and I had plenty of leg room, but at the moment, I was longing to be crammed in like a sardine with a hundred other poor slobs on their way to some anonymous destination.

At least then, I wouldn't be watching my boss get drooled on – or worse, if things progressed the way she obviously wanted.

As for me, I'd pulled out a paperback and was pretending to read while she continued to seek his attention. The sad thing was, I *wanted* to read. It's just that it was difficult to focus on anything when she looked ready to get down and dirty any minute.

Trying to be subtle, I snuck a quick glance at Zane. He looked bored and restless, even as he scrolled through his cell phone, checking messages – or hell, surfing porn for all I knew.

As for his companion, I didn't even know her name, mostly because Zane hadn't bothered to introduce us, and my own initial attempts at friendliness were either rebuffed or ignored as the brunette turned all of her charm on the billionaire sitting next to her.

The only saving grace was that I wasn't the only other passenger on the flight. Sitting next to me was the same blond guy who'd been sticking up for Paisley in the lobby.

This might've given me someone to talk to, if it weren't for the fact that he was obviously still miffed about the whole Paisley thing. Oh sure, he'd briefly introduced himself, giving his name as Theodore without mentioning a last name at all. But then, immediately afterward, he'd settled into a quiet sulk and said nothing to anyone.

From the look on his face, he hated us all – probably, me in particular, since I was apparently the ho-bag who screwed her roommate's boyfriend and made her cry.

Yup, I was a monster.

Across from me, the brunette gripped Zane's knee and said, "You're so tense. Should I rub your shoulders?" And yet, it wasn't a shoulder she had her eye on.

Zane didn't even look. "No."

Her hand moved higher on his thigh. "Something else then?"

Zane was still scrolling. "No."

Her hand inched a fraction higher. "Are you sure?"

He pulled his gaze from his phone and gave her a long, cold look. After an awkward pause, she pulled back and asked, "What's wrong? You weren't tense last night." She gave a throaty laugh. "Even if you *were* stiff."

Well, that was lovely to know.

Zane told her, "If you wanna fuck someone, try him."

She drew back. "What?"

Zane flicked his head toward the guy sitting next to me. "Looks like he could use it."

The brunette gave a huff. "I don't want *him*."

"And I don't want you," Zane said. "So try someone else, or keep your clothes on."

Her mouth tightened. "You wanted me fine last night."

"Yeah. And I told you it was a one-time deal."

She was openly pouting now. "But we had such a good time."

"And it's over. So move on." He looked back to his phone. "Or sit with the luggage. Your choice."

"But..." She paused, as if unsure what to say next.

The blond guy, who'd been watching this exchange with obvious disgust, looked to Zane and said, "Hey! I don't need your sloppy seconds."

The brunette turned to glare at him. "I'm not sloppy. I'm tight as a virgin. Ask anyone."

I looked around, longing for a flight attendant with a drink cart. Unfortunately, there were none, which only proved that I'd been right all along.

Private jets sucked.

The brunette's gaze snapped in my direction, "What are *you* looking at?"

"I, uh—"

In a bored tone, Zane said, "Leave her alone."

"Why should I leave *her* alone," she demanded. "It was supposed be just the two of us. *She's* the third wheel, not me."

I felt my brow wrinkle in confusion. "What?"

"Oh yeah," she said, giving me a smirk. "You didn't know?"

No. I didn't. In fact, everything about this trip had caught me completely by surprise.

Into my silence she continued, "It was *supposed* to be just me and Zane."

Was that true?

I looked to Zane, wondering what he'd say. But he didn't say anything. Instead, he leisurely got to his feet and headed past me, toward the front of the plane.

I didn't even turn to watch him go, but I was pretty sure that if he returned with a drink, I'd be ripping it from his clutches and guzzling it down before he could say, "Welcome to the flight from hell."

The brunette eyed me with clear disdain. "And then *you* show up." She glanced at the guy sitting next to me, and her mouth twisted into something surprising ugly for someone so beautiful. "With *him*."

I looked to the guy in question. "I'm not with him."

The guy grumbled, "That's for sure."

It was obviously an insult. I asked, "What's that supposed to mean?"

The guy looked to the brunette and announced, "She's sleeping with her roommate's boyfriend."

Oh, for God's sake. Through clenched teeth, I said, "I am not. I don't even like him."

The guy made a sound that I couldn't quite decipher. A scoff? A snort? What?

I told the guy, "If you have something to say, just say it."

As an answer, he reached into the inside pocket of his suit coat and pulled out a familiar-looking pink card. I snatched it from his fingers and gave it a quick glance.

Immediately, I felt color rise to my cheeks. It was the card that had accompanied the flowers. Apparently, he'd scooped it up from the lobby floor as some sort of secondhand keepsake.

I had to wonder, why would he do such a thing?

To humiliate me in front of Miss Tight-as-a-Virgin?

To prove to my boss that I was a terrible person?

Or, because the guy was just that annoying?

I was still staring at the card when it was abruptly snatched from my fingers. I looked up just in time to see the brunette scanning the hand-written message. With a laugh, she read the note out loud. "Wet yet?"

Hearing this, I couldn't help but cringe all over again. It was either the worst flower-watering instructions I'd ever heard, or something a whole lot more suggestive.

The brunette tossed the card aside. "This is nothing. What's the big deal?"

The guy next to me explained, "It's from her roommate's boyfriend." He looked back to me and said, "Or, are you gonna deny that, too?"

By now, I was pretty sure I hated the guy. I said, "What do *you* care?"

Ignoring my question, he looked back to the brunette and said, "So if I were you, I'd keep an eye on her."

Well, that was rich. Already, the brunette was giving me the squinty-eye, as if I were personally responsible for her failure to get down and dirty at fifty-thousand feet, or however high we were. About the altitude, I didn't know, and I didn't care. At this point, all I cared about was the drink cart – or lack thereof.

The thought had barely crossed my mind when Zane returned and settled himself back into his seat without uttering a single word.

I looked to his hands.

No drink.

Damn it.

I was still dealing with *that* disappointment when something in our flight seemed to change, like we were slowing down or maybe changing altitude. Being such a newbie, I couldn't quite figure it out until Zane said, "Buckle up. We're landing in ten."

Ten minutes? That couldn't be right. We were still a long way from New York.

Weren't we?

The brunette looked toward the nearest window. "We are?"

As for Zane, he was once again scrolling through his cell phone. He didn't answer the question.

The blond guy looked to his watch. "All right, I'll play along. Where are we landing?"

Zane didn't even look up. "Kalamazoo."

The brunette said, "Kalama-who?"

"Kalamazoo," Zane repeated. "Michigan."

"What? Why?" She looked toward the cockpit area. "Don't tell me there's a problem with the plane?"

Zane said, "All right."

Again, she turned to look. "So there *is* a problem?"

Zane was still scrolling. "No."

"I don't understand," she said. "We're going to New York."

"*We* are," Zane said. "You aren't."

CHAPTER 35

Zane's announcement hung in the air. No one made a sound. He couldn't mean what I thought he meant. He wouldn't seriously ditch her at a random airport and keep on going? *Would he?*

Then again, this *was* Zane Bennington. He did a lot of things that nice people didn't do.

The brunette blinked a couple of times and said, "What?"

Zane replied, "You heard me."

She glanced around as if searching for a hidden camera. "But why?"

Zane looked back to his cell phone. Almost under his breath, he said, "Because I didn't bring a parachute."

For himself? Or for her? He didn't say, and no one asked.

She gave a shaky laugh. "Oh, so you're kidding?" She blew out a long, unsteady breath. "Wow, for a minute there—"

"I'm not kidding," Zane said. "Now, buckle up." He scrolled through his phone. "Or not. Your choice."

The blond guy and I exchanged a look. For once, he looked utterly unconcerned with my apparent sluttiness.

Across from us, the brunette sputtered, "But I'm working that show in New York."

"Not my problem," Zane said.

She was glaring at him now. "Well, it's *gonna* be your problem, considering that you're one of the sponsors."

I had no idea what they were talking about. I heard myself ask, "What show?"

It was the brunette who answered. "A fashion show." She gave me a quick once-over and added, "Not that *you'd* know anything about that."

I felt my gaze narrow. "Excuse me?"

Next to her, Zane stopped scrolling only long enough to say in a low voice, "I *said*, leave her alone."

The brunette practically leapt to her feet, as if preparing to storm off, which was really stupid, considering that there was nowhere to go. "Well, this is just terrific," she told him. "What? You're sleeping with *her*, too?"

Oh, God. I looked toward the rear of the plane. If only there *was* a parachute. It would have my name all over it.

The guy next to me spoke up. "She's not sleeping with *Zane*," he said. *"*She's sleeping with her roommate's boyfriend. Remember?"

The brunette gave a snort of derision. "Oh, like that matters. You *do* know you can sleep with multiple people, right?" Her lips formed a smirk. "Sometimes, even at the same time."

She looked to Zane, and her tone softened. "Which reminds me... I've got a friend in New York. She's hot as hell and super-freaky, too." The brunette leaned closer to him and said, "If you want, she'll do things—"

"Don't," Zane said.

She blinked. "Don't what?"

"You know what."

Again, the brunette's gaze swiveled in my direction. "Is it because of her?"

"No," Zane said. "It's because you're embarrassing."

"Oh, so you're embarrassed? Is that what you mean?"

"No," he said. "You're embarrassing yourself."

"Hey," she said, throwing back her shoulders, "I'm not embarrassed by my own sexuality." When he made no response, she gave his crotch a pointed look and added, "And last I looked, you weren't either."

I sunk lower in my seat. Forget the parachute. Maybe I'd just jump out the emergency exit and pray for the best.

The brunette turned and gave me a particularly nasty smirk. "Can *you* suck a golf ball through a garden hose?"

I stared up at her. What did that even mean?

Next to me, the new guy muttered, "If you *really* wanna know, ask her roommate's boyfriend."

I'd had just about enough. I jumped to my feet and glared down at the guy. "What's your problem?" I demanded. "I didn't do anything to you – or to her stupid boyfriend, not that it's any of your concern."

Zane's voice cut through the commotion. "You wanna hit Kalamazoo, too?"

Just great. So now he was threatening to leave *me* behind? Cripes, at this point, he'd be doing me a favor, well, aside from the fact that I'd be stranded with the garden-hose golf-ball sucker.

I turned to glare at him, only to discover that he wasn't looking at me. He was looking at the new guy.

As I watched in stunned disbelief, Zane told him, "Now, apologize. Or grab your luggage."

After a long, awkward pause, the new guy looked vaguely in my direction and muttered a few words that might be considered an apology if I weren't too picky.

I was still trying to make sense of it all when the brunette demanded, "What about me? Don't *I* deserve an apology?"

I couldn't resist asking, "For what?"

"What do you mean 'for what?'" She straightened. "I'm being kicked off for no good reason."

This might've been true five minutes ago, but now, I could see plenty of reasons to kick her off. Wasn't it some sort of flight hazard when someone stood up and flipped out on a plane? The thought had barely crossed my mind when I realized that she wasn't the only one standing.

Unsure what else to do, I sank down in my seat and tried to pretend that none of this was happening. I closed my eyes in a desperate bid to block out everyone and everything, including my own jumbled thoughts.

In the background, I heard Zane say, "Are you gonna buckle up or not?"

The brunette snapped, "No. And you can't make me."

"I wasn't talking to you," Zane said. "I was talking to *her*."

My eyes flew open, and I looked to Zane. He looked to my seatbelt, and his voice hardened. "Now."

Well, that wasn't bossy or anything.

Still, I reached for my seatbelt and began fastening it over my lap.

The brunette gave a single stomp of her foot. "Doesn't anyone care about *me*? I'm still standing for Christ's sake!"

Next to me, the blond guy assured her, "I care."

"Yeah?" she said. "Well, up yours!"

I glanced out the window and bit my lip. We were definitely getting ready to land. True, I couldn't see the airport, but the ground was looking a whole lot closer than it had just a couple minutes earlier.

I looked up and told the brunette, "Seriously, I think you'd better sit."

"Oh yeah?" She crossed her arms. "What if I don't want to?"

I tried to think. "Well, um, if we have a rough landing, couldn't your face get mangled or something?"

Her hand flew to her face. She felt around as if imagining an ear where her mouth should be and vice-versa. She stopped in mid-motion and gave me the squinty-eye. "Oh, shut up," she said, before plopping back into her seat and fastening the belt over her lap.

It was a good thing, too, because Zane wasn't kidding. We were definitely landing.

Welcome to Kalamazoo.

CHAPTER 36

An hour later, we were in the air again, minus What's-Her-Name.

The blond guy looked to Zane and said, "You're a real asshole, you know that?"

Zane had set aside his cell phone and was now leaning back in his seat, looking at nothing in particular.

The blond guy said, "Well?"

Zane spared him half a glance. "Well what?"

"Aren't you gonna respond to that?"

"No."

The guy frowned. "Why not?"

"Because I don't care."

"About what?"

"That you think I'm an asshole."

"I don't *think* you're an asshole," the guy clarified. "I *know* you're an asshole."

Zane looked utterly indifferent. "Good to know."

"What does *that* mean?" the guy said. "Do you mean it's good that *I* know? Or it's good that *you* know?"

Zane replied, "Does it matter?"

The guy looked to me and said, "What do you think?"

Oh, so *now* he wanted to include me in the conversation? After he'd been treating me like trash from the get-go? I tried for a smirk. "I dunno...Does it matter?"

Yes, I realized that I was only repeating what Zane had said, but that was the whole point. It was annoying, and I *wanted* to annoy the guy.

Besides, I saw no reason to take his side, not after he'd been so eager to assume the worst of me.

With a sound of annoyance – score one for me – he looked toward a nearby cabinet and asked, "What happened to the drinks?"

Zane said, "I got rid of them."

"When?"

"This afternoon."

The guy frowned. "Why'd you do that?"

"Because I don't want to deal with a drunk."

"Hey!" the guy said. "I can hold my liquor just fine."

Zane leaned further back in his seat and closed his eyes. "Uh-huh."

The guy looked to me and said, "What about you? Wouldn't *you* like a drink?"

Boy, would I ever.

But stubbornly, I *still* didn't want to take his side. And besides, what was the point of complaining? It's not like we could hit a liquor store in mid-air.

I gave a dismissive shrug. "I'm not much of a drinker." In spite of my drink-cart fantasies, this was actually true.

The guy said, "Well, aren't you special?"

With his eyes still shut, Zane said, "Hey, Teddy."

"What?"

"Fuck off."

Teddy's jaw tightened. "What?"

"You heard me," Zane said.

As the guy replied with some profanity of his own, I felt my eyebrows furrow. *Teddy?*

I'd heard that name before. But where? And then it hit me. "Oh, my God," I said. "You're Teddy the—" *Oh, crap.* With a small gasp, I slammed my lips shut and looked away.

Like an idiot, I'd been about to say, "Teddy the Drunk."

My gaze landed on Zane, and I was surprised to see that his eyes were now open. Our gazes locked across the short distance, and I swear I saw a flash of amusement flicker in those green depths.

And then, it was gone, replaced by the bored indifference he seemed to favor when not being an outright prick.

In spite of this, I couldn't seem to make myself look away. Odder still, *he* wasn't looking away either. *Weird.*

Next to me, the blond guy demanded, "Teddy the what?"

With a start, I turned to look at him. Earlier, he'd given his name as Theodore. No wonder I hadn't made the connection. But it *did* make sense. Theodore, Teddy – yup, they *had* to be the same guy.

I should've known. After all, he'd been giving Zane all kinds of attitude for most of the flight. And yet, he hadn't been tossed out like What's-Her-Name.

Did Teddy get a pass because he was family?

Next to me, Teddy was still waiting for an answer. "Well?" he said.

Desperately, I tried to think. I recalled snippets of what I'd overheard from inside the catering van, not just from Teddy, but from that Bob guy, too. Finally, I settled on, "Teddy the Cousin."

Teddy's mouth tightened. "*Second* cousin."

This also made sense. On the Bennington side, Zane had those two uncles. Both had died childless, which meant that Zane *had* no first cousins, at least not on his father's side. As far as his mother's side, I had no idea.

So where did Teddy fit into all of this? I studied his face. He and Zane looked nothing alike. Where Zane had bold, angular features, Teddy had a fine, delicate mouth, light blue eyes, and pale eyelashes. It's not that Teddy was unattractive. It's just that, compared to Zane, someone like Teddy would totally fade into the background.

Was *that* the source of his animosity?

No, I decided. It had to be about the inheritance. Zane had gotten everything. And Teddy? What had *he* gotten?

Kicked out of his house, that's what.

No wonder he was hostile.

Suddenly, I was seeing him in a much more sympathetic light.

On the night of the party, he'd been drunk and belligerent. Today, he was sober, but nearly as hostile. But could I really blame him?

I heard myself ask, "So, why are you going to New York?"

As an answer, he looked to Zane. I looked, too. Once again, Zane's eyes were shut as he leaned back in his seat.

But if he was truly asleep, I was Little Red Riding Hood. Probably, he just didn't want to be bothered. That was fine by me. It's not like I wanted to talk to him, anyway.

In a quiet voice, Teddy finally said, "I'm going to be working in the New York office."

This surprised me. After all, the two guys obviously hated each other. So, why would Zane offer Teddy a job? And why on Earth would Teddy accept?

Then again, who was I to wonder such a thing? After all, I was working for Zane, too, and it's not like *I* was his biggest fan.

I said, "Really? Doing what?"

Teddy frowned. "Whatever *he* wants."

He hadn't said who "he" was, but it wasn't hard to guess. I gave Zane another quick glance. His eyes were still shut, and yet, I'd be a fool to forget that he could probably hear every word, assuming that he cared enough to listen.

At the thought, I did a mental eye-roll. Yeah, like *we* were so fascinating.

Turning my attention back to Teddy, I asked, "So, was the move a sudden thing?"

"No. We worked it out last week." He paused. "This trip was sudden though."

"Really? How sudden?"

"*Very* sudden." Teddy was frowning again. "Today, I show up at his office for a meeting, and he tells me to pack my stuff, because we're flying out in just a few hours."

I could so relate. I almost laughed. "Yeah, me too."

Teddy's face softened into something that might be considered a smile. "I guess I should say it, huh?"

"Say what?"

"I'm sorry."

"For what?" I asked.

"For the attitude earlier." He gave a slow shake of his head. "You want the truth? It's been one of those weeks."

My shoulders relaxed, and I returned his smile. "That's all right." And I meant it, too. After all, I knew – probably more than he realized – just how much he was going through.

With a sigh, Teddy added, "After all, it's none of *my* business who you're sleeping with."

And just like that, my smile was gone. "What?"

"I'm just saying, we all have our issues."

Oh, I had issues all right. Through gritted teeth, I told him for what felt like the millionth time, "I'm *not* sleeping with my roommate's boyfriend."

He held up his hands in mock surrender. "Hey, like I said, it's none of my business."

And yet, he kept making it his business.

I stared at the guy, wondering what his deal was.

At something in my expression, he gave a long sigh. "Sorry. It's just that, shit, I know what it's like to be cheated on." He looked toward Zane, and his eyes narrowed. "Especially when they cheat with your own cousin."

CHAPTER 37

I didn't know what to say. Was he saying what I *thought* he was saying? Did this guy's girlfriend – or wife, for all I knew – cheat on him with Zane?

I was dying to ask, but didn't dare. And now, I had no idea what to say. Once again, my gaze drifted to Zane. His eyes were still shut, and he showed no sign that he was listening, or even conscious for that matter.

I studied his face as I considered what Teddy had just implied.

In every possible way, Zane was unlike anyone I'd ever met. My own loathing aside, I could definitely see why someone – or cripes, *anyone* – would want to sleep with him.

And it wasn't for his money.

His hair was thick and lush – dark bronze, with golden highlights. His eyes were emerald green with flecks of gold. His lips – I felt myself swallow – oh yeah, they were definitely made for sin, just like that amazing body of his.

On top of that, I'd heard the rumors. The way it sounded, he put that body to most excellent use.

Next to me, Teddy gave a loud sigh. "Don't tell me she was right?"

I practically jumped in my seat. "What?"

"About you and Zane."

I drew back. "God, no."

"Are you sure?" Teddy's gaze narrowed. "Because you seem like his type."

Okay, now *that* was just plain ridiculous. I'd seen Zane's type. They were all tall and willowy with perfect hair and million-dollar cheekbones.

In contrast, I wasn't tall, willowy, or particularly gifted in the cheekbone department. I was no goblin, but I wasn't a supermodel either. Teddy's statement *had* to be a joke.

I almost laughed in his face. "Yeah, right."

"You think I'm kidding?"

My face was burning with embarrassment, especially because I was obscenely aware that the person we were so rudely discussing was right here, across from us, within earshot no less.

Again, I looked to Zane. His eyes were still shut, but that was no guarantee of anything.

And besides, he was my boss.

And a total jerk.

I looked back to Teddy and said, "Of course, I think you're kidding. Look at me compared to…" *Damn it.* I didn't even know the chick's name. But that was hardly the point.

I glanced away. "You know what? I don't feel comfortable discussing this."

"Why not?" Teddy asked.

As an answer, I looked to Zane.

Teddy said, "If you're worried about him, he's out cold."

"He is not," I said. "And even if he *is*, he's my employer, not, well, anything more."

Determined to end this conversation once and for all, I grabbed my paperback and opened it to a random page. I looked down and pretended to read, as if I could concentrate on a single word.

My thoughts were filled with too many questions. They all centered on one guy, who happened to be sitting across from me.

Ignoring my obvious hint, Teddy said, "Growing up, I saw him maybe once, twice a year. We used to talk sometimes." Teddy gave a low scoff. "He was a lot nicer back then."

This, I could believe, but only because Zane was such a jerk now. In comparison, *any* version of him would be nicer, right?

But this wasn't the time or the place to be discussing it, so I gave a small shrug and kept my eyes trained on my book.

Undaunted, Teddy continued. "Anyway, when it came to girls, he always went for the farmer's daughter type, so if you ask me, it's only a matter of time."

More heat rushed to my face, and of course, it didn't help that my parents were, in fact, farmers.

What were the odds?

Oblivious to my discomfort, Teddy kept on talking. "Zane's grandfather – a really nice guy, by the way – had this thing for old TV shows. *I love Lucy. Father Knows Best....*" He gave a small laugh. "...*Gilligan's Island*. So sometimes, we ended up watching along in his media room, you know?"

I gave a noncommittal shrug. It wasn't that I wasn't interested. It was just that I was so terribly conscious that Zane could be listening.

And besides, I wasn't sure how much of this I actually believed. Even as far as the grandfather, the guy had been absolutely loaded. I had no idea what rich people did in their free time, but for some reason, I couldn't imagine them watching old reruns on TV.

Then again, I was no expert. After all, it wasn't like we saw a lot of billionaires down on the farm.

Teddy was still talking. "But Zane? He was all for Mary Ann. Never Ginger."

It took me a minute to realize that he was referring to the characters on *Gilligan's Island*. I'd seen only a handful of reruns, but this was more than enough to know that Mary Ann was a farmer's daughter, while Ginger was a movie star.

Now that I thought about it, I *did* look a little like Mary Ann. Or maybe that was just wishful thinking. Either way, I was definitely no Ginger.

I gave a little shake of my head. Why was I even thinking about this?

More desperate than ever to end this conversation, I looked to Teddy and said, "Well, he likes Gingers now, so…" I let the words trail off, as if there was nothing else to be said.

"Oh yeah?" Teddy replied. "So why'd he kick Ginger off the

plane?"

Obviously, he was speaking metaphorically – unless her name really *was* Ginger, which I highly doubted.

I said, "That's an easy one. He kicked her off because she was being a pill."

"So were you. And *you're* still here."

"Oh, please," I said. "I wasn't the one who threw a giant hissy-fit. And besides, you were kind of a pill yourself."

He frowned. "I was not."

I returned my eyes to my book. "Sure, you weren't."

"All right, fine," he said. "But here's a fair warning. You *don't* want to get involved with that guy."

"I wasn't planning on it."

"You know he's an asshole, right?"

I gave Zane a nervous glance. "All *I* know is that he's my boss, and I don't feel comfortable discussing this."

Stubbornly, Teddy said, "Yeah, well he's my boss, too."

With a sigh, I set aside my book and turned to face him. "Oh, come on. He's not just your boss. He's your cousin."

"So?"

"So maybe you two should, I dunno, patch things up."

Teddy looked at me like I'd lost my mind. "With that asshole? You can't be serious."

I gave another shrug, but made no reply. After all, what could I say?

Teddy made a scoffing sound. "Are you forgetting? That asshole screwed my girlfriend."

Stupidly, I couldn't help but think, *"At least it wasn't your wife."* It's not that I was excusing Zane's awful behavior. He was a monster, plain and simple. But I *did* realize that it could always be worse.

Still, what could I say? Honestly, I had no idea. I was still searching for the right words when Zane's voice cut through the silence. "She was no girlfriend."

Teddy turned to glare at him. "Oh yeah? Then what was she?"

Without missing a beat, Zane replied, "A gold-digging slut."

I heard myself gasp. He did *not* just say that. But his eyes were now open, and he wasn't taking it back.

Teddy was still glaring. "What?"

"If you ask me," Zane said, "you're better off without her."

Teddy was sputtering now. "You've got to be fucking kidding me."

But Zane wasn't kidding. I knew this, because for fifteen whole minutes, Teddy tried – unsuccessfully, I might add – to get Zane to take it back.

Instead, Zane doubled down by telling Teddy that he should be grateful he learned the girlfriend was garbage before Teddy did something really stupid, like marrying her.

Teddy was practically yelling now. "I *was* gonna marry her!"

If Zane felt guilty, he sure as heck didn't show it. "Then consider it a bullet dodged."

The argument ended like two minutes later after Zane casually mentioned that Kalamazoo wasn't the *only* airport on the way to New York.

It was a threat, obviously. And no doubt, Zane would've made good on it.

Apparently, I wasn't the only one who thought so. From then on, Teddy said nothing to anyone.

The awkwardness aside, that was fine by me.

I was tired and confused, not only by what I'd just learned, but also because of my own conflicted feelings. I said a silent prayer that after we arrived in New York, everything would be smooth sailing.

And who knows? It might've been, if it weren't for the unexpected arrival of a certain senator and his wayward fiancée.

CHAPTER 38

It was an hour before nightfall, and I was alone in the elevator, going down. Already, I'd been in New York for three jam-packed days of accompanying Zane to countless interviews.

Just this morning, he'd appeared on two morning shows and a popular business channel. On air, he'd been surprisingly professional and yes, maybe even charming, at least by Zane's standards.

It made me wonder all over again, who *was* this guy, anyway?

We were staying, of course, at the Bennington Hotel in New York, which also housed the regional corporate offices, where Teddy would be working whenever he got settled in.

As far as anything we'd discussed on the plane, none of it was ever mentioned again – not by me, not by Teddy, and certainly not by Zane, who'd been even more unsociable than normal.

That was fine by me. Ever since that awkward flight, I'd been feeling nervous and unsettled for reasons that I couldn't quite decipher. Something between us had shifted, but I had no idea what.

I was still trying to figure it out when a sudden ding jolted me back to reality. In front of me, the elevator doors slid open, and I came face-to-face with someone I was surprised to see so far from home.

It was Tiffany, and she was toting a bunch of shopping bags. At the sight of me, she stopped and squinted across the short distance. "Jane? Is that you?"

I had to laugh. "As far as I know."

She bustled forward. "What are you doing here?"

"Working."

"Oh, like a catering thing?" She gave me an encouraging smile. "Good for you."

Obviously, she had no idea what I'd been doing, which was pretty surprising, considering how obsessed she'd been with Zane. Then again, she'd never been one to follow the news.

I was just about to explain when she said, "I'm going to the lobby. Could you please hit the button?"

I glanced at the panel. "It's already hit."

"Oh." She frowned. "You're not going there, too, are you?"

I gave her a confused look. "Why? Is that a problem?"

"No." She bit her lip. "Well, maybe. It's just that I'm meeting the senator."

"That's nice." I hesitated. "Right?"

"Sure, but..." She let her words trail off into silence.

"But what?" I asked.

She sighed. "Listen, I hope you don't take this personally, but could you scoot away a little?"

Scoot away? "Why?"

The doors had already shut, and the elevator was once again heading downward.

Tiffany replied, "Because he might recognize you from the catering stuff."

"And...?"

"And, well, I don't want him to think we're together."

I stared at her. "Together how?"

"Well, not together-together. I just mean, I don't want him to think we're, um..."

My jaw tightened. "Friends?"

She smiled in obvious relief. "Right."

I was so stunned that I didn't know what to say.

At something in my expression, Tiffany winced. "You're not insulted, are you?"

"Me?" My tone grew sarcastic. "No. Not at all."

"Oh come on, don't take it so personally," she said, glancing down at my clothes. "Honestly, you're dressed so nice *now* that he might not make the connection, but really, it would be *so* much better if I didn't have to risk it."

I looked down. Thanks to the busy interview schedule, this was my first stretch of real freedom, and I was on my way out to do some sight-seeing.

Not knowing where I'd end up, I'd skipped the more casual clothes in favor of a long black skirt and high leather boots, along with my favorite white cotton blouse.

This way, I figured, I was prepared for anything – except, of course, to be insulted yet again by Tiffany.

She gave another sigh. "Look, I'm not trying to be mean, honest. It's just that I need to consider my social standing. You know how it is."

I did *now*. Looking to make a point, I made a show of backing up until my butt hit the back wall. "Is *this* far enough for you?"

"I guess," she said. "I mean, not like you could go much further." She gave me a nervous smile. "But can you do me another tiny little favor?

I rolled my eyes. "Oh, suuuuure. Anything for a friend."

"See, that's just the thing," she said. "If he's waiting, can you pretend we're just strangers?"

Un-freaking-believable.

At this point, I didn't *have* to pretend. It's not like Tiffany and I had ever been best-buddies anyway. Obviously, she was no friend of mine. "Don't worry," I told her, "That *won't* be a problem."

The words had barely left my mouth when the elevator dinged again, and there we were, at lobby level. The elevator doors slid open, and right there, facing us, was a familiar male figure, dressed in dark tailored slacks and a cream-colored shirt, open at the collar.

But it wasn't the senator. It was Zane.

When he saw me, mashed up against the elevator's back wall, his brow wrinkled. "Jane? You okay?"

Probably, it was the nicest thing he'd ever said to me.

Before I could even think to answer, Tiffany squealed out, "Oh, my God! Zane!" She dropped her bags and lunged forward to claim his arm. "Imagine seeing *you* here."

As if his last name *wasn't* on the building.

She looked back to me and said in an off-handed way, "Hey, can you grab those?"

I blinked. "Excuse me?"

"The shopping bags," she said, "would you mind grabbing them and taking them to the front desk? I think they've got a giant safe or something." She gave a breezy wave of her hands. "If they ask, just tell them I'll pick them up later."

Well, that was rich.

I put on my clueless face. "I'm sorry, but who are you?"

She gave a nervous laugh. "Oh, stop." She looked back to Zane and then froze, as if finally putting two and two together. "Wait, so you two know each other?"

Wow. What a guess.

Zane had, after all, just called me by name.

Tiffany looked thunderstruck by the connection. As for Zane, his gaze returned to mine, but he said nothing.

Zane was a lot of things, but he wasn't stupid. He obviously realized there was a lot more to this story.

By now, the elevator doors surely would've slid shut again, if it weren't for a huge shopping bag blocking their path. Tiffany had dropped it during her mad lunge for Zane, and the bag was now lying on its side, smack-dab in the elevator's doorway.

The way it looked, it was triggering the sensors that were designed to keep the doors open until everyone was in or out.

Unable to resist, I edged forward and gave the bag a little nudge with my foot. The bag slid forward, and a moment later, the elevator doors began to slide shut.

Tiffany called out, "Wait!" Releasing Zane's arm, she lunged back into the elevator. Frantically, she gathered up her bags, glowering at me the whole time. Under her breath, she hissed, "Thanks a lot."

I gave her a cheery smile. "You're welcome."

With the bags in tow, she once again, exited the elevator.

Feeling surprisingly cheerful now, I followed after her. As for Zane, his gaze kept shifting from me to Tiffany and back again.

The way it looked, he wasn't nearly as happy to see Tiffany as she was to see him.

Utterly oblivious, Tiffany turned to Zane and said, "So, do you have any plans for dinner?" She leaned closer and practically purred, "Because I haven't eaten all day."

Oh, for God's sake. Hadn't she just told me that she was meeting her fiancé? What was she planning to do? Ditch the guy last-minute? Or make it dinner for three?

Zane gave her a cold look. "Yes."

Tiffany beamed up at him. "Great! We could eat right here in the hotel. I haven't been to the Skyroom, but I hear it's fabulous."

Obviously, she meant the restaurant on the rooftop. Supposedly, it *was* fabulous, but it took forever to get a table.

Then again, the hotel's owner would surely be able to snag a seat any time. Who knows? Maybe Tiffany wasn't as clueless as I thought.

Zane's gaze shifted to me. In a tight voice, he said, "I meant *yes*, I have plans."

Tiffany's smile faded. "Oh. With who?"

His gaze locked on mine. "With Jane."

I froze. *Me?*

Tiffany blinked a few times and said, "What?"

He said, "And we're late." He flicked his head toward the front desk. "So shove off. The senator's waiting."

I turned to look. Sure enough, the senator *was* waiting. Worse, he was watching us with an expression that told me *he* wasn't stupid either.

He knew exactly what had just happened, and he wasn't happy. In spite of everything, I actually felt bad for the guy.

But I had no time to dwell on it, because, to my infinite surprise, Zane hadn't been bluffing about dinner.

Unfortunately, I never did get to eat it.

Because of *her*.

And *him*.

The prick.

CHAPTER 39

Less than ten minutes later, Zane and I were sitting at a prime table in the glass-enclosed restaurant. The whole scene was entirely surreal, and not only because of our ultra-posh surroundings and the amazing cityscape view.

More than anything, it was the whole idea of being here, with *him*, in a social setting that didn't involve watching as he told someone to fuck off.

Then again, we hadn't yet eaten, so there was still plenty of time.

Zane, with his usual degree of politeness, was ignoring me as he texted someone on his cell phone. Who he was texting, he didn't say, and I sure as heck didn't ask, even after he claimed – falsely, I might add – that he'd be only a minute.

That was five minutes ago, not that I was counting.

Much.

While he tapped away at his phone, I took another slow look around. Outside our window, light from the setting sun glimmered off the windows of neighboring buildings, making the whole city sparkle and shine, at least to my inexperienced eyes.

Soon, it would be dark, and I had the whole night ahead of me. During those hours of freedom, I'd been planning to visit Times Square and do as many touristy things as I could.

In fact, that's where I'd been going when I'd been waylaid, first by Tiffany and then by Zane.

Talk about bad timing.

My only *good* luck was that I'd dressed up. But still, even in a skirt and blouse, I felt seriously outclassed compared to the formal cocktail dresses I saw all around me. And, as far as the men? Every single one of them wore a suit *with* a tie, except for Zane.

The dress code, like so many other things, apparently didn't apply to him.

Go figure.

If that weren't unfair enough, tie or not, he still looked better than any other guy in the whole place, including Paisley's favorite TV star, who was dining with a stunning redhead a few tables away.

Across from me, Zane was still texting, looking less enthused with every message he received in return.

Just great.

Probably, when he finished – *if* he finished – I'd be bearing the brunt of whatever news had irritated him. Who knows? Maybe in the end, he'd be telling *me* to shove off.

Between texts, he'd ordered a bottle of wine and dinner for both of us – without consulting me, I might add. It was bossy and arrogant, and yes, in a way, almost a relief, as much as I hated to admit it.

My menu had no prices, and I'd been oddly nervous about ordering the wrong thing, especially because most of the dishes were unfamiliar and written in a script that was so fancy, I could hardly read it.

I couldn't imagine why we were here at all, unless he wanted to discuss work – or to prove once again how rude he could be by texting throughout wine, dinner, *and* dessert, assuming we stuck around that long.

He'd been lying to Tiffany. Zane and I *didn't* have plans. And this, as much as anything, made no sense at all. Obviously, he didn't care two bits about sparing her feelings. So, why the lie? And why drag me up here at all?

Was it just because he could?

Finally, he finished texting and – *holy hell* – not only turned off his phone entirely, but said something that caught me off guard. "Sorry about that."

I blinked. "Excuse me?"

"Sorry," he repeated, "but it couldn't be helped."

Wow. *Two* sorries? Right in a row? From Zane Bennington? I almost didn't know what to say. I glanced around before murmuring, "That's all right."

He gave me a long, calculating look. "So, you know Tiffany."

There it was again, a question without a question mark. Funny, I was almost getting used to it.

I replied, "A little."

"So what do you know about her?"

"Not much," I admitted. "It's not like we're best friends or anything."

Especially now.

Zane said, "But you're more than acquaintances."

"I guess." Maybe I was being evasive, but honestly, there wasn't much to say.

"How about her fiancé?" he said. "The senator. You know *him*, too?"

I shook my head. "I've seen him, but that's it."

"Yeah? Where?"

I gave a shaky laugh. "Other than in the lobby a few minutes ago?"

"I'm not talking about tonight," he said. "You saw him before. Where?"

I bit my lip. I almost didn't want to say, mostly because that whole night had been so incredibly embarrassing. Still, there was no sense in lying about it. "Actually," I said, "it was the night we met. At your party."

Zane leaned back in his seat, and his mouth tightened. "Uh-huh."

The way it looked, he wasn't any happier with the recollection than I was.

Happily, I was spared from saying anything in response, thanks to the appearance of a wine steward, who went the whole ritual of opening the wine and pouring each of us a glass.

I was excessively grateful, and not only because I could definitely use a drink. The interruption, as short as it was, gave me some time to figure out why I was here.

At last, I thought I knew.

Obviously, for whatever reason, Zane wanted to know more about Tiffany and the senator. And, in true Zane fashion, he couldn't bring himself to wait until tomorrow.

So here I was, at his beck and call.

As usual.

Maybe he'd send me packing the moment he learned whatever it was that he wanted to know. No wonder he hadn't let me order. For all *I* knew, he didn't plan on letting me stick around long enough to actually eat.

It would be just like him, too. When the steward left, I couldn't stop myself from tormenting him, at least a little. "So, 'Shove off' huh? Is that your new catch-phrase?"

To my surprise, he didn't look tormented at all. In fact, he looked almost amused. He gave something like a shrug. "I was trying to be nice."

Zane Bennington? Nice? That would be a first. And yet, it did make sense in a Zane sort of way. After all, the phrase was a lot nicer than what he usually said to those who irritated him.

I had to admit, "I guess it *is* an improvement." I took a sip of my wine and savored its sweetness for a long, drawn-out moment before asking, "So, how do *you* know Tiffany?"

Yes, I was being bold, and maybe a little nosy, but the way I saw it, he had it coming. And besides, I *was* curious. Zane and Tiffany had, after all, been caught doing *something* at his own party.

Zane studied me from across the table. His gaze didn't waver as he took a slow drink of his wine and then set down his glass before saying, "How do you think I know her?"

I felt myself swallow. *Intimately.*

But I didn't say it, because even now, I didn't quite have the nerve. So instead, I tried to laugh. "No fair. I asked you first."

"Yeah? Too bad."

"Why?" I teased. "Because you're my boss?"

He shook his head. "Forget that."

It seemed an odd thing to say. "Forget what? That I work for you?"

"That's right."

Now, I was really confused. "Why?"

"Because I want the truth."

Was that an insult? I wasn't sure. "Hey, I'm always honest."

"Maybe," he said. "But honest and unfiltered aren't the same thing."

"So?"

"So, I want to know what you're really thinking."

I almost laughed. "No, you don't."

"Why?" He leaned toward me across the table and said in a low, compelling voice, "Because you think I'm an asshole?"

Talk about a loaded question.

Instinctively, I reached for my glass, but Zane snagged it first. He pulled the glass away and said, "First, answer the question."

I eyed the glass with a surprising amount of longing. I couldn't decide if I was annoyed or amused by his cunning move. "Or what?" I asked. "You won't give it back?"

As an answer, he gave my glass a slow, hypnotic turn, making the liquid swirl enticingly as I watched in stupid fascination.

It wasn't just the wine that had captured my attention. It was his fingers, long and firm around the stem of the glass. I recalled all those salacious rumors. It wasn't just that he was physically gifted. It was that he made very good use of his gifts – one gift in particular.

Against all logic, I felt my tongue dart out between my lips, even as I tried to form some sort of protest. He was holding my drink for ransom. I should be irritated. Instead, I was utterly hypnotized.

In hopes of breaking the spell, I looked up to meet his eyes.

Big mistake.

He wasn't watching the wine at all. He was watching me. And, if I didn't know any better, I might've believed, if only for an instant, that he found me incredibly fascinating, and maybe even beautiful.

It was official. I was going insane.

Distracted, I heard myself murmur, "You're not *always* an asshole." As soon as the words left my lips, I wanted to take them back – not because they were untrue, but rather, because just then, he did something I never would've expected.

He laughed.

And just like that, his whole face changed. Gone was the jerk who'd been making my life miserable. And, in his place sat a guy I'd never met. His gaze was warm, and his mouth looked so kissable that I could hardly think.

On my own lips, I felt the tug of a traitorous grin. "What's so funny?"

He stopped laughing and leaned forward to say, "If I've gotta explain…" He let his words trail off and once again, leaned back to study me from his side of the table.

In the process, he'd set down my glass, and I took the opportunity to snatch it up and take a long, desperate drink.

I needed something to calm my nerves, and for once, it wasn't because he was doing something awful. It was because, in his own personal way, he was drawing me in, making me see him as something more than a jerk, something more than my billionaire boss, and yes, simply, *something more*.

And it scared me half to death.

After all, I'd seen how coldly he treated the women in his life. Even if I hadn't known this all along, my firsthand view of him kicking What's-Her-Name off his private jet would've told me everything that I needed to know.

He was one of *those* guys – charming before and a prick after.

As a relationship type of girl, I'd never experienced that particular dynamic, but I'd heard plenty from my more adventurous friends.

I couldn't help but think of Tiffany. During our impromptu lunch date however many weeks ago, she'd mentioned that she was meeting up with Zane later on that same night.

At a hotel.

It didn't take a genius to figure out what they'd been doing.

And now, how was Zane treating her?

Badly.

Shove off?

At the time, it seemed rude enough, but now that I thought about it, it was more than rude. It was heartless.

And yet, it was exactly what I *should've* expected from the same guy who'd gotten me fired, who'd kicked his cousin out of his family home, and who'd given me way too much grief already.

I gave a little shake of my head. To think, I'd almost fallen under his spell.

Idiot.

Not him.

Me.

I felt my gaze narrow as I eyed him across the table. Oh sure, he was gorgeous. And rich. And sexy as hell. But inside, he was as cold as they came.

Nothing *ever* ruffled him, and it was easy to see why.

It was because he *had* no heart. And if he'd ever had a soul? Well, he'd probably sold it southward a long time ago.

As if reading something in my eyes, Zane's expression darkened, and an icy chill settled over the table. After a long, intense moment, he said in a low voice, "Whatever you're thinking, you're about to be proven right."

I felt my eyebrows furrow. Was that a warning? It sure sounded like a warning.

What was he truly telling me? That he'd seen the way I was looking at him? That he was getting ready to make his move? That I wouldn't be spared from his usual charm-them, fuck-them, dump-them routine?

Talk about arrogant.

I made a scoffing sound. "That's what *you* think."

Suddenly, I didn't care how sexy he was, or how utterly mesmerized I'd been for those few brief moments. I was no longer charmed. And, whatever he'd been anticipating, it wasn't going to happen, not that he'd outright asked.

But still, a girl knows, right?

His gaze shifted to the view outside, and for the briefest instant, I saw an expression that looked an awful lot like regret.

I gave a mental eye-roll. Regret? *Oh, please.* Probably, his only regret was that he'd bothered to order wine.

With a look of grim resignation, he returned his gaze to mine and said something that, once again, caught me off guard. "I'm sorry."

What was that? *Three* apologies? All in one night?

But the truth was, I had no idea what, specifically, he was apologizing for. For being a jerk? Or for making me forget, if only for an instant, that he wasn't a nice person?

Whatever it was, I wanted to make him say it. I said, "For what?"

He looked down and closed his eyes for a long moment before saying, "For what's about to happen."

CHAPTER 40

I gave a confused shake of my head. "Why? What's going to happen?"

As an answer, he pushed back his chair and stood. In a low voice, he said, "You should go."

I stared up at him. *What a total asshole*. I tried to laugh, but it came out hard and bitter. "Well, that's nice."

"No. It's not." His jaw tightened. "And I'm sorry."

What was that? Apology number four? That had to be some kind of record, especially for Zane.

I looked down at the table in front of me. On it, I saw silverware for food that hadn't yet arrived, two half-empty wine glasses, and of course, the bottle itself, with plenty of wine remaining.

Bummer for me, huh? Apparently, I was being dismissed.

True, I'd been half-expecting it, but it still bothered me more than it should've – not that I had any intention of showing it.

Instead, I summoned up a stiff smile and got to my feet with as much dignity as I could muster.

The effort was a total waste. He was paying me zero attention. Instead, he was staring past me, toward the restaurant entrance – or, exit as the case might be.

Hint taken.

Jerk.

I turned away, intending to march off with my head held high. Instead, I nearly collided with a tall, elegant blonde in a long, ice-blue dress.

I stepped back and somehow managed to mumble, "Sorry."

Her lips formed a sneer. "You should be."

Well, this wasn't humiliating or anything.

All I wanted to do was leave. But at the moment, I couldn't, not with the woman blocking my path. Nearly desperate now, I backed closer to the table and waited for her to pass.

But she didn't. Instead, she looked to my chair said, "That's *my* seat."

I froze. "What?"

Suddenly, a dark wall appeared in front of me. The wall was Zane, who'd stepped between us, with his back to me and his front to her.

In a quiet voice, he said, "I told you, we'd reschedule."

She gave a mean little laugh. "And I told *you* that no one 'reschedules' Maven."

She leaned around Zane and gave me a quick once-over. "Now, run along, sweetie. The *important* people are talking."

I felt my gaze narrow. "Important people?"

But already, she'd disappeared behind Zane. In a breezy voice, she said, "Now that we've cleared that away…" She paused. "Oh come on. You can't seriously be angry."

Zane said, "Can't I?"

"No," she said. "And you had plans with *me* first."

In a tight voice, he said, "Which I canceled."

My stomach twisted. Obviously, *she* was the person he'd been texting.

I should've known.

I wasn't sure what I found more revolting – that he'd ditch his date last-minute or that he'd ditch *me* now.

And why on Earth was I still standing here? With a sound of disgust, I pushed my way around Zane and began striding toward the exit.

I'd made it only a few steps when a tug on my wrist made me stop. I looked down to see Zane's hand, encircling my own.

In a low voice, he said, "Jane. Wait."

I glanced around. By now, everyone was staring, not that I could blame them. Near our table, Maven stood, eyeing our exchange with blatant satisfaction.

When she spotted me looking, she smiled and gave me one of those finger waves – the kind you give when you really want to piss someone off.

And I *was* pissed. No. Not just pissed. Royally pissed. I yanked my hand out of Zane's grip and hissed. "Your date's waiting."

"No," he said. "My date's leaving."

My thoughts were so jumbled, I wasn't even sure who he meant. Me? Because I was heading toward the door? Or her? Because he was planning to ditch her a second time.

Either way, I wanted no part of it. I glared up at him. "Thanks for the wine."

Asshole.

I didn't say it out loud, but from the look on Zane's face, he got the message loud and clear.

He leaned closer, "Jane—"

Behind him, I heard Maven call out in a sing-song voice, "Oh waiter. We'll need a new bottle of wine. And can you clear away this mess?"

Zane and I hadn't even eaten. There was no mess, at least not at the table. But inside, I felt conflicting emotions swirling and twisting into a toxic brew. Adding salt to the wound, I felt stupid and disheveled in comparison to Maven's cool elegance.

The way it looked, she was loving every minute of this – the drama, the spectacle, the fun of humiliating someone who wasn't remotely in her league.

Suddenly, I felt like crying.

I didn't want to cry, not in front of a crowd, and certainly not in front of Zane.

Or Maven, for that matter.

Besides, I told myself, none of this was a big deal. Zane was always a jerk. I was used to it. Or at least, I *should* be used to it.

And yet, now I wasn't. I looked back to Zane. As our gazes locked and held, I didn't bother hiding my disgust. Whatever *he* was feeling, I couldn't be sure.

But it wasn't happiness.

Good.

I lowered my voice to just a whisper, and said, "Zane, there's something you need to hear."

He leaned a fraction closer. "What?"

"Fuck off." And with that, I turned and walked away, pushing my way through the exit. In the distance, I heard Maven laughing as she said, "God, what a drama queen."

Bitch.

Outside the confines of the restaurant, I was walking faster now, heading toward the elevators. But when I arrived, a couple was already standing there, waiting for the next elevator down.

I didn't want to wait. And besides, the thought of breaking down in front of strangers was just too much to bear.

In a moment of blind panic, I ducked into the stairwell and let the door swing shut behind me. And then I stood, for a long moment, catching my breath and trying to figure out what had just happened.

Whatever it was, I never, *ever* wanted to repeat it.

As I stood there, in the bleak stairwell, I reminded myself that I didn't even like him. In fact, I was pretty sure that I hated him.

I'd hated him almost from the start. So why was it, I wondered, that I felt so awful now?

I didn't bother returning to my room. Instead, I caught a crowded elevator a few floors down and rode it to the lobby with a dozen other hotel guests who looked a lot happier than I was.

Still, I was glad to be lost in a crowd – alone, anonymous, where I could totally forget Zane Bennington, if even only for a few hours.

But in the end, I couldn't even do that, thanks to *more* bad timing.

CHAPTER 41

I'd almost reached the hotel's main doors when I heard a vaguely familiar male voice calling out my name. I turned and spotted Teddy, of all people, heading toward me in the crowded lobby.

Damn it.

I wasn't happy to see him. Already, I'd had more than enough of his attitude, and I was in no mood to make small talk with a guy who loathed me.

Still, I couldn't exactly duck and run. So reluctantly, I waited for him to catch up.

When he reached my side, he asked, "Heading out?"

I glanced toward the exit. If only I'd been two minutes earlier, I'd *already* be out. "Yes, actually."

Teddy paused and studied my face. "Is something wrong?"

I *so* didn't want to talk about it. "No. Everything's fine."

He lowered his voice. "Are you sure?"

No. I wasn't. And I was feeling less fine with every passing moment.

I'd been absolutely determined to forget what had just happened with Zane. And now, with just a few poorly timed questions from his cousin, I was starting to feel all those emotions bubbling up to the surface – the embarrassment, the humiliation, and a whole slew of other feelings that I couldn't quite decipher. But I did know that none of them were positive.

Still, I managed to say, "I'm sure."

He eyed me with obvious concern. "You're not fine. It's written all over your face."

I looked away. As if *he* cared.

I'd met the guy only a few times, and each time, he'd acted like I was some kind of degenerate. I glanced toward the exit. "Seriously, I really need to go."

His voice softened. "Hey, I'm sorry, okay? I'm just concerned, that's all." He gave me a hopeful smile. "Is there anything I can do to help?"

I blinked long and hard. *Shit*. Probably, I should've ducked into my hotel room for a shower or whatever – anything to pull myself together.

I said, "It's just been one of those days. That's all."

"You wanna get something to eat?" His tone brightened. "Dinner, maybe a couple of drinks? That always helps, right?"

I stared at the guy. "Look, don't take this the wrong way. But why would you care?"

He drew back. "Why wouldn't I?"

I was too irritated to be tactful. "Gee, I don't know. Because you think I'm a terrible person?"

"I do not." He was frowning now. "What gave you that idea?"

"Oh, please. You think I'm a ho-bag."

His eyebrows furrowed. "A ho-bag?"

I sighed. "You know, the kind of girl who jumps in the sack with anyone who asks."

He smiled. "Actually, that's one reason I want to take you to dinner."

My jaw dropped. I almost wanted to slap him. "Forget it."

Pig.

His smile vanished. "I wasn't talking about *that*."

"Oh yeah?" I crossed my arms. "Then what were you talking about?"

"I just mean, I owe you an apology."

I vaguely recalled him apologizing on the plane – only to insult me all over again. I didn't want another apology. I just wanted to be on my way. Stiffly, I told him, "Don't worry about it."

"Easy for *you* to say. I've been beating myself up for days." He gave a rueful laugh. "Believe it or not, I'm usually a pretty nice guy."

This, I could actually believe. But it didn't change a thing. In truth, he was probably *too* nice, considering his poor judge of character. He had, after all, believed Paisley over me – and picked a girlfriend who cheated on him – *damn it* – with Zane.

I wanted to scream. Lately, everything led to Zane. Every topic. Every thought. Cripes. I was even standing in *his* building.

Suddenly, I had a nearly uncontrollable urge to bolt for the exit and leave Teddy standing there to think whatever he wanted.

But I didn't. And why?

Because when Teddy mentioned that he had a few other things to tell me – mostly about Zane – I'd been unable to resist.

So there I was, fifteen minutes later, at a different restaurant with a different guy. And what he told me over the next hour made me feel more confused than ever.

CHAPTER 42

"So basically," Teddy concluded, "he stole everything."

I sat in stunned silence. According to what Teddy had just told me, this included the company, the houses, the cars, and everything else associated with the estate.

We were tucked deep into a little pizzeria joint a few blocks away from the hotel. Teddy had suggested eating someplace a lot nicer than this, but I'd had more than enough fanciness for one night.

It didn't matter, anyway. After everything I'd just heard, even the small slice of cheese pizza wasn't sitting quite right.

When I finally found my voice, I said, "You can't know that for sure."

"The hell I can't," Teddy said. "There were signs. I just regret I didn't see them sooner."

"What kind of signs?"

"Like with the company," he said. "A couple of years ago, there were problems with creditors. *Big* problems. With suppliers, too."

I knew what he was referring to. During that timeframe, there'd been talk of bankruptcy, but nothing had ever come of it.

I said, "But it all got worked out, right?"

"Sure," Teddy said, "but we don't know how. That whole time, the old man – meaning Zane's grandfather – was acting like a different person."

"How so?" I asked.

"Normally, he was the nicest guy you'd ever meet." A sad smile crossed Teddy's features. "He never had a bad thing to say to anyone."

Listening, I couldn't help but compare the grandfather to his only grandson. Unlike the "old man," Zane was a holy terror.

Teddy continued. "And he got reclusive, stopped taking our calls. Every time we tried to reach out, he gave us the brush-off."

"When you say 'we,' who do you mean?"

"Well, you heard about Cedric and Randall, right?"

I shook my head. "Sorry, but—"

"Zane's uncles."

"Ohhhh…right." I tried to recall what I knew. The grandfather had three sons total. There was Zane's dad plus two older brothers, the ones who'd died late last year. I gave Teddy a sympathetic look. "That must've been rough, losing both of them so suddenly."

"Yeah, it was." He gave a sad chuckle. "Those guys were real characters."

Now, *this* I believed. Both brothers had been notorious playboys. Between the two of them, they had nearly a dozen ex-wives, a slew of scandals, and no kids whatsoever. "I bet you miss them, huh?"

"You want the truth?" Teddy said. "I didn't see them a lot, because they were always traveling. But I *do* know they were worried. We *all* were. My stepdad in particular."

I tried to think. "You mean Bob?"

Teddy looked surprised. "You know him?"

Belatedly, I recalled that Teddy had no idea I'd been eavesdropping from inside the van. Out of sheer embarrassment, I wanted to keep it that way. Trying to be vague, I said, "I know that he used to work for Zane's grandfather, right?"

Teddy nodded. "Right. Until maybe a year ago."

"What happened then?" I asked.

"All of a sudden, he's forced into early retirement."

"By the grandfather?"

"Supposedly," Teddy said. "But even then, I knew Zane was behind it."

"What makes you say that?"

"Because everything was fine until *he* showed up."

I wasn't following. "What do you mean by showed up?"

"Lemme back up," Teddy said. "You've heard that Zane grew up in

Northern Michigan, right?"

I nodded. "Right."

"Well," Teddy continued, "it used to be, we never saw him, except maybe a couple times a year. But then, all of a sudden, around a year ago, we're seeing him all the time – hanging around the house, almost like he owns the place."

Funny, he did own the place. Now, anyway. Looking to confirm that I was thinking of the right house, I said, "You're talking about the estate, right? Where Zane's living now?"

Teddy nodded. "Yeah. The grandfather's place. And you wanna know what I think?"

"What?"

Teddy leaned forward across the table. "I think he moved himself in and never moved out."

"But how would you even know?" I asked.

"Like I said, Bob was worried, so he was keeping an eye out."

Based on what I knew of that neighborhood, this made a lot of sense. "You mean from the house on Longwood? The one that Zane, um…" How to put this? "…took back?"

Teddy didn't look happy to be reminded. "So you know about that, too?"

I nodded. "Yeah, I heard." *Literally*.

"Oh yeah, that was a real treat," Teddy said. "And you know who took it *really* hard?"

"Who?" I asked.

"Bob's daughter."

I recalled the young woman who'd been sobbing out on the front lawn. "Oh?"

Teddy gave another nod. "She loved that place, especially the pool, cried her eyes out when Bob told her about the move."

So the woman *was* Bob's daughter? At the time, I hadn't been so sure, but it did make sense.

At something in my expression, Teddy said, "You look surprised."

I *was* surprised, but I'd never tell him why. After all, who wanted to hear that their stepsister might've been mistaken for a live-in girlfriend? I said, "Well, it *is* a lot to take in."

"I know. But there's a reason I'm telling you."

Cautiously, I said, "which is…?"

"I see the way he looks at you."

I blinked. "What?"

"You know what I mean."

"No. I don't." I wasn't even lying. Oh sure, there *had* been a few moments when I might've wondered, but now, I saw things clearly for what they were.

Probably, Zane was *always* giving off that vibe.

In hindsight, Maven had probably saved me from a huge mistake, because for a moment there, I'd been almost ready to believe that there was more to Zane than I originally thought.

How stupid was *that*?

When Teddy said nothing in response, I added, "Honest. There's nothing between us."

He gave me a look. It was the same look he'd given me after I'd insisted that there was nothing between me and the professor.

I hated that look. "I'm not lying," I told him.

Right on cue, he gave me the same look *again*. "If you say so."

So much for his earlier apology.

I gave him a look right back. "I *do* say so."

"Hey, I'm trying to do you a favor."

Some favor. "Thanks. I guess."

He lowered his voice. "And, as long as we're talking, I'd like your help."

I felt my eyes narrow. "Doing what?"

"Just keep an eye out. That's all I ask."

He could ask all he wanted, but I wasn't going to spy for him. And besides, his timing sucked. I said, "Aren't you forgetting something?"

"What?"

"What I told you during the walk over." At his perplexed look, I added, "That my job's probably gone. You do remember that, right?"

"Of course I remember. But you never said why."

"Yeah, because you never asked."

At this, he had the good grace to look chagrinned for like two whole seconds before mumbling, "Well, maybe I didn't want to pry."

Or maybe, he just didn't want to bother.

I don't even know why I was irritated.

I wouldn't have given him the details, anyway. On top of that humiliating scene with Maven, it was beyond embarrassing that I'd told my boss to fuck off.

But it wasn't only embarrassment that was keeping me from sharing all the dirty details. I didn't trust Teddy *or* his intentions. And besides, I wasn't one to gossip.

And yet, in spite of that lofty sentiment, I wasn't blind to the fact that I'd just spent an hour listening to someone I barely knew divulge family secrets that were none of my business.

Part of me actually felt ashamed.

Across from me, Teddy was saying, "Yeah, but if you're still around, keep an eye out. That's all I'm asking."

His concern was oh-so-touching. It only confirmed what I'd already begun to suspect – that this dinner had been merely an excuse to run Zane into the ground *and* recruit me as a potential spy.

Idiot.

Once again, I was referring to myself.

I stood. "I really need to go."

Teddy frowned. "So soon?"

If I'd been smart, I would've left an hour ago – or better yet, declined his invitation entirely. Now, I was just eager to leave.

I wasn't thrilled when he insisted on walking me back to the hotel, supposedly for my own safety.

I was even *less* thrilled when he spent the first half of the walk theorizing that Zane had strong-armed the grandfather into rewriting the will, and the second half hinting that Zane might've had his uncles killed so he wouldn't have to share the inheritance.

Call me a sap, but I didn't believe either one of these things.

Was I being naïve? Maybe. But the way I saw it, Zane had plenty of bad qualities already without adding elder-abuse and killing to the list. Plus, when it came to both theories, I couldn't help but consider the source – Teddy, who seemed way too eager to believe all kinds of things that simply weren't true.

Who knows? Maybe I didn't trust any of them, including the uncles who, dead or not, didn't sound like particularly nice people.

By the time Teddy and I said goodbye at the hotel entrance, all I wanted was to crawl under the covers and forget the whole lot of them.

But I couldn't.

Why? Because when I was finally approaching my own hotel room, who did I see waiting for me?

Zane Bennington.

CHAPTER 43

I felt sweaty and worn out – partly from the walk and partly because I was more confused than ever.

Seeing Zane standing there didn't help.

And of course, *he* didn't look sweaty or worn out. No. Not him. He looked cool and determined, even as he stood, with arms crossed, facing the door to my hotel room.

Where his room was, I had no idea, but it didn't take a genius to know that it was surely located a lot higher up than mine.

In fact, come to think of it, he had a penthouse in New York. Was it right here? In this hotel?

Probably.

Well, goodie for him.

I'd just rounded the corner, and so far, he hadn't spotted me – or so I thought, until he turned his head slowly in my direction. At something in his expression, I felt myself swallow.

He looked pissed off, and not just a little.

But so what?

I was pissed off, too, and not because of anything I'd heard during my dinner with Teddy. Rather, it was the other dinner – the one I *didn't* get to eat – that was fueling my current hostility.

To think, I'd been taken to the top of the world, charmed for like ten whole minutes, and then dismissed like some kind of temporary seat-warmer.

In the back of my mind, I couldn't help but wonder how much worse I'd be feeling now – or heaven forbid, tomorrow morning – if

I'd been stupid enough to succumb to Zane's shallow charms.

I almost scoffed out loud. I didn't need to wonder. If I truly wanted to know, I could ask Tiffany or a dozen other girls, including the one he'd ditched in Kalamazoo.

The jerk.

Almost before I knew it, I was marching forward even as he strode toward me, meeting me more than halfway. I stopped within slapping distance and glared up at him to ask, "What are you doing here?"

"Waiting."

"For what?"

"You," he said. "Now, tell me something."

I almost laughed out loud. Oh, there were plenty of things I could tell him. But none of them were fit for public consumption. So instead, I crossed my arms and said, "What?"

"Your job – did you quit?"

What the hell?

I practically snorted in disbelief. "So *that's* why you're here?" I tried for another laugh. "Well, I guess that rules out apology-number-five."

"Just answer the question."

I didn't feel like doing anything he asked. So instead, I gave him a taste of his own medicine. Lowering my voice to match his, I mimicked, "My job – am I fired?"

He looked anything but amused. "Is that a serious question?"

Was it? I honestly didn't know.

When I said nothing in response, he gave me a hard look. "And how was Teddy?"

I froze. "What?"

"Over dinner, did he give you a good earful?"

He *had*, in fact. But that wasn't the point. I said, "How'd you know?"

"You're in *my* hotel."

"So?"

"So if I'm looking for you, it's not hard to find out when you left…" His jaw clenched. "…*or* with whom."

In spite of everything, I just had to ask, "Did you seriously just say 'whom'?"

"I know plenty of words, and they're not *all* four letters."

I paused. "But wait, that *is* a four-letter word."

His eyebrows furrowed. "What?"

"Whom," I said. "It has four letters."

"Forget the letters. Now, tell me something."

"What?"

"Do you believe everything you hear?"

Of all the questions, this was one I hadn't been anticipating. But it didn't matter. I already knew what I thought.

Sure, it would be incredibly easy to believe the worst of Zane "the Prick" Bennington. He was, after all, the most impossible person I'd ever met. But when it came to Teddy's claims, I had more than a few doubts.

I just didn't know how to explain it. After all, I didn't want to cause any more friction between the two cousins.

I was still trying to come up with a diplomatic response when Zane moved a fraction closer and said, "Or did he want something else?"

I stared up at him. "Like what?"

In a tight voice, he said, "You know what."

Oh. That. My face grew uncomfortably warm. "Even if he did, why would you care?"

Something about his look made me want to step back, or maybe step forward. Stupidly, I couldn't decide which. He looked raw and dangerous, and maybe even on the verge of losing it.

But that wasn't going to happen. I knew this, because Zane *never* lost it. Over the last few months, I'd seen this dynamic firsthand.

No, I reminded myself, what *he* did was make other people lose it. In fact, I felt dangerously close to losing it now.

And he *still* hadn't answered my question. It almost made me wonder. If Teddy was interested, *would* Zane care? I stiffened. If so, he had no right.

Again, he moved closer. "What do *you* think?"

I lifted my chin. "I think you had dinner plans of your own."

"You're right. I did. And they went to shit. So, let me ask you again." Speaking more slowly and deliberately, he said, "Did he want something else?"

Yes. He did. He wanted me to spy on Zane. Oh sure, he hadn't put it quite that way, but I'd received the message loud and clear.

Still, I knew what Zane really wanted to know, and I wasn't one to play games. I said, "Well, he didn't want to sleep with me if that's what you're getting at."

Zane studied my face, as if he wasn't so sure. Finally, after a long, tense moment, he said, "Good to know."

"Oh yeah? Why's that?"

"Because he's not the guy for you."

Like I needed Zane to tell me *that*. But I was in no mood to be agreeable. "And why not?"

"Because he's a pussy."

I might've laughed if I weren't so angry. But I *was* angry. And on top of that, I was getting more confused with every passing minute.

Why were we discussing Teddy at all? I'd joined the guy for a slice of pizza. *Big deal.* In contrast, Zane had dined in luxury with someone who made *me* feel like chopped liver.

Stupidly, I couldn't help but wonder if she'd eaten my dinner – or whatever it was that Zane had ordered. I looked away and tried not to think about it.

Zane's voice, softer now, reclaimed my attention. "I'm not gonna fire you."

I turned to look at him. "And why not?"

"Does it matter?"

"Of course it matters," I said. "For all I know, you just want to torment me."

His eyebrows lifted. "Torment you."

"Yes. Torment me," I repeated. "Speaking of which, I've just gotta ask…" I stared straight into his eyes. "Why'd you drag me to dinner in the first place?"

He didn't look away. "Because I wanted to."

"Why? To grill me about Tiffany?"

"Fuck Tiffany."

I gave a bitter laugh. "Did you?"

His gaze darkened. "Did I what?"

Once again, heat rushed to my face. I heard myself mumble, "Fuck Tiffany."

"No."

It was my turn to study *his* face. Was he lying? I didn't think so, but could I really be sure? And why did it matter, anyway?

Zane said, "You're forgetting she's engaged."

I wasn't forgetting anything. From what I'd seen so far, this wasn't always a deal-breaker. I gave a loose shrug but said nothing in reply.

"And," Zane added, "she's not my type."

I wasn't sure I believed *that* either. As much as I hated to dwell on it, Tiffany was undeniably beautiful. Probably, she *could* be a model if she weren't so busy seeking a career as a trophy wife.

I wasn't sure why, but it seemed very important to know the whole story. "So, you *didn't* meet up at a hotel a couple months ago?"

"No." But then, he paused, as if recollecting something long-forgotten. "Wait. You mean *my* hotel?"

"Apparently."

"Then the answer's yes."

Shit. The answer stung, although for the life of me, I couldn't figure out why. After all, I'd known this for weeks, months even. So why did it hurt, *now?*

Zane continued. "Yeah, I met her, but not in a room, if that's what you were told."

I tried to remember. Tiffany hadn't said it outright, but her implication had been pretty clear. I asked, "So, where *did* you meet?"

"In my office. *With* the senator."

Hearing this, I was stupidly pleased. "Really?"

Zane nodded. "And you wanna know what they wanted?"

"What?"

"Money for his campaign."

Now, I was even more curious. "Did you give it to him?"

"Hell no. The guy's an asshole."

Since Zane was an expert in that department, I didn't bother arguing. "So you declined on what? Some sort of moral grounds?"

"No. I declined, because he's a shitstorm waiting to happen. It would be a piss-poor investment, don't you think?"

I didn't know what to think. But it gave me a pretty good idea why Tiffany and the senator were here at all. Probably, he was still trolling for money.

And as far as Tiffany? Well, I knew what she was trolling for. And to my extreme annoyance, I discovered that I didn't like it.

When I said nothing in response, Zane said, "Satisfied?"

Was I? I'd be lying if I didn't admit that I felt at least a little better, but it didn't change anything. Not really.

And in truth, I couldn't help but wonder why I'd asked about Tiffany at all. After all, she wasn't the one who'd eaten my proverbial dinner.

And yet, in a crazy, twisted way, it did reinforce what I'd known all along. There were way too many women in Zane's life. If *I* couldn't keep track, how on Earth could he?

I still hadn't answered his question. Was I satisfied? No. But he had answered all of *my* questions, and he'd been a pretty good sport about it too.

Finally, I managed to say, "I guess so."

"Good. Now it's your turn to answer."

"Answer what?"

"My question. Did you quit?"

It was a simple question. But for the life of me, I couldn't come up with a simple answer. My own crazy mixed-up feelings aside, I had no idea how I'd get home if I decided to cut and run.

Oh sure, I could book a flight, but how much would *that* cost? If I were smart, I'd save my pennies, especially if I was soon to be unemployed.

When I made no response, Zane looked away and muttered, "Fucking Teddy."

"Wait, what does he have to do with this?"

Zane returned to his gaze to mine. "Lemme ask you something. Who do you think sent Maven?"

"No one."

He gave me a look. "You sure about that?"

"Well, you two obviously had dinner plans."

"Which I canceled."

"Oh sure," I said. "Last-minute."

"Wrong," he said. "Last *night*."

That made me pause. "What?"

"Last night," he repeated. "That's when I canceled."

"So then why'd she show up like that?"

His jaw tightened. "Guess."

I tried to put myself in Maven's shoes. Her reason for showing up was pretty obvious. Zane was rich, famous, and unbearably hot.

But I didn't say it. It was shallow and stupid, especially because Zane would surely assume that I was speaking for myself, and not Maven the Terrible.

I said, "I don't feel like guessing."

Zane looked away and was quiet for a long moment. Under his breath, he said, "Fuck."

On this, I could agree. "Yeah. No kidding."

He looked back to me and said, "You're not fired. And you can't quit. So forget it."

"Wait, why can't I quit?"

"Because I said so."

Talk about bossy. I reminded him, "I don't need your permission to quit."

"You do if you want a good reference."

My mouth fell open. "What are you saying?"

"You're smart. You'll figure it out."

"You wouldn't seriously sabotage me?"

"Wouldn't I?"

But I knew the answer to *that* question. He totally would. After all, I'd seen firsthand how he dealt with people who gave him grief.

I made a scoffing sound. "And how long do you expect *that* to work?"

"What to work?"

"Threats."

His expression softened. "I'm not threatening you."

"Are you sure? Because it sure sounded like it."

"If I were threatening you, you'd know it. Now, tell me."

"Tell you what?"

"Tomorrow. You're still gonna be here, right?"

I shrugged. "Honestly, I don't know."

"I'll take that as a yes."

Probably, I was lucky. After all, if I were going to quit, I'd be ten times smarter to do it *after* we returned back home. I just prayed that when that day came, I'd have a clearer idea of what was going on.

In the end, I didn't bother arguing. Instead, I looked toward the door to my hotel room. "Fine. Whatever. Now, if you'll excuse me, I've got plans."

"Yeah?" He frowned. "With who?"

Myself, that's who. But employer or not, that was none of his business, so all I said was, "No one you know."

It wasn't even a lie. The way I saw it, Zane didn't know me at all. And I sure as heck didn't know him. But I *did* know one thing. He wasn't thrilled with my answer. It was written all over his face.

Yeah? Well, so what?

Deliberately, I stepped around him and tried not take any satisfaction from the fact that nearly a minute later, he was still standing in the same spot, watching me as I opened my hotel room door and slipped inside without so much as a wave.

When I poked my head out five minutes later, he was gone.

Good.

CHAPTER 44

By unspoken agreement, we spent the next couple of days pretending that nothing had happened. As usual, I accompanied him to all of his media interviews, where things went surprisingly okay – at least while the cameras were rolling.

On the rare occasions we were alone, he was even colder than usual, which was fine by me – or at least, that's what I kept telling myself, even as he haunted my thoughts like the nightmare he was.

By midnight on the second night, I was so distracted that I found myself heading toward the hotel bar, looking for a nightcap or, cripes, even a distraction – anything to push Zane Bennington out of my thoughts.

I never did get the nightcap, but I *did* find one heck of a distraction in the form of Tiffany and the senator, who were arguing near the bar's entrance.

I stopped several paces away and tried not to stare as Tiffany practically yelled, "Hey, it was *your* idea!"

The senator was red-faced and disheveled, with his tie askew and his bald head shining with perspiration. He said, "I wanted you to get close to him. Not hump him in the damn elevator!"

Woah.

Him? Meaning Zane?

That was *my* guess.

I only prayed I was wrong. My own conflicted feelings aside, I was tired of explaining away Zane's bad behavior. Just within the past two days, I'd received nearly a dozen inquiries from reporters wanting to know why Zane and Maven had gotten into a screaming match in the Skyroom restaurant.

My answer? "No comment."

Normally, I used that phrase when I knew the information, but for whatever reason, couldn't reveal it. This time, however, I truly didn't know.

Obviously, the so-called screaming match had occurred sometime after I'd stormed off, leaving the two of them to enjoy each other's dubious company.

Other than that, I knew nothing. Why? Because Zane wasn't talking, and I wasn't asking.

But I *did* know one thing. Zane wasn't the screaming type, which led me to believe that Maven had been the one who lost her temper.

Good.

If nothing else, it was heartening to know that I wasn't the only one who'd had a crappy time that night.

Yes, I *was* that petty.

In front of me, Tiffany and the senator were still arguing, even as a small crowd began to form around them. Tiffany thrust out her chest and said, "Hey, I can't help it if men find me attractive."

The senator was looking a little unsteady, even as he told her, "You were half-naked for Christ's stake."

"I was not," she insisted. "It was a wardrobe malfunction, just like I said."

Oh, brother. This again?

It was the same excuse she'd used at Zane's party, when they'd been caught in the alcove, doing who-knows-what.

The senator said, "Wardrobe malfunction, my ass."

In that particular moment, I felt a strange sense of kinship with the guy. The statement was, oddly enough, the exact same thing *I* always thought when hearing that ridiculous excuse.

Tiffany said, "Yeah? Well, your ass is covered in fur, so I'll thank you not to mention it."

The senator looked ready to pop. "What?"

"I'm just saying, it's hairy. You ever think of waxing it?"

As the senator sputtered out some incoherent reply, I glanced around. It was a weekday night, which meant that the place wasn't nearly as crowded as it could've been.

This was good for the lovebirds, but bad for me, because the longer I stood here, the more conspicuous I felt, even in my jeans and dark long-sleeved shirt.

I *so* didn't want to get involved. And yet, I *did* want that drink. I gazed past them toward the bar. Maybe if I snuck off to the side, they wouldn't notice me?

No such luck.

I was just sidling past them when Tiffany said, "Jane knows. She'll tell you."

I froze in mid-step. Reluctantly, I turned to look. "Huh?"

Tiffany said, "A hairy ass. Hot or not?"

Oh, God. I looked toward the bar and wondered if they sold wine by the bottle, because I was pretty sure I'd be needing more than one glass.

Tiffany urged, "Go on. Tell him."

I looked to the senator and felt myself frown. The guy wasn't just unsteady. He looked almost ready to throw up. But why? Because he'd had too much to drink? Or because the topic of conversation was just that nauseating?

Tiffany gave me a look of impatience. "Well?"

I glanced around. "Uh, no comment?"

Tiffany beamed like I'd just given her the best participation trophy ever. She turned to the senator and said, "See! She totally agrees."

I made a sound of frustration. "That's not what I said."

But already, they'd moved on, yelling back and forth about her wardrobe allowance, even as the crowd around them grew.

Wanting no part of it, I hurried to the bar and ordered the first thing that came to mind. Surprisingly, it wasn't wine. It was a mimosa of all things.

A few paces away, the argument ended with Tiffany ripping off her engagement ring and hurling it onto the floor. I couldn't help but wince, even as she turned and flounced away, leaving the senator staring, unsteadily, after her.

I hadn't voted for the guy, but I still felt bad for him. While waiting for my drink, I watched as the crowd drifted away, leaving him standing alone, looking at the fallen ring.

He made no move to pick it up, and for some reason, that made the scene even more pathetic.

Unable to stop myself, I left the bar and returned to where he was standing. Silently, I picked up the ring and held it out in his direction.

But he didn't take it. Instead, he staggered forward, straight into my arms. He was a big guy – a pro football player back in the day, and I nearly fell backward under the weight of him.

He pulled back to mumble, "Sorry, guess I had one too many." He gave me a sad smile. "Walk me to the elevator?"

I glanced toward the bar, where my mimosa was now waiting on the counter. And then, I glanced toward the nearest bank of elevators.

Selfishly, I wanted to say no. But he looked so darned pathetic that I didn't have the heart. So I gave him a nod, and let him take my arm as we moved awkwardly in that direction.

As we walked, he muttered, "Fucking Zane Bennington."

My steps faltered, and I gave him a sideways glance. I wasn't even sure what he meant. Was it a description of what he thought Tiffany had done? Or was it merely a general observation on Zane himself? If that one was the case, I could definitely relate.

The senator slurred, "He's the reason we're here, you know."

This wasn't a surprise. And yet, part of me wanted to ask for details.

But I didn't. Gossiping aside, I hadn't sunk so low that I'd take advantage of a drunk guy.

Turns out, I was way too scrupulous, because less than ten minutes later, it was *him*, trying to take advantage of *me*.

CHAPTER 45

When we reached the elevators, he kept on going, like a sleepwalker in his jammies. I stopped and gave his arm a gentle tug. "Woah there. I think you missed your stop."

He turned to look. "Oh. Yeah. Sorry 'bout that."

And then, he turned in the *opposite* direction, as if preparing to head back to the bar – or into traffic for all I knew.

With a sigh, I gripped his arm and turned him toward the nearest elevator, which thankfully was already open. When he made no move, I gripped his elbow and practically dragged him into the elevator myself.

I asked, "What floor?"

He gave me a blank look. "Uh-huh."

Damn it. Speaking more slowly now, I said, "What floor are you staying on?"

His brow furrowed. "Fourteen-ninety-nine." He hesitated. "Or ninety-eight."

Obviously, he was giving me a room number, not the floor. But it was easy enough to figure out. I hit the button for the fourteenth floor and prayed for the best.

As the elevator carried us upward, he fumbled inside his jacket and pulled out the card key to his room. It slipped from his fingers onto the elevator floor. He stared, silently, down at the thing, as if he couldn't figure out where it had come from.

With a sigh, I reached down and plucked it up. But when I held it out in front of him, he made no move to take it. Instead, he only frowned as he slurred, "I hate those things. Used to be, you'd get a real key."

That was before my time, but I nodded anyway and held it out a little closer. And yet, he still made no move to take it. His bottom lip gave a quiver as he said, "Normally, Tiffany does that."

"Does what?" I asked.

"The card key thing."

Oh, for crying out loud. It wasn't that difficult. And if he didn't know how to use it, why was he carrying the card key at all?

I said, "Well, she's not here, so…"

Looking more unsteady than ever, he muttered, "Fucking Zane Bennington."

"I know," I said. "You told me."

He brightened. "I did?"

"Yeah. Downstairs."

"Oh. Okay."

He still hadn't taken the card, which was probably for the best. When the elevator doors opened onto the fourteenth floor, I grabbed his hand and practically dragged him out of the elevator and then down the hall, watching room numbers as I went.

When we reached room 1499, I asked, "Is this the one?"

When he replied with an unsteady nod, I swiped the card key into the slot and heard the telltale click of the lock disengaging. I gave the door a tentative push and breathed a sigh of relief when it actually opened.

Behind me, the senator slurred, "You're really nice."

I turned to look. "Uh, thanks."

"Not like *him*." He gave a snort of derision. "Or *her*."

He didn't say who he was talking about, but it was easy to guess – Zane and Tiffany, who'd been doing who-knows-what in some elevator.

As we stood there, I half-expected Tiffany to appear in the doorway at any moment. After all, this must be her room, too.

I had to wonder, if they didn't make up, which one of them would be sent packing?

I didn't plan on sticking around long enough to find out. So I wished the senator a good night and made a move to leave, only to have him envelope me in a giant bear hug. "You're really nice," he repeated.

I said the same thing I said the first time. "Uh, thanks."

"Smell nice, too."

"Uh, okay."

I made a move to pull back, but the senator only held on tighter. "I like your hair." He gave it a noisy sniff and mumbled, "Smells good, too."

I gave a nervous laugh. "Thanks, but I'd better get going."

As I spoke, it took me a moment to realize his hands were creeping lower. Almost before I knew what was happening, he'd cupped a cheek in each hand and gave them a firm squeeze.

I yanked myself backward just as I felt both of his thumbs going in for the crack.

I glared up at him. "What the hell are you doing?"

He looked to his room. "You wanna go inside?"

What the hell?

I gave a bark of laughter. "No."

He mumbled, "My ass isn't *that* hairy." He perked up. "If you want, you could shave it."

I didn't know whether to laugh or slap him. The only upside was that I highly doubted he'd remember any of this tomorrow.

I gave a shudder. If only I could say the same for myself.

I dodged past him and scurried down the hall, not looking back, even as he hollered out, "Come back, you fucking tease!"

At that particular moment, he sounded almost sober, and I couldn't help but wonder if the whole drunk-as-a-skunk thing had been only an act to get me up here.

But no. It couldn't be. After all, he'd been staggering when talking to Tiffany, too.

Hadn't he?

I decided not to dwell on it, and just thanked my lucky stars that I hadn't been even more foolish.

I made a mental note to avoid him like the plague in the future. And I might've managed it, too, if only it weren't for what happened the very next morning.

CHAPTER 46

Early the next morning, I was rushing around my hotel room when the telephone rang – not my cell phone, but rather the phone on the night stand.

I gave it a worried glance.

In five minutes, I was supposed to be meeting Zane in the lobby, where we'd be catching his limo to his next scheduled interview.

Still, vowing to make it quick, I answered the phone with a breathless, "Hello?"

It was Carla, the receptionist from the main office, who sounded a little breathless herself. "I'm terribly sorry to ask, but…" She hesitated. "Is Mister Bennington there?"

I felt my eyebrows furrow. "You don't mean in my hotel room?"

"I wouldn't even ask, but it's an emergency." She lowered her voice to just a whisper. "Everyone knows, so there's really no need to hide it."

I froze. "Everyone knows what?"

"That you two are…you know."

"No," I said. "I don't."

She sighed. "Oh great. Am I in trouble now?"

"Why would you be in trouble?"

"I don't know," she said. "For not pretending?"

"Pretending what?"

"Not to know."

I made a sound of frustration. "Not to know what?"

After a long moment, she whispered, "That you're his…" Again, she hesitated.

"His what?"

And then, in a low whisper, she dropped the hammer. "Mistress."

I sank to a sitting position on the bed. The term, as old-fashioned as it was, felt like a slap to the face, especially because Zane and I were barely on speaking terms. I said, "Excuse me?"

"Oh come on," she whispered. "You're the only one who pretends."

Where on Earth had *this* come from? "I hate to tell you this, but I have no idea what you're talking about."

She was still whispering. "Listen, you seem like a really nice person, and I'm just hoping I don't get in trouble for this, but you should probably know that he's already admitted it."

If I weren't already sitting, this would've knocked me on my ass for sure. "He has? When?"

"I dunno…Maybe a month after you were hired?"

That asshole. Trying not to lose it, I said, "And just *who* did he 'admit' this to?"

"To that bedding supplier from Cincinnati."

"Boris Feldman?"

"I think so."

"So, let me get this straight," I said. "Zane Bennington – our boss – told Boris Feldman that I was his *mistress*? Am I understanding that right?"

Sounding more nervous than ever, she whispered, "Oh, no. You're angry, aren't you?"

Yes.

I was.

But not at her.

On the phone, Carla muttered, "I knew I should've kept my big mouth shut."

By now, I hardly knew what to think. But I *did* know that none of this was Carla's fault. Absently, I murmured, "No. It's fine."

"Are you sure?"

"Uh, yeah." I paused. "Wait a minute. Was *that* why you were so nervous when that guy showed up with those flowers?"

"Well, wouldn't *you* be nervous?" she whispered. "I mean, I know Mister Bennington sees other people, but…" Again, her words trailed off.

"But *I* don't?"

How humiliating was this? I could only imagine what everyone thought of me. Not only was I the ho-bag sleeping with my boss, but I was so pathetic that I let *him* run around like some kind of horn-dog while I waited at his beck and call.

Carla sighed. "Well, I've never *seen* you with anyone else, except the guy with the flowers. And you seemed pretty eager to get rid of him, so I just figured…" She paused. "You know what? This is really none of my business."

All of this was giving me a headache. I reached up to rub my temples. By now, I hardly knew what to say. Somehow, I managed to mumble, "No. It's fine. I'm glad you said something."

"Oh, sure," she whispered, "*you're* glad, but what's gonna happen when Mister Bennington finds out?"

"Nothing's gonna happen. It's fine."

"If you say so." Carla said, sounding far from convinced. "And I'm sorry to push the issue, but I've gotta know. Is he around? Like, maybe in the shower or something?"

Oh, good grief.

Through gritted teeth, I said, "Did you try *his* room?"

"Sure, but—" Abruptly, she stopped. "Never mind."

"But what?" I asked.

After a long pause, she said, "But someone named Tiffany answered. She said he'd been gone for hours."

I felt my hand tighten around the phone. "Tiffany? As in the senator's fiancée?"

"I'm not sure. She didn't say." Carla paused. "So is he there?"

It seemed like a ridiculous question. After all, if Zane Bennington were here in my room, I certainly wouldn't be asking all of these stupid questions. And why? Because I'd be too busy throttling him.

"He's not here," I told her. "And in fact, he's never here."

"Oh." She hesitated. "Because the penthouse is that much nicer?"

"No," I said with all the patience I could muster. "Because I'm not sleeping with him. I don't even like him."

That made her pause. "Really?"

"Yes. Really." In the back of my mind, I started listing the reasons.

Because he's a total prick.

Because he lied about me.

Because he was awful in all the ways that counted.

And… Before I could continue with my mental list, a thud just outside my hotel room made me pause. This was quickly followed by a yelp, and then a scream. I looked toward the sound and felt my brow wrinkle in confusion. The screamer sounded like a guy.

Well, that was odd.

Into the phone, I said, "Sorry, but I've gotta go."

"But what about Mister Bennington?"

Fuck Mister Bennington. But I didn't say it, because none of this was Carla's fault. So instead, I promised to keep an eye out and quickly hung up before dashing to the door to see what on Earth was going on.

I poked my head out of the doorway and looked down the long corridor, just in time to see Zane Bennington – shirtless, no less – dragging the senator away by his ankle.

What the hell?

CHAPTER 47

My eyes widened, and I stifled a gasp. Why was he dragging the senator? And why on Earth wasn't he wearing a shirt?

Had he lost his freaking mind?

Unsure what else to do, I dashed out of my hotel room and scurried after them.

As for the senator, he was screaming like a girl. I could almost relate, because I felt like screaming, too.

All along, I'd known Zane was trouble. He was a prick. A liar. A total reprobate. And now, he was – I could hardly think of the word – a senator assaulter?

On both sides of the long, carpeted corridor, doors swung open as hotel guests leaned their heads out to gawk at the commotion. All things considered, I couldn't exactly blame them.

The senator was still screaming. "Help! Somebody!"

As I moved, I glanced down. I was still holding my little notebook, the one I used for my daily to-do list. If only I had time, I'd jot down a new top priority.

Kill Zane Bennington.

I called out after him, "What are you doing?"

The senator stopped screaming only long enough to holler back, "I'm being assaulted! What the fuck does it look like?"

Dumb-ass. I wasn't talking to him. I was talking to my future murder victim.

Yes. That would be Zane.

As they passed a random door on their left, a couple of teenage girls swiveled their heads to stare at the traveling spectacle.

They were still staring when I scrambled past their doorway. As I plowed forward, one of them called out after me, "Hey, was that–?"

"No comment!" I yelled, hoping to keep the publicity to a minimum.

Probably, too late for that.

Already, the other girl was finishing the question. "Zane Bennington? Oh, my God. I think it was."

Damn it.

Hustling away from the girls, I called out to Zane's receding back. "Where are you taking him?"

Zane didn't even pause. He just kept plowing forward, ignoring me *and* the guy twisting and screaming behind him.

By now, the friction had wreaked havoc with not only the senator's suit jacket, but with his dress-shirt too. The shirt came completely untucked and rode up his torso, revealing a stomach that was soft-looking and yes, pretty darn hairy.

The senator gave a particularly girlish scream. "Call security!"

I yelled, "Damn it, Zane! Will you *please* stop?"

After the events of the last couple of days, I wasn't even sure I'd be keeping my job, but I still couldn't afford to take any chances. If word of this got out, *I'd* be the one doing damage-control.

How on Earth would I explain *this*?

Maybe I should've felt bad for the senator. But I couldn't, not after what happened last night.

After ditching him at his doorway, I'd returned to the bar in desperate need of that mimosa – which of course, someone had snatched up while I'd been away.

I'd ordered a new one, and had almost finished it when the senator reappeared in the lobby looking surprisingly sober. He hadn't seen me sitting in the shadows of the bar, but I'd seen him, all right.

This led me to a pretty sad conclusion. The pig was, once again, on the prowl.

And now, even as I scurried down the hall, I shuddered with revulsion at the memory of his hot breath in my ear and meaty hands on my ass. And I *so* didn't want to think about his thumbs.

As I watched, Zane rounded the corner, still dragging the senator behind him. The way it looked, they were heading for the elevators – my steps faltered – or, *oh crap*, the stairwell.

I called out, "Don't you dare take the stairs!"

Whether Zane heard me or not, I had no idea.

A split second later, the screaming stopped, and I almost feared the worst. I rounded the corner just in time to see Zane yank the senator up by his jacket and shove him hard against the wall between the two nearest elevators.

Now that I'd actually caught up to them, I wasn't quite sure what to do. Silently, I edged forward, hoping to catch Zane's elbow and maybe ease him away from the senator.

And then, I reasoned, could murder Zane myself privately.

I was still moving forward when Zane finally spoke. In a voice filled with menace, he leaned closer to the senator and said, "If you *ever* touch her again, I'll break off those fucking fingers." His grip visibly tightened. "And then, I'll shove them down your fucking throat."

I froze. *What?*

Again, Zane shoved the senator against the wall. "Are we clear?"

I stood in stunned confusion. Who on Earth was he talking about?

He couldn't mean *me*.

No. Definitely not.

Probably, the senator had gotten grabby with someone else, like maybe an important guest or heaven forbid, Zane's latest squeeze, whoever she was *this* time.

My jaw clenched.

Tiffany?

Or someone else?

No. It couldn't be Tiffany, because the way it sounded, she'd been tucked away in Zane's penthouse doing who-knows-what with you-know-who.

Trying to make sense of it all, I studied Zane's face in profile. For as long as I'd known him, he'd been the epitome of control.

And yet, he didn't look in control now.

When the senator offered no coherent response, Zane gave him another shove and repeated his question, more slowly this time. "Are. We. Clear?"

The senator swallowed. "I, uh, what?"

More confused than ever, I stepped toward them.

Instantly, the senator's gaze snapped in my direction. He called out, "Jane! Go on! Tell him!"

My steps faltered, and I heard myself ask, "Tell him what?"

The senator gave me a pleading look. "Tell him that you liked it. You know, that it was voluntary."

My jaw dropped. *Huh?*

I gave a confused shake of my head. I *didn't* like it. But that wasn't the thing that had me reeling.

It was the implication of what he'd just said.

My gaze shifted from the senator to the guy holding him against the wall. As if feeling my gaze, Zane slowly turned to look. And when he did, I saw something new in his eyes – a possessive spark that caught me totally off guard.

My breath caught. *Oh, my God.* This *was* about me.

But why?

I mean, we were barely on speaking terms. And the way it sounded, he'd spent last night with another girl, the senator's fiancée, in fact.

In that instant, I almost felt bad for the senator – right up until he blurted out, "And seriously, *she* was coming onto *me*!"

I sputtered, "What?"

"Yeah," he said, turning desperate eyes on Zane. "It was all I could do to shove her away."

I glanced down at my notebook.

Item Number Two: Kill the senator.

Just as the thought crossed my mind, something horrible happened. I snickered.

Both guys turned to look.

My hand flew to my lips, and I looked from the senator to Zane. Nothing about this was funny. So why had I laughed? A nervous reflex? It had to be.

But for whatever reason, it seemed to break the spell. Already, the senator was reaching back to slap at the nearby elevator buttons, even as Zane continued to hold him tight against the wall.

I looked to the buttons. Both were now lit – the one with up arrow *and* the one with the down arrow. Probably, this was a good thing, because it doubled his odds of a quick escape.

As it turned out, luck was on the senator's side, because within mere seconds, the nearest elevator arrived with a ding.

Going down.

And not by way of the stairs.

Thank God.

Zane let go, and the senator practically dove into the crowded elevator. To no one in particular, he yelled, "For God's sake, hit the button!"

Someone did, and the doors slid shut, leaving just me and Zane – and, of course, a dozen other people who'd scrambled out of their rooms to witness the spectacle.

I looked around and tried to think of something useful to say. When nothing came to mind, I gave the crowd a nervous smile. "No comment?"

Of course, it was a stupid thing to say, because technically, no one had asked me anything.

They were all too busy staring at Zane.

From the looks on their faces, the females in particular, they liked what they saw. I pulled my gaze from the crowd and turned to see what I was missing.

And then, I felt myself swallow.

He stood a few feet away, facing me in all his shirtless glory. His muscles were deliciously defined, and his hair was tousled like he'd just had the sweetest sex in the world.

And then, there were his eyes, brooding and dangerous in a way that I'd never seen them. The cautious part of me wanted to back away, but I was way too mesmerized to go anywhere.

I simply couldn't. The sight of him was far too compelling.

His shoulders and pecs were perfectly cut and nearly bulging, whether from lingering tension or from the physical effort of dragging the senator down the hall.

Below *those* muscles, his abs formed a perfect six-pack, tight and lean against the waistband of his expensive slacks.

For some reason, I recalled the only other time he'd given me such a glimpse. On *that* day, I'd been standing on his doorstep, looking to chew him out for getting me fired. At the time, he'd been wearing a swimsuit and hoodie, unzipped far enough to hint at what was underneath.

Even then, I'd found it difficult to look away, in spite of the fact that I loathed him with all my being.

This posed a terrifying question. Did I still loathe him?

I knew I should, especially after what I'd just learned.

But it wasn't loathing that was making me stare.

It was something else. But what?

Lust?

No. Or at least, that wasn't all of it.

Even in my distracted state, I knew one thing for certain. It wasn't his glorious body, as stare-worthy as it was, that made my knees wobble and my breath hitch. It was the look in his eyes, dark and possessive, like a silent promise to destroy anything that tried to claim what was his.

Funny, I'd always known that about him. He never gave up anything, and he had a ruthless streak a mile long. But to have any of this apply to me, well, it was a concept that I couldn't seem to wrap my brain around.

Even as my thoughts swirled, I *still* couldn't look away.

But apparently, *he* could.

He pulled his gaze from mine and looked toward the crowd. His jaw tightened, and his gaze grew ice-cold. Was he embarrassed? He didn't look embarrassed.

But he *did* look pissed off.

With a muttered curse, he moved away from the elevator and strode straight toward me like a man on a mission. In those few short seconds, time stood still, and I held my breath, dying to see what he'd do next.

Take me into his arms?

Kiss me like there was no tomorrow?

Whisk me away to someplace private?

I waited.

For nothing.

Because *what* did Zane do? He kept on going, striding past me like I didn't even exist.

Wordlessly, I watched as he then moved past the crowd and disappeared around the nearby corner, heading back to wherever he'd come from.

I stared after him. What on Earth had just happened?

I had no idea.

But I intended to find out. ☐

CHAPTER 48

He'd barely disappeared when I felt my gaze narrow. *Not so fast, Zane Bennington.*

Determined to get some answers, I plunged after him. To my infinite frustration, the crowd followed along beside me, as if eager to see Act Two of this impromptu performance.

Without breaking my stride, I called out over my shoulder, "The show's over, okay? You should probably go back to your rooms."

Of course, no one did.

Like *that* was a surprise.

When I rounded the corner, I spotted Zane up ahead, striding purposefully down the hall. As I followed after him, I tried not to stare at his naked back and long legs, but it was embarrassingly difficult not to. Confused or not, I had to admit, his silhouette looked annoyingly fine, even as it grew smaller in the distance.

I wanted to yell for him to stop, but I didn't dare. After all, the last thing I needed now was an even bigger crowd.

From somewhere behind me, a female voice asked, "Are you his girlfriend?"

My steps faltered, and I glanced back to see who would ask such a ridiculous question.

It was one of the two teenagers from earlier. I didn't know which one of them had asked, but I *did* know the answer. "No. Definitely not."

Far from discouraged, they scampered up beside me. "Are you sure?" the first girl asked. "He looked *really* jealous."

"Yeah," the other one said. "I thought he was gonna kill that guy."

The first girl said, "Ugh, did you see that guy's stomach?"

The other one made a sound of disgust. "It wasn't a stomach. It was a freaking pelt."

Now, my steps *did* falter, but not because of anything they'd said. Rather, it was because, far ahead of us, Zane had stopped just outside the door to a hotel room.

It was *my* hotel room.

Now, I stopped moving entirely. I watched as he turned and opened a door. But it wasn't the one to *my* room. It was the door to the room directly across from mine.

I felt my eyebrows furrow. *Well, that was unexpected.*

Next to me, the first girl spoke again. "If you're not his girlfriend, what are you?"

Honestly, I had no idea. I was still staring down the hall. Absently, I mumbled, "Just his employee, that's all."

"No, I don't think so," she said.

"Yeah," the other one agreed. "You could totally tell he likes you."

"He doesn't *like* her," the first corrected. "I think he's loves her. You don't do that unless you're totally in love."

At this, I might've laughed out loud if I weren't so distracted. I heard myself mumble, "He doesn't love anyone."

And if he did, he wouldn't love *me*. After all, I was a total nobody, and he was a billionaire with the world at his fingertips.

As the girls chattered back and forth, I tried to tune them out as my thoughts continued to churn in my addled brain.

Zane wasn't seriously staying in the room across from me?

Was he?

I was desperate to find out, but not in front of a crowd. Reluctantly, I turned to face them. The crowd wasn't huge, maybe only a dozen people, but it felt like more as they watched me with eager, excited eyes.

From somewhere in the back, a guy announced, "I got the whole thing on video."

I almost flinched. "*What* whole thing?"

"Everything." His eyes were bright with enthusiasm. "I bet I can sell it for a million bucks."

I reached up to rub my temples. It wouldn't be worth a million, but it would net him some decent cash if he shopped it to the right people. I only prayed he didn't.

The guy standing next to him said, "You can't sell it for a million."

"Oh yeah?" the first guy said. "Why not?"

With a grin, the second guy held up his cell phone. "That only works if you're the only one who's got it."

The first guy gave a shrug. "I didn't mean a million literally. I meant a few thousand, you know?"

The other guy gave a slow nod. "Yeah, maybe we should team up, see what we can make happen. We'll get more if it's exclusive."

Watching this exchange, I had no idea what to say. But I *did* know that just down the hall was the person who started all of this. And I desperately needed to talk to him.

Alone.

I cleared my throat. "Well, there's nothing to see now, so…" I made a little shooing motion with my hands. "Please, uh, disperse."

Nobody moved.

A tall woman near the front asked, "Hey, why wasn't he wearing a shirt?"

Good question.

Another woman asked, "And who was the guy? The one with the hairy gut?"

I didn't know what to say. Technically, this was part of my job, dealing with questions and what-not. But I had no answers, and I told them so, over and over, until one by one, they wandered away, no doubt because Zane – the star of the show – was long gone.

Soon, it was just me, standing alone in the long corridor. Like someone in a trance, I walked down the long hallway and didn't stop until I reached the hotel room door.

Not *my* door.

His door.

And then, I knocked.

CHAPTER 49

When the door opened, I was almost surprised. After all, part of me hadn't really expected him to open up, at least not without some serious pounding and yelling first.

But now that he'd actually answered, I was utterly lost for words. And he didn't look particularly chatty himself – or thrilled to see me.

Silently, I stared up at him as he stood in the open doorway. He was fully dressed now, but not in the way I might've expected.

He'd ditched the slacks and was now wearing faded jeans, along with a gray T-shirt emblazoned with some university logo that I didn't recognize. The shirt wasn't tight, and yet, the thin cotton did little to hide the outlines of his defined pecs and bulging biceps.

At the sight of him, I felt unsettled and confused, even more than usual. Just like that day on his porch, he didn't look like a billionaire. He looked like an All-American golden boy, fresh from his senior year at college.

But he didn't look happy.

Finally, I found my voice. "That thing with the senator, what was *that* about?"

"Nothing," he said. "It's solved, so forget it."

As if I could. "But what happened?"

His gaze shifted to something behind me, and I turned to look. I saw nothing except the door to my own hotel room.

Was that a hint for me to leave? If so, he was in for a rude awakening, because I wasn't going anywhere until I had some answers.

I turned back to him and asked, "Is this *really* your hotel room?"

He gave me a look. "*Every* room is mine."

Technically, this was true, but he wasn't stupid. He knew exactly what I meant.

I pointed vaguely toward the interior of his room. "But you're not actually staying here, are you?"

"No." He glanced past me. "I'm heading out."

I made a sound of frustration. "Oh, come on. You're deliberately not understanding a single thing I'm asking."

And I hadn't even gotten to the hard questions.

"I understand you fine," he said. "But if you expect answers, you're in the wrong place."

"No," I told him, "I'm in the right place, because the person I need answers from is *you*, and this is where you are."

"Not for long," he said. "I'm flying back."

"You are? But we have those…" I gave a little gasp. "Oh, my God. The interview. The one with that morning show. We should've left already." I was nearly frantic now. "Hang on. Just let me grab my stuff."

"Forget it."

"You're right. There's no time. Should we just leave from…" I let my words trail off and looked to his clothes. "But wait. You're not dressed for it."

"Yeah. And I'm not gonna be."

"But what about the interview?" I asked.

He looked away. "Fuck the interview."

"What?"

"It's canceled."

I still wasn't following. "But who canceled it?"

"Carla."

And then I remembered. "She was trying to reach you. She said it was an emergency."

"Yeah. And it's handled. So forget it."

The more he talked, the less, I understood. "But if you were going to cancel, why would you have Carla call them?" I gave a shaky laugh. "After all, that's *my* job, isn't it?"

He was quiet for a long moment, and something in his gaze told me that I wasn't going to like whatever he was planning to say next.

Sure enough, his next words hit like a hammer. "You can't work for me anymore."

Of anything I'd been expecting, this wasn't even on my radar. "Why not?"

"You've gotta ask?"

"Yes." I lifted my chin. "Apparently, I do. Because I have no idea what's going on."

His gaze met mine. "Don't you?"

I sucked in a quiet breath. Something in his expression had changed. Gone was the familiar cold bastard, and in his place was the *other* Zane, the one I'd seen by the elevators – raw and ragged, like he might lose control any moment.

Suddenly, I was feeling a little out of control myself.

He loomed closer. "You wanna know what happened?"

My lips went dry, and I felt myself nod.

His gaze bored into mine. "That fucker – the senator – was camped out, waiting for you."

I felt my brow wrinkle. "He was? For how long?"

"Too long."

I got the point. Still, his reaction seemed a bit extreme. After all, it's not like the senator had been humping my doorknob or anything – I gave a shudder of disgust – at least, not that I knew of.

But what *had* he been doing? With a twinge of dread, I asked, "Is that all?"

Zane's mouth tightened. "You know it's not."

Oh, crap. So Zane knew what happened last night? Yes. He did. Now, I was absolutely sure of it.

Because I worked for the company, I knew a little something about the hotel's security. There was no shortage of surveillance cameras, especially in long hallways and near the elevators.

Obviously, Zane knew more than I'd originally thought. Reluctantly, I said, "So, you saw what happened last night? Between me and the senator, I mean?"

"That *and* other things." As he spoke, something in his tone suggested that if senator showed up now, he'd be dragged off a second time, and maybe chucked down the stairs for good measure.

I'd known Zane for months. He wasn't one to lose his cool. And yet, he had. Even now, he looked dangerously close to losing it again.

I winced. "He didn't hit on anyone else, did he?"

Zane looked at me like I'd lost my mind. "Hit on? That's what you're gonna call it?"

I sighed. "All right, fine. Did he get grabby with anyone else?"

"Don't know. Don't care." His jaw tightened. "But I *do* care that he was bragging that he fucked you. And, he was–" Zane looked away. "– touching himself outside your room."

CHAPTER 50

Instantly, an image of the senator popped into my brain. Much like the guy's stomach, it wasn't pretty. "No." I gave slow shake of my head. "He wasn't."

"Yes. He was."

Against my better judgment, I just had to ask, "Above, or…" I gave a little shudder. "…below his clothes?"

"Above," Zane said. "And lucky for him."

I reached up to rub the back of my neck. "Well, that's a relief."

Zane loomed closer to say, "He's lucky I didn't toss him down the stairs."

Now, *this* I believed. A traitorous smile tugged at my lips. "For a minute there, I thought you might."

Unlike me, Zane wasn't smiling. "If you want, I'll track him down, try again."

Now, I couldn't help but laugh – although for the life of me, I couldn't figure out why. After all, it wasn't funny.

Zane said, "You think I'm kidding?"

"Honestly, I don't know."

But I *did* know that for the first time since meeting him, it felt almost like we were just two regular people – not the client and the caterer, not the boss and the employee, and not even the bastard and the basket case.

I was mulling all of this over when something he said finally hit home. My smile faded to nothing. "Wait a minute, when you said that I couldn't work for you anymore, what did you mean?"

"You know what I mean."

I shook my head. "No. I don't."

Or more likely, I didn't want to know.

Zane said, "Trust me. I'm doing you a favor."

I made a sound of disbelief. "Some favor."

"Are you forgetting?" he said. "Just two nights ago, you wanted to quit."

"No," I said. "Two nights ago, I was *thinking* of quitting. But I didn't, because *you* wouldn't have it."

"Yeah? Well things change."

I made a scoffing sound. "Obviously."

"Don't worry," he said, "you'll get a nice severance."

"So you're really firing me? Seriously?"

He looked away and muttered, "Fuck."

"Yeah, tell me about it."

We'd been talking for how long now? Five minutes? Maybe ten? In that short timeframe, my emotions had bounced all over the place. And was it really any wonder? I was getting so many mixed messages that I didn't know what to think.

I said, "Are you going to give me a reason?"

He looked back to me and said, "You know the reason."

"I do not," I said. "All *I* know is I'm getting a little tired of you telling me that I know things when I don't."

On that note, I also didn't know why we were arguing out here in the hallway. So far, we'd been incredibly lucky that no one had come out to look, but our luck couldn't last forever, especially given the fiasco from earlier.

I looked past him, into his room. The bed was made, and everything was in pristine condition. The way it looked, he hadn't slept there at all. Either that or he had his own personal maid, which, of course, wasn't out of the realm of possibility.

When his only response was an icy stare, I said, "Seriously, you can't just fire me and not give a reason."

"Wrong," he said. "I can. And I did."

"But—"

"You remember what I told you."

"Yeah. Nothing."

Speaking slowly and deliberately, he said, "Read the fine print. *Always*."

And there he was, the prick I'd known all along. I muttered, "I should've known."

"Yeah," he said. "You should've."

I glared up at him. "And here's another question. Why do people at work have the impression that we're sleeping together?"

He frowned. "If they do, it's the first I've heard of it."

"Oh come on, at least be honest. Did you – or did you not – give Boris Feldman, that bedding guy from Cincinnati–"

"I *know* who he is."

"Good," I said. "So why'd you him tell that I'm your mistress?"

"Mistress?"

"You know. Your side-squeeze or whatever you'd call it."

Zane looked down and muttered, "Shit."

"So you did?"

He looked up. "No. I didn't."

There was something he wasn't telling me. That much was obvious. I made a forwarding motion with my hand. "But…?"

He gave a loose shrug. "But yeah, he might've gotten that impression."

"How?"

Zane gave another shrug, but said nothing.

I made a sound of impatience. "Well?"

"The guy's a pig."

This, I believed. I'd participated in exactly one meeting with the guy, and he'd been more focused on my breasts than the paperwork that he was supposed to be signing.

But that wasn't the point. I looked to Zane and said, "So?"

"And married."

"So?" I repeated.

"He was gonna ask you to show him around town."

This, I *didn't* know. And yet, I had to say it again. "So?"

In a quieter voice, Zane said, "So I didn't like it."

"Why?" My tone grew sarcastic. "Because you were worried I'd ask for overtime?"

"No. Because I didn't want his fucking hands on you."

Well, that was unexpected.

Trying to make sense of it all, I said, "So you did *what*, exactly?"

"Nothing."

I gave Zane a no-nonsense look. "It was more than nothing."

"All right. It's late Friday, and he tells me he's gonna see if you're busy."

"And?"

"And I told him you were. With *me*."

"So you lied?"

"No. I had you work late." At my confused expression, he added, "You remember."

Now that I thought of it, I *did* remember. He'd had me wait by the phone in case a certain newspaper called. I didn't recall the newspaper's name, but I did recall how annoyed I'd been.

And now? Well, now I was oddly touched.

Was I sap or what?

I said, "But why'd you give him that impression at all? I mean, I would've just told him no, anyway."

"Maybe. But I didn't want him hassling you."

At any other time, the statement would've made me laugh out loud. And why? Because nobody on this Earth had ever hassled me more than Zane. Oh sure, it wasn't sexual harassment, but he was the biggest hassler I'd ever met.

Short-tempered.

Foul-mouthed.

Stubborn.

And yet, I heard myself ask in amazement, "So you did it for me?"

"Hell no," Zane said. "I did it for me."

I drew back. "You? Why you?"

"Because I didn't want the distraction."

Obviously, I was missing something. But I had no idea what. I asked, "What do you mean?"

He loomed a fraction closer. "All right, you wanna know something?"

I sucked in a short breath and tried not to notice for the millionth time that his eyes were an amazing shade of green, and that his mouth looked annoyingly delicious, especially now, that he was so achingly close.

I heard myself murmur, "I don't know."

Zane's gaze met mine, and he was silent for a long moment. Finally, in a voice that was almost raw, he said, "I don't like how you make me feel."

Suddenly, I was finding it hard to breathe. "And how *do* I make you feel?"

He leaned another fraction closer. "Out of control."

The way he talked, he didn't like it. And yet, he wasn't moving away.

Funny, neither was I.

As I stood, silently staring up at him, my emotions swirled like a hidden tornado. I didn't even know what I was feeling – anger, betrayal, and an embarrassing amount of lust.

It made no sense. But there was something raw and compelling that was drawing me in. As much as I hated to admit it, it had *always* drawn me in, right from the start.

Shit. He wasn't the only one out of control.

Almost without thinking, I leaned closer to him and tilted my head just a fraction. His lips looked so kissable, so soft and full, and so very close.

But not close enough.

CHAPTER 51

I don't even know who moved first, him or me. But soon, our lips met in a kiss so sweet, and yet so savage, that it took my breath away. I felt his hands on my back, and then in my hair, sifting through its tendrils as his mouth claimed mine.

I lifted my arms and wrapped them around his neck. His body felt warm and hard, and so incredibly perfect that I couldn't help but press myself even tighter.

He was a great kisser, but of course, I'd always known he would be. I felt his teeth graze my bottom lip, teasing and tantalizing, before I felt his tongue brush against mine.

I gave a muffled moan and shifted my hands lower, sliding them down his back. Through the thin cotton of his shirt, I felt his lean muscles shifting slightly with the motions of his own hands as they moved to my waist. He yanked me closer, and I felt the proof of his excitement pressing hard against my hip.

In the back of my mind, I couldn't help but ponder the fact that just last night, I'd stood in a different doorway with a different guy. But everything now was so dissimilar that it was beyond silly to even consider comparing them.

With Zane, I wasn't pulling away. Cripes, with the way he made me feel, I *couldn't* pull away, even if I wanted to.

And heaven help me, I didn't want to.

What on Earth was wrong with me? I knew this was a bad idea. I knew that we didn't even like each other. I knew that he went through lovers the way some people went through napkins or paper plates.

And yet, I *still* couldn't pull away.

But too soon, *he* did. He pulled himself back, and held me literally at arm's length, as if determined to put some space between us.

Without his body against mine, the corridor felt cold and lonely, and I stifled a shiver. I glanced past him, into his room. It was only morning, and yet, I couldn't help but glance at the bed.

I never did this.

I never *wanted* to do this.

But I did now.

I wasn't even sure why.

Oh sure, he was beyond sexy, and he obviously knew what he was doing. But it still made no sense. I was smarter than this.

Maybe it was the aftermath of the thing with the senator. Maybe it was some sort of primal response to a guy who'd literally assaulted someone on my behalf. Maybe it all boiled down to some caveman thing that I would never understand.

Or, maybe, he was just too irresistible.

The silence between us stretched out longer than I might've expected. This was fine by me. After all, the voices in my head were practically yelling for me to run. But *to* him? Or *away* from him?

This is where the voices disagreed.

Finally, it was Zane who broke the silence. "Fuck leaving," he said, more to himself than to me.

I gave a little shake of my head. "So you're not flying out?" I was insanely relieved – and scared as hell.

Stupid voices.

Zane replied, "That depends."

I gazed up at him. "On what?"

"On you."

"Me?"

Zane nodded. "Now, say yes."

Almost in a trance, I felt myself nod. His gaze was warmer than I'd ever seen it, and I knew that no matter what he was asking, I'd find it utterly impossible to say no.

With his gaze locked on mine, he said, "Spend the day with me."

Even now, I wasn't quite sure what he was asking. But it didn't matter, because I already knew the answer, and I'd already given it with that simple nod.

Still, I felt a sudden urge to tease him. "Are you sure that was a question? It didn't sound like a question."

"I'll take that as a yes." He glanced past me, toward my room. "Get changed. Throw on jeans, shorts, whatever. I'll be knocking in ten minutes." He leaned tantalizing close. "And if you don't answer…"

I was smiling now. "What, you'll leave?"

To my surprise and delight, he actually smiled back. "No. I'll bust down the door. And *make* you say yes."

There were a million things I might've said in response. I might've pointed out that the owner of the hotel might be unhappy if he trashed the place. Or, I might've reminded him that the doors in *this* establishment were even stronger than they looked. I might've even suggested that as the hotel's owner, he surely had smarter ways to get inside without resorting to brute force.

But his suggestion – of actually going out instead of staying in – was so unexpected that all I could do was nod again. I had no idea what I was getting into, but I was too far gone to turn back now.

And the way it looked, I wasn't the only one.

CHAPTER 52

I was running a final brush through my hair when my cell phone rang. I grabbed it and glanced at the display.

It was Charlotte.

I hit the answer button and said, "Hey, I'm really sorry, but I'm on my way out. Can I call you back later?"

"Sure," she said, "if you don't mind waiting for scoop."

I paused. *Scoop? As in news?* "Scoop about what?"

"Not *what*. *Who*."

"Then who?" I asked.

"Your boss."

Now, *that* got my attention. "You mean Zane? What about him?"

"Oh, well," she said in that breezy way of hers, "I know you're in a hurry, so I'll just tell you later."

I felt my gaze narrow. "Now, you're just teasing me."

"I know," she said. "It'll build anticipation, right?"

Wrong.

I was literally on my way out with the guy she supposedly had news about. If I didn't find out now, I'd wonder all day. I asked, "Can you make it quick?"

"How quick?"

"I've literally got like two minutes."

"Oh, all right," she said, not sounding thrilled to be rushed. "You'll never guess who I ran into."

"Who?" I asked.

"Naomi."

"Naomi who?"

"*You* know," she said. "Your former co-worker? From the catering company?"

"Oh. *That* Naomi." The last time I'd seen her had been on the night of Zane's party. "But wait, how do *you* know her?"

"We ran into her at the coffee shop? Remember?"

"Right. Sorry." As I spoke, I took another look in the mirror. Outside, it was a beautiful summer day. Zane had suggested wearing jeans or shorts, which meant that we'd probably be wandering around the city. In the spirit of his suggestion, I'd thrown on navy shorts and a white short-sleeved shirt with little buttons down the front.

Would he like it? *I* liked it. But was it too casual?

On the phone, Charlotte said, "Hey, are you still there?"

"Uh, yeah. Sorry, I'm a little distracted."

This was a massive understatement. Just across the hall, Zane was waiting for me. I had no idea what I was getting into, but I *did* know that it was too late to turn back now – unless, of course, Charlotte told me something horrible about him.

I bit my lip. Knowing Zane, this was a distinct possibility. I pulled my gaze from the mirror and braced myself for whatever she was planning to say.

"Anyway," Charlotte continued, "you'll never guess what she told me."

With more than a little trepidation, I said, "What?"

After a long, dramatic pause, Charlotte said, "You weren't the only one who was fired."

My stomach sank. "So Naomi lost her job, too?"

Like an idiot, I'd assumed that Zane would've been satisfied with only getting *me* fired. Turns out, I'd been giving him far more credit than he deserved.

Crap.

I was almost afraid to ask, "Was anyone else fired?"

"Nope," Charlotte said, sounding annoyingly cheerful. "Just the two of you."

I glanced toward the door to my hotel room. Was I seriously going to hang out with that guy? I wanted to. But I *also* wanted ice cream for dinner every night.

Absently, I mumbled, "Well, that's good. I guess."

Charlotte laughed. "You *guess*?"

I sighed. "Well, knowing Zane, it's a wonder he didn't have everyone fired, huh?"

Because he was just that awful.

What the hell was I doing?

"See, that's the thing," Charlotte said. "It wasn't him at all."

I did a mental double-take. "Wait, what do you mean?"

"I *mean* he wasn't the one who complained."

"Then who did?"

"Well, according to Naomi, it was some guy named Robert Hunt."

I sucked in a breath. "You mean Bob?"

"So you know him?"

"Not really. But I know who he is…except, from what I saw, he seemed like a pretty nice guy."

Charlotte gave a snort of derision. "He wasn't *that* nice. Get this. He stiffed them on the catering bill."

I winced. "He did?"

I couldn't help but recall listening from inside the van as Bob complained about the cost of the party. At the time, I'd been worried he might not pay. But soon, I'd gotten so distracted by my own troubles that it completely slipped my mind.

In hindsight, it made me feel just a little ashamed.

On the phone, Charlotte was saying, "And it gets worse. Wanna guess who he blamed, for not paying, I mean?"

Knowing what I overheard, I actually had a pretty good guess. I said, "Zane?"

"No," she said. "You."

"Me? Why me?"

"You *and* Naomi," she clarified. "Get this. He told the catering company that the two of you trashed one of the serving stations and ruined a super-expensive rug."

I felt my jaw drop. "What?"

"And *that's* why he refused to pay. Because of the damage."

I felt my gaze narrow. I knew I hated that stupid rug. "But that's a lie," I said. "*We* didn't trash anything. It was Zane and Teddy." I paused. "At least that's what I heard."

"Who's Teddy?" she asked.

"You remember," I said. "The guy who was drunk?" When she made no response, I added, "You know, Zane's cousin? The guy on the plane? The one who thinks I'm a ho-bag?"

"Ohhhhh," Charlotte said. "Him? He sounds really annoying."

He *was* annoying – and from what I'd seen, he was a terrible judge of character. It was one of the many reasons I'd come to believe that his theories about Zane were just a little far-fetched.

Oh sure, Zane could be a hard-ass, but a cheat? And a slimeball? And hell, even a killer? I wasn't seeing it.

Or maybe, I just didn't want to see it. After all, I was so drawn to the guy that it was dangerous.

I blew out a relieved breath. "Wanna hear something funny?"

"What?"

"I was sure you were going to give me *bad* news."

She laughed. "I know. That's what made it so delicious."

I felt myself smile. Zane's lips were delicious – all warm and wonderful, like a sweet tantalizing dream. Would I be kissing him again?

Yes.

Or, at least I sure hoped so.

Into the phone, I said, "Thanks for letting me know, but I really do need to get going."

"But wait," she said, "there's one more thing."

"What's that?"

"Guess who finally paid the bill."

"Who?"

"Your boss."

Now, that surprised me. "He did?"

"Yeah, and he told the company flat-out that they had to hire back anyone who might've been fired due to the misunderstanding."

"Really?"

"That's what Naomi says."

I had to point out the obvious. "But they didn't hire *me* back."

"Right. Because you weren't part of the deal."

"Why not?" I asked.

"Well obviously, it's because you already had a job."

Yes. I did. Working for him. And it had been a roller-coaster right from the start. Again, I glanced toward my hotel room door. It was funny how many times my feelings about him had shifted.

Did I hate him? Or love him? I froze at the mere thought. *Love?* Of course, it was ridiculous. I didn't love him. It was only that, well, I didn't hate him nearly as much as I used to.

I might even like him a lot more than I cared to admit.

It was a terrifying thought, especially with the way he operated. And yet, only a minute later, I was off the phone and crossing the hall.

Whatever happened now, I vowed that I wouldn't regret it.

CHAPTER 53

As we walked along the city sidewalk, I asked, "So why didn't you tell me?"

Just like a regular couple, we were holding hands while we took in the sights. Obviously, the sights weren't terribly new to Zane, but they *were* new to me, and I was enjoying it like any other generic tourist – even if I didn't feel totally anonymous.

Why? Because around us, people occasionally stopped to stare.

Zane ignored them, and I did my best to ignore them, too. And yet, I couldn't deny how surreal it was to be out with him, pretending that he was just a regular guy.

Oh sure, in his jeans and university T-shirt, he was *dressed* like a regular guy, but he wasn't fooling anyone, me included.

No. Zane was anything but ordinary. He exuded confidence and power, the kind that you couldn't fake *or* hide, even along a crowded sidewalk in a city full of movers and shakers. On top that, he was practically a household name.

As the person who monitored his news coverage, I'd definitely know.

But at this particular moment, my job was the last thing on my mind. I'd just told him what I'd heard from Charlotte, and I was dying to hear what he'd say in response.

So far, he'd said nothing.

When the silence became nearly unbearable, I said, "So when I came to your house, why didn't you deny it?"

"That I got you fired?" he said. "I'm not gonna deny what's true."

I didn't quite understand. "But it wasn't you who complained."

"Maybe. But it *was* me who got the ball rolling."

In a roundabout way, I saw what he meant. The night of his party had been crazy in more ways than one. His fight with Teddy led to the catering station getting knocked over. And shortly thereafter, his argument with Bob had surely been a factor in Bob stiffing the catering company, even though we had nothing to do with it.

Still, I said, "But when I showed up, you didn't have to take *all* the blame."

"That's what *you* think," he said. "You scared the piss out of me."

At this, I couldn't help but laugh. It was too ridiculous to take seriously. "Oh, stop it. You weren't scared. You were annoyed."

But Zane was shaking his head. "You want the truth?"

More curious than ever, I felt myself nod.

"Ask me later," he said, "and maybe I'll tell you."

My jaw dropped. "Maybe?"

His lips curved into the hint of a smile. "Maybe," he repeated.

And no matter how hard I tried to talk him into it, he never would elaborate. And yet, it *did* seem to break the ice. Soon, we were just two tourists, enjoying a day in the city.

He was a different person, and so was I. Already, I'd thrown caution to the wind and was determined to simply enjoy the day for whatever it was. As for Zane, he was more civil than I'd ever seen him.

From what I could tell, he was treating this as an actual date. He told me a little about his family – meaning his parents, not anyone associated with the hotels.

The way he talked, his dad had become disgusted with the whole lot of them and decided that he'd rather deal with real snakes than human ones. As for Zane's mom, she'd been an aspiring actress until she'd chucked it all to run off with Zane's dad and live in a remote cabin of all places.

This might've made for a nice storybook ending, if only the mom hadn't gotten stir-crazy when Zane was still a baby, and returned to Hollywood, where she died in a car crash only a few months later.

Apparently, Zane's dad had been a total recluse ever since.

The more I learned, the more I saw Zane differently – and not only because of his tragic past. It was because here, in the present, he was showing me a side of him that I hadn't known existed.

I hadn't expected any of this – the conversation, the attention, and a multitude of other small courtesies that I never would've associated with someone like Zane Bennington – the biggest prick on the planet.

And yet, I wasn't seeing him that way anymore. Not today. And maybe not ever from now on.

Within just a few short hours, I knew more about him than I ever would've expected.

It wasn't like he told me everything all at once. Rather, as we wandered through the city, he'd let a detail slip here or there. This is how I also learned that he'd graduated from Michigan Tech University, where he'd earned a bachelor's in physics, and then a master's in civil engineering.

I gave his T-shirt a sideways glance. "So *that's* where the shirt's from."

He looked down as noticing it for the first time. "Well, it's not from Harvard, that's for sure."

I couldn't help but tease, "So, they turned you down, huh?"

"No. I turned *them* down."

"Really? So you were accepted?"

"Hey, it wasn't that hard," he said. "I had legacy on my side. I would've been the fourth generation to go."

I had to laugh. "Not that hard, huh? So tell me, what were your scores?"

After going back and forth a few times, he finally admitted that he'd gotten a nearly perfect score on his SAT, and that he'd graduated summa cum laude – for his bachelor's *and* his master's.

Although I hadn't recognized the university logo, I did know a little something about his alma mater. It wasn't Ivy League, but it wasn't a school for dolts either. The way I heard it, you had to be wicked smart just to get in – and legacy counted for zip.

Apparently, I was dealing with a certified genius. It shouldn't have been a surprise. After all, he'd been running a multi-billion dollar corporation without breaking a sweat – even if he did break an egg or two along the way.

As the hours slipped by, I told him more about myself, too, even though I strongly suspected that in true Zane fashion, he already knew more than he let on.

As we sat on a bench in Central Park, I happened to mention the location of my parent's farm and was surprised when Zane showed a genuine interest, even to the point of asking what crops they were growing this year.

At this, I had to laugh. "Oh come on. You're just being nice."

He lifted a single eyebrow. "Me? You're kidding, right?"

Was I? That word, *nice*, it didn't fit him at all – or at least, it hadn't until today. Maybe this should've worried me – the fact that he'd been such a bastard all along, and now, he was acting like a pretty decent guy.

We were sitting close, with his arm draped over my shoulders. I leaned into him and savored the feel of his hard body against mine. "Well, you're a lot nicer today than normal."

"Yeah? Well don't tell anyone."

Funny, he didn't sound like he was joking. I pulled back to study his face, even as I teased, "Why? Would it ruin your reputation?"

"Probably." His eyes held no trace of humor. "My grandfather? He was the nicest guy you ever met."

"I know." I paused. "I mean, it's what everyone says."

"Right." Zane was frowning now. "And you wanna know what it got him?"

"What?" I asked.

"Nothing but trouble. My uncles – meaning my dad's brothers? Guys were total losers. Drugs, women, you name it."

As far as I knew, Zane didn't do drugs. And he certainly wasn't a loser. But when it came to women, he was in no position to talk. The recollection was a cold splash on an otherwise warm day.

Next to me, Zane said, "What is it?"

"What's what?" I asked.

"What were you thinking?"

"When?"

"Just now," he said. "Tell me."

I didn't want to tell him. Because if I did, I'd have to face the reality of how fleeting all of this would surely be. I recalled What's-Her-Name from his private jet. She'd looked at Zane like he was the only guy in the world. And *he'd* looked at her like she was used goods.

And then, there was Maven from dinner. The way it sounded, he'd ditched *her* pretty quickly, too.

But I didn't want to dwell on it, just like I didn't want to dwell on Zane's earlier comments about my job. Maybe I *was* about to be fired. Or maybe, he'd been speaking rhetorically. Foolish or not, I didn't want to ask.

Not now.

I still hadn't answered his question. *What was I thinking?* I glanced around. The sky was blue, and the breeze was warm. Around us, the trees were rustling, and I was sitting with the most fascinating person I'd ever met.

Worrying, I decided, would be an absolute waste. After all, it wouldn't change a single thing.

Besides, I wasn't *that* naive. I already knew how this would end.

Badly.

Because with Zane, that's how it always ended. And yet, right now, I couldn't bring myself to care, or at least, not enough to ruin what was shaping up to be a pretty spectacular day. So I summoned up a smile and said, "Nothing."

He gave me a dubious look. "Uh-huh."

"What's that supposed to mean?"

"It means, I *know* what you're thinking."

"Oh yeah? What?"

"You're thinking, 'Who is this guy, judging his uncles when he's just as bad? Worse, even.'"

A nervous laugh escaped my lips. "That's *not* what I was thinking." *Not word-for-word, anyway.*

His mouth held the hint of a smile. "If you say so."

In spite of everything, I felt like smiling, too. "Okay, then I also know what *you're* thinking."

"Yeah? What's that?"

"You're thinking, 'How'd I end up on a park bench with some farmer's daughter.'"

His tone became flirtatious. "Hey, I like farmer's daughters."

Funny. On this, Teddy might've been right. Go figure.

I smiled up at him. "Oh yeah?"

Zane gave a slow nod. "One in particular."

It was such a lovely thing to say, especially from him. And, if he were anyone else, I might've believed that it was more than simple flattery.

Zane's gaze met mine. "And," he continued, "I know exactly why we're sitting on some bench."

"Why?"

"Because, if we're in public I *might* behave myself."

I had to laugh. "You? Behave yourself? Oh, please."

His eyebrows lifted. "Meaning?"

I gave him a playful poke to the chest. "You're a monster."

As I pulled back my hand, he reached out and captured my wrist. Slowly, he turned my hand so my palm was facing upward. And then, he lowered his head and grazed his lips across the tender skin between my wrist and palm.

It didn't feel like a kiss. It felt like a promise. My heart fluttered, and my mouth went suddenly dry. I heard myself say, "Was that a serious answer?"

Against my wrist, he said, "Which one?"

"That you wanted to leave the hotel so we'd behave?"

"Not *us*," he said, with another teasing kiss, this one to my wrist. "*Me.*"

"Seriously?"

With his lips still on my skin, he looked up and hit me with those amazing eyes of his. The way it looked, he was dead serious.

Again, I felt myself swallow.

I half-expected him to pull me close and kiss me on the lips, just like he had in his hotel room doorway. But he didn't. Instead, he got to his feet and tugged me up along with him.

He wrapped me in his arms, and brushed his lips against my forehead. We stood there like that one heavenly moment before he pulled back to say, "Monster, huh?"

I laughed. "Definitely."

He shrugged. "Eh, I've been called worse."

Now, this, I knew was true.

The next hours flew as we toured the Statue of Liberty, walked along Broadway, and rode to the top of the Empire State Building. Throughout all of this, he was a perfect gentleman.

I didn't know whether to be relieved or frustrated. Probably, I was a little bit of both, because I knew that whatever he asked me in private, I'd never be able to say no.

And yet, when we returned to the hotel, I *was* saying no. But it wasn't to sex. It was to something else.

CHAPTER 54

I stared down at the single sheet of paper. "I'm not signing that."

We were standing just inside the door to my hotel room. We'd returned to the hotel just a few minutes earlier, after an amazing day in the city, complete with a sunset dinner overlooking Times Square.

It had been one of the best days of my life, and now, it was turning sour so quickly, it was making my head spin.

I read aloud the first line of the document that Zane had retrieved on the way in. "Severance agreement?" I looked up. "Seriously?"

Zane said, "Is there a problem?"

"Of course, there's a problem. You're firing me."

If I'd expected him to look guilty, I would've been sadly disappointed. He looked as hard and determined as I'd ever seen him.

He said, "Technically, I fired you this morning."

I stared in stunned disbelief. "So, you were serious?"

"You know I was."

"That's not true," I said. "I mean, you *also* said you were going to fly out, and you didn't do *that*."

"I know. And that's a problem."

"Why is that a problem?" I asked.

"You don't know?"

I did. And I didn't. I gave a loose shrug and made no reply.

He loomed closer. "It's a problem, because I should've gotten the hell out of here."

"But why?"

His body was rigid and his eyes were hard. "Because I can't fuck you and be your boss at the same time."

I drew back. "What did you just say?"

His gaze softened. "Look, I didn't mean it like that."

"I think you did. And it seems to me, you're assuming an awful lot."

His gaze dipped to my lips. "Am I?"

Something in his look went straight to my core. And yes, in a sense, he was right. After all, I'd known exactly what kind of signals I'd been giving off. But in my fantasies, I didn't have to sign on the dotted line beforehand.

When I made no reply, Zane said, "So, if I asked you to my room, you'd say no."

I lifted my chin. "Yes, actually."

I wasn't even lying. I'd definitely be saying no *now*, since he was back to being a total prick.

He stepped back, putting more distance between us. It made me feel cold and alone, in spite of the fact that he was still within standing arm's reach. Suddenly, the gulf between us felt insurmountable in every possible way.

He asked, "So what are you suggesting?"

I sighed. "I don't know."

"Think," he said. "You wanna keep your job, pretend there's nothing there?"

I didn't know what to say. When no reasonable response came to mind, I gave yet another hopeless shrug.

In front of me, Zane looked as hard as ever. "You can't have it both ways. You know that, right?"

I looked down at the sheet of paper. What he was offering was actually pretty spectacular. Three year's salary, plus benefits. It was a fabulous deal by any stretch, especially considering that I'd been his employee for only a few months.

And yet, I hated this, and not only because of my job. Mostly, it felt like he was paying me for sex – and then, even worse, paying me to leave afterward.

Talk about insulting.

If I signed on the dotted line, what kind of person would I be?

Again, I glanced at the numbers.

Well, I wouldn't be cheap, that's for sure.

I asked, "So, what'd you do? Have your lawyers draw this up while we were out?"

Was *that* why he'd spent the day with me? Had he just been killing time while the attorneys worked to cover his ass? If so, it was incredibly disheartening.

But in front of me, Zane said, "No."

Well, that was informative.

I fluttered the sheet of paper. "So, you keep a stack of these lying around?"

"What do *you* think?"

"Right now?" I gave a humorless laugh. "Trust me. You don't want to know."

He pointed to the sheet. "Look at the date."

I looked down and felt my forehead wrinkle in confusion. The document was dated yesterday. I looked up. "So you were planning to fire me regardless?"

In a gentler tone, he said, "I'm not firing you. I'm terminating the contract."

I had to point out the obvious. "But that's the same thing."

"Not legally."

"And that's supposed to make me feel better?" I searched his eyes for some clue of what was really going on. "And I've gotta ask, why'd you hire me in the first place?"

"You want the truth?"

I nodded.

"I hired you, because I was a fucking idiot."

I stared up at him. "Gee, thanks."

"Jane, listen…" He blew out a long unsteady breath. "When I called you in for that interview, I told myself a shit-ton of lies – that I could keep it professional, that I was hiring you because you were honest and could keep a secret, and yeah, because I was short of people I could trust. But…"

With a low curse, he looked away.

"But what?" I asked.

He looked back to meet my gaze. "But I was lying – not to you. To myself. Because you wanna know the real reason I hired you?"

I felt myself nod.

"Because I wanted you near me, even if you hated my guts. Hell, if you hated me, even better."

I sucked in a breath. This wasn't anything like the answer I'd been expecting. And yet, it was so strange.

"But why?" I asked. "I mean, why would you want me near you *and* want me to hate you? That makes no sense."

He shoved a hand through his hair. "Yeah, tell me about it."

In spite of my confusion, I was stupidly pleased – until I recalled the parade of models and actresses he'd been dating from day-one.

If he'd been so interested in *me*, he wouldn't have been with *any* of them, much less *all* of them.

"I don't get it," I said, "if you were interested in me at all, why were you so awful?"

And why were you screwing other girls?

"I told you why," he said. "It was because I didn't *want* you to like me."

"But why not?"

"Because I've had to do things – ugly things – and I didn't want you involved. I shouldn't have hired you. It was a mistake, a *selfish* mistake. But I wanna make it right."

I shook my head. "By firing me?"

"Yes."

"But why?"

He reached for my hand. "Because I don't want you as an employee. I don't want you to say yes to anything, now or later, because you think your job is on the line."

At this, I wasn't sure if I should be touched or insulted. "You think I would?"

"No. But I'm not gonna take that chance."

"Technically, wouldn't it be *me* taking the chance?"

"Yeah," he said. "And I wouldn't like it."

"Why not?"

"All right, I'll spell it out. I don't want you to be the girl in the office that everyone knows I'm fucking. I don't want people to look at you, like you're trash, sleeping your way to the top. I don't want people to snicker behind your back or gossip when I call you into my office."

I stared up at him. "But you don't care about stuff like that."

His voice softened. "I would with you."

"But why?"

"Because *you'd* care, and if anyone hurt you – shit, if *I* hurt you – I wouldn't like it." He looked to the sheet of paper. "So yeah, I'm a selfish bastard. And you wanna know why?"

Almost in a trance, I felt myself nod.

"Because I want you to sign that thing now and get it out of the way, so I can drag you upstairs and do all the things I've been wanting to from the first time I laid eyes on you."

I was nearly breathless now. "What kind of things?"

He moved closer, and lifted my chin with his index finger. He moved very close until our lips were almost touching. In a low, seductive voice, he said, "I'm not gonna say. But I will promise you this…"

"What?"

"I'm not gonna stop 'til your throat's raw from moaning my name." His gaze dipped lower, and he said in almost a whisper, "And I can promise you this, you'll be plenty sore tomorrow."

That shouldn't have thrilled me. But it did. After all, I'd heard the rumors. I said, "You mean because you're, um, well endowed?"

"No, although I'm not gonna deny it. What I mean is, I'm not gonna stop until you're trembling so hard, your bones ache."

Holy hell.

That prick knew exactly what he was doing. Already, I was aching for him. I could feel my body responding. Wanting him. Craving him.

I glanced toward the window of my hotel room. I wasn't on a top floor, but the view was still pretty nice. I had a king size bed and fresh sheets. And in front of me, I had the sexiest guy I'd ever met.

In spite of my earlier protests, I reached for the pen he was holding in his free hand. And then, heaven help me, I signed.

CHAPTER 55

In a way, it felt like I was signing away my soul. But with a final flourish, it was done. I bit my lip as I silently handed him the paper.

The prick actually paused to read it.

And yet, it didn't dampen my desire for him. After all, I *knew* he was a prick long before tonight.

I gave the bed a nervous glance, wondering if I should fold down the bedspread or…?

Zane said, "If you think we're staying here, think again." He reached for my hand. "Now, come on."

While leading me out of my room, he mentioned, almost as an aside, that my severance pay was already deposited into my account.

So, he'd known all along that I'd say yes?

Talk about cocky.

Unwarranted? No.

But maddening? Yes. A million times yes.

As we walked, hand-in-hand, down the hall toward the elevators, I gave a final glance over my shoulder. "But what about your room across from mine?"

"What about it?"

"You weren't *really* sleeping there, were you?"

"Hell no."

"So what were you doing?"

"Watching to make sure that fucker didn't bother you."

Insane or not, a warm, happy glow settled over my heart. But too soon, I recalled something that Carla had told me just this morning. "But what about Tiffany?"

"What about her?"

I glanced away. "I, uh, heard she stayed in your room last night."

"You mean my suite? Yeah. She stayed there."

My steps faltered. *Crap.*

But then, Zane spoke again. "But *I* didn't."

"Really? Why not?"

He squeezed my hand. "You've gotta ask?"

I felt myself smile. "So what happened? Were you doing her a favor? Like in case the senator got belligerent or something?"

"No," he said. "I was doing *me* a favor."

"What do you mean?"

"If the senator showed up at their room, I had someone waiting."

"Why?" I asked.

"Because I wanted to talk to him." An edge crept into Zane's voice. "*Without* an audience."

That sounded vaguely ominous. I gave a nervous laugh. "Without a witness, you mean."

"Something like that."

Now, I just *had* to know, "What were you planning to say?"

"Nothing I want to repeat."

"Oh, please," I said. "There's nothing you could say that would shock me."

We'd just reached the elevators, and he turned to face me. "You think so, huh?"

As I looked up to meet his gaze, everything else faded into the background. In his eyes, I saw the promise of secrets and surprises, and all sorts of things that shouldn't be discussed in public.

Without breaking eye-contact, he reached to his side and hit the button to summon the next elevator going up. While waiting, he pulled me close and nuzzled my neck.

Into my ear, he whispered, "You're mine. You know that, right?"

If he meant to shock me, he'd definitely succeeded. I pulled back to study his face. He actually looked serious.

But what did that mean? His for one night? For a weekend? For longer? Or was it just a pretty thing to say?

I might've asked, if only a sudden ding didn't break the spell. I turned to see the doors slide open, revealing an elevator that was already crammed with people.

And everyone was staring.

At Zane.

Not me.

Thank heaven.

Oblivious to the attention, Zane guided me into the elevator and wrapped an arm around my waist as we turned to face the front. Together, we ignored the whispers behind us as the elevator carried us upward to whatever would happen next.

With every stop, the space became more sparsely populated, until it was just him and me. He was behind me now, cradling me against him as I watched the numbers climb until they reached the penthouse level.

He pulled away and took my hand, leading me out of the elevator and into the posh hallway beyond. I didn't know how many suites were up here, but I *did* know that the doors on *this* floor were spaced much farther apart than they had been below.

With every step, I was feeling more nervous – but not so nervous that I wanted to turn back. In hopes of breaking the tension, I said, "Wanna hear something funny?"

Before he could even respond, I plunged onward, "Charlotte thinks you dragged me to New York because of Professor Lumberjack."

He gave a gentle tug on my hand. "Dragged you, huh?"

I gave him a tug right back. "Oh, you know what I mean." At the memory, I had to laugh. "After all, you didn't give me a whole lot of advance notice."

When Zane said nothing in reply, I said, "But she's crazy, right?"

Almost to himself, Zane said, "Not any crazier than Fergus O'Neal."

My steps faltered. "Wait, how'd you know his last name?" I stopped walking and turned to face him. "*I* didn't even know his last name. Is it really O'Neal?"

Zane gave a tight shrug, but made no reply.

I didn't know whether to smile or frown. "Oh come on. Tell me."

"All right. You want the truth? He's your roommate's boyfriend, right?"

"You *know* he is." I studied Zane's face. "In fact, I'm wondering if *you* know more than I do."

"All *I* know is this." Zane squeezed my hand. "I couldn't leave you alone with those people."

"What do you mean?"

"The guy has access to your house."

"So?"

"So, I didn't want you sleeping – or hell – even walking around where he could get to you."

It was so sweet and so crazy that I didn't know what to think. "Wait a minute," I said. "Was that the reason you wouldn't let me leave the office to pack?"

He gave me a wry smile. "No comment."

I couldn't help but smile back. "Hey, that's *my* line."

"Not anymore."

This much was true. And the strangest thing was, I wasn't nearly as disappointed as I thought I'd be. I had to admit, Zane was right. Whatever happened next would change our work relationship forever.

In truth, it was already changed. There was no going back now – not that I would if I could.

He reached out and took my other hand in his. "Jane, listen..." He gave both of my hands a tender squeeze. "I don't want you going back there."

"Back where?"

"To your house."

"Why not?"

"For one thing, because I don't trust those people."

I tried to laugh. "Yeah, me neither."

"And, for another. You don't belong with them." His gaze was warm, and his voice was a caress. "You belong with *me*."

My lips parted, but I didn't know what to say. I wasn't even sure what he was getting at, but I didn't have time to dwell on it, because soon, his lips sealed mine with a kiss so tender, and so amazing that I could hardly think, much less speak.

That was fine by me. I didn't want to think, or even talk. I wanted to feel more of this – more of him. More of everything. And yes, I wanted to feel him inside me.

Like now.

CHAPTER 56

Together, we practically fell through the door to his suite. Already, I was desperate for him – wet and ready, even though all we'd done was kiss.

In the back of my mind, I still couldn't believe that I was doing this. And yet, I knew that *not* doing this was too impossible to consider.

I was in his arms, and his lips were on mine. The door swung shut behind us, and I gave a shiver of anticipation.

Zane pulled back to ask, "Are you cold? Want me to turn on the heat, or—"

A nervous giggle escaped my lips. "Actually, I'm pretty hot already."

He pulled farther back and gave me a long, appreciative look. "Got that right."

He *had* to be kidding. Belatedly, it occurred to me that I was still wearing the same clothes that I'd worn all day around the city. Probably, I should've changed, but at the time, I'd been in such a hurry to be with him that I hadn't even thought of it.

I glanced down at my wrinkled shirt and shorts. "I probably should've gotten freshened up, huh?"

But Zane was already shaking his head. "You're perfect just the way you are."

"Perfect? Now, I *know* you're joking."

"No joke," he said, looking surprisingly sincere.

I had to laugh. "Oh come on. Are you seriously telling me that I *don't* look like I need a shower and fresh clothes?"

He gave me a slow, secret smile. "Hey, I've got a shower."

Yes. He did. Actually, he probably had more than one, with multiple shower heads and everything. But that wasn't the thing that set my pulse jumping.

It was the look in his eye. It was a look that told me I wouldn't need to shower alone, not unless I wanted to.

And I definitely *didn't* want to.

Almost in a trance, I felt myself nod. To what, I wasn't even sure. *The shower? Him? Both?*

"And," he said, "who says you need clothes?"

I heard myself whisper, "Not me."

In spite of my best intentions, we never did make it to the shower.

In fact, we barely made it to the bed. It all happened so suddenly. One moment, we were standing there, like two regular people, with a decent amount of self-control.

And then, I reached for his shirt. And he reached for the buttons on mine. I tugged his shirt upward and savored the sight of his rock-hard abs with all their valleys and ridges.

Suddenly, I was desperate to see more. I moved my hands higher, taking more of his shirt with me as I went. Soon, it was over his head, and then, tossed onto the floor, giving me a nice close view of his upper torso.

Oh. My. God.

I felt my lips part, and my breath catch. I might've looked longer, except soon, something even more compelling claimed my attention. It was his lips on mine and his arms pulling me close.

His lips were full and oh-so sweet as they moved against mine, teasing and promising, just like the telltale hardness I could feel pressing against me through his jeans.

I wanted him like I'd never wanted anything else in my whole life. And if he were any other guy, I might've believed that he felt exactly the same way.

But like so many other things, that was too ridiculous for words, so I didn't dwell on it or let it consume me, even as he kissed and caressed me all the way to the bedroom, removing clothing as we went – a shirt here, shorts there, his jeans along the way, and socks who-knows-where.

Almost before I knew it, we'd tumbled onto the king-size bed, with me in my bra and panties, and him only in his briefs.

Already, I was finding it hard to breathe. I reached for his hardness, only to feel him pull back, leaving my hand way too lonely.

In a teasing tone, he said, "Remember the reason for going out?"

Already, I was so lost, I could hardly think. But then, I remembered. "You mean so you'd behave?"

He gave a slow nod. "And the rule still applies."

"What? Who said anything about rules?"

"Me." He ran a smooth hand over my bare skin. "You're like a present, and I want to unwrap you nice and slow." With that, he lowered his head and brushed his lips softly against my ear and then moved his lips downward, kissing his way to my throat and lower still, toward the center of my breasts.

With warm fingers, he nudged aside the lace of my bra and took a nipple into his mouth. His mouth was warm, and his tongue was enticing, teasing me to distraction, even as his hand trailed enticingly toward the intersection of my thighs.

I was beyond wet and craving him like I'd craved nothing else during my twenty-three years on this Earth. When his fingers grazed that special spot, I gave a moan of pure pleasure laced with frustration – pleasure because it felt too good for words, and frustration because I wanted him inside me like ten minutes ago.

He lifted his head and looked down toward his fingers. In a low, seductive voice, he said, "I like your panties."

I almost wanted to giggle. "You should. I'm pretty sure you bought them."

"Did I?"

"Maybe." My mind was growing fuzzier with every stroke of his finger. Somehow, I managed to say, "You should probably take them off and check."

"Or," he said, with a particularly enticing stroke, "I could watch you squirm like you've made me squirm."

If I weren't so breathless, I might've laughed. Zane Bennington, squirm? "Oh, please. You're so full of it."

"You think so, huh?"

Honestly, I was finding it hard to think at all.

It didn't help when he slipped his finger beneath my panties and then inside me. I was so hot and so wet that I literally ached for him, even as a second finger joined the first, and his thumb danced across my swollen clit.

I heard myself whisper, "I want you."

"I know."

"What?" Even as breathless as I was, I made a move to sit up, but gently, he pushed me back onto the bed. With a smile, he said, "Where do you think you're going?"

Already, his fingers were moving again. All I could say was, "Nowhere."

"Damn straight," he said. "Wanna know what I want?"

I only prayed it was me. Because if it wasn't, I was in serious trouble. Somehow, I managed to ask, "What?"

"I want to take you hard and fast…"

That sounded so good. I gave a little moan of encouragement.

And then, he said, "But not yet…"

My breath caught. "You are such a tease."

"So are you."

"Me? No way."

He leaned his mouth close to mine and whispered. "Yes." He grazed his lips across my mine, teasing me even now. You know what it's been like, wanting you, thinking of you, watching you, and knowing that I couldn't have you?"

I had no idea what he was talking about, but it sounded oh so good – and eerily familiar, because there was a part of me – a very shameless part of me – that had been feeling the same way for longer than I'd ever admit, even to myself.

But I refused to dwell on that now, because this had been one of the most wonderful days of my life, and it was getting better with every stroke, every whispered word, every motion of his fingers as they made love to me on that giant bed of his.

And then, just when I thought I couldn't wait another minute, he was tugging down my panties, even as I frantically worked to free his body from his briefs. Soon, he was poised above me, with his thumb still in motion, and his gaze on mine.

I reached between us, guiding his massive hardness to my opening, and then gave a moan of contentment when he finally entered me, claiming me like he'd already claimed the world.

Soon, I was lost to everything but him – his body moving with my own, his hands caressing my skin, his back muscles shifting in time to our motions.

I ran my hands down his sides, up his back, and through his hair, feeling like I couldn't get enough, even as he filled me almost to the point of bursting. When we reached our peak, he held me in his arms for the longest time, almost like he never wanted to let go.

If that was the case, he wasn't the only one.

And when we *did* let go? It was only to run a steaming hot bath in his massive whirlpool tub. Together, we lingered, chatting and laughing until the water grew cold and we grew hot – for each other, that is.

When the first hint of dawn began creeping through the windows, I drifted off, more satisfied than I'd ever been in my whole life.

And it was all because of him – Zane Bennington, the guy who was impossible to figure out, especially a couple of hours later, when reality came calling in the form of too many people I'd been hoping to forget.

CHAPTER 57

I woke alone in a cold and rumpled bed. Still naked, I sat up and looked around the luxurious bedroom. Sunlight streamed in through the massive windows, casting a pale glow on my posh surroundings.

I looked toward the bedroom's doorway, where the trail of discarded clothing brought back memories of the previous night.

Had I really done it?

Had I really slept with Zane "the Prick" Bennington?

A pleasant soreness, not only between my thighs, but also deep in my stomach, told me all I needed to know. Last night, I'd had so many orgasms, I'd literally lost count.

Did I regret it?

Yes.

And no.

Yes – because this wasn't me. I wasn't a jump-in-the-sack kind of girl. I was a relationship kind of girl. Until now, I'd successfully avoided guys like Zane – irredeemable man-whores with a list of lovers a mile long.

And yet, I also realized that regret cut both ways. If somehow, I'd found the willpower to walk away when I'd had the chance, I'd be dealing with regret of a different kind.

I had to face facts. I would've been screwed either way. But only one of those ways had given me a memory to last a lifetime.

There was no denying it. I'd wanted him.

I heard myself sigh. And now, I'd had him. *What now?*

Clutching the sheet close to my chest, I took another long look around, but saw no sign of him. I didn't hear him either. Was he gone? It sure seemed that way.

Was this my cue to leave, too?

I gave my discarded clothes a worried glance. There was no way I'd consider them clean *now*, especially my panties. Last night, I'd been so wet from wanting him that, for all I knew, they were still damp.

The thought was more than a little embarrassing.

I glanced at the clock on the nightstand. It was only eight o'clock. The morning was still young, right? Maybe he'd just popped out for coffee? Like the sap I was, I waited in his bed until nearly nine-thirty.

Finally, when it became painfully obvious that he wasn't coming back, I did the only thing I could. I got up and started gathering my clothes.

Ten minutes later, I was fully dressed, minus the panties, which I'd wadded up and tucked into the front pocket of my shorts.

Silently, I crept toward the main door of his suite, feeling incredibly self-conscious, even though I was utterly alone.

Unfortunately, that dynamic changed within five seconds of my departure. His door had barely shut behind me when who did I see rounding the nearby corner?

Tiffany.

At the sight of me, she stopped dead in her tracks. I stopped in mine. I wasn't normally a blusher, and yet, I could feel my face burning with raw embarrassment.

Her lips formed a smirk. "So, what'd you think?"

"What'd I think of what?"

She eyed me up and down. "Oh, forget it. It's not like I want to hear it, anyway." She glanced toward the door that I'd just come out of. "I'm missing a pink hairbrush. Did you see it?"

I had, in fact. The brush had been sitting on a marble-top table near the main door. "Uh, yeah. I think so."

She frowned. "You didn't use it, did you?"

Feeling more self-conscious with every passing moment, I ran a nervous hand through the tangles of my hair. "No. I didn't use anything."

This was only a slight exaggeration. I *had* helped myself to a splash of mouthwash and a quick look in the mirror. Unfortunately, this meant that I knew exactly what Tiffany was seeing – a girl who'd just stumbled out of Zane's bed.

But that wasn't the only thing bothering me. It was the visual reminder that Tiffany had slept in that same suite just one night earlier.

This posed a rather disturbing question. In that same bedroom? Or in the other one? And what if it *was* in the same bedroom. Was it in the same bed, under the same sheets? If so, had they been changed?

Zane had already assured me that nothing had happened between them. And foolish or not, I actually believed him. Was I being stupid?

No.

Or yes.

Damn it. Either way, I was wilting under Tiffany's scornful gaze. She gave my appearance another quick once-over. "Yeah," she said. "I can tell."

It took me a moment to recall the threads of our conversation. Obviously, she meant that she could tell that I hadn't brushed my hair or gone to any other trouble to make myself presentable.

But in my own defense, I'd been betting on a quick anonymous escape.

No such luck.

With a mumbled excuse, I moved past her and rounded the corner, only to collide into who?

Teddy, Zane's cousin.

Just shoot me, now.

As I stumbled backward from the unexpected impact, he stood, staring like he'd just caught me molesting the neighbor's cat. With a sound of disgust, he said, "I see you ignored my advice."

I was almost too embarrassed to think. "Huh?"

He gave me a smirk. "Or, maybe you were screwing him all along."

What the hell?

From somewhere behind me, I heard Tiffany say, "No. I don't think so."

I turned to look. She was now standing within arm's reach, giving

Teddy a knowing smile. "What *I* think," Tiffany told him, "is that she's wanted him all along, and he finally took pity on her."

I wanted to slap her. Determined to resist, I shoved my hands deep into the front pockets of my shorts. After all, there was no need to get violent – yet.

Tiffany said to Teddy, "Wanna know how they met?"

"How?" Teddy asked.

"She was like, a caterer's helper or something." She gave a little snicker. "You remember that party at Zane's place? Well, *she* was the one picking crab cakes off the carpet."

I spoke up. "Yeah? And *you* were the one humping him in the alcove."

Tiffany straightened. "So?"

"So your fiancé was at the same party."

"Ex-fiance," she corrected.

"Oh, please," I said. "Not at the time, he wasn't."

At this, she had the nerve to look insulted. "What are you saying? That I'm some sort of slut?"

"Oh, get real." I threw up my hands in frustration. "I'm just saying, you're in no position to talk."

In unison, Tiffany and Teddy turned to look at something near my right foot. I lowered my head to see what they were seeing, and felt my face burst into new flames of embarrassment.

Yup, those were my panties all right. With as much dignity as I could muster, I swooped them up and crammed them back into my pocket.

And then, what else could I do?

I turned and marched toward the stairway, trying to ignore Tiffany's laughter ringing out behind me.

CHAPTER 58

On the phone, Charlotte was still laughing. "But why'd you take the stairs when you could've grabbed an elevator?"

"Because," I explained, "I didn't want to risk seeing anyone else."

I *still* didn't want to see anyone, but I *did* appreciate hearing her voice, even if she wasn't giving me quite the reaction I'd been hoping for.

An hour earlier, after trudging down countless flights of stairs, I'd finally made it back to my own hotel room, where I'd taken a long shower and then called Charlotte for a dose of sympathy.

The only problem was, she wasn't terribly sympathetic. In fact, she spent most of the conversation telling me that she'd known all along that Zane and I would hook up eventually.

And *how* did she know this? It was because, in Charlotte's words, "You can't hate someone that much without loving them at least a little."

When she repeated this for the third time, I said, "What are you saying? That I'm in love with Zane Bennington?"

Heaven forbid.

"You must love him," she said. "He's all you ever talk about."

"Sure, because he's a monster."

Her tone grew teasing. "You mean a monster in bed?"

Well, he was big and powerful. And he'd made me scream. Did that count? I mumbled, "Yeah, well, that doesn't mean anything."

"Says you. And if he was such a monster, you wouldn't have slept with him at all."

Technically, this was true, but I wasn't ready to give in just yet. "You *do* remember that he fired me, right?"

"Yeah, and he gave you a three-years' severance. It's practically a vacation."

Well, there was that.

"And," Charlotte continued, "he was paying you a crap-ton of money, anyway."

"So?"

"So when you take *that* into account, it's more like a ten-years' severance, at least in normal-person dollars."

Damn it. She did have a point. Still, I wasn't blind to the fact that he was literally paying me to go away.

I sighed. "I dunno."

"Wanna know what I think?"

"What?"

"I think *he* loves *you*, too."

I almost dropped the phone. "Oh, please. He doesn't love anyone."

"But from what you said, he loved his grandfather. And his dad."

"Yeah, so?"

"And he loves his dogs."

"Well, everyone loves dogs," I pointed out.

"Not hardly," she said. "I'm just saying, I think you're reading it all wrong. I think he fired you so he could date you all legal-like."

At this, I felt an embarrassing surge of hope, especially because Zane had implied something very similar. Still, the whole situation scared the crap out of me.

I couldn't *really* be in love with Zane Bennington? *Could I?*

If so, I was in huge trouble. After all, he'd disappeared without so much as a note.

Charlotte and I were still talking ten minutes later when a knock sounded at the door to my hotel room.

On the phone, Charlotte said in a sing-song voice, "I know who that is."

"Who?"

She laughed. "You know who."

Obviously, she meant Zane. But I wasn't so sure. After all, we hadn't made any plans. Still, I called out, "Be there in a sec!"

In a rush, Charlotte said, "Hey, real quick…Don't forget to call me before you fly home."

Hearing this, it suddenly occurred to me that I had no idea *when* I'd be flying home. Considering that I was now unemployed, it could even be today. Still, I promised to let her know and ended the call feeling a lot happier than when I'd begun.

Probably, I should've relished it, because when I finally answered the door, it wasn't the guy I'd been hoping to see.

Instead, it was Bob, Teddy's stepfather.

And he looked like hell.

CHAPTER 59

From my hotel room doorway, I stared at the unexpected visitor. Until today, I'd seen Bob on only two occasions. The first time had been at Zane's party. The second time had been when I'd spotted him standing out on his front lawn, watching as the movers loaded up his stuff.

Both times, he'd looked immaculate, with tailored clothes and a perfect haircut sporting just the right amount of gray at the temples.

Back then, he'd looked like everybody's favorite rich uncle.

Now, he looked like a hobo who'd been turned away at the soup kitchen.

His face was unshaven, and his hair was a mess. He wore dark slacks and a gray dress shirt, but the slacks were rumpled, and the shirt had a dark, damp stain running down the front, like he'd been trying to take a drink and accidentally missed his mouth.

I gave the stain a closer look. *Coffee?*

Or something stronger?

He said, "Got a minute?"

Startled out of my stupor, I managed to say, "Uh, sure. Bob, right?"

He blinked. "You know me?"

I nodded. "We met at the party. You remember? At Zane's place?"

"Oh. Sorry." He squinted at me for a long moment. "Yeah. You were wearing a red dress, right?"

No. I'd been wearing work clothes and a frilly apron. Obviously, he had me mixed up with someone else, but I didn't have the heart to correct him, so I gave him a reassuring smile and said, "Something like that."

He murmured, "Right, right... Looked great on you, by the way."

"Uh, thanks."

He glanced toward the inside of my hotel room. "Can we talk inside?"

The question caught me off guard. I barely knew the guy. Plus, I had no idea why he was here.

Still, I couldn't help but feel sorry for him, in spite of the fact that he'd cost me my catering job. No wonder he didn't pay the bill. The way it looked, he could barely afford food for himself.

I gave him an apologetic smile. "I'm really sorry, but I can't have guests in the room. Maybe we can talk out here? Or maybe get a coffee downstairs?"

After all, he looked like he could use it.

He frowned. "Out here's no good. He might see us."

Who on Earth was he talking about? Zane? Teddy? Someone else? I had no idea.

I said, "Sorry, *who* might see us?"

From somewhere beyond my line of sight, I heard a different voice, lower and harder, say, "Me."

Bob whirled to look and went suddenly pale. A split-second later, he managed a shaky smile. "Heeeey, Zane. How's it going?"

Zane appeared outside my doorway, like he'd just come from somewhere down the corridor. He looked to Bob and replied, "Shitty. Now, get the fuck away from her."

I couldn't help but flinch. "Actually," I said, "it's fine."

Without so much as a glance in my direction, Zane said, "No. It's not. And stay out of this."

What the hell? "I can't stay out of it," I said. "This is *my* room."

Zane's mouth tightened. "Not for long."

I wasn't even sure what that meant. Before I could even think to ask, Zane returned his attention to Bob. "You heard me," Zane told him. "Now, find somewhere else to go."

"Like where?" Bob's shoulders slumped. "I was kicked out of my suite."

"Not *your* suite," Zane corrected. "*My* suite."

I'd heard this sort of logic before. The last time, I'd found it funny and charming. Now, I was only appalled.

In front of me, Bob was saying, "It was *supposed* to be mine."

"But it's not," Zane said. "So fuck off."

And there it was – Zane's favorite phrase.

Bob lowered his voice to a pathetic whisper. "Then how about a loan? Or maybe an advance? You know, to tide me over?"

Zane gave Bob a long, cold look. "No. But I *can* give you some advice."

With obvious reluctance, Bob asked, "What?"

"Get out before I drag you out."

I gave Zane a worried glance. Normally, I would've assumed this was merely a figure of speech. But Zane *did* have that history.

First the senator, now Bob?

I spoke up. "You know what? I might have a little something."

Both guys turned to look. Bob's expression grew hopeful. "Oh yeah?"

As for Zane, he looked more irritated than ever. "I *said* to stay out of this."

I glared up at him. "And *I* said it's fine. Remember?" I looked to Bob and said, "Hang on, okay?"

With the door still open, I turned and dashed into my hotel room. I yanked my purse off the nightstand, dug out my wallet, and pulled out all of my cash.

It wasn't a ton of money, but it would surely be enough for a decent hotel room and maybe even dinner.

I hustled back to Bob and thrust out the bills in his direction. He gave the money a worried look, but made no move to take it.

It was easy to see why. Next to him, Zane loomed large and hostile.

Ignoring Zane, I thrust the bills closer to Bob. "Go on," I urged. "We'll just consider it a loan or something."

Anything to preserve the guy's dignity.

Finally, with a mumbled thanks, Bob took the money, turned, and trudged silently away. Watching him go, I felt a wave of sympathy wash over me. Everything about this felt so incredibly wrong.

I turned angry eyes to Zane. And of course, the look in *his* eyes was all too familiar. It was the same look I usually saw right before he told someone to fuck off.

Already, he'd said this to Bob. And the way it looked, he was getting ready to say it again.

To me.

CHAPTER 60

From the open doorway, I stared at the guy who'd rocked my world only a few hours ago.

If he wanted to cuss me out, fine. He could go right ahead. But he'd be hearing some choice words in return.

I crossed my arms and waited.

Zane looked down and gave a slow shake of his head. When he finally looked up, all he said was, "You didn't answer your phone."

"What phone? The hotel phone?"

"No. Your cell. I called you maybe thirty minutes ago."

I *had* received a call while I'd been talking to Charlotte. But I hadn't recognized the number, so I'd let it go to voicemail.

I asked, "Did you leave a message?"

"No," he said. "I came in person."

I gave him a look. "Yes. You sure did."

"Meaning?"

I made a sound of frustration. "The thing with Bob, are we just going to pretend that it didn't happen?"

"If you're lucky, we are."

Was that a joke? It didn't *sound* like a joke. "What's that supposed to mean?"

"It means, you were supposed to stay out of it."

My arms dropped to my sides. "Why?"

"Because it's not your problem. And I don't want it to be."

This might've been a lovely idea, if only the so-called problem hadn't arrived on my proverbial doorstep. With a sigh of frustration, I looked away.

Zane said, "If you've got something to say, go ahead."

I looked back to him and said, "Well, I guess I *am* wondering how you can be so awful."

His mouth tightened. "To you?"

That was the million-dollar question, wasn't it?

What *was* the price of my soul? Even if this was more than a fling, *and* even if he *did* end up treating me wonderfully, would I seriously be able to stand by while he abused everyone else? And if so, what kind of person would that make me?

His question was more complicated than he realized. *Was he awful to me?* No. Especially not lately. But it *was* awful to see him kick someone when they were down. I murmured, "I don't know."

His voice was flat. "You don't know."

Obviously, he didn't get it. Desperately, I tried to explain. "I just don't know what to think, you know, after the thing with Bob."

"Forget him," Zane said. "He's gone."

"Yeah, but to where? I mean, you kicked him out of his house."

"No," Zane said in a tone of forced patience. "I kicked him out of *my* house. Big difference."

"But you're not even living there." I searched his face. "Are you?"

"You *know* where I live."

Yes. I did. He lived in a giant mansion with so many rooms, he probably got lost at night. And where was Bob living? I didn't even want to speculate.

"But seriously," I said, "aren't you worried? He looked so pathetic."

"Yeah. He did. And you wanna know why?"

"Why?"

"So he could take advantage of someone too dumb to know better."

I drew back. "Did you just call me dumb?"

Zane's expression softened. "I wasn't talking about you."

Sure he wasn't.

I almost felt like crying. And it wasn't only because I felt bad for Bob. All of this was making me remember – belatedly, it seemed – how heartless Zane could be.

I almost didn't know what to say.

As the silence stretched out between us, I couldn't help but recall my conversation with Charlotte. What if, heaven forbid, I *did* love this guy? What then?

The answer was obvious. He'd break my heart and stomp on the pieces. It was only a matter of time.

In front of me, Zane's expression grew stormier with every passing moment. Finally, he said, "Whatever you're thinking, you're wrong."

Was I?

In front of me, he looked anything but warm and welcoming. I snuck a worried glance over my shoulder. Behind me, all I saw was a temporary room, reserved for a job that I no longer had.

This posed a troubling question. Why was I still here, anyway?

From the look on Zane's face, he was wondering the same thing.

I heard myself say, "I'm going home."

"No."

"Why not?"

"Are you forgetting your roommate? *And* her boyfriend?"

I wasn't forgetting anything. But as far as a reason to stay, it was sadly lacking. Besides, I'd have to go home *sometime*, right?

I said, "It'll be fine."

His jaw tightened. "Will it?"

"Yes. Definitely." My throat felt tight as I went on to explain. "As far as Paisley, I've handled her fine so far. And, well, with the professor, he's probably already moved on."

"Uh-huh." Zane looked far from convinced. "To who?"

"I dunno. Someone else."

"And if he hasn't?"

"Then I'll deal with it."

After a long moment, he said, "Jane, listen. If it's the house that's bothering you—"

I held up a hand. "You know what? You don't need to explain. After all, like you said, it's none of my business."

"You're right. It's not."

I summoned up a stiff smile. "See? Problem solved."

Ignoring my comment, Zane continued. "But I'd rather tell you than have you look at me like you're looking at me now."

"It's not just the house," I said. "It's everything. And really, it doesn't even matter."

"Oh yeah? Why not?"

How to explain? I gave a hopeless shrug. "I guess, because we're so different."

"Yeah. We are. But that doesn't have to be a problem."

Maybe not for him. But it would be for me. After all, how many times could I watch him being awful to somebody before I ended up despising him?

Maybe it was unfair. Maybe I was being stupid. But at that particular moment, all I wanted was some time to think.

When I made no reply, Zane said, "Everything I do, I've got my reasons."

I gave a bitter laugh. "Oh, I'm sure you do."

Zane stiffened, and I felt a tiny twinge of guilt. It only reinforced what I knew all along. We were totally different people. He could chew someone up and spit them out without breaking a sweat. But me? I felt awful every time I hurt someone.

Even now, part of me worried that I might be hurting *him*, as crazy as that sounded. I heard myself murmur, "This would never work."

Zane's posture grew rigid. "What?"

"I'm just saying…" I blinked long and hard. "I really need to go."

Zane looked at me for a long moment before saying, "All right. You wanna go home? I'm not gonna fight you."

Good. It was, after all, for the best – or at least, that's what I kept telling myself, even as the heaviness grew in my heart.

Still, I gave a quick, silent nod.

"Fine," he said. "We'll leave at five tomorrow. And that's morning. Not night. The car will be waiting out front." As he turned to go, he added, "Be there. Or I'll come and get you myself."

I gave a quick shake of my head. "But wait, you said *we* – as in both of us – leave tomorrow?"

He turned back to say. "Right. That's what I was coming to tell you."

"Sorry, I don't get it. You were coming to tell me *what* exactly?"

"That we're done here. No need to stick around, right?"

Ouch.

What could I say? In barely a whisper, I said, "Right."

With a tight nod, he turned and strode away, leaving me standing in the open doorway. As I watched him go, I couldn't help but wonder if I was incredibly lucky that Bob showed up when he did – or if it was the worst thing that could've happened at the worst possible time.

But obsessing wouldn't change anything. And besides, I hadn't expected this to be a long-term thing, anyway – or at least, that's what I kept repeating to myself over and over, even as I packed my bags for the trip home.

While hurling things into my suitcases, I tried to take some satisfaction from the fact that, unlike the rest of Zane's flings, I'd at least shown a little dignity.

But dignity – or any other lofty ideal – didn't keep me warm that night as I tossed and turned in the cold and empty bed, wishing like crazy to turn back the clock.

After that restless night, followed by a tense ride to the airport, Zane and I boarded his private jet before the sun even peeked over the horizon.

And then, we were off.

Across from me sat Zane, grim and silent, staring at nothing in particular. Stupidly, I found myself longing for the dubious company of Teddy or even What's-Her-Name – anything to break the lingering tension.

After two silent hours, Zane looked to me and said, "Tell me."

I almost jumped at the sound of his voice. "Tell you what?"

"What you're thinking."

I tried to smile. "Right now, I'm thinking that I'd better keep my mouth shut."

"Yeah? And why's that?"

"Because," I said with a glance toward the window, "I think we're like ten minutes from Kalamazoo."

He frowned. "Was that a joke?"

Was it? I couldn't be sure either way. I gave a small shrug. "Maybe. Honestly, I'm not sure."

His gaze locked on mine. "So that's what you think? That I'd ditch you at some random city?"

"Well, you ditched *her*."

"Yeah, I did." His voice hardened. "And admit it. You were glad."

I stiffened. "I was not."

"You wanna keep telling yourself that? Fine by me. But we both know what you were thinking."

"Yeah. I was horrified."

"Maybe," he said. "But you were glad, too, whether you'll admit it or not."

"And what if I *don't* admit it?" I said. "Will you be dropping *me* in Kalamazoo?"

He looked away. "No."

"Oh yeah? And why not?"

"Because we passed it five minutes ago."

Now, it was my turn to ask, "Was *that* a joke?"

He was still looking away. "Hell if I know."

As an answer, it was oddly unsatisfying, but I was smart enough to not press the issue. After all, the flight wasn't over yet, and unless I wanted to cool my heels in Fort Wayne or wherever, I knew better than to push my luck.

So instead, I leaned back and tried to think of anything but him – not that I had any success.

When we landed, another limo was waiting. To my lingering despair, he told me flat-out that he was seeing me home. Just like so many other things, it was sweet and terrible all at the same time.

But I knew better than to argue – because from the look on his face, it was pretty obvious that I wouldn't win.

Through all of this – all of the tension, all of the silence, all of the unanswered questions – I tried to console myself with one single thought. Soon, I could crawl into my own bed, have a good cry, and then forget that Zane Bennington ever existed.

There was only one problem. When we pulled up to my house, it looked nothing like it had when I left. In fact, I wasn't even sure how to describe it.

As I stared at the destruction, only one word came to mind.

Squashed.

CHAPTER 61

As we pulled into the driveway, I stared, dumbstruck, at the place I used to call home.

Squashed was definitely the right word. The roof was caved in, and the exterior walls were slanted inward, like the house had been stomped on by a mythical giant.

Encircling the entire mess was bright yellow tape, like something yanked from a crime scene.

The limo had barely stopped when I lunged for the door handle, intending to jump out for a closer look. But something made me stop. It was a hand on my elbow – Zane's hand.

He said, "Don't."

I whirled in my seat to face him. "Don't what?"

"Don't go out there."

I was nearly frantic. "Why not?"

"Because I'm gonna look first."

"Why?" I demanded.

His mouth was grim. "Because, you don't know what you'll find."

"I don't care. I'm going." I made a move toward the door. Again, he pulled me back. Again, I whirled to face him. "Will you stop that?"

He rapped on the glass that separated us from the driver. When the glass slid aside, Zane told the guy, "When I get out, secure the back."

And then, almost before I knew what was happening, Zane slipped out on the opposite side and slammed the limo door shut behind him. A split second later, something clicked. *Damn it.* The door locks? It had to be.

I lunged for my door and yanked on the handle. And then, I pushed. Nothing happened. The glass separating me from the driver had already slid shut.

I reached up and rapped on the glass.

When it slid aside, I said, "Hey, unlock the doors."

"Sorry. Can't."

"I mean it," I told him.

"Sorry," he repeated. "Just following orders."

I made a sound of frustration. "Not *my* orders."

"I'm terribly sorry."

I spent the next five minutes practically begging for him to let me out. *He* spent the next five minutes apologizing, but refusing to open up.

The whole time, I kept glancing at the house, watching as Zane circled the front and then disappeared around the side, heading into the back yard.

He emerged sooner than I expected, and strode back to the limo. He rapped on the driver's side window, and exchanged a few words with the guy before I heard the telltale click of the locks opening.

Immediately, I bolted out of the limo and ran up to the house, not bothering to close the car door behind me. I stopped short at my front door – or rather, what was left of it.

Behind me, Zane said, "That's close enough."

Obviously.

I mean, even *I* could tell that it wasn't remotely safe. I heard myself say, "What happened?"

"It was a tree."

"What?"

"A tree," he repeated. "It fell on the house."

I shook my head. "I don't think so. I mean, wouldn't there be branches or something?"

"Yeah, but they're gone now."

"Then how do you know it was a tree?"

"Because part of it's still in the back yard."

Almost in a daze, I walked around the side of the house, barely noticing as Zane kept close to my side. Sure enough, the giant oak tree that had previously taken up most of the yard was gone, replaced by a jagged stump and not much else.

I turned away from the stump and looked toward the house, only to feel the color drain from my face. If anything, the back was more squashed than the front.

This was where the bedrooms were. If I'd been asleep in my own bed, I would've been squashed, too.

I bit my lip. "Do you think anyone was hurt?"

I held my breath and waited. If anyone had been home, the answer to *that* question was obvious.

Yes.

But next to me, Zane replied, "No."

Relief coursed through me. Still, I had to ask, "But how can you be sure?"

"I'm not," he said. "But the way it looks, it happened a few days ago. Seems to me, you would've heard if anyone was injured."

All I could do was scoff. "Yeah. You'd think." I made a useless gesture toward the house. "But no one called to tell me *this.*"

I cringed. *Oh, no.* Unless the person who *would've* told me was dead or in the hospital.

Already, I was pulling out my cell phone. I found Paisley's number and hit the call button.

No answer.

Shit.

With an effort, I reminded myself that it was still early in the morning. Probably, she was fine. She was a late sleeper. Even under the best of circumstances, she wouldn't be up for hours yet.

I mean, just because she didn't answer, that didn't mean she was dead *or* in a coma or anything.

I kept telling myself this, even as I called my sister. Unfortunately, *that* call went straight to voicemail. With increasing desperation, I tried Paisley a second time, and then a third, and a fourth after that.

On my fifth attempt, she finally answered with a cranky, "What?"

I breathed a sigh of relief. Never had I been so happy to hear her voice. Breathlessly, I said, "I'm here at the house. What happened?"

"Gee," she said, "thanks for your concern."

I stiffened. "I *am* concerned. That's why I'm calling. Are you okay?"

"No," she said, "I'm not."

"Oh, my God. So you were hurt?"

"I wasn't *hurt*," she said. "I was asleep. Why'd you keep calling?"

I glanced at the destruction. "Gee, I wonder why."

"I'm just saying, if someone doesn't answer the first time, you don't need to keep calling."

Oh, for God' sake.

"I'm ever so sorry," I said through gritted teeth. "I'll keep that in mind the *next* time our house is squashed while I'm out of town."

"I hope so," she said, "because you know I'm not a morning person."

"Right," I gritted out. "And like I said, I'm sorry. But seriously, what the hell happened?"

It took ten full minutes to get the story out of her, but apparently, the tree had fallen during a storm four nights ago while she'd been out at some art show with the professor.

Her ten-minute explanation included nine full minutes of gushing at how incredible Fergus had been in cleaning up the debris.

She concluded by saying, "He even bought a chainsaw. You should've seen him." Her voice became almost husky. "He was magnificent."

The professor? Magnificent? I couldn't even imagine. "Uh, yeah. Well, that's good."

She gave a little giggle. "I know, right?"

Funny, I'd never heard her sound so happy. Maybe the lumberjack life *was* for her. Still, I had to say, "I don't want to be critical here, but there's something I've gotta ask."

"What?"

"Why didn't you call and let me know?"

"Because Charlotte said *she'd* tell you."

"She did? When?"

"The day after it happened, when she stopped by to check on the place – which I didn't appreciate, by the way." Paisley gave a snort of disbelief. "What is it? You don't trust me?"

Considering that I'd spent the final few minutes *before* my trip stuffing all of my valuables into a suitcase, this was a question better left unanswered.

I cleared my throat. "Well, she was probably in the neighborhood."

"Yeah, right," Paisley said, sounding decidedly disgruntled again. "But anyway, she saw the damage and said she'd let you know."

"She did? Are you sure?"

"Of course, I'm sure. In fact, she told *me* not to worry about it."

Paisley? Worry?

About anyone but herself?

I couldn't even imagine.

Even now, I knew she was lying. After all, I'd talked to Charlotte just yesterday, and she hadn't mentioned a thing.

Still, there was no point in arguing, so I ended the call with as much grace as I could muster. And then, I shoved the phone back into my pocket and tried to think.

What now?

Zane's voice interrupted my thoughts. "You want me to get anything?"

Funny, I'd almost forgotten he was there. It was the strangest sensation, because every other time we'd been together, I'd been obnoxiously aware of his every move.

I gave a mental eye-roll. Finally, I knew just the thing to push Zane Bennington out of my mind.

A squashed house.

Now, if only I had a million more.

Almost in a daze, I turned toward the sound of his voice. He was standing next to me, frowning as he eyed the damage.

I said, "Sorry, what was the question again?"

He gestured toward the house. "You want me to grab anything?"

I looked toward the mess and tried to think. Oh sure, I had a few dishes and clothes, but the place had come already furnished, and I couldn't see the point of sifting through the rubble now.

After all, not much of it was mine. And, in a weird twist of fate, everything I truly cared about was already packed, thanks to my distrust of Paisley.

I shook my head. "No. But thanks." I glanced toward the front of the house. "I guess I should grab my suitcases, huh?"

He gave me a look. "What?"

"From the trunk of the limo."

"I *know* where they are," he said. "But you're not unloading them here."

I was only half-listening. In the back of my mind, I was still trying to come up with a plan.

Stupidly, I'd sold my old beater of a car. And the other car, the nicer one, wasn't even my own. Rather, it was a company car for a job that I no longer had. This meant, of course, that I had no vehicle at all.

But surely, *someone* would be willing to pick me up – if not my parents, then definitely Charlotte, assuming she ever answered her phone.

I mumbled, "It'll be fine. I'll just wait here with my suitcases."

"Wrong," Zane said. "What you're *going* to do is stay with me."

CHAPTER 62

I turned to face him. "What'd you say?"

He looked dead-serious. "I *said* you're staying with me."

Instantly, an image of Bob popped into my brain. I couldn't help but wonder, why hadn't *he* been offered a place to stay? After all, he needed shelter way more than I did.

And yet, Zane's offer was so very tempting.

Embarrassingly, it wasn't even because I had no options. It was because, even now, I wanted to throw myself into his arms and forget everything else – the squashed house, the tension between us, and worst of all, the slump of Bob's shoulders as he shuffled away.

It was that final image that stiffened my resolve. I shook my head. "No. Thanks, really. But I'm not."

"That's what *you* think."

"No," I told him. "That's what I know."

"We'll see." With that, he turned, once again, to look at the house.

I looked, too. As I took in the damage, I couldn't help but compare this place to Zane's estate. Unlike the mess in front of me, Zane's place was big and luxurious. It even had a swimming pool.

Plus, it wasn't squashed.

But it wasn't his house that was tempting me. It was Zane himself. Heaven help me, I probably did love the guy – because the longer this went on, the more I wanted to cry at the thought of life without him.

I was pathetic.

But I wasn't *so* pathetic that I'd actually jump on his offer – or *him*, as tempting as he was, standing beside me, looking annoyingly fine in the morning light.

I *had* to end this now, before I forgot all of the reasons why this would never work. With that in mind, I turned and began striding toward the front of the house, planning to grab my suitcases and settle this once and for all.

As I moved purposefully toward the driveway, Zane silently kept pace, never letting me out of arm's reach.

When I reached the back of the limo, I paused as a realization hit home. The trunk was locked. Trunks were always locked. I knew that. I'd just forgotten, that's all.

Undaunted, I strode to the limo's driver's side and rapped on the window. When the glass slid down, I said to the driver, "Could you please pop the trunk?"

The driver looked to Zane, who gave a slight shake of his head. The driver looked back to me and said, "I'm sorry, but no."

"Oh, for God's sake." I turned to glare at Zane, even as the window slid back up. Through gritted teeth, I said, "Give me my suitcases. Please."

He shrugged. "All right."

I felt my gaze narrow. Knowing Zane, there had to be a catch, because nothing with him was this easy. I crossed my arms and waited.

He flicked his head toward the limo. "Get in."

"What do you mean?"

"Get in the car," he said, "and I'll give you the suitcases."

"When?"

"When we get there."

"Where?"

"My place. Like I said."

And there it was. *The catch*.

I couldn't help but sigh. "I'm not staying with you." I stared up at him, silently begging him to understand. "I can't."

But the look on Zane's face suggested otherwise. In a tight voice, he said, "I've got a guest room."

Stupidly, the statement *didn't* make me feel any better. In fact, I was pretty sure it made me feel worse. *Talk about messed up.*

I shoved a nervous hand through my hair. "You've probably got ten guest rooms, but that's hardly the point."

"Then what is?"

"Do I really need to explain?"

He made a forwarding motion with his hand. "Go ahead."

Desperately, I searched for the words. "Well, we had, I dunno, a fling I guess, and now it's over. Don't you think it would be a little awkward if I stayed at your place *now*?"

His jaw tightened. "A fling."

I gave a hopeless shrug. "I just don't know what else to call it." I offered up a weak smile. "I'm not very good at this, am I?"

He didn't even try to smile back. "No. You're not."

Well, at least we agreed on *something*. Unfortunately, it wasn't anything that made me happy.

From the look on Zane's face, he wasn't feeling so cheerful himself.

Under his hard gaze, I started to wilt like soggy lettuce. Over the last day, I'd barely slept and hadn't eaten in hours. Plus, my house was squashed, and no one had bothered to let me know.

If this wasn't a crappy morning, I didn't know what was.

Just like too many other times today, I almost wanted to cry. In truth, it was kind of surprising that I wasn't crying already.

I looked away and tried to think. But my thoughts were a cloudy, distorted mess, and the whole effort seemed like a giant waste of time.

From beside me, Zane's voice cut through the clutter. "All right."

I turned to face him. "Great." It was a lie, of course, because nothing about this was good, much less great.

Zane glanced toward the limo. "You don't wanna stay at my place? Fine. I've got somewhere else. Stay there instead."

Where? In one of his hotels? Oh sure, like that would end well.

Summoning my last bit of resolve, I declined his offer and pulled out my cell phone. Again, I tried to reach Charlotte, and then my parents. As I made the calls, one after another, Zane watched in stony silence.

Obviously, he wasn't thrilled with my decision. Neither was I, especially when nobody answered *or* called me back.

In the end, what else could I do? I let Zane guide me back into the limo – not because I thought the idea was so terrific, but rather, because I was too worn out to argue.

Turns out, that was a big mistake, because the moment we pulled up to the place he had in mind, I knew I couldn't stay there, not if I wanted to keep my sanity.

CHAPTER 63

From inside the limo, I stared silently at the house. It was huge and beautiful, with a brick exterior and manicured lawn. And yet, I was almost too horrified to speak.

Why? Because I knew the place. I'd even walked by. And what had I seen? Bob's daughter sobbing on the front lawn.

And *why* was she sobbing? Because Zane Bennington, the guy sitting next to me, had kicked them out with zero guilt, zero kindness, and almost zero notice.

In my mind, I could still see her, the young woman crying as the family's furniture was loaded onto the moving truck.

And now, I couldn't help but wonder, where was she staying now? I had no idea. Probably, neither did Zane. The only difference was, I cared, where he didn't.

I was still looking at the house. "I can't stay here."

"Why not?"

"Because this is Bob's house, isn't it?"

"No," he said, "it's *my* house, just like I said. And I'm telling you, you can stay."

He was wrong. I couldn't. Regardless of my own situation, I couldn't see myself building a nest, even for a single night, on the foundation of someone else's misery.

I was still staring at the place. "You know what? I'll just get a hotel or something."

"No. You won't."

"Why not?"

His voice hardened. "Because you owe me."

I whirled to face him. "For what?"

Zane leaned back in his seat. "I told you I'd be calling in a favor."

I remembered no such thing. "When?"

"Before New York."

I tried to think. And then, it hit me. He must be referring to that conversation we'd had in his office, right after the Fergus flower fiasco. All too well, I recalled how relieved I'd been to learn that I wasn't being fired.

In hindsight, it was almost funny. After all, it had only delayed my dismissal by less than two weeks.

I told Zane, "You've got a lot of nerve. You know that?"

"Maybe. But you're staying, anyway."

I turned to look in the general direction of the guard shack. From what I'd seen as we pulled through the gate, security had been noticeably upgraded. The guard manning the gate *now* had looked more military than mall cop, and I couldn't help but wonder if this new, upgraded security could be used to keep people *in* as well as keep them out.

It wasn't a comforting thought.

Testing my theory, I said, "Let's say I *do* stay. Can I leave whenever I want?"

Zane's jaw tightened. "You're not my prisoner, if that's what you're asking."

Heat flooded my face. Of course, it had been a stupid question. If he *really* wanted to keep me prisoner, he'd be dragging me into his basement, not offering me the use of a luxury home.

In spite of my irritation, I couldn't help but feel just a little bit ashamed. Already, he'd gone to a good bit of trouble on my behalf, and here I was, acting all paranoid.

I was so confused, I didn't know what to do.

Apologize?

Thank him?

Or run for the hills?

I squeezed my eyes shut and tried to think. Maybe I'd just stay for the night and figure everything out tomorrow, after a good night's sleep – assuming that I could sleep at all.

In the end, I let him lead me out of the limo and into the house.

Unfortunately, what I saw there only made me feel worse.

CHAPTER 64

Just inside the front door, I stopped and looked around, surprised to see that the place was fully furnished, complete with stunning artwork and an impressive array of Victorian antiques.

This might've been a lovely thing, if only I hadn't seen these exact same pieces weeks ago, sitting out on the front lawn.

I turned to Zane and asked, "Whose stuff is this?"

He looked toward the far corner of the front room, where a stack of boxes sat near a stunning brick and marble fireplace. He frowned. "Don't worry. I'll have them hauled away tomorrow."

I wasn't worried. I was disturbed. "I'm not talking about the boxes," I said. "I'm talking about the furniture. Whose is it?"

He moved deeper into the front room. With his back facing me, he said, "It goes with the house."

I followed after him. "This isn't Bob's furniture, is it?"

He turned and gave me a long, penetrating look. Something in his eyes made me feel transparent and silly, like I'd been caught skulking around where I didn't belong.

Still, I had to ask, "So, did you buy it off him or something?"

"No." Zane looked away. "It's not his."

Right. Just like this wasn't Bob's house. Funny how all that worked.

And yet, I *had* seen the furniture being loaded up. Hadn't I? But if so, why was it still here?

Zane said, "By the way, your car's in the garage."

That made me pause. "What car? You don't mean the company car?"

"It's your car now."

"But—"

"The fine print," he said with the ghost of a smile. "You should read it sometime."

Obviously, he was referring to the severance agreement. At the time, I'd been too aroused to read much of anything. Now, I was beyond stunned. "Are you serious?"

"I had someone bring it over," he said. "And just so you know, there's a parking pass on the windshield and an electronic card to open the gate. If you go out, you'll need them to get back in."

I recalled Zane texting someone from inside the limo, but I hadn't realized it involved me. The whole thing was surprisingly thoughtful, which only made me feel worse.

I reached up to rub my temples. "Thanks, but I actually feel kind of guilty."

"Don't."

But I did. And the mental whiplash was making me crazy. Zane was being incredibly generous and thoughtful. And yet, he'd been so heartless with everyone else.

Once again, I had to wonder, *"Who is this guy?"*

Desperate for clues, I said, "About the boxes, who do they belong to?"

He turned to give me another long look. "Does it matter?"

"Well, yeah…" I gave a nervous laugh. "Like if someone stops by to get them, I'd need to know what to do, right?"

From the look on his face, he thought the odds of this were pretty low. Still, in a tight voice, he said, "Hey, if their name's on it, they can have it."

I asked no more questions, even as Zane showed me the alarm system and told me in no uncertain terms that he expected me to use it. He also assured me that in spite of the boxes, the house had been cleaned weekly, including the sheets, so I should take my pick of the bedrooms and make myself at home.

Before leaving, he leaned close, almost like he might kiss me. But he didn't. Instead, he said, "We'll talk later."

Was that a promise? Or a threat? Either way, all I could do was nod.

And then, he was gone, leaving me sitting alone in the quiet house. Even with the furniture and boxes, the place felt big and empty, and nothing like an actual home.

This shouldn't have been surprising. After all, this wasn't anyone's home – not anymore, and all thanks to Zane.

And yet, I couldn't help but love the other side of him – the side he'd shown me not so long ago. If I wasn't careful, I'd be falling hopelessly under his spell.

I sighed. Who was I kidding? I already had.

That realization only confirmed what I knew all along. I'd be smart to leave as soon as possible. Cripes, if I were *really* smart, I'd leave now, but I didn't quite have the nerve, not after he'd gone to so much trouble.

I spent next couple of hours wandering through the house, opening the windows to let in the fresh air, and trying to pass the time while I figured out what to do – not just with my living situation, but with my whole life.

Utterly overwhelmed, I finally sank down on the nearest sofa – which *wasn't* an antique, thank God – and closed my eyes, hoping it would help me think.

It didn't.

Instead, I drifted off, thinking of Zane, only to be startled awake by the sound of ringing.

I sat up. It was a phone. But it wasn't my own.

Well, that was odd.

CHAPTER 65

I sat up. The phone sounded like a landline. Funny, I didn't even realize the house had one – not hooked up, anyway.

I stood and looked around. The ringing was coming from somewhere near the rear of the house.

Suddenly curious, I began walking in that direction, listening as I went. I found the phone in the far corner of a small sitting room, jam-packed with boxes.

The phone was cherry red in a classic, retro design. It was still ringing.

I stared down at the thing. Should I answer it? Or let it ring? After all, the call *couldn't* be for me – unless, maybe it was Zane?

Reluctantly, I scooped up the phone and answered with a tentative, "Hello?"

But it wasn't Zane's voice that greeted me on the other end. It was the voice of an unfamiliar female, demanding, "Who's this?"

"Uh, Jane. Who's this?"

"Jane who?"

I really didn't want to say, especially considering she still hadn't answered *my* question. "Sorry," I said, "but I think you might have the wrong number."

"I do not," she said. "You're in *my* house."

I cringed. *Oh, crap.* She sounded close to my own age, which meant that I was probably talking to Bob's daughter, the one who'd been crying out on the front lawn.

I still hadn't responded when she spoke again. "And you're talking on *my* phone. Aren't you?"

Heat flooded my face. "Actually, I'm not sure."

"Is it red?"

"Maybe," I admitted.

"What, you don't know?"

I did know. I just didn't want to say.

She said, "So, what's the deal? Are you living there now?"

I glanced around. *Was* I living here? Zane might say yes, but I'd say no. Splitting the difference, I settled on, "Not really."

"What kind of answer is that?"

Her open hostility was hard to stomach. And yet, I couldn't exactly blame her. After all, I was in her space, using her things.

Still, I couldn't help but sigh. *Why on Earth had I answered?*

She said, "I can hear you breathing, you know."

I winced. "Sorry, it was just a sigh."

"It didn't sound like a sigh to me."

"Well, it was," I insisted.

"So, what are you?" she asked. "His new squeeze?"

And just like that, the house felt several degrees warmer. If she was talking about Zane, I'd been his so-called squeeze for one unforgettable night.

But what was I now?

I had no idea – well, other than some sort of mouth-breather, apparently.

I told the caller, "I'm not his anything. But if this is about the house, I have no idea what's going on. So if you have any concerns, you should probably talk to Zane."

"That prick?" She gave a bark of laughter. "You're kidding, right? Have *you* ever tried reasoning with him?"

The question hit a little too close to home. "Maybe."

"Oh yeah? And how'd *that* go?"

I *so* didn't want to say. In too many ways to count, Zane was the most unreasonable person I'd ever met. Unfortunately, he was also the most fascinating. And sexy. And yes, sometimes, so protective and generous that he took my breath away.

The caller said, "You don't have to answer. I *know* how it went. Terrible, right?"

I bit my lip. "Maybe."

"You keep saying maybe, but I know what that *really* means. You *do* know he only cares about himself, right?"

I shoved a hand through my hair. "Honestly, I'm just a former employee, so—"

"So, what'd he do? Fire you?"

I mumbled, "Maybe."

"I knew it! He does that all the time, you know." She made a scoffing sound. "I hope you got a good severance."

My gaze shifted toward the front of the house. *Oh yeah. I got a car and triple a year's salary.* Actually, it was pretty amazing, and yet, the whole arrangement still made me uncomfortable. After all, what exactly had I been paid for?

The caller gave a sudden gasp. "Oh, no. If *you're* there, what happened to my stuff?"

"What stuff?" I asked.

"Well, the boxes for one thing."

"Nothing happened," I assured her. "They're still here, probably right where you left them."

She made a sound of derision. "And why should I believe *you*? For all I know, you're using my stuff right now."

"Trust me, I'm not using your stuff."

"Oh sure..." Her tone grew sarcastic. "...says the person using *my* phone."

Oh, for God's sake. "Well, I wouldn't be using your phone if you hadn't called."

"Hah! You didn't know it was me. I could've been anyone."

"Maybe," I said through gritted teeth, "but you weren't."

"But I could've been."

We went back and forth a few more times, and I had to remind myself that her paranoia might be at least a little justified. After all, she'd been dealing with Zane for who-knows-how-long.

He was enough to make anyone crazy.

Finally I said, "Look, if you want the boxes, just come and get them." I hesitated. "I mean, of course, when Zane's around."

"Oh suuuuure," she said. "And put them where, exactly? It's not like I've got room *here*."

I didn't know where "here" was, but I saw what she meant. I tried to put myself in her shoes. How would I feel if some stranger was living in my house, using my things?

I'd hate it. And I might even hate the person who was living there.

In spite of my own troubles, my heart went out to her. "I'm really sorry. If there's anything I can do…"

Apparently, that was the wrong thing to say.

Because she pounced on my offer faster than I could say, *"What the hell was I thinking?"*

CHAPTER 66

A half-hour later, I was parked at a gas station just a few miles away from Zane's neighborhood. Already, Kayla – meaning the caller – was ten minutes late, which gave me far too much time to consider the foolishness of what I was doing.

And yet, on the phone, her request hadn't sounded *too* unreasonable. Had it?

Even now, her words made a compelling case.

"I just want to look."

"It'll only take a few minutes."

"I'm really worried. Can't you help?"

But it wasn't until she started to cry that I crumbled like a stale cookie. So here I was, watching for a little red car and praying that I wasn't making a huge mistake.

I was still waiting when my cell phone rang. I lunged for it and took a look.

It was Charlotte.

Finally.

I skipped the hello and went straight to a frantic, "Hey, I've been trying to reach you."

"Uh, yeah. I got your messages."

I'd left at least a dozen, each more desperate than the last. "So about the house," I said, "Paisley said you knew, but she was lying, right?"

Charlotte hesitated. "Uh, well..."

"Oh, my God. She wasn't? So you *did* know?" My voice rose. "And you didn't bother to tell me?" I knew I was ranting, but I couldn't seem to make myself stop. "Do you know what it's like to show up one morning and find your house squashed?"

"No, but..."

"But what?"

"Well..." Charlotte hesitated. "You were supposed to call me."

"What do you mean?"

"I kept asking you to call me before you came back. Remember? I even said it yesterday."

I squeezed my eyes shut. *Yesterday.* After the thing with Bob, and then my argument with Zane, I hadn't been in the mood to talk to anyone, especially Charlotte, with all her sunny storybook predictions for me and you-know-who.

When I made no reply, she asked, "So, why didn't you call?"

"I don't know," I snapped. "Why didn't *you* tell me about my house?"

After a long pause, she mumbled, "It isn't *really* your house."

"What?"

"I mean, it's just a rental. And you told me that you already packed everything you care about." She hesitated. "You know, because of your fight with Paisley?"

As if I could forget.

I sighed. "But according to Paisley, the house was squashed *days* ago. How long have you known?"

"I dunno," she said. "A few days?"

"You're kidding, right?"

"Uh, not really."

"But I've talked to you almost every day. And you never thought to mention it?"

"Well, yeah," she said. "I *thought* about it."

I made a sound of frustration. "But you didn't actually do it?"

"I would've, but seriously, what could you do, anyway?"

I resisted the urge to bang my forehead on the steering wheel. "Gee, I don't know. Maybe come home and figure things out?"

"Figure *what* out?" she said. "It's not like you can put the house back together."

"Yeah, no kidding."

Her voice picked up steam. "And I don't know why you're so mad at me. *I* didn't squash your house."

"Oh, I thought it *wasn't* my house."

"You know what I mean."

I just had to ask, "But why on Earth didn't you tell me?"

"Because I didn't want to ruin your trip."

"What?"

"Yeah," she said. "It sounded like you and Zane were really hitting it off."

Not anymore.

Through gritted teeth, I said, "It wasn't a vacation. It was a work trip."

"Oh, please," she said. "You *know* he just agreed to those interviews as an excuse to drag you away with him."

Funny, he'd practically admitted as much. But that wasn't the point.

In a tone of forced cheer, Charlotte said, "So, did you have a nice trip?"

"No," I snapped. "I didn't."

Not in the end, anyway.

She hesitated. "So, where are you now?"

"A gas station." I sighed. "Don't ask."

"So you're staying at a gas station?"

"No. I'm *meeting* someone at a gas station."

"Who?"

"Kayla."

"Kayla who? I don't know any Kayla."

"Yeah, me neither," I muttered. "And she's already late."

But just then, I spotted a little red sports car pulling into the lot. In the driver's seat, sure enough, sat the same young woman who'd been sobbing on the front lawn. "Anyway, she's here, so I've gotta go."

And with that, I ended the call without saying goodbye. Of course, I instantly felt like crap.

Sure, I was still angry, but I also realized that Charlotte's heart was probably in the right place.

Unfortunately, good intentions were no guarantee of a good outcome, as I soon discovered for myself – the hard way.

CHAPTER 67

Kayla was all smiles as she leaned her head out of her driver's side window to call out, "Hang on. I'll just grab my purse."

I tried to smile back.

Well, at least she wasn't crying anymore.

And I knew why. Against my better judgment, I'd agreed to let her pop into the house for just a few minutes to make sure that her things were still there *and* unmolested – by me, apparently.

Our plan was simple enough. We'd leave her car at the gas station and take mine to the house, where she could take a quick look around to ease her mind. Afterward, I'd drive her back.

Simple and quick.

In theory, anyway.

In spite of my nervousness, I tried to look on the bright side. I was doing a good deed, right?

And yet, when she emerged from her car, I felt my eyebrows furrow. Her clothes – or rather, lack of clothes – made me wonder what exactly she was thinking.

She was wearing a skimpy red bikini, with a black something-or-other that might be considered a skirt, if only it weren't so short and so sheer that it was mostly transparent.

On her feet were sassy white sandals with thick, chunky heels. Over her left shoulder was draped a long white purse with long leather fringes. As she opened my passenger's side door, she said, "You are *such* a life-saver."

I bit my lip. No, I was an idiot.

I hadn't even checked with Zane, but he *had* given me permission in a roundabout way. After all, he *did* say that if someone's name was on a box, they could have it. And I'd seen plenty of boxes with Kayla's name.

Still, I wasn't going to take any chances. "I hate to ask," I said, "but I can see your driver's license?"

Her smile vanished. "What?"

"Your driver's license," I repeated. "I just want to make sure that your name matches the name on the boxes."

"Why?" she said. "I'm not taking anything. I'm just making sure everything's still there."

"I know, but..." How to explain? "Zane left pretty clear instructions."

She gave an irritated sigh. "Oh, whatever." She pulled out her purse, and began digging through it. "It totally figures. He is *such* a prick."

It was then that the strangest thing happened. I felt my hands clench around the steering wheel, almost like her statement actually bothered me. But it *couldn't* bother me, because she had a point.

Zane *was* a prick.

Most of the time, anyway.

I pulled my hands off the wheel and tried not to think about it.

As for Kayla, she pulled out her driver's license and thrust it out in my direction. I took it from her hand and pulled it close to study the details.

Yup. It was all there. Kayla Hunt, 241 Longwood Drive – just like I'd seen on a whole bunch of moving boxes.

When I returned the license, she said, "So, are you satisfied?"

Not really. "Uh, yeah. Thanks."

Kayla glanced around. "Hey, I don't wanna be rude, but I'm kind of on a schedule here." She glanced down. "Pool party and all. Do you think we could get going?"

Well, that explained the clothes.

About leaving, she didn't have to ask *me* twice. The sooner we finished, the better.

Ten minutes later, we rolled through the gate without a hitch. When we reached the house, I pulled the car straight into the attached garage, cut the engine, and shut the garage door behind us.

The door was barely down before Kayla scrambled out of the car and into the house. Over her shoulder, she called, "I'm gonna check upstairs first, okay?"

I didn't want to be nosy. This was, after all, her stuff. But I *did* feel a certain responsibility for anything that might go wrong, so I scrambled after her, feeling more like a security guard than any kind of helper.

But if she minded, she didn't show it. Silently, I trailed behind her as she wandered from room to room, first upstairs, and then back to the main floor, where she took a quick look around and even opened a few boxes for good measure.

When we reached the final room – a small den near the front of the house – she said, "Well, it looks like it's all here."

"See?" I said, feeling the first hint of relief. "You didn't have anything to worry about."

She gave me an apologetic smile. "Sorry if I was kind of bitchy." She looked heavenward and said. "But Zane is *such* a prick."

And there it was *again*. That twinge of annoyance.

Damn it.

I made a noncommittal shrug, but said nothing in reply.

But Kayla was on a roll. She leaned against a Victorian roll-top desk and said, "Do you know, he's been giving me grief right from the start? God, I *hate* that guy."

This posed a troubling question. Did *I* hate him? No. Definitely not. In truth, I felt quite the opposite.

This *wasn't* good.

Across from me, Kayla was saying, "And don't get me started on the furniture."

I looked around. *That's right. The furniture.* The reminder was the perfect cold splash for the annoyingly warm feelings that kept creeping into my heart.

How could I keep forgetting? Zane hadn't only kicked them out.

He'd kept their furniture, too.

Kayla gave an epic eye-roll. "You should've seen him on the night we moved. He was all like, 'Put it back. It's not yours.' And I was like, 'Fuck you, asshole.'"

I blinked. "Wait, what?"

She gave me a look. "What, you never heard the word 'asshole' before?"

"Uh…"

"Or was it the 'fuck' that bothered you?"

I gave a confused shake of my head. "It wasn't either one. I'm just trying to understand. If the furniture's not yours, whose is it?"

"It *is* ours." She glanced away. "Or, at least, it should've been."

"You mean yours and your dad's?"

She frowned. "What does my dad have to do with this?"

I froze. *Oh, crap.*

Still, hoping for the best, I said, "Because… he lived here, too?"

She gave me a look. "No, he didn't."

Uh-oh. This wasn't what I wanted to hear. Still, I summoned up a hopeful smile. "But we *are* talking about Bob, right?"

"Bob?" She laughed like I'd just said something funny. "He's not my dad."

"He's not?"

"No." Her laugh turned into a giggle. "But he *does* like it when I call him Daddy."

CHAPTER 68

I stood very still. *She calls him Daddy?*

I almost didn't know what to say. "Wait, so Bob *doesn't* have a daughter?"

"Oh, he totally does." Kayla looked heavenward. "But she is *such* a crybaby."

I felt my gaze narrow. "Is that so?"

"Totally," Kayla said. "She's like the most spoiled girl I know. Thank God she doesn't live with us."

"She doesn't?" I said. "So where *does* she live?"

"Right now? She's a senior at Purdue."

"The university?"

"No. The chicken plant."

"Huh?"

"I'm kidding," she said. "Of course, the university. She's like older than me, so you'd think she'd be past the whole crying thing, you know?"

What could I say to that?

Hell, what could I say to *any* of this?

Fortunately, I was spared the need of making a reply when my cell phone rang in my pocket. I yanked it out and glanced at the display, only to feel the color drain from my face.

It was *him*. Zane.

I glanced in the general direction of his estate. If I didn't answer, would he come over in person?

Now?

Yikes.

I said to Kayla, "Can you excuse me for a moment?" And then, without waiting for an answer, I practically dove for the nearby powder room and slammed the door shut behind me. I answered with a hushed, "Hello?"

Zane said, "What's wrong?"

"Nothing."

"I'm coming over."

"What, why?"

"Because you sound scared."

"I'm not scared." I forced a laugh. "You just caught me by surprise, that's all."

He was quiet for a long moment. "All right."

Did he believe me? From his tone, I couldn't be sure.

But I hadn't been lying. True, I *was* surprised that he called, and yeah, maybe a *little* nervous, but that wasn't the same as scared.

I forced a smile into my voice. "Seriously, everything's fine."

"Uh-huh." And yet, he didn't sound convinced. "So, where'd you go?"

"What do you mean?"

"An hour ago, you left. But the alarm wasn't engaged."

I stifled a curse. He was right. In all the confusion, I'd totally forgot. "Oh, jeez. Sorry about that. I dashed out for a minute."

"You were gone thirty."

"Was I? How do you know?"

"I got a report from the guard."

"Wait, so you're spying on me?"

"No," he said in a tone of infinite patience. "I'm making sure the house is secure."

"Oh, because you're worried about the stuff?"

"Fuck the stuff," he said. "There's only one thing in that house that *I'm* worried about."

Something about his tone made me feel just a little bit breathless. "Really?"

"Yeah, and I'm talking to her."

My heart fluttered, and I felt myself smile. I wanted to say something, but I had no idea what.

I was still searching for a decent response when he said, "Listen, I told myself I'd stay away, because you looked like you needed some space. But..." His words trailed off into silence.

I was dying to know what he'd say next. "But...?"

"But fuck that. You know what you need?"

"What?"

"Me."

That single word sent my world spinning.

Yes. Him.

Holy hell. He was right. I heard myself murmur, "I know."

With a smile in his voice, he replied, "Yeah?"

I was still smiling, too. "Definitely." And to my surprise, I realized that I meant it with all my heart. Maybe he *was* a prick, but now, I could totally see why.

On the phone, Zane said, "The hell with this. I'm coming over."

I practically gulped, "Now?"

"Is that a problem?"

Was it? Suddenly, I was desperate to see him. We hadn't resolved anything, and I had no idea what he had in mind. And yet, the longing was so strong that I could hardly control myself.

Still, I forced myself to say, "How about I'll come to your place?" On instinct, I reached out turned on the faucet. "I need to get cleaned up, maybe take a shower or something."

"Or," he said in a voice that was way too compelling, "you could come over and shower with me."

I swallowed. I *could* shower with him. Even now, I could imagine his body all slick and lathered – and his hands – *oh, boy* – he had nice hands. And the places they could go...

Already, sweet, warming sensations were creeping upward from my toes, and downward from my face. If I kept on thinking, I knew exactly where all that warmth would settle – right in the middle.

I murmured, "That sounds *really* nice."

A sudden pounding on the door made me jump. A split second

later, Kayla's voice carried from the other side. "Hey! You didn't forget I'm here, did you?"

On the phone, Zane said, "Who's that?"

Stupidly, I said, "Who's who?"

"Was that your sister?"

"Uh, nope." And then, in a rush, I said, "But I've gotta go, so I'll catch you in a bit, okay? Alrighty then. Bye." I disconnected the call before he could say a single word in response.

I wasn't going to lie to him, but the way I saw it, a little delay would be a very good thing – if nothing else, to give me some time to clean up my mess – and I didn't mean the normal kind.

No. *My* mess was still pounding on the door. "Hey!" she called. "You didn't fall in, did you?"

Into where? The toilet? I stifled a shudder and called out, "I'll be out in a second!" I turned off the faucet and yanked open the door to see Kayla standing like two inches away.

She said, "You *do* remember that I'm in a hurry, right?"

Through gritted teeth, I said, "Oh, I remember, all right."

"And do you *always* talk on the phone when you've got company?"

Company? She wasn't company. I wasn't sure *what* she was, but I intended to find out. I resisted the urge to roll my eyes. "Gee, I'm ever so sorry."

"Whatever. I'm just saying, it's pretty rude."

I stared at her. *Speaking of rude...*

"And anyway," she continued, "I need your help."

"For what?" I asked.

She glanced around. "As long as I'm here, I figure I might as well grab a few things."

"You mean from the boxes?"

She gave a breezy wave of her hand. "Nah, I'll worry about that stuff later. But I wouldn't mind snagging a few paintings."

I blinked. "What?"

"The paintings," she repeated. "They'd go great in our new place."

I didn't even know what particular paintings she meant, but I *did* know that if she started ripping stuff off the walls, we were going to have a serious problem.

I said, "I can't let you do that."

"Why not?"

Did I really need to explain? "Because I don't have the authority. I mean, I'm just a house-guest."

Her mouth tightened. "Yeah. In *my* house."

"Look," I said, "I've gotta be honest here. I'm not understanding any of this."

"What's so hard to understand?"

"Well, like Bob. If he's not your dad, that means he's your…?"

She looked at me like I was a complete moron. "Husband. You didn't know?"

I did now.

In truth, I'd begun to suspect as much. "So, that would make Teddy what? Your stepson?"

She drew back. "Hell no. That's disgusting."

I gave her a confused look. "Why? Because he's not your type?"

"No, because he's my ex."

CHAPTER 69

Woah. I hadn't seen *that* coming. I stared at Kayla. "Ex-*husband?* Or...?"

"Oh, please," she said. "We were never married. I mean, he's a nice guy and all, but he lacks that killer instinct, if you know what I mean."

Funny, I *did* know, especially when I compared him to Zane. This reminded me of something Teddy had said on the plane. He'd accused Zane of sleeping with his girlfriend. And worse, Zane hadn't denied it.

Was Kayla the girlfriend?

I shuddered at the thought. "So, let me get this straight. You *were* with Teddy. And now, you're with his stepdad?"

Her gaze narrowed. "You're giving me a look."

"I am?"

"Yeah. And I don't like it."

"What kind of look?"

"It's the same look *he* always gives me."

"Who?" I asked.

"The prick. Zane. Have I ever told you, I hate that guy?"

Through clenched teeth, I said, "You might've mentioned it."

"And it's all *his* fault we're not living here anymore." She grimaced. "You should see our new place. It's *way* worse than this."

What could I say to that? "Gee, that's too bad."

"Yeah. Tell me about it." She perked up. "But the paintings might help." She looked around. "Hang on, I'm gonna see which ones I want."

She could look all she wanted, but grabbing them? Well, that was another matter. I told her, "If you want to make a list, I'll check with

Zane."

"Screw him," she said. "He says no to everything."

Funny, I could totally see why.

Barely stopping for breath, she said, "Get this. A couple of months ago, I get *so* mad that I go down to his fancy office to try to reason with him. And what does he do? He has me tossed out, literally."

She looked down to her feet. "I even lost a shoe."

I froze. A shoe? In Zane's office?

In my mind, I could still see it – that red "fuck-me" shoe that I'd tripped over during my job interview.

I hated that shoe.

"This shoe," I said, "by any chance, was it red?"

Kayla looked surprised. "Yeah. How'd you know?"

Good question. I pointed vaguely toward her red bikini. "Red *does* seem to be your color."

"Oh sure." She rolled her eyes. "Not that *he* noticed."

"You mean Zane?"

"Who else?" she said. "I go down to his office, and I'm wearing these great heels and this awesome red dress, with a matching red thong and everything." She gave a little shimmy. "No bra, by the way. And he practically ignores me."

I was almost afraid to ask, "Did he, uh, see the thong?"

"Well, yeah." She shrugged. "He might've gotten a peek or two."

"How?"

"Well, it wasn't from anything *he* did. That's for sure. I could've been wearing a paper sack for all *he* noticed."

I felt myself smile. "Really?"

She gave me a look. "Why are you so happy about it?"

I wiped the smile from my face. "Um, because it's a really good story?"

She grumbled, "I'm glad *someone* thinks so. But I guess I shouldn't take it personally. I mean, I *know* why he wasn't interested."

"Oh yeah? Why?"

"Because he was screwing all those models. With all *that* action, it's a wonder his dick didn't fall right off."

And just like that, my urge to smile was gone. For starters, I liked his dick right where it was. Plus, her statement was a grim reminder of how many girls Zane had gone through, just within the last few months.

Kayla said, "But you wanna know what I think?"

By now, I wasn't so sure. Still, I said, "What?"

"I think he's been banging them for information."

No. He was "banging them" because they were gorgeous. That much was obvious. I said, "Sorry, but I'm not seeing it."

"Why not?" She licked her lips. "If he were banging me, I'd tell him anything."

What? I gave a confused shake of my head. "But I thought you hated him."

"Well, yeah, but he's still smoking hot, right?"

Yes. He was.

But more than that, he was actually a pretty decent person, all things considered.

Imagine that.

"But wait," I said. "You said he wanted information? About what?"

"About who killed his uncles."

Okay, that was unexpected. "But they both died in accidents."

"Oh, please. *Two* freak accidents in *one* day?" She gave a little laugh. "You don't believe that, do you?"

It *had* seemed suspicious. But it wasn't something I'd been dwelling on. "So you think he's looking to do what? Solve the crime or something?"

"No," she said. "I think he's looking to make sure *he's* not next."

I swallowed. "You mean to get killed?"

She gave an enthusiastic nod. "Oh yeah. I mean, if someone whacked the uncles, why not him, too?"

I swear, my heart stopped beating. "You don't think he's in any danger, do you?"

"I hope not," she said.

"Yeah," I whispered. "Me, too."

"Because seriously, I doubt he'd leave us a thing."

I stared in absolute horror. "You mean in his will?"

"Well yeah," she said. "We were screwed once. No need to get screwed again."

Well, that was nice.

Kayla gave a long, sad sigh. "But I guess *I'll* have to be satisfied with the paintings."

I stiffened. "Not today, you won't."

"Excuse me?"

"I can't let you take them."

Her gaze narrowed. "And who's gonna stop me? You?"

If it came down to that, I would. But I still had this blind hope of reasoning with her first. "Look, why don't you have Bob call Zane? Let *them* work it out."

"No way," she said. "Bob's in New York. He won't be back 'til tomorrow. And why should I make a special trip?"

With that, she turned and started heading deeper into the house. Over her shoulder, she said, "There's a really nice one in the den."

Oh, God. Was I really going to have to wrestle her for the paintings? With increasing desperation, I scrambled after her. "But Kayla, wait. I need to tell you something."

With a sigh, she stopped and turned around. "What?"

Yeah. What?

Grasping at straws, I finally blurted out, "I heard that Bob's going through a tough time. Maybe you should give him a call. Like, now."

She was frowning again. "What do you mean?"

"Well, I didn't want to say anything, but I heard he's in bad shape."

Her frown deepened. "You're not talking about his beer gut, are you?"

Huh? I didn't notice a beer gut. "Uh…no?"

"Oh, so you mean that flab under his chin?" She waved away my concern. "I'm not worried. He's having lipo when he gets back."

Liposuction? Really? I couldn't even imagine. For starters, he didn't need it. And besides, wasn't that expensive?

But already, Kayla was turning away.

"Wait," I called. "You never said. Why was Bob in New York?"

Again, Kayla stopped and turned around. With a sound of impatience, she said, "Because Zane was there…*with* his P.R. chick."

I froze. P.R.? As in Public Relations? Was she seriously talking about *me?*

CHAPTER 70

It suddenly struck me that Kayla had never even asked my name. Did she truly not realize that *I* was the so-called P.R. Chick? *Apparently not.*

I shook my head. "Sorry, but I'm not following."

"Look, it's not that complicated. Zane had all these interviews set up, right?"

As the person who set them up, I'd definitely know. But how was *she* so well informed? I said, "And you knew this, how?"

"From Teddy," she said. "So anyway, Bob and I get to talking, and we decide that what Zane needs is a little reminder that *we* can hurt *him*, too."

I *so* didn't like the sounds of that. "What do you mean?"

Kayla smiled. "Two words. Bad publicity."

"Oh?"

Kayla nodded. "Yeah, Bob figures he'll put a good scare into her, meaning the P.R. chick."

"But how?"

"By showing her the kind of publicity she'll be dealing with if Zane doesn't cooperate."

Funny, I hadn't been scared. Concerned? Yes. But scared? Not even a little, unless I counted Zane's reaction, which, yes, was a little scary.

I gave her a perplexed look. "What kind of publicity do you mean?"

"Interviews, appearances...whatever to show the world how Zane Bennington left us dirt poor *and* kicked us out of our home."

"So, Bob wanted revenge?" I said. "Is *that* what you're saying?"

"No." She looked at me like I was stupid. "He wanted money – which he should've been getting all along."

"So, you were planning to do what? Blackmail him?"

She gave me a cheerful smile. "Right."

There was no way I'd be smiling back. Aside from the sliminess, that had to be one of the dumbest plans I'd ever heard. "But Zane doesn't care about bad publicity." I hesitated. "Does he?"

Kayla's smile faded. "Apparently not." And then, she brightened. "But he *does* care about the P.R. gal."

I felt myself go very still. "What do you mean?"

"Well, according to Teddy, he's boning her on the side."

Okay, now that was just plain insulting. "Boning her?"

"You know. Fucking her."

Through gritted teeth, I said, "I *know* what boning means."

"Really? Because you looked confused."

I *was* confused, but not because of the terminology. I said, "So, this plan, did it work?"

Her shoulders slumped. "No. Zane ruined everything. As usual."

"How?"

"For starters, he kicks Bob out of Teddy's suite –"

"Wait. *Teddy's* suite?"

"Yeah. Technically, Zane owns it, but it's always been Teddy's place." She glanced around. "Kind of like the house."

"Wait a minute. *This* house? The one we're standing in?"

"Right." She waved the subject away. "But anyway, Zane catches Bob in the middle of his pitch and gets all pissy about it."

"Pissy?"

"Mad. Whatever. And get this. Afterward, he tracks Bob down and tells him that if he ever bothers his precious P.R. gal again, he'll live to regret it him." Kayla made a scoffing sound. "Like *she's* so special."

Against all logic, I wanted to smile. Oh sure, the story was terrible, but it still made me feel embarrassingly warm all over.

Kayla was still talking. "Although, *here's* something funny. This P.R. chick? She's so stupid, she doesn't even realize that it's all an act."

"Excuse me?"

"Yeah." Kayla gave a little laugh. "Get this. She pulls out like two-hundred bucks and hands it over, like she's saving Bob's life or something." Kayla rolled her eyes. "God, what an idiot."

My jaw clenched. "Yeah. No kidding."

And I meant it too. Zane had told me. But had I listened?

No. I hadn't.

But I should've. After all, he knew these people a whole lot better than I did.

Damn it.

Did I owe him an apology?

Probably.

In front of me, Kayla was still laughing. "Two hundred bucks? In Manhattan? I mean, that won't even get you a decent dinner."

I had no idea what to say to that, mostly because everything I *wanted* to say was loaded with profanity.

Kayla gave another quick glance around. "You know what? Forget the paintings."

I breathed a sigh of relief. "Really?"

She nodded. "Yeah, they're a lot of trouble. I think I'll just grab the silverware."

I gave her a look. "You can't have the silverware."

"Why not?"

"Because, as I keep telling you, I'd need to check with Zane first."

"Screw *him*," she said. "He can shove a fork up his ass for all I care." And with that, she made a move to go around me.

I sidestepped to block her path.

She moved to the other side.

I moved again.

Her gaze narrowed. And then, she pulled a fast one, faking to the left, but then dodging to the right. A moment later, she was sprinting toward the kitchen with me on her heels.

I caught up, just as she was yanking open the silverware drawer, and reaching for the tray inside.

Sure enough, she yanked out the silverware, tray and all, and then turned to make off with it. To where, I had no idea, unless she was planning to sprint back to the gas station.

Not so fast, sister.

I lunged forward and grabbed the tray's other end, making the silverware jangle precariously. I gave the tray a tug.

She gave it a tug right back. "Let go!"

I tugged again. "No!"

"I mean it!"

The next thing I knew, the tray was flying upward, with all the silverware inside. Just as the tray almost reached the ceiling, the tray itself started to fall even as the silverware kept on going, crashing into the ceiling, and then falling hard and fast, until the mass of forks, knives, and whatever came to a clattering crash all over the tile floor.

Kayla yelled, "You did that on purpose!"

"Yeah? Well, you're a skank!" I gave a little gasp. I'd never called anyone a skank before. Or a slut, or even a bitch, come to think of it. Oh, sure, I'd thought such things. But saying them out loud was a different matter entirely.

Kayla was glaring at me now. "What'd you call me?"

I cleared my throat. In a quieter voice, I said, "A skank?"

Just then, I heard a yip at the nearby kitchen. I turned to look and spotted two furry faces with big floppy ears.

It was Flint and Lansing. I swear, they were smiling.

I knew why, and I hated to disappoint them. I gave them an apologetic look. "Sorry." I winced. "I don't have any meatballs."

When I turned back to Kayla, she was still glaring, but not at me. Rather, she was glaring past my left shoulder.

I turned to look and saw who? Zane Bennington – the most wonderful guy on the planet.

He moved close and pulled me into his arms. Into my hair, he whispered, "You okay?"

I almost didn't know what to say. He felt warm and wonderful, and just the thing I needed.

I wasn't just okay. I was *more* than okay. With a happy sigh, I nodded against him.

Behind me, I heard Kayla say, "Hey, don't you care about *me?*"

Without missing a beat, he replied, "No."

"But she called me a skank!"

He shrugged against me. "Well, if the shoe fits…"

CHAPTER 71

An hour later, it was just him and me. At Zane's insistence, he'd been the one to give Kayla a ride back to her car – minus the silverware *or* any paintings, for that matter.

As for me, I'd spent that time waiting at Zane's place, mostly playing with the dogs, who'd apparently just arrived home from their doggie vacation up north.

Of course, I spent *some* of this time rummaging through Zane's massive freezer in search of – yup, you guessed it – stray meatballs.

Did I find any?

I'll never tell. But I *will* say that two microwavable minutes later, along with a few bad throws, the dogs were in no mood to complain, and soon settled down for a nap in the shade.

I was in no mood to complain either. Somehow, after wandering from the kitchen, I'd ended up on the same exact rug that I'd been cleaning however many months ago.

In fact, that's where Zane found me when he returned from taking Kayla back to the gas station. With an amused smile, he asked, "What are you doing *there*?"

I was sprawled on my back, gazing up at the high ceiling. "Just thinking."

"About what?"

"My question." I gave him an impish smile. "You never *did* answer it, you know."

He sank down onto the rug beside me and pulled me into his arms. "What question?"

"Earlier, you *claimed* you were terrified when I showed up on your doorstep. But you weren't really, were you?"

"Hell yes, I was terrified."

I gave him a playful swat to his arm. "Oh, stop it."

"I was," he insisted. "And you wanna know *why*?"

"Why?"

He pulled me closer. "Because even as mad as you were, I still didn't want you to leave."

I laughed against him. "Wow, that *is* scary."

"Yeah. Tell me about it." He ran a hand along my back. "And it wasn't just me. It was the dogs, too."

"Now, I *know* you're joking."

"No joke," he said. "You should've heard them when you left. They howled for an hour." His voice softened. "You *do* know they're crazy about you."

I was still laughing. "They're not crazy about *me*. They're crazy about meatballs."

"Nah, they can get those any time. But *you*? You're something special."

His words made me feel warm and gooey all over, and I smiled against the cotton of his shirt. "So are you."

"Yeah?"

"Totally." Still, I had to tease him. "But I've gotta say, if you didn't want me to leave, you sure had a funny way of showing it."

"Hey, I did what I had to."

"What do you mean?" I asked.

"You want the truth?" His tone grew serious. "I didn't want you coming around."

"Why not?"

"Because I didn't know who I could trust, and I didn't want you on anyone's radar."

"But why?"

"Because I didn't want anything to happen to you."

That sounded ominous, and I just had to ask, "You're not *still* worried about that, are you?"

"No. Because I'm a lot better informed."

"About what?"

"Just between you and me?"

I nodded against him.

After a long silence, he said, "I know who killed my uncles."

"Seriously?" I pulled away and sat up. "Who?"

"They did."

"What?"

"Two hits," he said. "One on each other."

"Oh, my God." It was almost too terrible to contemplate. "How did you find out?"

"I got some hints, hired some people. Truth is, I just found out a couple of hours ago."

"Wow." I studied his face. "Was *that* why you were so worried about the alarm?"

His gaze met mine. "One of the reasons."

"Speaking of that house…" I hesitated. "Whose is it, really?"

"Mine." He smiled. "Legally, anyway."

I gave a confused shake of my head. "So, are you planning to keep it as a guest house or something?"

"Nah," he said. "I'm planning to let Teddy live there, well, whenever he pulls his head out of his ass."

"Really?"

"Yeah," Zane said. "After all, it's *his* house."

"But wait, you just said it was yours."

"Technically, it's part of the estate, but my grandfather wanted him to have it."

"He did?"

Zane nodded. "He hated what Bob and Kayla did, driving Teddy out like that."

Oddly enough, I hated it, too. "I can see why."

"And before he died, I promised to make it right."

"But I don't understand," I said. "If that's what he wanted, why didn't *he* deal with it?"

Zane looked away. "People are different, you know. The things I've had to do – well, I guess he didn't have it in him."

I knew exactly what he meant. But this posed another question. "Sorry, but I've gotta ask, why didn't just tell me what was going on, with the house, I mean?" I gave a shaky laugh. "I was *so* mad at you."

"Really?" he said. "I didn't notice."

I rolled my eyes. "Oh, please."

"All right. You wanna know why? It's because you had dinner with Teddy."

"So, you were what? Punishing me?"

"No," he said. "I was trying to keep you from getting dragged into the mud. The whole thing, it's like this messed up freak show, and I wanted to keep you the hell away from it."

I smiled in spite of myself. "But what about Teddy? Why didn't you tell *him*?"

"You know Teddy," Zane said. "Let's say I give him the house today, how long before he's out again?"

I saw what he meant. I had to admit it, "Not long."

"Right. But if the house is mine, they're gonna have a lot harder time taking it."

"You mean, because…" I wasn't quite sure how to put this.

Zane flashed me a grin. "Because I'm a prick, and Teddy's not."

At this, I had to laugh, because it was so terribly true. Teddy wasn't an awful person, but the odds of him hanging onto anything? Well, they weren't great.

As for Zane, he was obviously willing to fight for the things that were important to him. And for whatever reason, this seemed to include me. My voice softened. "You're not *always* a prick."

"Yeah?" He reached up and pulled me back into his arms. "Well don't tell anyone."

His body felt hard and warm against mine. I couldn't help but say, "Speaking of pricks…"

"Yeah?"

I almost giggled. "Have you ever had sex on this rug?"

CHAPTER 72

He pulled back to gaze into my eyes. "Not yet."

"Well, don't you think you should?"

"That depends," he said.

"Oh what?"

His lips curved into a wicked smile. "If you don't mind rug burn on your ass."

I stifled a giggle. "Well, maybe *I'd* be on top. And *you'd* get the burnt ass."

"Or maybe," he said, "I could take your sweet ass upstairs and make you forget this rug ever existed."

My breath caught. That sounded *really* good. "Come to think of it," I said, "I've always hated this rug."

"Yeah?" He was still smiling. "Say the word, and I'll burn it."

"You wouldn't."

His voice was nearly a caress. "I would if it made you happy."

The truth was, I actually believed him. And I might've told him so, if only he didn't, just then, get to his feet and pull me up with him. "Come on," he said, leading me toward the main stairway. "Let's pick out our bedroom."

"*Our* bedroom?"

"Well, yeah," he said. "If you think I'm letting you leave this place, you're crazy."

Whether he was kidding or not, his enthusiasm was contagious, and together, we bounded up the stairs like two college kids on Spring Break.

Embarrassingly, we never made it past the very first bedroom where, after glimpsing its luxurious bathroom, I suddenly recalled that I'd been promised a shower – with *him*.

And this is where we found ourselves two minutes later, naked and lathered as the steaming water cascaded down from multiple shower heads on both sides.

Zane's hair was wet, and his body was glistening. As far as his hands, those *wonderful* hands, they were slippery with soap as they ran slowly up and down my body, lathering my breasts, my back, my stomach, my legs, and everywhere in between.

As for *my* hands, they had some serious exploring of their own to do, and I wasn't going to let this opportunity pass me by.

He'd been my own personal fantasy for longer than I'd been willing to admit, even in the deepest, darkest parts of the night, when he'd been haunting my dreams with fantasies like the reality in front of me now.

He was undeniably beautiful, with his sculpted body and perfect face. And yet, that wasn't why I'd fallen for him. It was his inner beauty – hidden like a treasure reserved for the cherished few who claimed a special place in his heart.

Did this include me? It sure seemed like it. If so, this made me the luckiest girl in the whole world.

I couldn't help but smile as I ran my soapy hands along his back and down his ass, loving the feel of his hard muscles shifting in time with the motions of his own hands, which were, even now, caressing me to distraction.

More eager than ever, I reached for the soap again and lathered my hands until they were overflowing with white, scented foam. After returning the soap to its holder, I reached out, washing his chest with both of my hands – loving the feel of his pecs, hard and firm, under my smooth fingers.

Through all of this, my eyes were exploring too – relishing the sight of his body, his face, and best of all, his eyes, filled with an expression that looked a lot like love.

And then, he spoke. "Jane?"

"Hmmmmm?"

His hands had returned to my breasts. His palms were cupping them while his fingers captured the nipples, giving them a tender, maddening squeeze that sent a warm tingle all the way to my toes.

His voice was quiet and sincere. "You're made for me. You know that, right?"

I *did* know that, and yet, I swear, I would've been thrilled to hear it a million times over. I gave him a secret smile. "And *you're* made for me."

"Got that right."

I ran my own hands lower, skimming my fingers along his rock-hard abs before reaching for his length. He was massively hard in my soapy grip, and I gave his erection a tender squeeze, and then a long, smooth stroke, followed by another.

In front of me, Zane closed his eyes and gave a muffled moan that blended so sweetly with the sound of the water cascading over our naked bodies.

I tightened my grip, loving the feel of him, the sound of him, the look of him, especially when he smiled in a way that was almost sweet.

At any other time, I might have laughed at the very idea. Zane Bennington, sweet?

And yet, being with him was the sweetest thing I'd ever known, especially a few minutes later when we tumbled, wet and eager, from the shower onto the four-poster bed.

I felt clean and warm and so very desperate to have him inside me. At that moment, I might've even been willing to beg him, but happily, I didn't have to. When his body claimed mine, I felt full and complete in a way I never would've thought possible.

I drifted off, happy and sated, in the quiet afternoon, only to wake however long later to see Zane propped up beside me, gazing at me with an expression that made me smile all over again.

I couldn't help but ask, "What are you thinking?"

"I'm thinking of the first time I saw you." He pulled me into his arms and whispered into my ear. "I noticed you right away, you know."

"At the party?" I had to laugh. "It would be hard *not* to notice me, considering that you caught me eavesdropping."

"Maybe. But that wasn't the first time I saw you."

"It wasn't?"

"No. I saw you from an upper window."

"You did? When?"

"That afternoon, when you were playing with the dogs."

At first, I didn't get what he meant, but then, I realized. "Oh, my God. You mean when I was throwing those stupid meatballs?"

"Yeah," he said. "It amused the hell out of me."

"Well, if *that* amused you, I can only imagine how funny it was to find me in some van." I nuzzled closer. "Admit it. You hated me."

"I didn't hate you," he said, "but I *was* suspicious."

"Why?" I had to laugh. "Just because you caught me hiding out in the dark?"

"No. Because you were just my type."

"Oh, stop it," I said. "I was not."

"Wanna bet?" He ran a warm hand along my hip. "In fact, you were so exactly my type, I figured it *had* to be a setup."

"Seriously?" I laughed against his bare chest. "So you thought I was a spy or something?"

"No." A smile crept into his voice. "I thought you were trouble."

"Me?" I couldn't help but scoff. "Compared to you, I'm an angel."

"Yeah." His voice softened. "You are."

Of course, I knew this wasn't true, but it was sweet to hear just the same. "Well, I'm glad *you* think so."

"And, as long as I'm confessing," he said, "I was happy as hell that your house got smashed."

I made a move to pull back. "Wait, what?"

"I'm not kidding," he said, refusing to let go. "If I had an ax, I'd have chopped that tree down myself."

I shouldn't have laughed, but it struck me as incredibly funny. "It wasn't smashed," I said. "It was squashed."

"Smashed, squashed, same difference to me. I'm just pissed I didn't think of it myself."

"Easy for *you* to say. You're not the one who's gotta find a new place."

"So don't."

"What do you mean?"

"I mean, don't go."

I snuggled tighter against him. At the moment, I wasn't sure I could go anywhere, even if I wanted to.

And I *didn't* want to.

Still, there was something I wanted to know before I lost my nerve. I pulled back to study his face. "Can I ask you something?"

"What?"

"Was there ever anything between you and Kayla?"

"Hell no."

I wasn't surprised, but I *was* curious. "But if that's the case, why didn't you deny it? To Teddy, I mean?"

"I *did* deny it."

"You did not. I was there, remember?"

"On the plane?" he said. "Well yeah. By then, I'd already denied it a dozen times. That stuff gets old fast."

On this, I could totally relate. After all, Teddy was still convinced that I was "boning" Professor Lumberjack. From now on, I decided, I'd take Zane's approach and let Teddy think whatever he wanted – because heaven knows, he would, anyway.

Tentatively, I asked, "And what about all those models?"

"What about them?"

"Well, you dated a whole bunch of them."

"Yeah. I did. And I'm not gonna lie. I had some good times."

I could only imagine, except I really didn't want to.

Zane added, "But you wanna know the truth?"

Bracing myself, I nodded.

"Stuff like that?" he said. "Well, that gets old, too."

"So what happened?" I asked. "You got tired of them?"

"No." His gaze met mine. "I fell in love."

My breath caught. "Oh?"

He gave a slow nod. "Jane?"

Suddenly, I felt almost too breathless to speak. "What?"

"I love you."

"Really?"

He laughed. "Is that such a surprise?"

Yes.

And no.

Either way, it was wonderful to hear. I felt a mischievous smile tug at my lips. "Well, as long as we're confessing…"

"Yeah?"

I almost giggled. "I'm pretty sure I love you, too."

He lifted a single eyebrow. "Pretty sure, huh?"

"All right. *More* than pretty sure. Actually…" I gazed deep into his eyes and confessed the undeniable truth. "I love you, Zane Bennington."

He flashed me a sudden grin. "You'd better."

I smiled back. "Oh yeah? Why's that?"

"Because I've got a question."

"What?"

"Will you marry me?"

And just like that, the world stopped spinning. After a long, wonderful moment, I asked, "Is that a serious question?"

He looked absolutely sincere. "What do *you* think?"

I gave a happy laugh. "I think you're crazy."

"Got that right. And you wanna know why?"

"Why?"

"Because I've waited too long already."

"For what?"

His voice was very quiet. "For you."

I was so overwhelmed, I could hardly breathe. "I know exactly what you mean."

"Yeah?"

I nodded. "Oh yeah."

"So, is that a yes?"

I knew it was beyond crazy. I knew that only a month ago, I thought I hated him. I knew that Zane was foul-mouthed, stubborn, and yes, at times, a total prick.

But I knew other things, too. Topping that list? I loved him, and he was positively perfect exactly the way he was.

I gave a happy nod and said the word that would change everything. "Yes."

He pulled me close and kissed me like I'd just given him the world on a silver platter. But in reality, it was *him* giving me everything I never realized I wanted.

It was official. I was positively pricked – and always would be.

EPILOGUE

Just three months later, Zane and I were married in the same place where we'd first met – back when I'd been a lowly catering assistant and he'd been, well, Zane Bennington, the biggest prick on the planet, who also happened to have the biggest heart in the universe, at least when it came to me.

The day after his impromptu proposal, we were back in New York City, where he picked out the biggest diamond I'd ever seen and proposed all over again at midnight in Times Square.

We spent half a week there, taking in the sights all over again, this time with two furry companions and a whole bunch of doggie bags. We spent the remainder of that week back in Indianapolis, entertaining my parents and Charlotte, who grew to love Zane nearly as much as I did.

Soon, I learned a whole lot more about those awful meetings – the ones I'd attended during my short stint as Zane's employee.

Turns out, those original contracts had been drawn up by who else, but Bob, who'd written the fine print so craftily that the hotels ended up paying inflated prices while Bob netted some sweet kickbacks on the side.

But those days are long-gone. Today, Bob and Kayla are on the talk-show circuit, where they tell anyone who will listen how Zane screwed them out of what they truly deserved.

No one's buying it, not even Teddy, who's found love all over again, this time with a girl who loves him back with a ferocity that's just a little bit scary.

Teddy's officially our neighbor now, living in the same house that Zane's grandfather had wanted him to have all along. We're no longer worried about Teddy keeping the place, because his new fiancée is ten times more aggressive than Kayla on her worst day.

The fiancée's name? Paisley.

Yup, my former roommate.

In the end, she gave up the lumberjack life for good, in favor of something ten times better – her own personal knight in shining armor who loves her just the way she is.

Heaven help him.

As far as our wedding, it was attended by everyone I loved and at least one person I didn't. That person was Tiffany, who showed up on the arm of the lieutenant governor, a guy with even larger political aspirations than Senator Grabby-Ass, who's currently cooling his heels in a sex addict clinic for repeat offenders.

The footage of Zane dragging the senator never did show up on the news, and it wasn't until a few weeks afterward that I finally learned why. The guys had, in fact, sold the footage for a pretty penny. But the buyer was a certain somebody who preferred to keep that particular incident just between us – along with yes, a dozen other witnesses who saw the spectacle in person.

As for me, I'm the newest member of the Mile High Club – and not only because I've had sex at fifty-thousand feet. No, *I'm* a mile high because with Zane, every day is a walk in the clouds, and I wouldn't change a single thing.

THE END

Other Books by Sabrina Stark
(Listed by Couple)

Lawton & Chloe
Unbelonging (Unbelonging, Book 1)
Rebelonging (Unbelonging, Book 2)
Lawton (Lawton Rastor, Book 1)
Rastor (Lawton Rastor, Book 2)

Bishop & Selena
Illegal Fortunes

Jake & Luna
Jaked (Jaked Book 1)
Jake Me (Jaked, Book 2)
Jake Forever (Jaked, Book 3)

Joel & Melody
Something Tattered (Joel Bishop, Book 1)
Something True (Joel Bishop, Book 2)

ABOUT THE AUTHOR

Sabrina Stark writes edgy romances featuring plucky girls and the bad boys who capture their hearts.

She's worked as a fortune-teller, barista, and media writer in the aerospace industry. She has a journalism degree from Central Michigan University and is married with one son and a pack of obnoxiously spoiled kittens. She currently makes her home in Northern Alabama.

ON THE WEB

Learn About New Releases & Exclusive Offers
www.SabrinaStark.com

Printed in Great Britain
by Amazon